MW01273477

EJFS:
ELITE JUSTICE FORCE SQUAD SERIES

Episode 2: The Shadow State

Michael J. Beasley

Michael Beasley
3/11/2024

BookLocker
Trenton, Georgia

Copyright © 2021 Michael J. Beasley

Print ISBN: 978-1-64719-909-8
Ebook ISBN: 978-1-64719-910-4

All rights reserved. No part of this publication may be reproduced, stored in a retrieval system, or transmitted in any form or by any means, electronic, mechanical, recording or otherwise, without the prior written permission of the author.

Published by BookLocker.com, Inc., Trenton, Georgia.

Printed on acid-free paper.

The characters and events in this book are fictitious. Any similarity to real persons, living or dead, is coincidental and not intended by the author.

BookLocker.com, Inc.
2021

First Edition

Library of Congress Cataloguing in Publication Data
Beasley, Michael J.
EJFS: ELITE JUSTICE FORCE SQUAD SERIES - Episode 2 -
The Shadow State by Michael J. Beasley
Library of Congress Control Number: 2021923214

<u>Dedication</u>

This book is dedicated to all who feel oppressed by tyrannical regimes and suffer great hardship from corrupt leadership worldwide.

My hope for this book will convey that all forms of corruption, terrorism, and tyranny should never be tolerated by anyone ever.

Table of Contents

Acknowledgments...9

Preface..11

Prologue...13

1: The Set-Up 17

2: Call to Action: Abhu's Stunning Revelation......................29

3: EJFS Emergency Briefing: Kim Taken in for
  questioning..43

4: Judson Clayborn's Re-education: EJFS Questions Kim......56

5: Kim's Questioning Begins: POTUS Hill's Dark Secret.........66

6: Enter Kim's Doppelganger: Zima and Gyan plot
  America's Election Day Demise 80

7: EJFS Stonewalled: Vritra's Remains Unsealed.................. 90

8: POTUS Hill National Address: Kim's Doppelganger's
  First Act of Sabotage 97

9: EJFS Arrives in NYC: The Storm to End All Storms is
  Created 109

10: EJFS Readies Assault on Gyan's Compound: Kim's
  Doppelganger Strikes Again..120

11: Gyan's Home Under Siege by the EJFS 126

12: Gyan in Custody: The USA In Peril 135

13: Gyan Interrogated: Zima Flees to Budapest..................142

14: Kim Learns of Caleb's Dual Identity: Alicia's Latest
  Sabotage 159

15: The Second Briefing: Kim Scorned by POTUS Hill's
  Duplicity 171

16: Drake's Defection and Escape: POTUS Declares War on EJFS 185

17: Drake Meets Khali Under Ultimatum from POTUS: EJFS TAC Teams Deploy to Budapest............................. 197

18: Gyan's Escape: Nicolas and Logan Make Amends........... 213

19: Drake Departs for EJFS Zurich Ghost Site: EJFS Vacates US Airspace...225

20: Midnight Thunder Activated: Nationwide Blackout 235

21: POTUS Hill's Video Conference with Canada and Mexico: Drake Arrives at Zurich EJFS Ghost Site 248

22: Anastasia Zima Arrives in Budapest: EJFS TAC Team Stakeout at Russian Embassy 263

23: Abhu's Ominous Dream: Black Sparrow Zero's Identity Revealed 274

24: A New Day Dawns: EJFS TAC Team Arrives in Warsaw, Poland 292

25: Abhu's and Durga's Dual Device Scan: Zima Interrogated 308

26: Warsaw EJFS Under Attack: Tragedy Strikes the EJFS 317

27: CIRB Director Confronts Matthews: Vritra's Necklace Resurfaces 330

28: Zima and Bradford Face-Off: EJFS TAC Team Attacks Rumbeke Castle 339

29: EJFS Returns to Atlanta: Richer Makes His Move 351

30: Shadow State Sleeper Cells Activated: Kim Begins Training.. 361

31: Kim's Transition into EJFS Superagency Begins: Richer Targets EJFS Atlanta Base 370

32: Atlanta-EJFS Thunderhead Base Defense from Hill's Wrath: Amir Laments Naveen's Death 383

33: EJFS Strikes Back: POTUS Hill and Shadow State Exposed 394

34: EJFS Oversees Hill's Impeachment: Another Government Mole Operative Activated 408

35: Khali Arrives in D.C.: Drake Assumes Command 419

36: Khali Testifies in Congress: EJFS TAC Team Forms Boundary Along US East Coast 429

37: EJFS Strikes Richer Manor: Shadow State Seizes Offshore Oil Rig 438

38: The Last Hurrah over the Southeast Atlantic: Vritra's Cataclysmic Return 448

39: Vritra Consumes Midnight Thunder 456

40: The Final Battle in The Atlanta Skies 465

41: Hill Learns His Fate: Khali in Dire Straits 472

Epilogue: Three Days Later 479

After-Story 482

   1: Khali Missing: Singh Overcome with Grief 482

   2: Abhu Debriefed: Singh Seeks Sharma's Counsel 490

   3: Singh Debriefed: Khali Bound for Siberian Prison 501

   4: Singh Makes the Call: Hill's Parting Shot 509

Acknowledgments

I want to thank all the editors, proofreaders, and beta readers as they helped shape my book into a fantastic work of art. These people have offered invaluable assistance in refining my craft, including my best friend, Joshua Glassmyer. My editor, Jeanette Chaplin. I also want to recognize the following friends and individuals that helped me chart a course in the publishing world: Adam Plenkovich, Armez Jackson, Paul Berry, Matthew Sterling, Dawn & Erik Claflin, Chuck Goodwin, Seth Barronian, and Sue Hughes.

I also want to extend my gratitude to all my family, friends, coworkers that believed in me and gave me continual advice and counsel. These people include Chuck Goodwin, Solomon Lemma, Jim Wadhwani, Christina Lease, Jeanette Chaplin, Dawn Claflin, Armez Jackson, Adam Plenkovich, and Joshua Glassmyer.

I would also like to thank Angela Hoy, CEO of BookLocker, and her team of publishers for their continued exemplary work. I am forever grateful to be a part of the BookLocker family and for the fantastic opportunity to publish my second book in this novel series.

Lastly, I want to thank my mother, Cindy Beasley, for putting up with so much from me and give me another chance to continue my dream to become a multi-published author. Thank you so much for helping me see this through to the culmination.

Preface

Much like my first book, I didn't anticipate and couldn't fathom this second installment to become another publication in the way that the first one did. Even as I write this passage, it never ceases to amaze me how things can line up into place so perfectly.

Thanks primarily due to the COVID-19 pandemic that has overtaken the world, it has somehow accelerated my publishing timeline. The stimulus money from the past couple of years has sped the process for completing this second book and consulting with a professional editor for a final copyediting and review.

This endeavor that I undertook back in 2015 has been a wild journey, and I fully intend to see it through to the conclusion of publishing the entire EJFS series into a trilogy.

The underlying theme in the story has not departed much from the first one. This book will cover previously encapsulated elements of Episode One, but on a much more profound scale that tackles corruption, tyranny, and terrorism, with additional subject matter areas surrounding secret societies and ecoterrorism.

My heart feels burdened with the urge to expose and illustrate what kind of near-future plausibility in a fictional setting will, hopefully, bring awareness and a sense of revelation to things happening in this subject realm right this minute.

I certainly hope and pray that this novel's underlying theme will continue to inspire many and resonate with readers who have a degree of awareness of the vast corruption and tyranny occurring on a massive scale.

Prologue

Fourteen months after the events of Vritra's Rebirth, a new global threat has taken shape.

By the plunging of the Gatekeeper's Blade, the evil dragon was released into the world by Ravan Kanda Ganesh: Vritra and subsequently defeated by Agents Abhu and Singh of the EJFS Atlanta Branch. Vritra's remains are unaccounted for after being surrendered to US control by Anastasia Zima, a biotech engineer from Russia. Zima used to work for the now-defunct Final Wave Terrorist Organization that disbanded late in 2023 after the death of their leader, Ravan, at the hands of the Elite Justice Force Squad.

Some say the necklace containing the remains may have been stored in a secure facility in Washington, D.C., while others say it vanished mysteriously.

Much uncertainty enshrouds Vritra's lost remains, which have changed hands from the Russian Government to the US Government in their newfound partnership through the vast network known as The Shadow State. This dark network rivals the hierarchy of the Elite Justice Force Squad. It threatens the agency's ability to manage and retain order, justice, and prosperity for the world's nations.

The story is set in early November of 2024: The US Presidential Election is imminent. A hard-fought campaign has been waged between POTUS Kenneth Hill and the Republican challenger, Mississippi Senator Wes Grisham. The incumbent POTUS, Kenneth Hill, has led the polls throughout much of the campaign trail with support from many wealthy donations to Hill's campaign. Coupled with FLOTUS Lacey Hill, the financial supporters team up to make the final push in the weeks leading up to the general election.

The friendship of Caleb Porter, a.k.a. EJFS Agent Abhu Dhuval Sandeep, and fellow Agent Singh Puneet Sherpa blossomed as they formed love interests with two women in the agency: Agents Durga Deshmukh and Gangi Bhanuni. Both couples have been dating since November of 2023, fourteen months following the events of Episode One.

At large, the Shadow State is an evil, elusive, underground network of world leaders who have banded together to form a New World Order. They aim to satisfy their own lust for power and control.

A technological genius named Jagmohan Gyan oversees his enterprise to help the Shadow State become a significant evil entity in the twenty-first century. He serves as a government sponsor of corruption *and* terrorism. Gyan provided technology to the Shadow State, which allowed the organization to wreak havoc on the world with chaotic weather phenomena.

Meanwhile, the EJFS has expanded its influence as a public agency aimed at mitigating terrorism, corruption, and tyranny extensively across the globe.

Khali remains at the Atlanta Branch's helm while many new faces join the superagency and old-timers return to action.

The EJFS maintains election integrity and ensures an honest election with the upcoming election less than a week away. The agency's intent is twofold: to guarantee that the electorate understands the nominees and illuminate any nominee's evil agendas, which could be harmful to the country. They want to be sure such things are brought to light and expose the nominees' ill-will toward the voters.

The story starts in the final days before the election on the first of November. Acts of terrorism have increased dramatically in the weeks leading up to the election and struck fear into Americans' hearts and the world population. EJFS is about to be called back into action.

Another tumultuous and turbulent time has descended upon the world, and the EJFS is about to thrust itself into an epic showdown with the Shadow State. It would be the most significant case they will undertake in their nine-year existence.

During the ten o'clock hour, the story begins in New York City. A cloaked individual tries to sell inside information to an interested buyer who sought out details on Vritra's remnants' whereabouts. The buyer seeks to acquire the ancient heirloom dragon-shaped vessel necklace and to research its terrible power.

However, things are about to take a turn for the worse, bringing Abhu and Singh back into action after their serendipitous break from intense work in the field.

1: The Set-Up

Judson Clayborn

R-Line

Lexington Avenue 59 Street Subway Station

Lower East Manhattan

New York City, New York, USA

November 1, 2024

10:00 PM EDT, Friday Night

On one rainy night in the lower east side of Manhattan, a slender middle-aged man in his 40s, named Judson Clayborn, walked down the street. At the late hour in the evening, he wore a brown leather trench coat in the pouring rain.

Judson Clayborn was a buyer from a local expedition group, hoping to locate the necklace containing Vritra's remains after the willfully human-caused seal breach at the hands of the fallen Final Wave terrorist organization in Siberia during the previous year. He wanted to see the full extent of its power.

Clayborn boarded a subway train, heading to the Western Hotel by the Grand Central Station. He was to meet with a courier for inside information on the whereabouts of the lost item.

Clayborn briskly but carefully trekked down the stairs to the Lexington Avenue subway station in the pouring rain.

The torrential downpour created tangled traffic in the city. Land-based and flying cars overhead honked at each other in the distance.

After Clayborn made it down the stairs to the subway station, he boarded the R-Train to the Grand Central Station on the Lower East Side, hoping to bypass the traffic jams throughout the city.

Meanwhile, a cloaked, athletically-built female arrived at the Western Hotel near the Grand Central Station area and retired to her hotel room. She had already booked it hours earlier, after running an errand.

The cloaked figure was the courier offering the sale of valuable information. The intel would lead to the whereabouts of Vritra's remains encased in the ancient dragon-shaped necklace vessel, which contained its evil power from eons ago.

The cloaked woman brought a sealed file inside a locked fingerprint-scannable courier case onto the elevator to the Western Hotel's fourth floor.

She unlocked the hotel room door with a key card and tapped on the reader device to enter the private suite.

The courier set up the room with a table, and two chairs prepared, one for the buyer and one for the courier facing the doorway to the suite.

***

Meanwhile, the R-Train arrived at Grand Central Station. Clayborn disembarked from the train and left the station to go to the nearby hotel.

After Clayborn crossed the street to the entrance of the Western Hotel, he walked in. As he wiped his feet on the rug, he discreetly picked up an identical access card beneath it. The courier had placed it to give him exclusive access to the room.

Clayborn took the elevator to the fourth floor and walked down to the hall where Room 477 was located. He tapped in his key card and walked into the room, causing the shadowy figure to draw her handgun. Clayborn reacted and drew his pistol, and they both stood off, gazing at each other.

"Is this how you treat your potential buyers?" Clayborn asked intently.

"Only to those that show up over five minutes late," The cloaked figure in the hooded jacket retorted in a sick, deranged voice.

"You sound demented," Clayborn replied.

The cloaked woman cackled and lowered her handgun, which led Clayborn to holster his pistol.

"I'll let this slide. I know the weather is horrid tonight." The cloaked woman responded in a calmer tone.

"Who are you anyway?" Clayborn asked bluntly.

"That's a very forward question, Judson." The courier in the shadowy outfit replied with hostility.

"I want to know if you are human," Clayborn added.

"I suppose I'll let you judge for yourself," The courier replied and took off the hood of the coat, revealing a lifeless, sullen face with pale skin and dark circles under her eyes.

"My name is Anastasia Zima," The courier revealed her name to the buyer as her haunting face came into view.

"You look like a ghost," Clayborn rudely pointed out.

"I would be cautious about your line of conversation, Judson. I could have had you eliminated by now if I wanted. But enough of this foolishness. Let us get down to business. Take a seat in front of me," Zima dictated in a pressing tone.

Clayborn was hesitant at first but approached the table.

"Take off your trench coat so that I know that you are not wearing a wire," Zima demanded sharply.

"Seriously?" Clayborn's face soured as he grew tired of the treatment from the courier.

"I'm always serious. Take it off," Zima continued, and her eyes narrowed to slits.

"Okay, fine," Clayborn took off his trench coat and showed Anastasia that he was not wearing a wire.

"Happy now?" Clayborn asked irritably.

"I'm satisfied. Now take a seat," Zima insisted.

Clayborn made a hostile facial expression and took a seat in front of Zima.

Zima retrieved her courier case and placed it on the table in front of Clayborn.

"Here are the terms of the deal. They are non-negotiable: I require that you wire transfer money to my offshore bank account in Macau, China, in the amount of $50,000. You will be given three minutes total to read the file. If you exceed that time limit, I will kill you, and the information I offer will remain in my control."

"Jeez, talk about sudden death," Clayborn shuddered as a chill ran down his spine.

"Those are the terms. You can take it or leave it. Need I remind you that your expedition company has been looking for leads on this ancient artifact for months? If you walk away now, you will have wasted those months and this meeting. There's no guarantee that you will find this information anywhere else," Zima enticed the buyer to remain committed to the sale.

"You know what? I'm out. I don't believe you are legitimate. I will tell all my partner companies to stay away from doing business with you," Clayborn replied and abruptly got out of his chair to leave.

"I'm sorry we couldn't complete the sale. Maybe you will have better luck in...another lifetime," Zima forewarned.

Clayborn was wary of her words, prompting him to put on his trench coat quickly. He hastily left and slammed the door.

Clayborn raced down the hall to the elevators as a housekeeper wandered down the hallway with a cleaning cart. He stared intently at the fleeing expeditor.

Clayborn briskly passed by the housekeeper and boarded the elevator.

After Clayborn boarded the elevator, the housekeeper pulled out his smartphone and speed-dialed an associate.

"The buyer has left the suite. Keep close and watch his movements," He instructed quietly.

CIRB Asset, Grant Bradford

"Acknowledged." The asset representing the corrupt CIRB, the Counterintelligence Response Bureau, Grant Bradford, watched the security footage from the surveillance van outside the hotel.

Bradford noticed Clayborn briskly storm out of the hotel to the Grand Central Station. Clayborn was seen rushing to board a train bound to Upper Manhattan.

Bradford suspected Clayborn was about to notify the authorities of what just happened. Clayborn could not have known that the US Government set up the failed deal orchestrated by the CIRB.

CIRB vehicles doubled back around the street, surrounding the station, as Clayborn noticed the increased activity. At the same time, he darted inside the station and reached the R-Train platform for northbound to upper Manhattan.

Clayborn, scrambling in a panic, tried to elude the CIRB agents on his tail as he waited to board the R-Train. However, the train was not due to arrive for another minute.

***

Zima packed up her gear at the hotel suite, loaded and placed her handgun in her holster, and lowered her hood to conceal her face.

She sought to hunt down her failed buyer, whom she contemplated killing after he stormed out of her hotel suite. She suspected that Clayborn would become a whistleblower.

***

At Grand Central Station, the CIRB agents received reinforcements and searched the building to find their target. In the shadows, Clayborn continued to wait for the train to take him north.

Finally, the train arrived at the R-Line platform, and he quickly boarded to return home several miles north.

The train closed its doors before the CIRB agents arrived on the scene and quickly departed.

One of the CIRB agents contacted Zima. "The target is on the R-Train going northbound. What do you want us to do?"

Zima quickly answered her smartphone. "Pursue the target down to the Lexington 55 station. He doesn't live far from there. Stay on him until I get to his residence."

Zima hung up as she briskly walked down the hall with her gear and courier case she kept secure in her messenger bag. From there, she hurried down the stairwell to the parking garage.

***

Clayborn rested on the subway train, under the impression that he had escaped the heat.

However, another CIRB asset was onboard the subway train and kept a close eye on the target. Clayborn caught a glimpse of a darkly-clad agent.

Clayborn was still in a slight panic and noticed out of the corner of his eye that another possible CIRB asset watched him in one of the rear-view mirrors.

Clayborn sat in his seat and felt anxious about what was happening around him. Other travelers were looking at him, confused by Clayborn's neurotic demeanor.

The CIRB asset kept his line of sight locked onto Clayborn. The agent planned to apprehend him as soon as the subway train arrived at the destination, where Clayborn would disembark to go home.

Meanwhile, Zima made her way to the parking garage by the hotel and boarded her motorbike. From there, she departed the garage heading to Clayborn's residence to pin him down.

On the subway train heading northeast, the CIRB asset accessed the subway operations program on his smartphone. He prepared to cause a derailment on the R-Line to cover up what they were doing in a false-flag operation.

The CIRB asset accessed the NTSB operations manifest on his smartphone. He then changed the train's course to a blocked railway in an under-construction station.

Soon after, the train stopped at the Lexington 55 station under its new guided path.

Clayborn was placed in handcuffs as the CIRB asset stopped him on the train. The asset escorted Clayborn off the train as other CIRB assets were on location to take Clayborn to his residence. Zima was destined to confront her buyer, who had reneged on the failed deal.

Flanking him on all sides, the CIRB assets walked Clayborn out of the station.

The assets escorted Clayborn to a black SUV with tinted windows. Clayborn was placed in the backseat to be taken to his residence.

Clayborn was terrified of what the CIRB assets wanted with him, but he remained silent, not knowing what was happening or why he was in the custody of the CIRB.

The black SUV arrived at Clayborn's residence, where Zima was waiting with several other CIRB agents awaiting Clayborn's arrival.

The CIRB assets escorted Clayborn inside his residence. Zima and her CIRB agents' team followed them inside.

One of the CIRB assets used a skeleton key to unlock the front door to Clayborn's home. They took him to his living room, sat him down on the couch, and prepared to question him while they searched his home for anything incriminating.

Zima and a few CIRB agents stayed behind while others searched the entirety of Clayborn's home.

"Do you know why we've brought you here?" Zima asked in a haunting tone.

"I can wager a guess. I think you are setting me up," Clayborn retorted in defiance.

Agent Grant Bradford, one of the athletically-built CIRB agents, punched Clayborn on his left cheekbone, causing him to groan in pain.

Zima leaned forward as she sat on the coffee table, trying to get into Clayborn's head.

"Why did you want to set up an information exchange when you walked out? Are you afraid of what you have gotten yourself into? Do you even know the history behind this necklace and its terrible powers?" Zima asked him.

"What do you people want with me?! Why are you rummaging through my home?!" Clayborn shouted.

"Quiet! We ask the questions, not you!" CIRB agent Bradford barked at Clayborn.

"I think you don't know what kind of trouble you have gotten yourself into. But I think you can be of use to us. Our network is looking for participants to sway the election to keep the current President in power for another term, perhaps beyond. We cannot let you go if you plan to expose us," Zima continued.

"Look, I don't want any part of what you people are planning. Let me go!" Clayborn pleaded.

"That's not possible at this point. You've dipped your toes into forbidden waters. You are now aware of our operation. You cannot continue to live your life without us on your tail. So, you can choose to either oppose us or work with us, and we will let you stay here, but on a short leash. Whether you like it or not, you have involved yourself in this organization. Join us, and we'll give you whatever you want as long as you stay out of our way," Zima scolded Clayborn.

Clayborn remained silent. He felt backed into a corner.

Suddenly, one of the CIRB agents, searching Clayborn's home, entered the living room with a piece of evidence that he wanted to share.

"I found a trip itinerary for a vacation in Guadalajara, Mexico, this weekend." CIRB Agent Cortez handed over the itinerary to Zima to inspect.

"Why are you taking a trip to Mexico this weekend? Did you intend to sell the information that you were going to buy to another party?" Zima asked as she reviewed the information on Clayborn's itinerary.

"Okay, I was going to put the information on the black market. I was looking to make money on return investment. Are you happy now?" Clayborn confessed.

"Very much so, Judson. You have just given us a reason to keep you in our custody. You are part of this operation for the long haul now," Zima snapped her fingers to her associates, and CIRB Agent Bradford covered Clayborn's face with a blackout blindfold.

The last words Clayborn heard before losing consciousness were chilling:

"Welcome to the Shadow State."

The CIRB agents and Zima took Clayborn out of his residence and boarded black SUVs. Their destination was a remote black site where the Shadow State operated in the upstate New York region.

***

Later that night, the same subway train that Clayborn once rode, sped down the wrong line and derailed off the tracks, causing everyone onboard to be killed in the wreckage. Along with first responders and the NYPD, DHS agents swarmed the area to examine the incident scene.

Around 11:00 PM on the US's east coast, the Elite Justice Force Squad saw the events unfold on the news in Atlanta's skyline. This spurred the EJFS super-agents and tech analysts to respond to the Manhattan incident after the train derailment.

Master Khali, the Chief Commander and Head of the EJFS, spoke on their network's AERIAL VOIP video calling system with the Chief of Police at the NYPD and the Deputy Director of Homeland Security.

Khali contacted all EJFS agents who were off-duty to return to action as a developing situation unfolded in New York City throughout the late-night hours.

2: Call to Action: Abhu's Stunning Revelation

EJFS Agent Abhu Dhuval Sandeep

Singh's Beachfront Villa

Savannah, Georgia, USA

November 1, 2024

11:10 PM EDT, Friday Night

EJFS Agents Abhu Sandeep and Singh Sherpa were vacationing with their love interests: Durga Deshmukh and Gangi Bhanuni. They were in Savannah, on the beachfront property owned by Agent Singh.

Agents Abhu, Durga, and Gangi were houseguests staying at Singh's villa during the week on their vacation period.

Agent Singh brought out a chilled bottle of white wine from the blast chiller.

The foursome relaxed in their comfortable beach clothes. They lounged on the patio overlooking the ocean, listening to the pounding waves hypnotically beating the shores.

The four agents gathered around a fire pit and spent the late evening hours having a little liquor to spice up the night while making s'mores.

"This brings back so many memories of my childhood years, except there was no Zinfandel involved." Agent Abhu scorched his marshmallows on the metal skewer over the fire pit.

"Well, let's make this a new time-honored tradition." Agent Singh toasted, and they all took a drink from their stemmed wine glasses.

"Here, here!" Gangi cheered for the new tradition.

"I'll drink to that too," Durga raised her glass and took a sip of her wine.

"So, Abhu, when did you have your first legal drink?" Gangi asked openly.

Abhu licked the nearly-incinerated marshmallow mess from his fingers. Abhu started to assemble his s'more sandwich treat. "Probably back when I had to move out of my family house. I think I had about two or three shots of rum and cola."

Singh took a bite out of his s'more sandwich and felt young again. "Mine was after I graduated from college. I enjoyed an East Indian Negroni with some friends from Georgia State. It was a real treat."

Gangi candidly spoke after she took a bite out of her s'mores treat. "I often drink mimosas and screwdrivers. I love citrus-based drinks mostly."

Durga took moderately big bites out of her toasted marshmallow treat that smelled like burnt sugar. "I'm more of a wine type of girl. All I need is a nice bottle of pinot noir by the fireplace, and I'm all set for the evening."

Abhu reflected on the events from the time he first enlisted in the EJFS.

"Man, I can't believe it has been over a year since Singh and I defeated Vritra. Now, we are amidst another presidential election in a few days," Abhu marveled.

Singh replied. "Indeed, my friend. This has been an incredible lead-up to the ensuing election. It's vital that our organization be a voice for truth and justice in this political season."

Durga spoke on the subject matter. "Does anybody think President Hill could win a second term?"

Gangi scoffed as she took another sip of her beverage. "Ugh, I would hope not. I think he is a menace."

Singh reacted. "Only time will tell. He *is* leading the polls, though."

Abhu interjected, "Sometimes, the polls are inaccurate. The last days of the campaign could be make-or-break for either nominee."

Singh concluded the political banter. "We must not be too biased in our line of work. Everyone in the EJFS knows that we must determine the truthfulness of each nominee. The electorate will have the final say on the outcome."

The four of them finished their late-night desserts and polished off their wine.

Agent Singh started to feel sleepy from the late hour and alcohol consumption.

"It's getting pretty late. We should head off to bed for the night. Have a good rest, everyone. I'll see you all in the morning,"

Singh washed his hands in the kitchen sink then wiped them with a dry towel.

The four of them entered the kitchen to wash up and clean their wine glasses.

Shortly after, the foursome went to bed in the beachfront home property for the night, relaxing to the waves pounding the beach. The foursome split up for the night, each pair eager to enjoy a romantic evening on the beachfront.

A gentle, fresh sea breeze blew through the open windows and made the environment comfortable.

When everyone was asleep, Abhu started having an intense dream involving an oppressive shadow government in another country.

Abhu saw images of captives being put into internment camps, forced into slave labor. During the vision, Abhu was a spectator in the dream.

Then, Abhu heard a raspy voice behind his ear that uttered: "You can't escape your destiny. This is your future!"

Abhu witnessed a scoundrel who stood tall with an upgraded Victorian-style building as the backdrop. A tyrannical leader's statue overlooked the building's main entrance, which was located near a clearing in the woods.

***

Suddenly, Abhu woke up to the sound of Master Khali's vibrating ringtone. The tune had an exotic Indian flair.

Abhu was startled out of his slumber, and he saw the time display on his phone, indicating it was 6:07 a.m.

Abhu answered the call after he sat up in bed to grab his phone from the nightstand.

"Hello?" Abhu answered his smartphone with a lethargic look on his face and his long wavy hair disheveled.

EJFS Chief Commander, Master Khali

"Agent Abhu, it's Khali. I am sorry to inform the four of you that your vacation has been cut short. We have a situation that is an ongoing development. Everyone is being called back to the base. We have an emergency briefing at 9:00 a.m. I need the four of you to get back to the Thunderhead Base right away. That's an order."

Master Khali spoke from his office in the EJFS Thunderhead Base over the Atlanta skyline while watching morning news coverage out of New York City.

During Abhu's call from Khali, Durga woke up at Abhu's side. She checked her phone and saw a flash message ordering all Atlanta EJFS agents back to the Thunderhead Base Palace immediately.

Abhu complied. "I understand. We'll be there soon."

Abhu rubbed the slumber from his eyes while Durga rustled out of bed to get dressed.

"Thank you, Agent Abhu. I'll see you all when you get back here." Master Khali ended the call and continued calling on all the veteran EJFS agents on vacation to return to action.

Abhu and Durga outfitted behind some changing screens in their room. Both grabbed their badges and guns from their nightstand drawers. They equipped both items after they donned their EJFS uniforms with strapped-on accessory belts and assorted gear-holders on their black cargo pants.

Abhu knocked on Singh and Gangi's bedroom door to inform them that Khali had ordered all agents to return to the base headquarters stationed over Atlanta.

EJFS Agent Singh Puneet Sherpa

Singh was already getting clothed in his uniform when Abhu knocked on his door.

"Khali needs us back at the base," Abhu informed them from the hall.

Singh and Gangi were getting clothed out of view behind the two changing screens facing each other.

"We know, Abhu, we've got the flash message." Singh spoke in a breathy tone as he quickly suited his Herculean body up in his uniform.

Singh's breath made the wind blow towards his love interest Gangi, frustrated with the windy draft originating from Singh's mouth.

"Ugh, Singh, you're messing up my hair," Gangi moaned in frustration.

"Sorry," Singh apologized.

Singh finished suiting up and staggered to his nightstand to retrieve his badge and handgun from the drawer.

Singh wrapped his holstering equipment around his thigh and stored his handgun in the concealed holster.

Gangi fixed her hair before she finished getting dressed, and she grabbed her gun and badge from underneath her pillow.

Singh noticed her habitual storage routine and called her out on it.

"Seriously? You keep your gun and badge under the pillowcase?" Singh arched his brow.

"Old habits," Gangi responded coyly.

Singh chuckled softly and kissed Gangi gently on her lips, and they packed their gear to depart.

As Abhu and Durga finished packing, Gangi followed Singh outside to his car parked in the driveway.

The four agents entered Singh's car and ascended to the EJFS Thunderhead Base, hovering above the Atlanta skyline.

***

EJFS: ELITE JUSTICE FORCE SQUAD SERIES

The four agents made their ascent into the Thunderhead Base, no longer in stealth mode as in previous years before the EJFS went public.

Singh drove down the automatic parking garage on the second sub-level floor with Abhu in the passenger seat and Durga and Gangi in the backseat riding along.

Agent Pranay greeted them with the briefing materials circulated to their tablets when the two dating couples entered the main lobby hallways.

"Welcome back, lovebirds. Here are your briefing materials. I have sent them to your tablets in a batch email to all agents. The briefing begins in less than a few hours. All of you better start studying the reports."

Returning Agent Pranay Prem grinned at them as he walked by his partner, Agent Garjan Bankim, who welcomed the returning agents.

Agents Abhu and Singh said goodbye to their lovers as they returned to the Level Four Opal Quadrant Unit, joining the other residents in a quick meeting.

Abhu and Singh returned to the Level Five Residential Quadrant Sapphire Unit after tapping their key cards and scanning them to enter.

The gate opened, and the duo entered the quadrant and witnessed their old friends as they hustled and bustled down the halls, settling back in after some had taken vacation time for a week.

"Hey! Welcome back, guys!" Agent Naveen greeted Abhu and Singh as they shook hands and hugged their colleague.

"It's good to be back," Agent Singh spoke and reciprocated the hug, and Abhu did the same.

"Good to see you again," Agent Abhu greeted him after a quick embrace from Naveen.

Agent Darsh stepped out of the quadrant office and welcomed the returned agents from their vacation in Savannah.

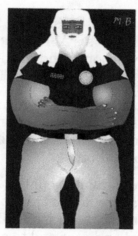

EJFS Agent Amit "Darsh" Darshan Vivek

"Ah, welcome back, you two. Both of you can head to your rooms and unpack, then meet us in the dining hall for a quick huddle this morning," Darsh welcomed both agents Abhu and Singh.

Both outstanding operatives arrived in their private quarters, which were next door to each other.

Both agents unloaded their luggage from their little vacation. They placed their dirty clothes in their laundry bags. The sorted laundry would be picked up by the crewmembers in the sub-level cleaning center of the Thunderheads for washing and cleaning.

They each placed their dirty clothes down a chute attached to a bin designated for every floor and quadrant unit. Then, workers began processing their clothes to sort and clean. After they were cleaned, they would be returned to their proper agents' quarters.

After both Abhu and Singh settled back into their respective rooms, they reviewed the briefing materials on their tablets and looked through the field reports composed by EJFS agents who had been on-site in New York City during the events the night before.

Inside the first section was a dossier file for Judson Clayborn, captured by the CIRB. Both Abhu and Singh studied the summary alone in their rooms and read through the reports submitted jointly by the EJFS and the NYPD.

Both flipped to the next page on their tablet screen, showing surveillance footage of the hooded individual in the Western Hotel, as they checked into their suite in preparation for an exchange of inside information.

Abhu and Singh individually continued to examine the documents, viewing surveillance photos at the New York Subway Station in Manhattan, which exhibited Clayborn being taken away in handcuffs and escorted to a black SUV.

Both agents turned to the next page in their digital briefing, showing crime scene photos from the subway crash and an illegal search and seizure of property by the CIRB as its agents searched the home of Judson Clayborn.

Both agents panned through the photos and examined all the evidence collected thus far.

The last photo in the digital briefing piqued interest: it featured a spray paint tag on the subway station wall near the derailed train with the acronym TSS.

There was a poster of a shadowy, athletic, feminine creature wearing a hooded striped jacket and holding up a palm facing forward, which showed a triangle and the acronym 'TSS.' Also visible was a tagline that read, "Destroy from Within" on the bottom caption of the poster.

After Abhu and Singh individually studied the advance briefing documentation on their tablets, they exited their quarters and gathered in the dining hall to reunite with their fellow agents.

Abhu and Singh sat next to each other along with the other agents in the unit. Amit "Darsh" Vivek, Pranay Prem, Naveen Kamboja, and the remaining agents assigned to the quadrant unit gathered at the long table for a discussion before the briefing later that morning.

Agent Darsh opened the symposium.

"Welcome back, gentlemen. I hope you have had a good time off. But it is now time to get down to business. Last night, there was a situation in New York City involving the CIRB, an unidentified party, and a man named Judson Clayborn. Here is what we will be scrutinizing in the briefing today: We will be reviewing evidence submitted by the NYPD Chief of Police to examine key elements involved in last night's events and the subsequent subway train derailment in New York. Then we will plan a mission outline and set of objectives. Finally, we will reconvene and revisit our assignments later."

"Now, I suggest everyone grab some breakfast downstairs and kick yourselves into high gear. This is a top priority case. The all-agency briefing will take place at 9:00 a.m. Don't be late," Agent Darsh warned.

The EJFS agents exited the dining hall and headed down to the main floor cafeteria for a homecoming breakfast banquet for the returning veteran agents.

The returned agents and new agents became acquainted after they had returned from their vacation.

Agents Abhu, Singh, Darsh, Pranay, Basu, and Naveen sat at one end of the table with the new EJFS agents.

All agents were given a stack of pumpkin pancakes as an autumnal treat with butter, maple syrup, and some pumpkin-spiced coffee with cream and sugar.

The agents indulged in their breakfast treat and familiarized themselves with the newest class of agents in the EJFS.

"Where are y'all from?" Agent Abhu asked between bites.

"My name is Anil, and I'm from Atlanta."

"I'm Baadal, and I'm from Marietta."

"Hi, I'm Daarun. I'm a transplant from the New York Division."

"Hello, I'm Ettan. I'm from Savannah."

"My name is Garjan, and I'm from Columbia, South Carolina."

"Hi, I'm Meghnad. I'm from Galveston, Texas."

After getting to know each other, the topic shifted to what was gathered from the brief they analyzed from their tablets.

Darsh asked the group of twelve seated at their table. "Has anyone been able to decipher what this acronym "TSS" represents?"

Tech Analyst Ettan gave his insight. "I think it could be the name of a secret society type of an organization. I have a few names running through my head right now, and it appears dire."

Agent Anil suggested. "I think it might have been a government-run false flag operation with the intent to distract the public from voting in the upcoming election."

Agent Singh asked. "Have we vetted everyone in both of the nominees' campaigns?"

Agent Garjan indicated. "We ran everyone in the database, and there were a handful of staff members on President Kenneth

Hill's campaign who appear to have some extreme views about which direction they want America to go."

Agent Abhu inquired. "Such as?"

Agent Pranay chimed into the discussion. "There are a few liaisons and interns on their payroll that have some active involvement in separatist groups opposed to a 'fascist government regime' in their mission statements."

Agent Meghnad pulled out a file folder containing dossiers of campaign staff members on the incumbent President's payroll.

Meghnad elucidated. "There are staff members on Hill's team who have had some questionable political affiliations in their career history."

Agent Meghnad began but paused. "There are a few of them who aren't very well-known. However..."

Agent Daarun whispered to Meghnad. *"Should we really be telling him this?"*

Agent Darsh insisted. "Go ahead, Meghnad. Abhu has the right to know."

Abhu asked abruptly. "Right to know what?"

Agent Meghnad paused again. "Well, Abhu. I'm sorry to have to inform you this but..."

Abhu stared blankly and expected horrible news.

"...Your sister, Kim Porter, is on this list of questionable affiliations. She is an event planner in the President's campaign, and she has been involved in some liberal extremist rallies this past summer at her alma mater. She advocates for some political activist groups considered by many to be domestic terrorists. They identify as a socialist uprising group known as "Upheave Fascism," Agent Meghnad continued grimly.

Agent Abhu disputed. "Wait a minute, I know my sister, and she would not get herself entangled in this mess. I mean, I know she is, you know...A bit...out there in her political ideology, but she is not that extreme."

Darsh countered. "That doesn't change the fact that she has a relatively politically active lifestyle. We must interview her later today, but you cannot be involved in her questioning since she is your sister. However, we will not go overboard on her interrogation out of respect for your family. We currently have a watch team hovering over her in her apartment to keep her surrounded."

Abhu was stunned. His appetite disappeared. He could not imagine that his sister would be engaged in this sort of political extremism.

Darsh continued. "She will be brought in later this morning for interviewing. Khali has permitted you to observe during the questioning, but you must exercise restraint or excuse yourself if you need to blow off steam. I'm sorry."

Abhu held his head in his hands and sighed, "This is going to be another long one."

Singh felt empathetic and comforted Abhu before the breakfast period was over.

Singh consoled Abhu, who felt sick to his stomach. "I'll make sure that they go easy on her. We need answers to find the ones responsible for this. Then we will let your sister return home. We have to follow protocol."

The twelve agents somberly exited the cafeteria and reported to the Level One auditorium for an emergency briefing regarding the last night's events.

3: EJFS Emergency Briefing: Kim Taken in for questioning

EJFS Second-In-Command, Agent Raj Ajith Kalidas

EJFS Briefing Auditorium – Level One

EJFS Palace Base Headquarters – Atlanta Branch, Eastern US Division

20,000 feet over Atlanta

Atlanta, Georgia, USA

November 2, 2024

8:55 AM EDT, Saturday Morning

The entire EJFS roster gathered into the main auditorium foyer to check into their assigned seats inside the Atlanta subdivision.

Agents Abhu and Singh signed in on the alphabetical sign-up tablets sorted by the first letter of their last name. The receptionists then transmitted the briefing materials to their tablets and other devices.

Once all the EJFS agents had assembled in the auditorium, the lights dimmed. The head of the EJFS superagency, Master Khali, entered the stage connected to the center of the odeum with his entourage: Second-in-Command Agent Raj Ajith Kalidas at his right, Agent Kumar at his left, Agent Devdas behind Raj, and Khali's new adviser Tanveer Bhattacharya.

The top brass of the EJFS took a seat at the curved table in the center of the chamber.

Agent Raj curled his index finger towards Singh to cue him to the curved table to join him. Agent Singh had since been promoted to Raj's task force team (the most elite team possible in the agency).

Singh rose from his seat, joined the elite five, and sat next to his partner, Agent Devdas, at the far end of the curved table.

Master Khali led the briefing to open, "Good morning, ladies and gentlemen. Thank you for attending this emergency briefing on such short notice. We have received word from our New York subdivision that there was an incident late last night involving an inside information exchange. Taking part was a key player in the apocalyptic events that transpired over a year ago. We will be issuing assignments to all units shortly. But first, Agent Raj will be giving us a briefing report and mission overview to explain the situation and our unified approach to correct the problem."

Agent Raj took control of the briefing, and Kumar enhanced the high-resolution digital presentation on the screens.

The first graphic displayed on the screens showed a surveillance video obtained from the Western Hotel in Lower East

Manhattan, indicating a cloaked figure entering the hotel with a courier case and checking into their suite.

The facial recognition software picked up a glimpse of the suspected perpetrator. A dossier report appeared, showing the description and headshot of Anastasia Zima, an ex-KGB operative, and a former biotech engineer for the defunct Final Wave Terrorist Organization. The network had since been disbanded over a year ago following the defeat of their leader, Ravan Kanda Ganesh, and their zealous monstrous dragon figure, Vritra, in September of 2023.

Raj spoke into his Bluejaw and provided the first set of details from the failed information transaction from the night before in New York.

"Good morning. Last night around 10:08 p.m. EDT, an inside information deal was supposed to go down inside the Western Hotel in Lower East Manhattan of New York City. We have obtained surveillance footage indicating a hooded character carrying a courier case seen entering the hotel. When the suspect entered the hotel, our facial recognition technology collected a partial frame of the suspect's face obscured by their hooded jacket. We processed the partial in the database. We found a match to a key player tied to the events of 14 months ago during the operation against the fallen Final Wave terrorist organization," Agent Raj began.

"The suspect is Anastasia Zima, a KGB operative during the end of the Cold War. She is now believed to be working with the CIRB in New York, forming a shadow government in some aspect of this network. I will explain more about that shortly," Agent Raj continued as the agents in the EJFS followed along and took notes on their tablet devices.

The presentation continued: another graphic was displayed on the screens that showed another player involved in the buy. A man in a trench coat was shown entering the Western Hotel. He acquired a hidden access card to the hotel suite number 477, where the failed transaction occurred.

The facial recognition technology pulled his profile out of the database, a 42-year-old male from Manhattan's Upper East Side. His profile and dossier report displayed on the screen showed his description and affiliations.

Agent Raj continued the briefing, "In this next slide, we have surveillance footage from around 10:13 p.m. EDT, showing a man that we have identified through facial recognition software as Manhattan native, Judson Clayborn. This man was believed to have been involved in the brokered meeting orchestrated by the CIRB in Upstate New York, where he runs his expedition operation involving ancient artifacts," Agent Raj began.

Information about Clayborn's company was displayed on the screens as part of the high-resolution presentation slides.

Raj continued, "Judson's company, named Expro Incorporated, is a well-known expeditor based in the Greater New York area. Judson stormed out of the hotel suite, passing by a housekeeping worker on the fourth floor. That housekeeper was then seen calling another contact on his phone, dialing a number registered to a CIRB asset named Grant Bradford. After Judson left the hotel, he rushed to Grand Central Station to board a subway train several blocks northeast to the Lexington 55 station. This is where CIRB assets apprehended Judson and escorted him back to his residence, presumably to search Judson's home and interrogate him."

The following graphic was displayed on the screens inside the auditorium. After a 911 call from a concerned neighbor, the images showing the crime scene established that something happened at Clayborn's house, which also appeared to be related to the subway train derailment in Manhattan around 11:00 p.m. EDT.

"In this next slide, we have obtained crime scene photos in partnership with the NYPD from Judson's residence. The area was mostly wiped clean before the forensics team arrived to respond to the emergency call. This is where the trail dead-ends for Judson. He has been declared missing after multiple failed contacts from his family and authorities. However, his registered phone has been disconnected. There may be indications that he was transported out of town to a remote site cut off from the grid. The next slide that I have prepared gives us clues on the identity of this group operating against the West."

Agent Raj switched the graphic over to the next in the presentation.

The wreckage from the subway train derailment in Manhattan close to the Brooklyn Bridge had graffiti tags. A poster showed a triangular logo bearing the acronym "TSS" on the palm of the shadowy figure's hand on the photo. The graffiti tag read "Destroy from Within" in the crime scene photos obtained from the NYPD.

"This last slide in the series shows that following an orchestrated terrorist attack on the subway metro system in New York. Items of interest to the NYPD and our agency provide clues into this network's identity connected to the failed buy at the hotel and the train derailment. Anastasia Zima and the CIRB appear to be part of a vast, global, underground network working against Western societal values to undermine freedom and peace to tip the world's balance into a perpetual state of civil unrest and dissent. The acronym "TSS" as seen on the palm of the hooded figure on the poster represents a terrible, formidable network that challenges the EJFS infrastructure to its very core..." Agent Raj trailed off.

The EJFS agents watched and listened with heightened interest and anxiety.

Agent Abhu sat with his tablet stylus pen pressed against his lips, vexed about what Raj explained in the briefing.

"This network is known as The Shadow State. They ostensibly mimic our technology in modifying weather patterns, resulting in more disruptive and menacing than the intended design we have adopted and safeguarded for almost a decade. A notorious tech giant and corporate owner, known as Jagmohan Gyan, has spearheaded the project and has been funding research and tests to advance the technology to control the weather. This man is coordinating with The Shadow State to equip them with this tool in a method that is detrimental to the entire world."

Agent Raj continued as the EJFS agents watched and listened with intent and fear.

"As you all know, the 2024 US Presidential Election will be held on Tuesday of next week. Our network all over the country has been monitoring, vetting, and researching all background information on both nominees. There is a troubling matter involving sitting President Kenneth Hill's campaign. Several of Hill's campaign staff members are tied to a political extremist group known as "Upheave Fascism." They are analogous to the Bolshevik Uprising and much more disruptive. The longstanding operation of ensuring a corruption-free and honest election is still in effect until the time after the election and the votes have been tabulated. We are going to crack down on this extremist group and put an end to any of the campaign staff members' careers that have been deliberately engaging in this activity," Raj continued.

Agent Abhu looked on in dismay, knowing that his sister, Kim Porter, had been implicated in political extremism.

"Finally, in the coming days of the election, all agents and analyst teams are to remain watchful and vigilant for any terror threats that may impact the election. Continue to monitor the darknet and the radio chatter to indicate possible terrorist threats that may surface in the final days of the campaign trail. This has been an intense election cycle that has proven contentious on every level. I will hand the floor back over to Master Khali to close out the briefing. Thank you all for your continued active service," Agent Raj concluded, passing the floor to Khali.

"Thank you, Raj. Now, I will assemble joint task force teams in conjunction with the New York Subdivision to handle the active case against The Shadow State. Raj's task force team and other assigned units will be responsible for bringing in the President's campaign staff members suspected of involvement to Upheave Fascism. The remaining agents and analysts will continue to monitor the developments surrounding the election. It is the home stretch until the peak of the action occurs. Stay sharp and on task. This briefing is adjourned," Master Khali concluded.

Agent Raj insisted Singh stay behind and called forth Abhu to join him regarding the agent's sister Kim Porter and the plan to bring her in for questioning.

"Agent Abhu, please join us. We need to speak with you," Agent Raj asserted in his thick and powerful thunderous voice.

Abhu joined Singh and Raj on the stage as the EJFS agents headed back to their assigned locations.

"I understand that you have been made aware of the fact that your sister, Kim, is going to be picked up by our agents to be questioned, correct?" Agent Raj asked Abhu calmly.

"That's what I've been told. I still do not think Kim is that extreme on the political spectrum. I can't picture her going that far left," Abhu responded, still in denial that Kim would be involved in political extremism.

"I'm sorry that this has caused you such grief. I am willing to grant you the option to entrust the task of picking Kim up by the agents of your choice. We will go easy on her, given the fact that she is your sibling. If she is cleared of wrongdoing, we will take her back home to her apartment after we have questioned her and her testimony is confirmed," Agent Raj consoled Abhu. He felt terrible for the junior agent during his disturbing revelation.

"I request that you and Singh pick her up. I think she'll be willing to talk with agents like you that she'll recognize," Agent Abhu entreated.

"Fair enough, Singh and I will fly over to Kim's apartment and pick her up. If she is not involved, you two will not have anything to worry about. She'll be safe in our care," Agent Raj comforted Abhu and hugged him to soothe his emotional anguish. Abhu felt comforted after the embrace from Raj and was given another soothing embrace from Singh.

"Don't worry, my friend. We will be kind to her," Agent Singh consoled his best friend, Abhu.

Abhu felt a little more at ease but still experienced some anguish, knowing his sister would be brought to the EJFS Detention Center not far from the main Thunderhead.

"Thank you both," Agent Abhu smiled weakly even though many thoughts were racing through his mind.

"Well, Abhu. You can head up to the command center to work a shift for the time being. You will be issued an assignment within the next hour to assist in the Anastasia Zima case. Keep an eye out on your email account for your mission brief. We will be back in about a half-hour. Let's go, Singh," Agent Raj finished.

Agents Raj and Singh left the auditorium while Abhu lingered, still in a state of bewilderment.

Abhu grabbed his tablet from his seat and left the auditorium to head up to the command center briefly. Abhu hoped that Kim would not resist, knowing she carried an oppositional attitude, in particular, toward those in law enforcement.

Raj and Singh entered an elevator to the parking garage to ride a white ICV (Interchangeable Vehicle) down to Central Atlanta's surface, not far from the University of Georgia.

Agent Raj took the driver's seat, and Singh rode in the passenger seat. Raj started up the ICV and drove down to the parking garage's exit bay housed in the Thunderhead's sublevel floors.

Raj entered Kim Porter's address into the GPS overlay in the manifest screen, then carved a route to her apartment building in the Atlanta Metro area. Immediately, the wheels were locked into place by the metal stoppers on the floor.

The two agents scanned out, and the timer on the screen counted down from five to zero.

After the timer reached zero, Raj floored the gas pedal and launched off the exit ramp to descend to the surface in Atlanta, Georgia.

***

Kimberly Porter

Meanwhile, in Kim's apartment suite in Central Atlanta, Kim was getting dressed for meetings with campaign staff to plan the election night festivities in Washington D.C. for Tuesday. She had a private flight booked to depart at 10:45 a.m.

Kim packed her portfolio in her travel bag and suddenly heard a rumble of thunder in the distance. Kim did not seem too concerned. Her flight may be delayed, but that was all that worried her.

The rain started pouring down gloomily as a storm summoned by the EJFS watch team modified the weather to obscure the apartment building area, which was suddenly surrounded by a thundercloud.

Kim grabbed her smartphone and her charger. She checked the weather forecast and the current conditions, which indicated a strong storm was blowing through the city.

Kim received notification from her flight tracking app that her flight had been delayed due to stormy weather in the airport's vicinity.

"Uh-oh. Not now," Kim whined as she grabbed her coat from her walk-in closet to dress for the stormy weather.

She would not settle on staying in her apartment suite. She needed to get past security for her check-in at Hartsfield-Jackson International Airport at 10:00 a.m.

Suddenly a louder clap of thunder resounded in the apartment. The occurrence caused the building's lights to shut off, and Kim's phone powered down on its own.

"Lovely," Kim sarcastically muttered as she left her closet and decided not to chance it.

Kim stayed put while the storm remained intact and quasi-stationary for well over fifteen minutes.

Suddenly, Kim heard another considerably deep rumble of thunder followed by a brief police siren wailing. The sound came from a white ICV, which had arrived from the EJFS Thunderhead Palace Base above.

Raj pulled the white ICV into a guest parking space as Singh grabbed raincoats to stay dry in the inclement weather.

Kim looked out the window and saw two incredibly powerful Indian super-agents wearing EJFS uniforms and reflective navy-blue raincoats with the EJFS acronym on the back.

Kim started to panic inside as she saw the two huge agents enter the apartment building and head upstairs.

Agents Raj and Singh lumbered up the stairs inside and reached the apartment complex's third floor. Both agents located apartment suite 302. Raj knocked on Kim's front door with authority.

"EJFS, open up!" Agent Raj commanded in his authoritative, booming voice.

The agents' arrival startled Kim, who deduced she was about to be arrested by the world-renowned Elite Justice Force Squad for something they had on her.

Kim felt shaky as another peal of thunder boomed in the sky.

Kim walked to the front door and opened it. She saw the two gigantic super-agents standing twice as tall as her 5'10" frame and felt intimidated by their presence.

"Why are you two here?" Kim asked fearfully while looking up at the two behemoth EJFS super-agents towering over her.

Agent Raj revealed his EJFS badge and identification to Kim, "Miss Porter, my name is Agent Raj, and this is my partner Agent Singh. We are from the EJFS. We first met you during the crisis events 14 months ago. If you do not mind, we would like to talk to you back at our base. We have some questions to ask you regarding your alleged involvement with the extremist group Upheave Fascism. We need to talk to you about it."

"I'm sorry, but there seems to be a bit of confusion. I do not know what you are talking about with that group. Now, if you do not mind, I have a flight to D.C. I need to catch in less than an hour." Kim resisted the two, but Singh wedged his large and robust size 18 6E boot in the door to prevent it from shutting.

"Kim, please don't make it hard for us. Your brother requested to have both of us bring you in after hearing about your alleged extremist activities. We will not arrest you if you cooperate with us, but we have a subpoena order from the EJFS to take you in for questioning. We will notify your people that you may need to take a later flight, if necessary. You must come with us and answer some questions," Agent Singh pleaded to Kim, who remained motionless with disbelief.

"I, *uh–*, okay. Let me grab my stuff. I want you to give me a ride to the airport once you clear me of any wrongdoing. If Caleb insisted on me coming, I will comply," Kim acknowledged as she surrendered to the EJFS agents.

"We will have that arranged for you. Just come with us." Agent Singh beckoned to Kim to bring her up to the EJFS Thunderhead Base.

Both agents escorted Kim down the stairwell with great care and placed her in the back seat of the white ICV.

Kim buckled her seatbelt, and the two immense agents entered the front seats and soared to the EJFS Thunderhead after Agent Raj engaged flight mode causing a tube to emerge from the steering wheel.

Raj blew a strong gust of wind into the tube, which summoned a wind vacuum to suck up the ICV, and they started flying upward toward the EJFS Detention Center.

After the vehicle shot up into the air, the strong thunderstorm cleared up. The clouds parted, showing some sunbreaks after the storm had hovered for 20 minutes over Kim's apartment building during her interaction with the EJFS agents.

4: Judson Clayborn's Re-education: EJFS Questions Kim

Program Participant Reprogramming Center – Compound Building One

Shadow State Black Site No. 44

Albany, New York, USA

November 2, 2024

10:18 AM EDT, Saturday Morning

Later in the morning, the Shadow State operatives transported the newest participant in their network to a local black site.

Judson Clayborn, while held captive, had been forcefully escorted to a reprogramming center for new members.

Clayborn was still becoming acclimated to mind-altering drugs the CIRB had injected before they transported him to their local black site in Albany, New York.

Before she departed, Anastasia Zima, the Shadow State's foreign asset, conferred with the site director, Clyde Patton.

Patton was reasonably athletic and well built. He wore a black suit and black pants. His hairstyle was thick and wavy black, trimmed neatly with a slightly apparent mustache and goatee. The palm in his left hand bore the triangular tattoo with the acronym "TSS" on his palm, which he held up to greet Zima.

Zima returned the sign with her hand bearing the same symbol.

"Do what you need to do to break him in. He's a resistant one, but I think he may be of good use to us." Zima relinquished custody of Clayborn to the site director.

"I will fix him up good, don't you worry," Patton reassured Zima in a creepy tone.

Zima mounted her motorbike and left the area to return to her secret hideout in Upstate New York.

Meanwhile, Patton entered the reprogramming center where other members devoted to the Shadow State operated: the place where Clayborn was held captive.

Clayborn was barely conscious during the transfer to the black site.

"Remove his blindfold," Patton ordered his men.

They complied, and Clayborn could barely see Patton's figure among the others in his warped vision.

"Who the hell are you?!" Clayborn shrieked in fear.

"My name is Clyde Patton, and I'm the director of this site. You will be our newest member of a growing, influential underground network: The Shadow State. In the next 24 hours, you will soon be a loyal devotee to this network, and you will help us crush all that oppose us. But, before then, we need to reprogram and rewire your mind to think as we do. Indeed, you may be of good use to us."

Clayborn was terrified of what pain the three men were going to inflict upon him.

Patton ordered his men to prepare the re-education set-up for Clayborn to develop him into a Shadow State Agent. "Get the programming materials started. We must not waste any time."

Patton's assistants, Alec Hawthorne and Lukas Hightower, procured the educational reprogramming materials.

The objective was to break in Clayborn and poison his mind into thinking as one entity in alignment with the Shadow State's ideology.

Alec prepared videos and brain-warping drugs to prepare Clayborn for the transition. Alec placed a vintage projector behind Clayborn to be displayed on the white screen.

Lukas injected Clayborn with another mind-control drug in the back of his neck before the session proceeded. The drug increased agitation, awareness, and elasticity in Clayborn's altered mental state.

"Start the cycle and clear the room," Patton ordered his men.

"Yes, sir," Alec and Lukas prepared a continuous influx of synthetics to be pumped into the room to accelerate the process. The three operatives left the room and turned on the "active session" light above the doorway.

The door locked shut, and Clayborn cried out a primal scream in response to the bombardment of mind-altering chemicals that invaded the room.

***

Meanwhile, Abhu worked in the command center on the top floor of the EJFS Thunderhead Base in the main building.

He received a text message from Agent Singh, his best friend, informing him that his sister, Kim Porter, had been picked up and was en route to the detention center for questioning.

Agent Singh sent the following text message to Abhu:

"My dear friend, Abhu. Raj and I have picked up your sister Kim, and we're heading to the EJFS Detention Center. I have informed Agent Lochan of the developing situation and have

advised him to let you observe the questioning on your lunch break if you choose. Please know that your sister will be taken good care of and treated with respect. You may take a vehicle to the Detention Center to meet with me in Interrogation Room Three's observation room. Much love to you. ~Agent Singh."

Abhu silently viewed the text message on his smartphone. He ascended the staircase to speak with the AIC, Agent-in-Charge, Lochan Nair, to request an early lunch break to rendezvous with Singh off-site at the Detention Center.

***

Agent Lochan sat at his desk, working on his computer station, in the upper-level section of the EJFS Bullpen. This is where most of the action took place in the final days before the US Presidential Election. Also on his mind was the appropriate tactical response to the Shadow State's looming threat.

Agent Abhu reached the upper area to Lochan's glass door and knocked gently to enter.

"Come in," Agent Lochan permitted.

Agent Abhu opened the glass door and met with Agent Lochan to chat about Kim Porter's situation, his sister.

"Hello, Abhu. I am sorry about the situation with your sister. I presume you are here to ask me to be excused from work to observe the questioning. Am I correct?" Agent Lochan asked empathetically.

"Yes, that's right. I received a text from Singh that both he and Raj are taking Kim to the Detention Center now," Abhu explained with distress on his face.

"You have my permission. Again, I am sorry that this situation is occurring. If you need anything or need to talk to someone, I am here," Lochan reassured Abhu.

"Thank you. I appreciate that. I'll be back to finish out my shift later," Abhu smiled weakly and headed downstairs to clock out and take his vehicle to the Detention Center not far from the base.

After Abhu clocked out by using his fingerprint on the time kiosk to punch out for an hour, he exited the Command Center and entered an elevator, descending to the main floor to pick up the keys.

While Abhu was at the reception desk, Abhu's girlfriend, Durga, checked in and tried to comfort him.

EJFS Agent Durga Gopal Deshmukh

"I'm sure everything will be okay with your sister," Durga assured Abhu while she hugged him.

"I hope so. It just seems so surreal to me. I have a hard time picturing Kim going to this level of political extremism," Abhu remarked in disbelief.

"I think they'll be considerate of you and go easy on her. I am sure your sister will be fine. If you do not see her being a political extremist, then maybe your instincts are right," Durga reassured Abhu.

"The truth will always prevail in the end," Abhu proclaimed.

"That's right, Abhu," Durga nodded her head.

"Thanks, honey. I'll talk to you later," Abhu retrieved his keys from the receptionist and left to go to the parking garage in the sublevels of the Thunderhead Base.

"Be well!" Durga bid farewell to her boyfriend as Abhu trudged to the elevators.

***

Agents Raj and Singh continued their approach to the Detention Center with Kim Porter in the flying vehicle's back seat.

Kim felt somewhat lost and seemingly perturbed by the heights and the location of the base. She wondered how all the areas of the complex functioned so high in the troposphere.

Agents Raj and Singh remained quiet as they made their final approach to the Detention Center's landing zone. Agent Raj prepared to descend upon a helipad on the outer section of the entrance.

Agent Singh received a text message from Abhu.

Singh quietly informed Raj:

"He's on his way."

"Good, you can bring him in, and I'll take Kim inside to be questioned."

"What are you two talking about?" Kim queried curiously.

"Your brother is on his way to meet with us to observe your questioning," Agent Singh informed Kim, partly turning his head to face her in the backseat.

Kim felt her stomach drop. She was horrified that her older brother would watch her during the interview process.

The vehicle lowered the landing gear and jetted forth a set of chopper wings to descend onto the helipad. The car landed gently on the helipad, prompting Raj to retract the landing gear and the chopper wings. The hulking agent drove up to the security gate.

The security guard, Tungar, defended the entrance from intruders and admitted Agents Raj and Singh inside after Tungar scanned their access cards to gain entry to the Detention Center.

Raj drove the vehicle into a parking space and pulled into his reserved spot near the front entrance.

Agents Raj and Singh exited the vehicle and helped Kim step down from the large ICV on a cloudy, cold, and windy day in the lofty heights over Atlanta.

Kim's coat was only slightly helpful in staying warm in the bitterly cold altitude.

Singh grabbed a thermal blanket from the back hatch and placed it around Kim to warm her up.

"Better?" Singh asked kindly.

"Yes, thank you," Kim graciously accepted the blanket.

"You're welcome. Raj will be taking you inside," Singh informed her as Raj escorted Kim into the Detention Center.

Agent Singh noticed that Agent Abhu's vehicle started to land not far from where he was standing.

Singh held his hand as a visor over his face to protect his eyesight from the glare in the bright gray skies while watching Abhu land his vehicle on one of the other helipads.

Agent Abhu landed his vehicle and drove up to the security gate, scanning his access card to enter.

Agent Singh took a few steps backward to give Abhu space to pull into a parking spot. The wind occasionally whipped Singh's long, thick, wavy black hair around. He wore his flannel EJFS coat for warmth.

Abhu pulled into a parking space and exited the vehicle in his outerwear jacket, approaching Singh. The two conversed as they began to head inside the facility.

"Kim knows you're here to observe, and she seemed a bit stunned that you were coming to watch her while she is interviewed," Agent Singh began as they neared the entrance.

"Does she know that I'm in my alternate form?" Abhu asked.

"She only knows what she understands after we went public last year. I didn't tell, and she didn't ask me about your current form," Singh assured Abhu.

"I don't know if she would be able to understand how the transition process worked. She might not take it too well if she finds out that I have a split identity," Agent Abhu replied as he and Singh scanned their badges to unlock the front doors and enter the Detention Center.

"At this point, that decision is entirely up to you. I would advise you to exercise your best judgment and take care when it involves divulging your identities to your sister. You've known her longer than we have," Agent Singh advised.

"I'll probably have to keep my distance in my current form as it is. I don't want Kim to freak out on us," Abhu replied.

Agents Abhu and Singh entered the observation room adjacent to Interrogation Room Three, where Kim would be interviewed in a vitals-based interrogation session with no pain involved.

Abhu had not been actively involved in the detention center operations until the present moment. He felt nervous for Kim, knowing she would be in the hot seat, answering uncomfortable questions regarding her political affiliations.

Abhu saw from the other side of the two-way mirror that Agent Raj brought Kim into the Interrogation Room. The powerful agent seated Kim at the steel table's front-end while Raj's fellow associate Agent Devdas prepared to set up Kim with wireless nodes to detect her vitals.

Kim was given a bright blue, translucent capsule device to ingest to help distinguish the facts from her memories and subconscious.

"What is this thing?" Kim asked with a slight tone of horror in her voice.

"It's supposed to help tell us whether or not you are telling us the truth," Agent Devdas answered calmly.

"Wow – big brother-like," Kim retorted.

She hesitantly swallowed the capsule device and was given a water bottle to help her ingest it.

On the other side of the two-way mirror, Abhu and Singh were joined by Master Khali and Kumar with an interrogation tech-in-training, Yukti Dubashi. The new agent would become an interrogation tech under Kumar's direction.

Khali greeted Abhu with a loving embrace to console him in his inner anguish about his sister.

"I'm sorry that this had to happen. Don't worry. We'll be delicate to Kim as long as she can agree to comply with us," Master Khali comforted Abhu.

"What if she doesn't comply?" Abhu asked Khali.

"We'll do all that we can to have her cooperate. You have my word that I will make sure she is treated with special care," Khali assured Abhu.

"I will take you on your word. Just do what you can that will not be too much for Kim to bear," Abhu accepted Khali's assurances.

5: Kim's Questioning Begins: POTUS Hill's Dark Secret

EJFS Detention Center – Interrogation Room Three

EJFS Palace Base Headquarters – Atlanta Branch, Eastern US Division

20,000 feet over Atlanta

Atlanta, Georgia, USA

November 2, 2024

10:39 AM EDT, Saturday Morning

The EJFS was about to question Kim with Abhu observing the entire interrogation.

The capsule device inside Kim had no harmful capabilities and only served to distinguish the truth from what Kim verbalized to the interrogators.

Kim was hunching in her uncomfortable seat with her purse on the floor by her left side. She was nervously waiting for a phone call from her superiors in the Hill campaign, inquiring about her delayed flight to Washington, D.C. She was also waiting for her boyfriend to call her about meeting up at a local four-star restaurant in D.C. for dinner that evening.

Around 10:41 a.m., Agent Raj opened the door from the observation room and entered with Agent Singh. They were prepared to interview Kim regarding her alleged ties to the political extremist group known as Upheave Fascism.

Both agents towered over Kim as she remained seated in her chair, dwarfed by their size.

"Am I going to need my attorney for this?" Kim asked.

"You haven't been formally charged. We're only gathering information," Agent Raj assured Kim.

Kim felt a little uneasy surrounded by the agents in the unsettling environment. Her vitals started to spike on the tablet screen with Kumar and his trainee, Yukti, watching side-by-side through the two-way mirror.

Abhu watched intently while the questioning commenced.

"Kim, I've reviewed your file, and you don't have much of a record against you. So, given the fact that you have no prior arrests, we might be able to clear you from the investigation if you fully cooperate with us," Agent Raj continued.

"Ask away," Kim said cautiously.

"Very well, we need to ask you some questions regarding your alleged involvement with Upheave Fascism. Are you aware that their practices are classified as political extremism?" Agent Raj asked Kim.

"I haven't seen any indicators that they were an extremist group. I just heard about their unified message against fascist leaders in our country and the ongoing mission to expose them," Kim responded.

Agent Singh interjected. "How long have you been familiar with the group?"

"I've heard about them earlier this past summer," Kim answered.

Agents Raj and Singh took notes from the responses received from Kim.

Raj handed out a printed photo of Kim holding up a sign from a summer protest at her alma mater.

"Could you explain this photo here that shows what appears to be you participating in a protest rally last summer at your college?" Agent Raj asked as he slid a photocopy to Kim of what appeared to be her engaging in a protest at the University of Georgia.

Kim was astounded upon seeing the photo.

"I don't know how that is possible, but that is not me," Kim pleaded her innocence.

"Kim, the person in the photo looks exactly like you. How could you say that wasn't you?" Agent Singh asked sternly.

"Look at the photo of the girl's face. She has a little birthmark. I don't have a birthmark on my face," Kim defended herself.

Agents Raj and Singh glanced at each other. Considering Kim's plea for innocence, Raj responded by paging Kumar to review Kim's medical records and her most recent photo.

"Kumar, run a check through the database and see if what she said is true," Raj asked while he paged the intercom next to the door.

"I'm on it," Kumar responded and ran a search through the database for a recent photo of Kim.

However, once Kumar managed to locate Kim's official record, the access was restricted by a Level 10 SCI Access key.

Kumar called on Khali to intervene.

"Master Khali, could you assist us, please?" Kumar requested.

Khali veered around and approached Kumar and his trainee, Yukti.

"What's wrong?" Khali asked calmly.

Kumar pivoted his tablet screen to face Khali. Access to Kim's records had been locked with a security clearance.

"Kim's record is under a security clearance, Level 10. Are you able to bypass this?" Trainee Yukti inquired.

"I can try to access it with my credentials," Khali replied.

Khali logged on to his system and pulled up Kim's secured records. He was prompted to enter a master security passcode that he had acquired to access all networks' available data.

Khali entered his usual passcode to gain access to the data. However, the passcode was rejected.

Khali was mystified as his passcode had never been rejected by any agency requiring authentication and used by the EJFS to clear suspects.

"This is strange. My credentials were rejected," Khali remarked in confusion.

Abhu overheard what was going on, concerned that something was not adding up.

"What's going on?" Abhu asked.

"Your sister's records have been secured by a Level 10 SCI Access. I am looking for the person who operates the clearance, and it seems like President Hill's Chief of Staff, Nicolas Hastings, has restricted Kim's records. I'll run a check on Hastings and look up his information," Khali explained.

"Nicolas Hastings? Isn't that the father of Kim's boyfriend?" Abhu pondered aloud.

"Let me check into that," Khali responded and looked up the chief of staff's dossier.

The dossier for Hastings was accessed by Khali and listed Hastings' son Logan in the Chief of Staff's genealogy profile. Khali searched Hastings' son Logan, aged 23, and located his romantic interest, Kim Porter.

"You were right, Abhu. She is dating the Chief of Staff's son, Logan Hastings. I wonder if Logan has any involvement in this group," Khali conjectured.

Khali was forced to keep Kim on ice until they could reach President Kenneth Hill's Chief of Staff, Nicolas Hastings. Khali had no other choice but to go through the proper channels until Kim's statements were verified.

With this in mind, Khali decided to examine Kim's memory from the past summer, trying to A) find any clues to the date that the Upheave Fascism protest took place and B) whether she was involved.

"Kumar, run a search in Kim's memory to see if you can find out whether there is any shred of evidence that Kim was not involved in the protest last summer," Khali ordered.

"I'll see if I can find anything," Kumar replied.

Kumar ran a retroactive scan from August 2024 and searched through a handful of images. The results came back inconclusive, as indicated by the computerized male Indian voice on the tablet speakers.

RETROACTIVE MEMORY SCAN COMPLETE, RESULT: INCONCLUSIVE. INSUFFICIENT DATA REPORTED.

"This doesn't make sense to me. Is someone hacking into our database and modifying our systems again?" Kumar questioned in a tone of frustration.

"I don't know, but this is a troubling development. Unfortunately, I am going to have to keep Kim here longer than she may prefer. At least until we can sort this issue out," Khali explained with a pressing tone in his voice.

Abhu was distressed and did not relish what was transpiring.

Khali paged Agents Raj and Singh into the observation room while Abhu stayed out of Kim's line of sight.

Khali explained his next move with Kim after the roadblock set in the EJFS's path of finding out the truth.

"I tried to search for Kim's records, but somehow her profile has been safeguarded with a Level 10 SCI Access. Not even my credentials were able to bypass it. Alternatively, we ran a retroactive scan of her memory to the timeframe of the protest last summer. The results were inconclusive," Khali reported to the two agents as Abhu joined in on the conversation.

"How is that even possible? That rarely happens," Agent Singh remarked in disbelief.

Raj interjected, "I think somebody must be trying to set her up, but we have no way to verify her statements if we can't access the data."

"Perhaps we should dig a little deeper about her relationship with the Chief of Staff's son. In the meantime, I will call the Langley EJFS office to have them request immediate access to Kim's records," Khali decided.

Abhu objected to the decision, "I don't think my sister is genuinely involved in this group. Let me see the photo in question, please."

Master Khali hesitated before showing the picture to Abhu for a closer examination.

Abhu noted that the woman in the photo was not his sister. He compared it to his sister's profile and observed that the birthmark on the woman's face did not match Kim's face.

"The woman in this photo is a fraud. That is not my sister. Someone must have been posing as her. Kim doesn't have that birthmark on her face like this woman in the photo does!" Abhu proclaimed.

"If that's so, who would do that, and why?" Agent Raj asked.

"Someone must have mimicked her and tried to frame her," Abhu explained.

The four agents stood at a loss for words as Kumar and Yukti sat in the background, each trying to contemplate their next plan of action. All agents stared blankly into the interrogation room.

***

In Washington D.C., the First Family was gathered in the White House to watch President Hill issue a statement condemning the terrorist attack in Manhattan's subway system the night before.

President Hill was joined by his wife, Lacey, and their son and daughter, Trevor and Allison Hill, both in their freshman year in college. Vice President Peter Drake and his wife, Suzanne, accompanied them. They all sat in the tearoom to have a light snack before a long day of meetings, campaign events, and a press conference.

During the late morning tea, a White House staffer named Libby Daniels entered the tearoom to interrupt the visit with an impromptu conference call from the Chief of Staff, Nicolas Hastings, and his son, Logan.

Libby managed to catch the President's attention after working her way into the tearoom.

"Pardon me, Mr. President, but you have a conference call waiting on Line One," Libby informed him.

"Can it wait? I'm spending time with my family," President Hill answered passively.

"It's the Chief of Staff and his son. They said it's an urgent matter," Libby explained.

The President whispered in Drake's ear, and they both arose from the davenport to excuse themselves.

"Please forgive us, but I need to take a conference call. I'll be back soon," President Hill informed his family.

"Don't take too long, honey. The kids aren't going to stay all weekend," First Lady Lacey Hill warned.

"I'll be back, I promise."

President Hill kissed his wife on the cheek before storming to the conference room down the hall while accompanied by Vice President Drake, leaving the First Lady disappointed that her husband could not set aside time for their family visit.

President Kenneth Hill and Vice President Peter Drake entered the West Wing conference room close to the Oval Office in the White House conference room.

Another staffer named Sedgwick Barnes greeted the President and Vice President upon their arrival to the conference room.

"Good morning, Mr. President. I have the Chief of Staff and his son on the line for you," Sedgwick informed.

"Put them through on speaker," President Hill ordered.

"Yes, Mr. President," Sedgwick responded.

Sedgwick put the conference call on speakerphone and engaged both Chief of Staff Nicolas Hastings and his son Logan in the phone conversation.

"Mr. Hastings and Logan, you're on the line with the President and Vice President. What is your status?"

Chief of Staff Hastings was the first to speak. He was in a motorcade limo en route to Langley, Virginia, to meet with the CIRB's Deputy Director.

"Mr. President, I regret to inform you that we have a situation with one of your campaign staffers based in Atlanta this morning. I have received word that the Atlanta Branch of the EJFS has taken one of my staffers into custody, and my son Logan's romantic involvement with this particular staffer has been exposed," Hastings reported.

"Who is this staffer?" President Hill asked.

"Her name is Kim Porter, Mr. President," Hastings answered hesitantly.

"That last name sounds vaguely familiar. When was her last check-in with her boss? Why was she taken into custody?" President Hill inquired.

"She's our campaign events liaison. She was last seen in her apartment earlier this morning until a storm cell developed over the building. She planned to take a flight to D.C. to coordinate election night festivities. After the storm broke, she was gone.

Her phone appears to be disabled. Her boss, Veronica Baylor, has repeatedly tried to reach her to no avail," Hastings explained.

Logan interjected himself into the conversation. "Mr. President, this is Logan. Kim and I were going to meet up for dinner at the Metro Café in D.C. later this evening. She hasn't answered my texts for the past two hours."

The President and the Vice President looked at each other with mutual concern on their faces.

"Nicolas, what can I do on my end? What do you know about EJFS's case against Miss Porter?" President Hill asked.

"My chauffeur is driving me to Langley now to respond to this agency's request for a Level 10 SCI Access. I'm going to try and stonewall and keep them away from Kim's record," Hastings explained.

"Why are you not going to allow the EJFS access to Kim's dossier? What does she know?" Vice President Drake queried with confusion.

"Mr. Vice President, this is a matter I cannot discuss over the phone. Trust me, you should let me handle it myself," Hastings insisted.

Drake was stunned by Hastings' refusal.

"When you get back from your little trip, I want a full update on this situation in person. That's an order!" Drake dictated angrily.

"When I get back tonight, I will explain everything to you. Now let me do my job and clean up this mess before it does irreversible damage to Hill's re-election campaign," Hastings finished the conversation and disconnected from the White House phone tree.

The line at the White House disconnected, and the vice president was visibly upset with President Hill.

"How did you not know about this? What are you hiding from me?!" Drake angrily fumed.

"Peter, this is a complicated matter. I can explain, but not right now. Not while you are this upset," President Hill attempted to de-escalate.

"You're right. I am upset. Do you know how much damage this could do to our re-election? Our careers, and not to mention our reputation, are on the line here. I don't know what you are hiding from me, but I think you need to figure out where we stand in this administration," Drake spat.

"What exactly are you saying, Peter?" Hill asked.

"Allow me to rephrase: Let me know what's going on, or you can find another VP on the re-election bid."

Drake stormed out of the conference room and did not return to the tearoom but went instead to his private quarters to let off some steam.

Meanwhile, President Hill received a silent notification on his smartwatch and saw that it was from a saved contact with a cryptic name.

New Unread Message from 'Shadow Four Cobra':

Cobra checking in for new task assignments. TSS Identification Code: Alpha Hotel Zulu, 293205. Direct call requested. ~S4CAHZ

President Hill excused himself for a private phone call in the Oval Office.

"Tell my wife that I need to make one more phone call. I'll be back in the Tearoom in 20 minutes," President Hill spoke to a Secret Service Agent upon entering the Oval Office.

"Yes, Mr. President," The Secret Service member nodded to his Commander-In-Chief.

The President entered the Oval Office, locked the doors, and uncovered a hidden switch in a discreet location behind his Presidential Portrait. He flipped it and disabled all the recording devices in the room. Afterward, the President blackened the windows from the outside, facing the White House Lawn, and sat at the Resolute Desk.

President Hill calmly and methodically unlocked a hidden drawer in his desk containing a burner phone with a scrambler device and retrieved it from the secret drawer.

He speed-dialed a contact in a New York area code.

***

The President dialed Anastasia Zima's phone number. She was in her hideout underneath the intricate piping and conduits of the New York subway system in an old maintenance office for subway workers.

Zima used a computer operating system with software integration developed and engineered by The Shadow State and their tech leader, Jagmohan Gyan.

Zima was hacking into the EJFS database to cover her tracks and place obstacles to impede the EJFS in finding her. She also used her CIRB credentials to restrict access by block-listing the superagency.

Suddenly, Zima's burner phone rang, and the Caller ID displayed "SE1." Zima answered the phone using her cryptic moniker.

"SC4AHZ. Identify yourself."

"SC4, this is Shadow Eagle One, Codename Kilo Echo Hotel 851303," President Hill identified his moniker using his role in the Shadow State's network.

"Hello, *Mr. President*," Zima ended the formalities and outed the President in the phone call.

"Hello, Anastasia. How did the operation go?" President Hill asked in a smarmy tone.

"Judson was difficult at first, but a little tough talk and MK-Ultra style synthetics did the trick simply fine. He is being reprogrammed at the Black Site in Albany right now. My estimation is he will be operational by tomorrow morning after Clyde's crew breaks him down and works his wonders on the expeditor," Zima ominously hinted at Clayborn's capture the night before.

"If he doesn't adapt, he's damaged goods, and you'll have to count him as a lost cause," The President intimated.

"He's a pawn. We have greater things to worry about, such as our rival agency's star rookie agent's sister. She is a liability. They took her into custody, and she could unknowingly expose us. But do not worry, your Chief of Staff will do what it takes to keep your secret out of the public eye," Zima assured President Hill.

"Very good. I do believe it's time for your next assignment," President Hill hinted.

"What are your orders?" Zima asked chillingly.

"Go meet with Mr. Gyan. Collaborate with him to equip yourself with all that you need to bring down the EJFS for good. His office is located at the One World Trade Center. Tell him Shadow Eagle One sent you," President Hill commanded Zima.

"I will comply. I accept your assignment." Zima gave her assent to her international sponsor and handler.

"Good luck, and I'll contact you again soon," President Hill dismissed Zima to her new assignment.

The President ended the call. He hid the phone back in the secret hiding place in his desk and returned to the Tearoom.

Less than fifteen minutes remained until his live address to the nation. He would speak in condemnation of the terrorist attack the night before, an attack which Hill had allowed to take place with his weaponized branch of government, the CIRB, as an apparent member of the Shadow State.

***

Meanwhile, Zima maintained her stranglehold on the EJFS systems and packed up her laptop and gear.

She prepared to travel back into the Manhattan area to the One World Trade Center. There she would meet with the Shadow State's tech giant, Jagmohan Gyan, in a joint effort to bring down the EJFS.

6: Enter Kim's Doppelganger: Zima and Gyan plot America's Election Day Demise

Langley, Virginia, USA

November 2, 2024

11:01 AM EDT, Saturday Morning

President Hill's Chief of Staff, Nicolas Hastings, was being driven to the CIRB Headquarters Office in Langley, Virginia. He was accompanied by two Secret Servicemen and his closest staffer, Laura Matheson.

Hastings and Matheson conferred with each other in the backseat of a government-issued vehicle about their damage control strategy with one of their newest staffers, Kim Porter. She was romantically involved with Hastings' son, Logan.

Matheson spoke her mind while the vehicle was in motion. "This Porter girl is quite a liability with her relationship to your son. Let us cut her loose to salvage our chances at the re-election bid. What dirt does she have on the Hill Administration?"

Hastings explained. "I'm afraid that is classified. I will leave it like this: She is related to someone who is part of a vast network that the CIRB considers a vigilante group. This specific group is a threat to America's sovereignty and to that end around the world. They went public last year after a series of coordinated strikes and operations against government officials and terror groups without any congressional oversight or accountability from world leaders."

"The EJFS?" Laura asked.

Hastings nodded. "Correct, they have been data mining terabytes of data for nearly a decade. They have unabated access to files from every government agency database in the world. Now, do you see wherein the problem lies?"

Laura seethed. "What a constitutional nightmare! This is unacceptable. How do you plan to stop them?"

Hastings replied. "Let us say that I have some connections in the tech industry that could pull some strings. They might be able to render their systems defenseless with the proper tools and methods."

Laura asked. "What are you going to do with the Porter girl?"

Hastings answered. "I suppose we'll have to cut our losses. She is too much of a public relations risk to keep around. We'll let her sweat it out for a while before we have her freed from her detainment."

Soon after, the vehicle containing Mr. Hastings and Ms. Matheson pulled up to the CIRB Headquarters Office Building in Langley, Virginia. The car driver and a couple of secret service members escorted the Chief of Staff and his most trusted staffer from the car. They both sauntered to the front entrance of the building after they cleared through security.

Hastings and Matheson arrived at the Deputy Director of the CIRB's office on the building's third floor, along with their security escort.

The Deputy Director's secretary greeted the Chief of Staff and his most loyal staffer.

"Mr. Hastings, the Deputy Director is terribly busy right now. Do you have a meeting scheduled?" Secretary Erika Cole asked firmly.

Hastings handed over a four-page order detailing the repeated attempts by the EJFS to access the CIRB Database.

"I'm afraid it's an urgent matter. I need to speak with Matthews right away. I am here to respond to the unauthorized server access by an entity unrecognized by the state."

Secretary Cole skimmed through the documents.

"I'll escort you both to his office. Follow me."

The secretary beckoned both Hastings and Matheson to the Deputy Director, James Matthews' office.

The secretary led both government officials to the CIRB Deputy Director's office while two Secret Service members stood outside guarding the double glass doors.

Deputy Director James Matthews was at his desk looking at the crime scene reports from the events of the night before, studying them intently. At the same time, he saw the photos from the train crash and Judson Clayborn's disappearance from the other night.

Suddenly, Matthews' secretary tapped the back of her knuckles gently on the glass door leading to his office.

Matthews curled his finger to gesture his permission to enter.

While both Secret Service agents stood posted outside the Deputy Director's office, Erika opened the double doors for Hastings and Matheson to enter.

Matthews greeted the two with half-hearted enthusiasm. "Hastings, what a semi-pleasant surprise. What brings you here?"

"You know why we're here. For starters: you could explain why the CIRB is up to their neck in this Clayborn disappearance. On top of that: why did the subway crash in New York have prior NTSB access by a CIRB Asset?" Hastings demanded answers.

"I'm afraid I can't discuss that with you. It's an ongoing investigation," Matthews explained.

Hastings countered. "Of course, you would say something like that. James, you're in charge of one of the most clandestine agencies in the world, that is, until some of your assets meddled with this disappearance and subway train derailment."

Matthews continued to deny his involvement in the incident.

"I don't think you know what you are talking about. Now, do you have a reason why you have come here to interrogate me about this development, or is there something that you want?"

Hastings continued. "There is something: Whether you accept it or not, your agency muddied itself in this false flag operation. Now, if you do not want your face plastered all over the news, I suggest you give me a quid pro quo. I need to call in a favor from you."

Matthews asked. "What do you want?"

"I need you to do your best to stonewall this entity known as the EJFS, the Elite Justice Force Squad. They are poking their noses into your operation, and now they have my son's girlfriend in custody somewhere up above. She was supposed to be on a plane to D.C. at this hour, but she was taken away. They have been piggybacking our database and servers for who knows how long. For all I care, they could be mining data from all over the country to across the globe. They are using some backend credential system to attain access to our system. We need to cut the pipeline feeding information to them," Hastings advised.

Matthews paused as he removed his bifocals and rubbed his eyelids.

"You're telling me that the EJFS that went public last year has been in our systems gathering our data for their use?" Matthews' face turned green.

"That's exactly what I'm saying. Maybe you should beef up your system security and continue to wage war against the EJFS. They have too much power over the nations. It is a violation of our country's sovereignty. You started this, and now you're going to finish it," Hastings asserted.

"I'll call a meeting with all other agencies and see what can be done to stop this. As far as your son's girlfriend, we have a plant that can take her place in the meantime." Matthews stated.

"Explain," Matheson prompted.

"She has a doppelganger that took part in a planned protest last year in Atlanta, Georgia. She can be used as a decoy until we can find a way to shore up our systems. Your son's girlfriend is someone related to an EJFS agent, correct? Miss Kimberly Porter, sister of Caleb Porter?" Matthews asked.

"So, you *do* know about them," Hastings affirmed.

"You know we have procedures that we need to follow to know how much someone internally knows about an ongoing case. I'll tell you what. I'll keep Kim out of play for the next two hours, but at some point, I'll have to give this agency the information they need to clear her name," Matthews explained.

Matheson interjected. "Who is Kim's decoy? Where is she now?"

Matthews answered. "She's here, and we can bring her in."

The Deputy Director paged his secretary to call Kim's decoy into the office.

Suddenly, an almost identical lookalike of Kim Porter entered through a side door in the office and stood to face both Hastings and Matheson.

"This is Alicia Blaze. She's Kim's doppelganger. She is a trained, incognito agent. She can work stealth and cause controlled chaos whenever and wherever we want," Matthews explained.

Alicia was the same girl pictured in the photo in question, which led to Kim Porter being suspected of political extremism.

"Alicia, you're going undercover as Kim again. You are going to meet with her handler, Veronica. Then you will have to keep Hastings' son Logan under the impression that you are the real Kim. Are we clear on that?" Matthews dictated.

"Crystal," Alicia answered.

"Good, now go to Washington, D.C., and meet with Kim's boss. Remember, act natural," Matthews ordered.

"You got it," Alicia complied and left the room to take an identical car to the one that Kim drives to D.C.

"I will make sure this gets taken care of. You both can leave now," Matthews dismissed Hastings and Matheson from the room, and they left to return to the White House.

***

Anastasia Zima

Meanwhile, in New York City, Anastasia Zima, codename Shadow Four Cobra, was en route to the One World Trade Center in Manhattan to meet with a tech genius working for the Shadow State, Jagmohan Gyan. Her goal was to draft a plan to disrupt the Presidential Election in the next few days with Gyan's help.

Zima drove her motorbike through downtown Manhattan while passing through Times Square. It was a cold, cloudy, but dry day in New York around 11:17 a.m.

Zima arrived at a metered parking spot near the OWTC. She tucked her hood down on her motorcycle jacket, plodded up to the building entrance, and then took the elevator to the 110th floor, reaching Gyan's startup office in the Northern portion of the building.

Gyan noticed Zima from across the room and went to greet her formally.

Gyan was a bit socially awkward at times but was one of the world's most intelligent men, with an IQ of over 250. He was known as the evil, dorky genius, helping the Shadow State.

"Miss Zima?" Gyan asked.

"Please don't call me that," Zima chided quietly.

"Sorry, Anastasia. I'm guessing you're here to consult with me on a co-op project?"

"Correct, I have an assignment from Shadow Eagle One for us to complete by Tuesday."

"This Tuesday? That is Election Day. What do you have in mind?"

"We're going to bring the Western world to its knees while obliterating the EJFS."

"Ooh, intriguing. Let us meet in my office. Right this way," Gyan excitedly beckoned. "Tina, please get some cold-brewed coffee for Anastasia. We're having a consultation in my office for a half-hour."

Tina was a bespectacled lady who was short and stout but very sassy and sarcastic.

"Oh good, maybe you can tell her about your in-depth relationship with your robotic kitty prototype that you created," Tina sarcastically quipped.

"Ahem—Not the time for that," Gyan countered with a forced smile.

"Oh, you're upgrading to a human companion. Excellent." Tina rolled her eyes as she prepared cold-brewed coffee for Zima.

"Don't mind her," Gyan quietly remarked.

Zima turned her eyes to the side and had a creepy smirk on her face.

Both Gyan and Zima entered Gyan's office.

"So, what is your plan?" Gyan asked as he poured some black tea.

"Here's what I have planned: I need you to upgrade your geoengineering projects to create a massive hurricane covering the entirety of the continental United States. That is the first phase of this plan," Zima began to explain.

"And?" Gyan asked.

"Secondly, you have to disable the power grid for a day. We need America to be blind and in the dark," Zima explained further.

"My investors are going to be pissed," Gyan quipped after almost spitting out his tea.

"It gets even better: Are you familiar with the remnants of Vritra, the ancient dragon from Siberia?" Zima asked.

"The name rings a bell. I had lost a few prototypes during his rampage last year," Gyan lamented.

"The last part of the plan involves Vritra's remnants. The hurricane you create should bring life to the dragon again," Zima continued.

"How are you going to manage to do that? The remnants of Vritra are missing and haven't been accounted for in a year," Gyan began to lose interest as he turned facing away from Zima while fiddling with his prototypes on the back table.

"That's where you are wrong," Zima refuted, causing Gyan to drop his cup of tea, shattering it to pieces.

"I know where Vritra's remains are stored," Zima explained.

"Now you have my full attention," Gyan remarked.

"You'll have to come with me to see it," Zima hinted.

"This is going to leave a mark on the world," Gyan declared.

"Exactly. Now, are you in with me on this?" Zima asked him.

"You can count me in," Gyan affirmed.

"Come with me then," Zima enticed.

Gyan joined forces with Zima, and they took a drive to Zima's hideout.

7: EJFS Stonewalled: Vritra's Remains Unsealed

Interrogation Room Three – EJFS Detention Center

EJFS Atlanta Branch – Eastern US Division

November 2, 2024

11:48 AM EDT, Saturday Morning

At the EJFS, Kim was still held in detainment. Simultaneously, Khali and his team of superagents investigated Abhu's claims that his sister, Kim Porter, may have a doppelganger impersonating her.

Khali was encountering difficulties while struggling to establish a connection into the CIRB database to access Kim's record but to no avail.

Because of this problem, Khali was forced to come up with a backup plan.

"I've tried every method I could think of, and I still can't access the CIRB network. I'm going to have to contact the Director to remedy this unless any of you agents have alternative suggestions," Khali spoke with frustration in his powerful, booming voice.

Abhu interjected. "Wait, let me see if we can pinpoint the problem. Maybe the Shadow State has something to do with this. I can figure this out, but I need to have the command center grant me access to their hacking tools."

Khali was hesitant to accept Abhu's assistance, especially since he had a family connection with their interrogatee.

"I'm unsure whether that is a good idea, given your sibling relationship with Kim. But, if you insist that you know what you are doing, you may work with Basu to collaboratively re-establish a connection to the CIRB database." Khali hesitantly permitted Abhu to remotely access the command center's system interface to prove his sister's innocence.

Abhu happily thanked Khali. "Thank you so much, Master Khali. I won't let you down."

"Kumar, put Basu on Line One and put him on speaker," Khali ordered.

"Yes, Master. Right away." Kumar assented.

Kumar accessed the multiline phone system and dialed Basu's extension at his station in the top-level command center in the Thunderheads' main building.

***

Meanwhile, in the EJFS command center, Basu was working on responding to the Shadow State's involvement in the election when Agent Abhu called his extension.

Basu's phone rang, and he saw the caller ID indicated that the phone line in the detention center was on the line. Basu answered the call using his last name as a moniker.

"EJFS, this is Madhav."

"Basu, it's Abhu."

"Hey, Abhu. How can I help you?" Basu asked with a friendly tone.

"I need you to help me re-establish contact with CIRB servers. Somehow, EJFS access has been terminated. I think the Shadow State may have been involved, but I won't know for sure unless we conduct a thorough backtrace in our system," Abhu explained.

"Why do you think the Shadow State was involved? Do you think they would sabotage your sister?" Basu asked.

Khali interjected. "Basu, do you have any way of trying to pinpoint what is causing the cutoff of access to the CIRB database? Are you able to find a way back into it?"

"I can try, but it would be a long shot. You might have to contact the CIRB director to restore your clearance. But we all know that may be a dead-end solution," Basu replied.

"Understood. If I must, I will go through the proper procedures to obtain a clearance. In the meantime, do what you can on your end to break through the impasse. Time is of the essence. You have to find a way in by any means necessary."

"Acknowledged, I will do my best," Basu concluded and went to work on finding another way into the CIRB database.

Agent Basu opened a command prompt and ran a program to search for a blocking agent that may have accessed the EJFS servers while also looking to manufacture a security clearance to access the CIRB database until their access could be fully restored.

***

Zima returned to her hideout with Gyan accompanying her. They took a secret entrance to descend into the subway's depths.

Deep within the underbelly of the belowground maintenance and utility section, tucked away from the subway system above, the ceiling tremored continuously during the occasional clamoring and clanging from the subway trains traversing the tracks consistently echoed throughout the office in the subway metro system in New York City.

Gyan stood in awe and fear of the dank surroundings.

"So, this is the belly of the beast, as they call it," Gyan observed.

"This is my humble little abode. It serves its purpose, but this place is a temporary home until the eve of Election Day. After what my handler is planning, the entire network of the Shadow State will lay waste to this world," Zima giggled menacingly.

Zima opened her laptop case and set her computer back up. She checked to ensure that her CIRB-loaned software's stranglehold still maintained its cutoff of data flow to the EJFS.

"Wow, you have tapped into the EJFS servers and stopped their data mining operations. How have you managed to do that?" Gyan asked.

"I suppose a technological genius like you will just have to figure it out," Zima hinted with her sultry Russian accent.

Suddenly, a warning prompt showed up on Zima's laptop screen, indicating that someone was trying to hack into her private network. A beeping tone went off on her computer as she struggled to locate the source of the hack.

"I thought this system was hack-proof!" Zima exclaimed.

"Can you track down the source of the hack?" Gyan asked with increased urgency.

"Let me check," Zima looked through her external connections. She discovered an IP address was tapped into her network while trying to access the CIRB database, which Zima hoped to prevent the EJFS from accessing.

"It's the EJFS! They're fast," Zima remarked out of heightened concern.

"Can you find a way to seal off your network?" Gyan asked.

"I don't know! Can you help me out, Mr. Genius Extraordinaire?" Zima mocked Gyan out of desperation.

"All you had to do was ask. Step aside. I got you covered," Gyan assured Zima.

***

Meanwhile, in the EJFS command center, Basu and Abhu hustled laboriously to hack into the CIRB database. They were able to pinpoint the source of the stranglehold over their data mining operations.

"Agent Abhu, I found the source of the disruption. I'm about to deploy a spike signal to neutralize the origin." Basu continued typing away at a brisk pace at his computer terminal to quickly dispatch the source and re-establish a connection to the CIRB database.

Suddenly, the signal disappeared, and the EJFS lost the connection with Zima's computer interface.

Basu frantically tried to reopen the trace, but all access was sealed.

"Abhu, I'm sorry, we lost connection to the source of the disruption," Basu regretfully lamented.

"Crap!" Abhu cursed.

Khali jumped into the conversation. "Basu, were you able to pinpoint the geographic location of the signal trace?"

"The signal originated from the Lower East Manhattan area, but it was within a one-mile radius," Basu replied.

Khali and Abhu exchanged glances, and Khali made an executive decision to act.

"All right then. Call engineering: instruct Nitin and Prabodhan to chart a course to New York. This might be a chance to find the Shadow State actor. If my suspicions are correct, we might be able to locate Judson and Anastasia potentially, and they may lead us to the leader of the Shadow State," Khali hypothesized.

"I'm on it," Basu complied.

Basu hung up to relay the order to Engineering in the thickest section of the EJFS Thunderhead Base to deploy to New York City.

***

At the NYC metro subway maintenance department, Gyan finished sealing off Zima's connection with military-grade encryption, and he put her system on his virtual private network.

"There, that should keep them out for quite a while," Gyan spoke with optimism.

"Gyan, we're going to have to leave. Do you have a place where we can hide?" Zima asked grimly.

"I have a place on Staten Island. We can hide there," Gyan suggested.

"I hope your security system is as extensive as your intellect," Zima quipped.

"Good one. Now, where can we find the necklace?" Gyan asked.

"Follow me," Zima insisted.

Zima led Gyan to a secure vault in the supervisor's office. She unlocked the safe and retrieved a sealed black case that contained the necklace containing Vritra's remains.

Gyan's eyes were wide open with awe as he saw the black case pulled out of the vault with the inked inscription that reads: *PROPERTY OF THE US GOVERNMENT, HANDLE WITH EXTREME CAUTION.*

Zima grimaced as she carefully unsealed the case that contained the lost necklace of Vritra's remains encased in a dragon-shaped vessel. It once adorned the neck of the late Ravan Kanda Ganesh of the defunct Final Wave Terrorist Organization.

"You are the first person to feast their eyes on this necklace that once belonged to my late commander, Ravan. He entrusted me to carry out his legacy from generations past to fulfill the prophecy of the dragon," Zima explained in detail.

"My ears are tingling. I can't believe my eyes." Gyan was astonished.

"You've seen what Vritra was capable of doing, although the utter destruction of this world was delayed for a short time. But together, we are going to bring him back to life to help him build his world. You and I, and the entire Shadow State, will be unconquerable and unstoppable. Vritra will destroy all who oppose us," Zima explained as she gazed into the dark amulet necklace, which contained the dormant power of Vritra's evil essence.

"This power will be heavily sought once the public eye sees it. We must keep it well-hidden. The EJFS would stop at nothing to undermine our plans," Gyan warned.

"They can try all they want, but their efforts will be futile. Once the Shadow State takes over the world, the election will amount to nothing. You are the perfect prospect to lead Vritra back to his resurrection. We must go. It's no longer safe here," Zima beckoned.

"Let's get out of here and take shelter in my compound. You drive, and I'll navigate." Gyan offered.

The two villains vacated the area, and Gyan mounted Zima's motorbike in the parking garage with Gyan riding behind her as they fled to Gyan's home on Staten Island.

8: POTUS Hill National Address: Kim's Doppelganger's First Act of Sabotage

White House – South Lawn Garden

Washington D.C.

November 2, 2024

12:02 PM EDT, Saturday Afternoon

After the clock struck noon, President Hill made his way to the South Lawn to address the nation to condemn the terrorist attack from the night before. However, the public was unaware that the President was behind the attack in some fashion.

Members of the press, including the EJFS press corps, watched and observed to gather notes and soundbites. EJFS Press Corp member Sanjay Ruta paid close attention to analyzing and evaluating the President's speech. The aim was to find any clues and supplementary information about the elusive Shadow State.

President Hill approached the podium and started to speak.

"Good afternoon, members of the press, my lovely wife and children, Vice President Drake, and his wife, Suzanne..."

Drake did not return eye contact with his running mate for his re-election bid when Hill began speaking. After the heated exchange in a conference call with the President's Chief of Staff Hastings several moments ago, it was still a contentious relationship.

President Hill continued. "My fellow Americans, last night around 11:00 p.m., a terrorist attack on the New York subway system in Manhattan occurred while most Americans were asleep. The NYPD and a world-renowned superagency, the Elite Justice Force Squad, have worked together to discover who is responsible for this horrendous attack. Whoever committed these gross and heinous acts will be brought to justice."

Members of the press continued to jot down notes, and Sanjay, the EJFS Press Corps Agent, gathered clues on his smartphone. Sanjay noticed that President Hill kept wiping sweat from his brow and appeared to be bothered.

The President continued his address. "Furthermore, I am ordering all federal agencies to investigate the incident, and I am releasing emergency funding to all agency offices to handle the case head-on. I ask that all citizens remain vigilant. If you know anything about possible leads to the individuals responsible, please do not hesitate to come forward. Thank you, and God Bless America!"

The press clamored to ask questions, but then the President walked away with his Secret Service detail and left the news media astounded that the President did not take a Q&A session.

The President and Vice President and their families returned to the White House to reconvene in the Oval Office while their families stayed in one of the East Wing staterooms.

The EJFS Press Corps Agent, Sanjay Ruta, speed-dialed Master Khali at the Atlanta-based EJFS Thunderhead Base Complex.

Master Khali was still at the Detention Center when Sanjay called. Khali heard his smartphone ringing and answered it.

"EJFS, Khali."

"Master Khali, President Hill wrapped up his speech. He did not give very many details as his secret service members took him back inside, and he did not take any questions from the press. He left before anyone could raise a question," Agent Sanjay reported.

"That's very odd for a sitting president not to take questions from the press after a terrorist attack. What is your overall analysis from the president's speech?" Khali asked.

"If you want the scary version, here it is: I think Hill perhaps knows more than he's asserting. I must review the film, but the telltale signs are present in his demeanor. I'll see what I can gather from my team on the notes we've collected, and I'll report back to you later today," Sanjay continued as he was walking off the South Lawn and prepared to end the call.

"Very well, keep me informed if you find out anything more," Master Khali directed.

"I will keep you posted on anything I find, and I'll send you real-time updates to your priority inbox. I must go. The White House staff are directing everyone off the South Lawn. I'll be in touch."

Sanjay ended the call and rejoined his press corps team as he boarded a shiny white ICV, an interchangeable transformative vehicle that could fly at most altitudes.

The ICV transformed into a flying car, departed the area, and headed to their EJFS Satellite Office in the Beltway of D.C.

***

President Hill and Vice President Drake held a private discussion at Hill's insistence.

"Peter, we need to have a conversation about our partnership. I know you are still upset about earlier. But let me try to explain my side of the story," President Hill began.

"Okay, let's hear it," Vice President Drake insisted.

"First off, what I am about to say is to stay between us. I need to make it clear that this is highly confidential information," President Hill emphatically stated.

"I will respect that," Vice President Drake continued.

"Very well, I will tell you everything." President Hill prepared to divulge information on what his administration was hiding from Drake.

"Kim Porter is in EJFS custody because she is part of a pilot program conducted to insert incognito spies into enemy nations to gather intel on their affairs of state. They are body doubles planted in the countries at war to obtain secret information about their military, economic strategies, and government. These duplicates travel worldwide at any moment's notice when they have received orders to go to another location and spy on them. Kim has a doppelganger that is a state crisis actress who is used as a weapon of chaos to disrupt the schemes of our enemies," President Hill explained.

"This doesn't make any sense. Why would you use your staffer as a body double or a state actor? Staffers are not trained to be national spies. My God, Ken, how long has this pilot program been running?" Drake asked in a sense of disgust and horror, considering international implications.

"This is the first year of it being tested for implementation. If the pilot program results are promising, other agencies will adopt similar tactics," President Hill elaborated.

"I cannot believe this. This violates international law. You are putting this great country in serious jeopardy," Drake spoke angrily.

"I'm afraid that in today's increasingly dangerous world, this is a necessary evil. Now, all I ask is that you keep quiet about this until after whatever happens on Election Day. If you want me to answer for what I have done in front of Congress, that can come later. But there is too much at stake right now. We have to snuff out this threat and put a stop to it," President Hill continued.

"I will not support something like this. You have caused irreparable damage to this country by what you are doing: Using your staffers as body-double spies for your trivial operation is despicable, and I won't stand for it!" Drake rebuked President Hill sharply.

"Peter, listen to me, we have all made sacrifices in our careers, but I can't let you destroy them," President Hill contended.

"Give me one good reason why I shouldn't have you impeached for this?" Drake asked.

"Well, you could torch your career in the process after the media finds out that you lied about your medical deferment in the war in Afghanistan," President Hill threatened his running mate.

"You can't be serious!" Drake shouted in anger.

"Peter, calm down," President Hill spoke patronizingly to the Vice President.

"I never lied about my medical moratorium, and I have flat feet. That is a legitimate reason why I could not enlist," Drake argued in a quieter tone to avoid being heard.

"That's not what it said in your file," President Hill argued mockingly.

"Okay, then why did I get deferred from the military?" Drake frustratingly replied.

"It's because you aren't a natural-born citizen. That also means you were never eligible to hold office," President Hill continued.

"You're blackmailing me into keeping your presidency going? You've got some nerve!" Drake fumed.

"You've left me with no choice. Either stay with me, or I will report you to the US Attorney General, and you will be facing a tribunal and risk deportation," President Hill coerced Drake.

"You're unbelievable," Drake mumbled with disgust as he sat back down on the couches with his arms enfolded.

"Now, are you going to cooperate with me or not? Are you still thinking about resigning as Vice President of the United States?" Hill whispered in Drake's ear.

"I guess you leave me no choice but to comply at this point," Drake spoke with a look of displeasure on his face.

"Good, let us go meet up with our families. We shouldn't keep them waiting," President Hill insisted.

They exited the oval office and kept their appearances up while they rejoined their families in the staterooms.

Drake continued to internalize his disgust for President Hill. He soon regretted running for office with Hill as his running mate.

***

Kim's doppelganger, Alicia Blaze, pulled her silver luxury car into a parking space. She checked her makeup and made sure the birthmark on her face was less noticeable before she met with Veronica.

She grabbed her purse and her briefcase and exited her car. She set her car alarm and walked up to the front door before retrieving her access card to unlock the front door of the building.

She swiped her card, and the door clicked and opened. Alicia entered the front office, and the receptionist, Olivia, was the first to get on her case, not knowing it was an imposter.

"Kim, where have you been?! Veronica has been trying to contact you all day. You missed your flight to D.C.," Olivia spoke with worry in her voice.

"It's okay. The EJFS agents gave me a ride to the airport. Where's Veronica?" The imposter asked.

"She's in the back office," Olivia replied.

The imposter briskly walked down the hallway to Veronica's office.

"Your boyfriend has been calling us all day long. You need to call him back and tell him you're okay," Olivia added out of earshot.

"I'll deal with him later," The imposter answered.

Veronica Baylor, Kim's boss, was at her desk, worried sick, trying to contact Kim. She contemplated notifying the Missing Persons Bureau that Kim might be missing until she heard a knock on her door.

"Come in!" Veronica entered.

The imposter opened the door and met with Veronica, who was enthralled to see Kim safe in her presence.

"Oh, my God. Kim, where were you? I've been trying to reach you all day," Veronica spoke with emotion as she hugged her subordinate out of genuine worry.

Alicia smirked slightly and patted Veronica on her shoulder, who then chastised her like a concerned parent.

"You've missed your flight. How were you able to get here so fast?" Veronica asked.

"I took a standby flight after the EJFS agents gave me a ride to the airport. It figures that after they kept me for questioning for so many hours, they were kind enough to get me a flight from ATL to D.C.," The imposter explained.

"Why were you being questioned?" Veronica asked.

"I don't want to talk about it right now. Let us get back to our jobs." The imposter deflected, trying to avoid breaking her cover.

"Well, that will be a discussion we will be having later. But let us talk about the election night festivities. Have you come up with a budget to plan the re-election party?" Veronica asked.

"Yes, I have. We are budgeted out for $4,000 for the festivities. Is that manageable for you?"

"Is that all you could scrounge up? We need to get it to at least $7,500 if we want to book a Western ballroom. Hotel ballrooms in D.C. Metro are not cheap. This is unacceptable, Kim. You are going to have to rework the budget for the party. Go to the campaign headquarters and try to increase that budget," Veronica reprimanded.

"Okay, I'll see what I can do."

Alicia replied and left Veronica's office to head to the campaign headquarters to budget more money for Election Night.

Alicia, posing as Kim, left the room before Veronica spoke to her once more.

"Also, please call your boyfriend and tell him never to call here again, or you are out of a job. Do you understand?" Veronica asked as she was sorting through papers on her desk.

"Yes, I understand," The imposter sighed heavily and left the office.

Alicia, Kim's doppelganger, left the office without saying goodbye and headed back to her car before driving to the campaign headquarters.

Alicia dialed her real boss, James Matthews, to provide him an update.

James met with some staff members and excused himself when he saw Alicia on his Caller ID.

"Excuse me for a moment," Matthews exited the meeting, retreated to his office, and answered the call from Alicia.

"Hello, Alicia. What's your status?" Matthews asked.

"I just performed sabotage at Kim's job, and her boss rejected her budget. Kim won't know that she has fallen out of favor with Veronica today, but she will soon," Alicia answered as she was sitting in her car, driving while speaking on a hands-free calling program on her screen.

"Excellent, now I need you to lay low for a while until later this evening," Matthews smiled.

"You got it. I'll be at my apartment, call me for my next assignment when you are ready," Alicia spoke while driving home.

"I will contact you later. Good work, Alicia!"

Matthews ended the call and rejoined the meeting in the conference room.

***

At the Detention Center interconnected with the EJFS cluster of Thunderheads, Khali, Abhu, Singh, Raj, and Kumar, alongside his trainee, Yukti, were planning their next move with Kim Porter, who was still in detainment.

Khali and Raj considered allowing her to be released because there was not enough evidence to charge her with a crime beyond all reasonable doubt.

Khali hoped to make one final attempt to access Kim's records to corroborate her statements since using the capsule device was rendered useless without access to the databases. However, Khali had an idea.

Basu, who was still at the command center running the logistics to find Zima and Clayborn, received another call from Khali's smartphone.

"EJFS, Madhav."

"Basu, it's Khali. I have an idea that might clear Kim's name. Are you able to access the cache memory of our backup servers to work around the impasse and find a record for Kim Porter?"

"I was thinking about doing that, and yes, I can. Just let me search the cache memory. Stand by," Agent Basu replied.

Basu ran a search for past information on Kim. He located one file showing some info on her and obtained a photo of Kim from the previous year before Vritra's rebirth.

"I found an old photo of Kim, and I am going to enhance the image and look for any birthmarks on her face. Give me a few moments," Basu insisted.

Basu pulled up the image in the question of Kim's doppelganger and compared them with each other. Basu finished enhancing the image, and Kim's claims were substantiated. She had a double somewhere in the US impersonating her.

"Khali, Kim was right all along. She does not have a birthmark. Whoever this woman is, she appears to be impersonating Kim," Basu informed him.

"Very good. Kim's name should be cleared. But we need to find her doppelganger and stop her from doing any more damage to Kim's reputation. I suggest we keep her here at the palace until we can plan to take care of her imposter. Outstanding work, Basu!" Khali commended.

"My pleasure," Basu replied, and then Khali hung up.

Khali, Raj, Singh, and Abhu conferred with each other and updated Abhu on what happened.

"Abhu, your sister has been exonerated. We can let her go, but I am afraid your sister's life may be in danger. I suggest we should keep her up here a little longer but in the palace base to make her comfortable, at least until we can find and apprehend Kim's doppelganger," Khali informed Abhu.

"I knew it. Thank you, guys, for working to clear her good name. I want to transform back into Caleb so that I can see her. May I?" Abhu asked.

"Of course, go right ahead," Khali permitted gladly.

Abhu accessed his smartwatch profile settings and changed back to his likeness as Caleb Porter.

During the transformation process, Khali, Raj, and Singh entered the interrogation room where Kim sat in her chair, feeling uncomfortable after sitting for an extended period.

"Hello, Kim. My name is Khali, and I am the Head of the EJFS. I want to start by apologizing to you personally that we had you taken up here for so long. You were right. That woman in the photo was not you. We were able to check a cache file from last year to corroborate your testimony. You are cleared of all wrongdoing," Khali began.

"Will I get to go free now?" Kim asked.

"Well, unfortunately, we believe you were targeted in a plot of some kind to destroy your reputation. It would be best to take you to our palace and let you stay with us until we can sort this out. It might not be safe for you to return to the surface at this time. I am offering you a temporary shelter in our palace base until we can apprehend your doppelganger," Khali explained.

"I don't know if I can. I am part of the President's campaign staff. I must go to meetings to plan the election night party," Kim replied, feeling uncertain.

Singh decided to interject.

"Kim, I know you have prior engagements, but we need to establish whether it is safe for you to return," Singh calmly clarified.

Agent Raj also interjected.

"Our base complex is bound for New York City for mission deployment. We are not far from Washington, D.C. Once we have guaranteed your safety, we will take you wherever you want to go," Raj assured.

Kim was feeling apprehensive but decided to trust their judgment.

"Okay, I suppose I'll stay here," Kim reluctantly accepted Khali's offer.

Suddenly, the door from the observation room opened, and Caleb, with his retained colossal physique, entered and reunited with his sister Kim.

"Caleb?" Kim muttered.

"You were always the rebel in the family, huh?" Caleb chuckled jokingly.

"Oh, you big lovable nerd," Kim laughed as she got up out of her seat and wrapped her arms around her huge older brother for a tremendous hug.

The other three EJFS agents, Khali, Raj, and Singh, smiled as they witnessed the two siblings' tender moment.

Khali placed his large hands gently onto Caleb and Kim's shoulders. "Let us head back to the palace for lunch. Kim can ride with Caleb, Singh, and Raj. I'll meet you all back at the base."

Master Khali warmly welcomed their guest and headed outside to the parking lot to return to the main Thunderhead's nearby palace base.

9: EJFS Arrives in NYC: The Storm to End All Storms is Created

Jagmohan Gyan's Smart Home Compound

Staten Island

New York, New York, USA

November 2, 2024

12:41 PM EDT, Saturday Afternoon

Later in the day, in New York City, Gyan rode along with Zima driving her motorbike, arrived at Gyan's Smart House on Staten Island.

Gyan pulled the bike up next to the voice recognition and thumbprint scanner next to the front gate. Gyan was prompted by his security system to announce his name and occupation while scanning his thumbprint on the reader device.

"Jagmohan Darjun Gyan, President and CEO of Phoenix Tech Enterprises Unlimited," Gyan announced his identity. At the same time, he placed his left thumb onto the reader device next to him. The voice recognition and thumbprint analysis software, that Gyan himself had created, confirmed his identity and permitted entry into his high-tech smart home, tucked away from the city.

The front gates unlocked and slid open, allowing Gyan and Zima to enter the premises. Zima drove her bike into the garage and turned off the engine before they both dismounted the bike.

Gyan and Zima entered the back door through the garage. Both arrived at the house that felt like a scene out of a Sci-Fi movie. The rooms were futuristic and felt warm and cozy in the late autumn months.

"Wow, you outdid yourself in building this place, haven't you?" Zima remarked with a hint of cynicism.

"You know me too well. This place is where I built my company from the early years. It is my baby. This is where I can engineer the weather events in the Eastern Seaboard. I have some cloud-making farms across many islands in the Atlantic Ocean and off the West Coast of Africa. I can engineer any cluster of storms into mega-charged hurricanes of brute force and destruction. Just think, if Hurricanes Harvey and Irma got together and had a baby, this would be their apocalyptic love child. The hurricane to end all hurricanes." Gyan smiled gleefully and menacingly.

"Intriguing. I like a man who has mastery over the weather." Zima gushed over Gyan's weather technological developments.

"So, this is the perfect time to start forming a powerful hurricane to rampage through the entire continental US, the likes of which humanity has never seen before until the coming days ahead. Let me show you my weather-making system. You're going to love this!" Gyan could barely contain his maniacal excitement.

Gyan and Zima arrived in the backyard of Gyan's house, where there were vast amounts of antennas and a tall contraption billowing out rain clouds to boost grain production over the farmlands up north.

There was also a greenhouse that contained many hydroponic herbs and medicinal plants. The purpose was to create and store live insolvents to inhale liquid solutions to expand any life form's lung capacity vastly, animals and humans alike, to blow very intense bursts of air for an extended period.

If the participant continued to inhale three puffs of the insolvent orally three times a day as directed by anyone who would purchase the product, they would be able to blow storm-force winds out of their mouths. However, the patent had hit a snag on the US Food and Drug Administration board.

"I have a couple of tricks I want to show you, and I'll let you experience the technology I have mastered over the past decade. Let us go to the greenhouse and pick up some inhalant solutions. This will blow your mind," Gyan excitedly explained.

Gyan and Zima entered the greenhouse. Gyan retrieved a refrigerated case of inhalers that he recently drew up in a substantial batch creation of the insolvable inhalants. He mastered the formula to increase lung capacity.

"First, I will prove how this breathable solution can be used in random, freak occurrences in livestock. Do not worry. This will not harm any of the animals. I have a Clydesdale horse that is very accustomed to this breathing treatment after suffering from shortness of breath and wheezing. This stuff cured that right up in no time at all," Gyan explained in detail.

"So, this solution has health effects as well for those who have trouble breathing?" Zima asked with an arched brow.

"I suppose you could say that. At this point, the FDA will not allow my formula to be distributed among pharmaceuticals because of the high risk for human-made wind disasters. But that will not stop me from testing them in a controlled setting for the time being," Gyan remarked, followed by a grumbling sound.

Zima turned her right eye as if she were looking at Gyan with confusion and wonder.

"Anyways, enough of my ramblings. Let me show you what this stuff could do. You'll be amazed!"

Gyan approached a horse that was feeding on a very tall stack of hay. The horse itself was robust and muscular after presumably undergoing extensive health conditioning.

"I'm going to administer one dose on this horse and reveal to you the potency of this solution. Watch."

EJFS: ELITE JUSTICE FORCE SQUAD SERIES

Gyan put an inhaler of the solution in the horse's mouth and delivered three puffs. Soon enough, Zima began to witness the chest and abdominal muscles of the horse expand within a minute. The horse drew and expelled breath. It was as if the horse was breathing a stiff breeze through its nose and mouth, rippling through the hair and clothes of Gyan and Zima.

"Now, get a load of this."

Gyan plucked a dandelion from the ground and placed it near the horse's nose, causing it to feel allergenic, and soon started to gasp before preparing to sneeze. With each breath the horse took, his lungs expanded further, and less than thirty seconds later, the horse sneezed, causing a hefty gust of wind to expel from the horse's nose and mouth, blowing the large stack of hay miles away and sweeping some trees over in its wake.

Zima's eyes widened in amazement.

"Uncanny!"

"Now, let's both try it out," Gyan suggested.

Gyan and Zima took in three inhalations of the powerful insolvent, and their chests and abdominal muscles increased in mass as their lungs filled out.

"You see that ugly barn over there? Let's blow it away," Gyan insisted breathily.

Zima and Gyan looked at each other intently and then glanced over at the barn not too far from them.

Gyan took the lead and started inhaling enormous amounts of air. Zima followed suit, then they puckered their lips and expelled mighty storm-force breath toward the barn, which began to rattle violently.

The roof tore from the barn, and then the entire barn blew away down the field and became destroyed in one fell swoop.

The duo laughed evilly and menacingly at the new power that Gyan had developed and mastered.

"Do you know what you've managed to do, Gyan?" Zima asked excitedly.

"Match the same power as the superagents of the EJFS?" Gyan replied with a question.

"You know them very well, it seems," Zima's smile faded slightly.

"I know plenty about them, and they are about to meet their match," Gyan hinted as he glanced back toward the rain cloud machine that was still spewing out thick rain clouds.

"Yes, soon, both of us will bring this world to its knees in a well-orchestrated fashion," Gyan added as they soon headed back inside to hunker down and prepare for the storm to end all storms.

***

Meanwhile, the Atlanta-based EJFS Thunderhead palace arrived in New York City so the agents could search for Anastasia Zima, determine the whereabouts of Clayborn, and unearth any clues on the identity of the Shadow State's leader.

Kim Porter, the sister of Caleb Porter, who was alternatively known as Abhu Dhuval Sandeep, rode along with Singh and Raj. They drove across to the main palace attached to the Thunderheads interconnected to the Detention Center less than a mile away.

Once the vehicle landed back at the palace, Kim was awestruck by the sheer size of the palace that housed all Atlanta-based EJFS superagents and field specialists operating in the massive, towering base.

"What an enormous place! How does it stay afloat?" Kim pondered.

Raj answered. "It's best that our agency doesn't divulge all of our secrets. Maybe one day, you'll know."

Singh spoke with Caleb as the four of them walked up to the massive front door to the palace's interior.

"Caleb, your sister, Kim, will be protected in one of the guest suites on Level 12. You can help her feel welcome as she stays here for however long as deemed necessary," Agent Singh explained to Caleb.

"Ahem, Singh, aren't you forgetting to do something before we enter?" Raj asked subtly.

"Oh, right," Singh pulled out his car keyring and chirped the remote twice to cause the car to park itself in the parking garage automatically.

"Wow," Kim was impressed with the technology that the EJFS had cultivated.

"Let's head inside and get you settled," Agent Singh added as they pushed open the tall, heavy door for Caleb and Kim to enter the palace base.

Kim was amazed by the highly ornate and technologically advanced interior of the base. There were superagents briskly walking through the corridors of the hallways on the first floor of the palace while two of the agents that Caleb knew very well, Darsh and Durga, came up to welcome Caleb's sister, Kim.

"Welcome aboard, Kim. I am so glad we were able to clear your good name. Your brother was exceedingly confident that you weren't involved in political extremism," Durga greeted Kim with a warm embrace.

Darsh interjected. "We know you have an imposter out there somewhere, and we'll track her down as soon as possible. But, at this moment, we are focused on a growing threat that will put the election and the world into serious jeopardy. We need to stop this network that we believe is responsible for the terrorist attack in New York last night and a false arrest of an artifact expedition expert in Manhattan. In the meantime, let us serve your lunch. You may eat with your brother in the cafeteria."

Caleb and Kim entered the cafeteria while Raj and Singh went to the command center on the Thunderhead base palace's top floor. Darsh and Durga returned to their assigned posts inside the base.

Raj and Singh rode the elevator up to the thirteenth floor. Along the way, Raj spoke to Singh about his concerns with Caleb retaining his old form and approaching the strategy of reintroducing Kim to Caleb's alternate persona, Abhu Dhuval Sandeep.

"We need to discuss how we're going to factor in Caleb's alternate identity of Abhu to his sister. We know from Kim's history that she was somewhat opposed to how we used to operate as a former secret agency. Kim might not take kindly that her brother has been living a double life for the past year," Raj mentioned.

"I already spoke with him earlier this morning that he is free to reveal his alternate identity whenever he feels the timing is appropriate. I know Abhu has matured over the past year after everything that he has been through. I trust his judgment, but I will continue to coach him if you feel that is a concern," Singh responded.

"If you feel that he will handle the situation accordingly, and given your close friendship with him, then I won't worry about it too much. But I need you to watch the situation if Kim changes her tone after finding out about Caleb's alternate identity. It could derail our agency and Abhu's career as well if she reacts negatively," Raj answered.

"Duly noted. I will keep my eye on them," Singh reassured.

Suddenly a soft tone followed by an announcement on the elevator speaker system whirred.

"NOW ARRIVING AT THE LEVEL 13 EXECUTIVE FLOOR AND LOGISTICAL COMMAND CENTER"

Agents Raj and Singh entered the command center.

Devdas rejoined them as they clocked onto their shift. Both agents were briefed by Agents Lochan and Basu about the developments following the impasse of the EJFS access.

Raj began, "So, where do we stand at this data blockage?"

Lochan explained, "We are still unable to enter the database. However, we have found a way to tap into the device's GPS function to stonewall us. We have pulled the user information for the owner of the device. It is an encrypted laptop that is leased to a User ID of SC4AHZ. Basu was able to trace that username through other databases internationally and found out to whom the username is registered."

Basu beckoned Singh and Raj to his station to show them his findings. He opened a record of information from the Hungarian Government and dug up data about the laptop owner.

"The laptop belongs to Anastasia Zima. However, it is surprising to see this listed in the Hungarian Intelligence database. Maybe whoever she is in contact with could be based out of Hungary. Whoever that person is could be the top leader of the Shadow State," Basu explained.

"Were you able to find out anything else?" Singh questioned.

"There's more to it: the issuer of the laptop is none other than Jagmohan Gyan, the technological genius who has been creating geoengineering projects, emulating our technology to manipulate the weather patterns, but in a way that is far more catastrophic and dangerous. We were able to pull his financials, and he runs his enterprise in two locations: Gyan's main headquarters at the One World Trade Center in Manhattan and in his Staten Island home. His home compound is highly secured with a home defense system that he designed and created," Basu continued.

"Where was the last known device location, are you still connected to the GPS function of the device?" Raj asked.

"We were able to bypass some of their firewalls and have narrowed down the location in the Staten Island area, so there is a high probability that Ms. Zima and Gyan are working together in a scheme for the Shadow State," Basu concluded.

"Then we need to head over there and stop them," Singh interjected.

"But that's where it gets tricky. We have detected an extraordinarily high level of electromagnetic disturbance near Gyan's residence. If we get too close to the disruption, it could cause our palace to shut down and crash to the surface. This may have been pre-planned as a deterrent to keep us away from him," Basu warned grimly.

"Then how are we going to go about apprehending them?" Singh asked.

"We'll have to find another way in, offsite, and storm the compound at a distance. We can still send in Situational Response Surveillance Drones and Recon One Sentinels as those aircraft are EMF proof. We will have to find a way to storm the area covertly without alerting Gyan. His security system is nearly impenetrable. So, we must be mindful of this in carrying out the assault," Lochan explained.

"I'm going to notify Master Khali. He needs to be informed about this," Raj asserted.

"What do you want me to do?" Singh asked Raj.

"You and Devdas need to coordinate with each other to apprehend Gyan and Ms. Zima. We must stop them from whatever chaos they are planning to inflict upon the nation. We will meet in the conference room shortly to go over our next plan of attack," Raj explained, then left the Command Center to meet with Khali.

***

At Gyan's Smart House, Gyan was preparing the weather manipulation system inside his compound to create a monstrous-sized and powerfully catastrophic human-made Category Five hurricane off the coast of Africa.

The terrible maelstrom was expected to slam into the continental United States' entirety and make landfall within four days.

Gyan worked alongside Zima was to harness it into the powerful energy of the human-made mega hurricane to revitalize Vritra's power to its full terrifying potential in a stormy apocalyptic scenario if successful.

Zima worked on her laptop at a desk next to Gyan when she suddenly noticed a GPS tracker alert on her system notification tray, prompting concern.

"Gyan, we have a problem. The EJFS is back on the hunt. Can you lock them out again?" Zima asked.

"Move aside," Gyan insisted as he slid his office chair over to Zima's desk.

Gyan was surprised that the EJFS quickly disabled their firewalls and had managed to crack the codes to get into the laptop and stay connected through the GPS.

"Damn!" Gyan cursed as he struggled to lock out the tracking signal. After that, Zima's computer was spiked and disabled.

"What, what happened?" Zima stuttered.

"They got you, and soon enough, they'll track us down. We must put the plan into action. I am going to summon the superstorm now. Once the machines are in hyperdrive mode, they will not be reversed. I'm issuing the command now before they shut us down."

Gyan urgently issued a command to a nearby satellite transmitter across the West Coast of Africa and the surrounding islands and archipelagos to start forming the mega hurricane.

***

Off the coastline of West Africa, on Cape Verde, near the Riviera of São Miguel, there was a massive contraption that Gyan supported to fund the building of a storm cloud machine capable of creating extremely dangerous human-made hurricanes.

The storm cloud-making engine received the command transmitted by Gyan's satellite transmitter in New York to engage the storm cloud creation's maximum strength. Thus, a broad, densely thick band of storm clouds started to stream slowly into the Eastern Atlantic Ocean, and the action was repeated across the Azores and many other locales leading up to the Caribbean Sea.

Soon after, a monstrously sized hurricane formed off the West Coast of Africa and began to churn westward towards the Continental United States, as seen on the satellite and infrared radar loop on Gyan's computer.

The storm to end all storms was barreling towards them, and the plan of America's demise was set forth into motion.

10: EJFS Readies Assault on Gyan's Compound: Kim's Doppelganger Strikes Again

Jagmohan Gyan's Smart Home Compound

Staten Island

New York, New York, USA

November 2, 2024

1:22 PM EDT, Saturday Afternoon

Gyan and Zima prepared to hold off the EJFS from putting a halt to their activities.

Gyan activated his home security system for a lockdown.

Simultaneously, both Zima and Gyan staged a defensive posture in the basement, where Gyan's workshop den was hidden away and sealed off by an impenetrably heavy door.

"It won't be long until the EJFS starts their invasion of your compound. We need to hold them off for as long as possible. Do you have an armory on-site?" Zima asked.

"I have a weapons stockpile in my workshop closet. Grab what you need," Gyan insisted.

Zima briskly walked to Gyan's closet and armed herself with numerous weapons, some of which she was unfamiliar with their use.

"You have some highly sophisticated weaponry. I'll stick with the conventional side of things," Zima grabbed some heavy artillery weapons along with some long-range sniper rifles and an AK-47 rifle.

Gyan maintained his watch over his compound surveillance to keep an eye out for any EJFS operations vehicles perusing the area.

"When they come, we'll be ready. Let the fun begin!" Gyan chuckled maniacally.

***

At the EJFS Command Center, Master Khali and Second-In-Command Raj met with Top EJFS Agents Singh and Devdas to coordinate the strike operation on Gyan's compound. The four of them were joined by Agent-In-Charge Lochan and Darsh to oversee the mission.

Raj directed the closed-door meeting to begin in the lower-level situation room attached to the Logistical Command Center's main floor.

Raj explained with his gruff voice, "Gentlemen, Khali and I have drawn up a plan of attack on Gyan's compound. We will be taking an indirect invasion approach. I will be ordering TAC Teams to assemble at a nearby safehouse not far from the target location. We will have backup posted nearby for reinforcements if necessary."

Khali contributed, "Singh and Devdas will be commanders of each TAC Team. Both of you will collaborate as one collective unit to disrupt Gyan's schemes. You two can decide together which agents you want to draft into your teams."

Lochan warned, "We will fly in as close to the Staten Island area as our grid system allows, but we cannot approach within 400 feet of the field, or the EMF disturbance on Gyan's antenna farm will disable our base."

Singh assented. "Affirmative, Devdas, and I will collaborate to develop a unified approach to complete this operation."

Darsh wrapped up the quick briefing. "Master Khali, we have a podium waiting for you to address the agency."

Khali and Raj, followed by Devdas, Singh, Darsh, and Lochan, exited the lower-level conference room in the command center. Khali took his stance at the podium to address the entire EJFS.

"Good afternoon, my subordinates. My task force team has been briefed on the evolving situation connected to the Shadow State's development. I am ordering my top two agents: Devdas and Singh, to call on all active field specialists and operatives to join their TAC Teams in a joint effort to storm the home compound owned by Jagmohan Gyan. We believe both Gyan and Zima are working together in a tangible effort to disrupt the elections. It is confirmed that these two are responsible for the stoppage in our access to the CIRB database. The mission objective is to apprehend both Gyan and Zima, and then we will interrogate both in the Detention Center. Please be prepared to give your full cooperation to both commanders of each TAC Team. Assignments will be issued within the hour. Thank you, and God bless!" Khali ended the address.

Devdas was the first to call on his selected TAC Team Alpha members, Agents Prabodhan, Garjan, Baadal, Durga, Anil, and Daarun.

Singh was the second to call on his selection of members to make up TAC Team Bravo consisting of Agents Abhu, Gangi, Naveen, Vasu, Nitin, and Chand.

Both TAC Teams Alpha and Bravo would answer to their respective team captain.

Abhu, while still in his original identity, Caleb Porter, finished up his lunch with his sister, Kim.

Since Singh called Abhu's name, Caleb had to depart for his TAC Team B assignment to the deployment bay. However, Kim was still unaware of her older brother's dual identity.

"Hey, Sis, I have to go. I will ask Agent Pranay to escort you to your room. He's a good friend of mine," Caleb whispered at the table with his sister, Kim.

"But I didn't hear them call your name," Kim was nervous about being separated from her brother.

"I'm still actively involved. I can explain later, but not now. I will talk to you then. I love you, Sis," Caleb gave Kim one last hug before he bolted to the locker room to change into his alternate persona, Abhu Sandeep, out of Kim's sight.

Pranay approached Kim and briefly introduced himself to her.

"Hi, you must be Kim, Caleb's sister, right? My name is Agent Pranay. Let me take you to your guest suite for the time being to get situated. I'll lead the way."

Kim hesitantly followed Pranay to the elevators as a mad dash by many agents rushing to their assigned stations ensued.

***

Meanwhile, in Washington D.C.: Kim's doppelganger, Alicia Blaze, waited for a phone call from CIRB Deputy Director James Matthews regarding her next act of sabotage.

Alicia was in her apartment unit, watching the news following President Hill's address, when her phone rang. She answered the call when she recognized the Caller ID show up as Matthews.

"Hello?" Alicia answered.

"Hello, Alicia. Did I call during a bad time?" Matthews asked from his desk.

"No, I was waiting for the next mission to stir up trouble," Alicia replied.

"Good, I need you to go and meet with Logan, Kim's boyfriend. I need you to end the relationship between the two. Come up

EJFS: ELITE JUSTICE FORCE SQUAD SERIES

with whatever reason you can imagine. The President and his Chief of Staff are adamant that you break off the relationship because it could hurt President Hill's chances on Election Day," Matthews demanded.

"I see. I wonder if that's why Hill was sweating it out on the national address earlier," Alicia noted while she prepared to deploy.

"Pardon?" Matthews asked in confusion.

"Never mind. Is there anything else?" Alicia asked.

"Yes, when you are finished with this task, come back to Langley. I need to equip you for a larger-scale operation that was planned many weeks ago. I need you to come back in and have a chat about it," Matthews continued.

"That sounds ominous. But, very well, I'll call you when I am done," Alicia accepted her assignment, not knowing what exactly Matthews was implying.

"Good. I'll see you soon." Matthews hung up.

Matthews slumped at his desk listlessly, staring at a mission brief on his desktop computer that would put Alicia on a trip overseas to an international espionage operation in Brussels, Belgium.

Alicia packed her gear and headed out to meet with Kim's love interest, the Chief of Staff's son, Logan, to sabotage their relationship.

***

Gyan and Zima were still holed up in Gyan's basement at Gyan's compound on Staten Island.

Gyan watched security cameras from neighboring portions of town, keeping watch for any signs of the EJFS.

However, there were none so far.

"They must know about the electromagnetic field from the antenna farm. They're biding their time," Gyan theorized.

"Do you think they won't adapt?" Zima asked as she kept an eye outside on the farmlands.

"It's not a question of if but when they'll adapt. We might need some more help," Gyan suggested.

"I know a group who might be able to help us, as do you, I'm sure," Zima hinted subtly.

Zima gave a suggestive nod toward Gyan and revealed the Shadow State tattoo emblazoned on her palm.

Gyan formulated a new plan and texted a flash message to the CIRB Deputy Director, Matthews.

Matthews read his flash message marked with high priority.

"EJFS is preparing to attack my home. SC4 is compromised. I need reinforcements posted at my address NOW!" ~Gyan

Matthews quickly heeded the message. The CIRB Deputy Director conscripted sleeper agents in the field and dispatched agents' teams to be posted at Gyan's residence.

Soon after, half a dozen CIRB agents, suited in combat gear, boarded armored vehicles to Gyan's private home on Staten Island, and a helicopter flew near to the location.

Gyan and Zima overheard the helicopter and grinned as they knew that backup from the Shadow State-backed CIRB had joined the party.

"Let the games commence!" Zima declared as she smiled wickedly upon hearing the helicopter flyovers.

11: Gyan's Home Under Siege by the EJFS

Jagmohan Gyan's Smart Home Compound

Staten Island

New York, New York, USA

November 2, 2024

2:02 PM EDT, Saturday Afternoon

Helicopters continued to whir over Gyan's home as CIRB agents established a holding pattern to prepare against the EJFS onslaught from mobile TAC Teams.

Gyan kept a close eye on the surveillance cameras outside his home, waiting for the EJFS TAC Teams' first indication to storm the compound.

***

At the EJFS Logistical Command Center, Khali, Lochan, Basu, and Darsh observed the military operation from the EJFS Thunderhead Palace Base that originated from Atlanta.

Lochan ordered, "Basu, dispatch Recon-One Sentinels, and Situational Response Surveillance Drones to the target location."

Basu complied. "Yes, sir. I'm sending out dispatch orders now."

Meanwhile, in the EJFS Paramilitary Aircraft Exit Bay, Recon-One Sentinels and Situation Response Surveillance Drones received transmitted orders from the Command Center. It launched into the skies to monitor the area over Staten Island.

The EMF-proof aircraft flew over Gyan's home and surveilled the area, as those in the EJFS Command Center noticed the increased CIRB presence on location.

Khali spoke. "We've got company. It looks like Gyan and Ms. Zima summoned assistance from the CIRB. We will have to take a different approach. We must disable their power grid. That's our only equalizer in this fight."

Basu replied. "You've got it. I'll hack into his utilities and deactivate his power."

Basu accessed the Staten Island power grid and pinpointed the target location to perform a power grid shutdown. However, there was a remote backup power source feeding on the antenna farm near Gyan's home. The power source was isolated from the primary grid system.

Basu noted. "I can disable his power, but it will take much more effort to disable his backup source. Even if I disable his electrical system, he will still retain electricity from his antenna farm nearby."

Lochan encouraged. "Do what you can. The other analysts will support you."

Basu complied. "Yes, sir!"

The Command Center analysts collaboratively initiated a power shutdown to the area of Gyan's home and extensively worked to disable the antenna farm.

***

Meanwhile, at Gyan's residence: Gyan and Zima noticed a rumbling sound overhead, and the lights in the house began to flicker.

"They're here," Zima remarked.

"Yep, they are quick. But do not worry. The antenna farm will keep the compound powered up. Even if the EJFS manages to disable both the grid and antenna system, the cloud machine runs on a solar-powered system. We must match the technology of their wind breath. Take one of my inhalant solutions with you. We're going to give the EJFS a hell of a struggle," Gyan insisted.

Zima grabbed an inhaler of the lung-expanding solution and stuffed it into her coat pocket.

Suddenly, the power deactivated for a few seconds and then came back on again.

"They've got the grid down, but the antenna farm will help keep us going for the moment," Gyan assured her.

"Do you have a plan in place in case they manage to disable your antenna system?" Zima asked.

"I'll have to join the battle and help ward off the EJFS. You must get out of here and take the necklace with you and flee the country. Go to the Russian Embassy in Budapest, Hungary. Stay there and wait for the Shadow State to offer you safety at their headquarters."

"What about you?" Zima asked.

"I've got a plan. Do not worry about me. You need to get out of here now. Use your inhaler to keep the intruders at bay," Gyan dictated urgently.

Zima packed up her gear and prepared to escape from the area. Suddenly, the power system went down and stayed off.

"Go now!" Gyan shouted.

Zima fled the den and carved her path up to the garage as she heard loud rumbles of thunder from the summoned storm above. She mounted her motorbike and started up the ignition.

The EJFS Thunderheads loomed over the area as the deterrents were disabled. The Sentinels and Drones flew overhead while the TAC Teams remotely stormed the compound from the EJFS Safe House nearby.

Suddenly, the wind began to howl as the storm above, summoned by the EJFS, gained strength.

TAC Teams led by Agents Singh and Devdas encircled the area, and a gunfight between the CIRB agents and the EJFS TAC Teams ensued.

Zima drove her motorbike in the direction of the exit, but soon realized that the gate system was rendered useless, and she had to find an alternate way out.

Agents Singh and Abhu noticed that Zima was making her escape as she revved her motorbike, veering around Gyan's house's backyard.

"That's Ms. Zima! We have to stop her!" Agent Singh exclaimed.

"She's on her motorbike. How are we going to stop her?" Agent Abhu asked.

"We need to summon our motorbikes. Get out your phone and activate your FOB key function!" Agent Singh commanded.

Both agents summoned their motorbikes from the EJFS Thunderhead Base Palace and prepared to pursue Zima.

The transformative motorcycles launched off the ramp from the top of the Thunderhead Base and descended to the surface while in guided flight mode.

Singh addressed his co-captain. "Agent Devdas, you have to call for more backup from the New York City EJFS Branch. This is going to be a tough fight. Abhu and I are going to chase down Anastasia to stop her."

EJFS Agent Devdas Bheru Tandon

Devdas answered. "Acknowledged, Captain! Good luck and Godspeed!"

Singh continued. "You have control over my TAC Team. Use all available tactical strategies, as necessary."

Devdas replied, "Understood."

Both motorcycles touched down on the street by Gyan's home. Agents Abhu and Singh boarded their bikes and took off to pursue Zima as she veered around the compound's backyard.

Agent Devdas and the remainder of Agent Singh's TAC Team and Devdas' team began to fire their weapons at the CIRB agents as the battle continued.

Meanwhile, Gyan initiated his plan of action. He equipped himself with some high-tech weapons of weather warfare, packed an inhaler of the lung expanding solution in his pant pocket, and propelled his way to join the battle alongside the CIRB.

Gyan took three puffs of the inhalant solution and used his enhanced breathing to blow down the reinforced door to his den. He gathered his weapons and sprinted to the roof of his home.

Several CIRB agents were shot dead by EJFS superagents as the storm continued to rage.

During the gunfight, the New York EJFS Subdivision joined for reinforcements to increase the odds in the EJFS's favor.

EJFS superagents from New York used their wind breath to blow away the helicopters and the heavily armored vehicles belonging to the CIRB.

Meanwhile, Gyan took a position from the roof and began to fire his high-tech weapon at the EJFS, which impacted several EJFS agents from the New York subdivision, causing them to be profoundly subdued, but they were not killed.

The Atlanta-based EJFS TAC Team overwhelmed the CIRB line of defense and stormed the compound to apprehend Gyan.

Devdas ordered. "Go after Gyan, now!"

The twelve agents battered the front gate down, raced into the compound building, and headed up to the roof to take Gyan into custody.

Upon witnessing the large team of superhuman superagents storm his residence, Gyan knew he was cornered and had no other options.

The TAC Team of twelve blew open the roof access door and reached Gyan.

"Gyan, don't move! You're coming with us!" Devdas shouted thunderously.

Gyan held up his hands in surrender as Agent Devdas approached Gyan and placed him in handcuffs before escorting him out of his residence to an EJFS transformative vehicle.

The EJFS Agents sedated Gyan and injected a crimson-colored capsule down his throat before they boarded their vehicles to return to the Detention Center.

Meanwhile, EJFS Agents Abhu and Singh caught up with Shadow State operative Anastasia Zima, but she led them on a high-speed chase through the streets as she made her escape.

Zima took three inhalations of her lung-expanding inhaler. She turned her head around and blew intense bursts of wind toward Abhu and Singh as they tried to maintain pursuit.

Agents Abhu and Singh continued to chase Zima through the Lower East Manhattan area and drove through the Brooklyn Bridge, where a CIRB roadblock was in place, trapping the EJFS agents on the bridge.

Abhu and Singh had no other choice but to retreat to the Atlanta-based EJFS Thunderhead situated over the New York skyline.

At the same time, Zima escaped to John F. Kennedy International Airport to take a flight to Budapest, Hungary, to seek asylum in the Russian Embassy.

Meanwhile, Gyan was transported to the EJFS Detention Center attached to the EJFS Thunderhead Complex not far from the base palace.

As the TAC Team brought in Gyan to be questioned, Khali and Raj stood waiting at the Detention Center.

"Place Mr. Gyan into Interrogation Room One," Khali ordered.

Agents Devdas and Raj escorted an unconscious Gyan to the interrogation room.

During this time, Agents Abhu and Singh returned to the EJFS Thunderhead Base, disappointed that they could not stop Zima from escaping.

"Singh, what are we going to do now? Anastasia escaped, and she is probably going to flee the country. How are we going to find the leader of the Shadow State with her gone?" Abhu asked.

"I must contact Master Khali and let him know what transpired," Singh informed his most loyal agent.

Singh speed-dialed Khali, who was at the Detention Center. Khali heard his adopted son, Singh, calling him. The ringtone sounded on his smartphone, and Khali answered the call.

"Singh, what's your status?" Khali inquired with urgency.

"Abhu and I were pinned down on the Brooklyn Bridge by the CIRB. They established a roadblock in place. Anastasia escaped. She must be fleeing the country," Singh lamented.

Khali sighed, holding his head in disappointment.

"Well, we've captured Gyan, so we managed to put a wrinkle in the Shadow State's plans. I need you to join me at the Detention Center to assist with Gyan's interrogation. Tell Abhu to return to the Command Center for the time being. We'll regroup and try to stop Anastasia later," Khali directed.

"Yes, Master. I understand. I'll be at the Detention Center shortly," Singh replied and ended the call.

Agent Singh turned to face Agent Abhu as his best friend appeared subdued.

"We have Gyan, so all hope is not lost. We're going to extract Gyan's memory, and we should be able to uncover their plans," Singh began.

"What are we going to do?" Abhu questioned.

"I have to go to help with the interrogation. You must return to the Command Center and track Anastasia to avert this predicament. Also, other agents are struggling to track down your sister's doppelganger. We also have yet to find Judson. He may be in danger. Time is short. We must work fast to sort these crises out," Singh urged.

"Be careful. Gyan is extremely quick-witted. Keep your guard up," Abhu advised.

"I will, and same to you, my friend," Singh gave Abhu a quick hug and quickly departed for the Detention Center.

Abhu returned to the palace and boarded an elevator to the top floor Command Center.

***

Meanwhile, at the Command Center, Basu made a startling discovery on its radar system. He noticed the massive hurricane that formed off the West Coast of Cape Verde, churning toward the Atlantic Ocean.

"Agent Lochan, you need to see this," Basu urged with a grim tone in his voice.

Lochan approached Basu's station and gazed into the computer screen in horror.

"Oh, my goodness! Phone Khali and tell him to inform the President right away!" Lochan ordered with extreme urgency.

The incredibly intense hurricane was nearly the size of North America as it continued to gather strength from the geoengineering operations at Gyan's hands.

12: Gyan in Custody: The USA In Peril

Level 13 EJFS Logistical Command Center

EJFS Atlanta Branch – Eastern US Division

Current Location: Staten Island, New York, USA

November 2, 2024

2:49 PM EDT, Saturday Afternoon

Lochan and Basu contacted Master Khali to alert him of the developing superstorm barreling westward toward the continental US, originating from Cape Verde, Africa.

Khali was at the Detention Center, prepping the interrogation of Jagmohan Gyan, the evil genius who facilitated the engineering of the superstorm in the Atlantic Ocean.

Khali's smartphone rang, and he noticed that Lochan was calling him. Khali accepted the call.

"EJFS, this is Khali."

"Master Khali, it's Lochan. I have some terrible news that I need to tell you," Lochan answered somberly.

"What is it? What's wrong?" Master Khali asked.

"Basu has discovered a monstrously massive hurricane that formed quickly off the west coast of Africa, and it is barreling towards the East Coast of the US. It is already a Category Five hurricane, and it is expected to strengthen much more into a historic supersized cyclone," Lochan replied grimly.

"How big is it, roughly?" Khali inquired.

"It is already the size of half of the lower 48 states and is expected to strengthen and expand rapidly. You need to brief the President and advise him to take emergency action right away. This could be the worst hurricane to hit the continent in centuries. See for yourself on your computer radar," Lochan exhorted with great concern.

Khali accessed the satellite and radar interface on his computer and found the growing mammoth hurricane churning quickly towards the US East Coast.

"Good Heavens! This is not a natural storm, from what I see. I know Gyan has modified the weather patterns over the East Coast of New York to perform cloud-seeding. But this is a grossly extreme act of weather warfare and ecoterrorism that I cannot allow to take place. There will be a tremendous loss of life with this event occurring so close to the election." Khali struggled to maintain his composure out of fear for the American population in harm's way.

"What do you suggest we do to counteract?" Lochan asked.

"I don't know. This might be beyond my capabilities. I will interrogate Gyan and find a means to force him to reverse this potential catastrophic weather event. But first, I will call President Hill and advise him to address the nation," Khali continued.

"Very well, we'll continue to track the storm's path. Currently, it is estimated to impact the US Coast by Monday night," Lochan responded.

"That's the night before Election Day. We do not have much time to respond. Instruct your analysts to look for a way to weaken the storm before it makes landfall," Khali instructed.

"Acknowledged." Lochan complied and disconnected the call.

Khali made another call to President Hill's secure line.

***

President Hill was eating lunch with his family in the dining room when Sedgwick Barnes, one of his staffers, came forward to capture the President's attention.

"Mr. President, you have a phone call from Khali, the Head of the EJFS, on Line One. He says it's extremely urgent," Barnes informed him.

President Hill lingered for a few seconds and then reluctantly extricated himself to be escorted by Barnes to a briefing room.

Barnes closed the double doors and placed the secure call on speakerphone.

"Mr. Khali, this is Sedgwick Barnes, one of the President's staffers. You are on speakerphone with President Hill and me. What is the purpose of this urgent call?"

Khali explained the emergency. "Mr. President, I regret to inform you that we have discovered an incredibly dangerous and massive hurricane bearing toward the US East Coast. My team of agents suspects that a prominent individual named Jagmohan Gyan has geoengineered a superstorm to impact the US right before the election. I implore you to take emergency action to protect from loss of life," Khali began.

President Hill was noticeably fear-stricken after hearing the news.

Barnes interjected. "Mr. Khali, where is this storm located now?"

Khali continued. "It just crossed the Azores, and it has completely leveled the islands. There were no survivors. Wind speeds exceeded 250 mph according to the buoys offshore."

President Hill interjected, "I thought you guys could affect the weather. Don't you have a way to stop it?" President Hill asked.

Master Khali responded, "Unfortunately, not when we are dealing with a storm of this magnitude of severity. At this point, the only thing the EJFS could do is try to weaken it gradually, but we cannot mitigate it in its current strength. I am sending you the GPS coordinates now to catch a glimpse of it for yourselves."

Barnes and Hill exchanged horrified looks after seeing the sheer monstrosity of the hurricane spinning toward the East Coast on satellite and radar.

President Hill was nearly speechless but became defiant and accusatory toward Khali.

"Mr. Khali, it is my understanding that you have been modifying and manipulating the weather for some odd number of years. I also understand that your agency has been data mining terabytes of data over the past decade. You should know that it is a blatant violation of our country's sovereignty. I think you formed this hurricane to engage in the act of weather warfare against the US and the free world," Hill alleged.

Khali was caught off guard and became defensive.

"Mr. President, with all due respect, you don't know what you're saying, and your rhetoric is highly belligerent. I strongly insist you focus on preserving innocent lives and protect your citizens from imminent disaster. Now, you can work with us rather than against us to let us help you evacuate and provide safety from the hurricane," Master Khali responded gently.

Hill interrupted. "No, you people have done enough damage to our climate already. I will declare martial law and have everyone take shelter in the underground tunnels. We are finished with you all. I declare your agency a rogue enemy of the state, and I am giving you 72 hours' notice to take your operations out of US airspace. Do I make myself clear?"

Khali was fuming internally. "If that is your intention, then so be it. You are making a grave and unconscionable mistake by not letting us help you. But we will operate with or without your approval from other locations. May God be with you and your people."

Khali ended the call and pondered his next move. Khali decided to consult his advisor, Tanveer Bhattacharya, to seek his expertise.

***

Meanwhile, at the White House, President Hill and White House staffer Sedgwick Barnes remained in the briefing room.

"Mr. President, are you sure you want to go against the EJFS, given their history in government meddling?" Barnes asked nervously.

"You're not questioning my authority as commander in chief, are you?" President Hill asked in a heated tone.

"Uh, I'm just saying…that maybe we should not oppose the EJFS knowing what they can do," Barnes gulped out of fear.

"You better get your mind in the right place, or you can find yourself on a plane back to New York. Do I make myself understood?" Hill asked sternly.

"Yes, Mr. President," Barnes stuttered with fear.

"Good, don't question my authority ever again," Hill warned.

President Hill exited the briefing room and rejoined his family to break the news to them.

"Ladies and gentlemen, we're taking shelter underneath the White House. I have been informed that a historic hurricane is barreling toward the US East Coast. All staff and personnel are to relocate to the bunkers downstairs for at least the next three days, effective immediately," President Hill ordered.

Before the first family could finish their lunch, both families and staff made a beeline toward the secret hallways leading to the underground bunker and war room.

***

At the EJFS Thunderhead Base stationed over New York City, Khali spoke with his advisor, Tanveer, at the Detention Center through an AERIAL VOIP video call to discuss the next plan of action.

"Tanveer, the EJFS is in a bind after my heated conversation with President Hill. He has refused to accept our help and has declared us a rogue enemy of the state. He has ordered us to leave US airspace in the next 72 hours, and he's going to declare martial law to protect his citizens," Khali explained.

"I see. What are your thoughts on that? Do you think he has something to hide?" Tanveer asked.

"It is a possibility that he might be a Shadow State actor, but I'm going to give him the benefit of the doubt until we can question Gyan with the conditions that we've been given. Regardless, we do not have the luxury of time to stay here for much longer. Clayborn's whereabouts are still unknown, and Anastasia is in the wind. However, Gyan might give us an opening to the schemes of the Shadow State."

"Then you must already know what needs to be done. You have a mandate and an impending catastrophe coming upon a country whose leader is unwilling to accept our help. I suggest we make good use of it before they would take military action against us. President Hill is very temperamental and maybe a corrupt politician. This means we have the prerogative to investigate him under our standards," Tanveer continued.

"It's a huge risk to defy the President's order. However, I feel compelled to act on behalf of his citizens to protect their lives and homes. During that time, we will investigate him.

Nevertheless, we must send our bases to find the Shadow State leader and then eradicate the superstorm. Although I can't help but think there is a bigger plan at hand."

"Do you have an idea of what this could mean for our longevity?" Tanveer inquired.

"I don't know. This might only be the beginning of what's to come," Khali concluded with ambiguity.

13: Gyan Interrogated: Zima Flees to Budapest

EJFS Detention Center – Interrogation Room One

EJFS Atlanta Branch – Eastern US Division

Current Location: Staten Island, New York, USA

November 2, 2024

3:07 PM EDT, Saturday Afternoon

As Gyan remained confined in one of the interrogation rooms, he formulated a plan to escape from his detainment. He hoped to use his superior intellect to cause a massive disruption in the EJFS's plan to stop the Shadow State's evil schemes.

Gyan was hooked up to some enhanced interrogation equipment with some extreme elements involved. All his belongings were seized during the takedown and arrest earlier at Gyan's Staten Island home.

Agent Raj and his top agent, Singh, huddled in the observation room. The objective was to strategize on breaking down Gyan and extracting his memories to obtain further intel on the Shadow State's plans to cause catastrophic destruction and disrupt the election.

Master Khali returned from a video teleconference with his advisor, Tanveer, and joined up with Singh and Raj along with Kumar, Devdas, and Yukti Dubashi.

Khali briefed the others in the room about the developments in the past hour.

"I'm afraid I have some bad news. I spoke with Basu, and our satellites and radars have detected a large and intense Category Five hurricane heading toward the East Coast of the continental US. I have briefed President Hill, and his tone toward me became rather hostile. To add insult to injury, Hill has ordered all EJFS operations to cease and disperse from US airspace in less than 72 hours," Khali explained grimly.

Singh interjected. "This is terrible news. All those people in the path of the hurricane will not survive a storm of this magnitude. How are we going to stop it?"

Raj added. "I have a hunch that Gyan is behind this. We know he has a geoengineering project in his repertoire. But maybe there is something bigger at play here."

Singh asked. "Like what?"

Raj explained. "I'm not certain, but I have to wonder if they are trying to create an energetic storm for more than just destruction of the Eastern US. I have a theory that the Shadow State may have the remnants of Vritra stored somewhere, and maybe they intend to reconstitute his remains into harnessable terrible energy used as a doomsday weapon against the free world."

Khali chimed in. "From what we know, Vritra's remains have been unaccounted for since the fall of Final Wave last year. We still have Ravan's damaged laptop in the archives at the lower level of the Detention Center. I will pull it from the evidence lockers and run some analysis to see if we can find out what we are confronting. In the meantime, you two can question Gyan, but don't start the pain stimulators until I finish my findings."

Raj responded. "Acknowledged. We must act quickly. Time is working against all of us."

Master Khali left the observation room, boarded an elevator to the Detention Center's bottom level deep in the Thunderheads, and headed to the archives where old evidence was stored for future use.

Khali searched the containers and found a box marked as "RKG Laptop." Khali retrieved it and stood at a computer terminal displaying multiple screens and USB connectors with many devices at the disposal of the EJFS to hack into any computer or electronic device to gain access to its files.

Khali powered on the damaged laptop after plugging in the power cord. The system booted up as the screens connected to the EJFS Central Database began to hack into the password to log in to Ravan's computer unit. The process was expected to take five to seven minutes to pick out the password and override the settings.

***

Meanwhile, Second-In-Command Agent Raj walked through the doorway to the interrogation room, accompanied by Singh.

Gyan remained in his uncomfortable seat while his crimson capsule device was hooked up to the EJFS system.

Devdas was prepping vials of chemicals that would stimulate the pain receptors in Gyan's brain.

Gyan mocked the two powerful agents.

"Oh, I guess it's time for my torture session already?" Gyan quipped.

"Don't be a smart mouth, Gyan. You are in a precarious position, legally speaking," Raj admonished Gyan sternly.

Singh contributed to the interrogation. "We know that you are responsible for creating a superstorm off the West Coast of Cape Verde. You have put the East Coast of the US in grave danger by your actions."

Gyan remained defiant and unapologetic.

"That's rich, coming from a group of vigilantes that can also control the weather." Gyan scoffed at the brute agents.

Raj responded heatedly.

"The difference between what we're doing and what you're doing is that loss of life is usually minimal. But what you have done is endanger a substantial portion of the American population on the eve of the election, no less. You are facing notable charges of conspiracy to commit mass murder and ecoterrorism. Now, we are going to extract your subconscious thoughts and memories to determine what your motives are and who you are working for," Raj spoke sternly.

Gyan's smirk faded slightly after realizing his thoughts would be downloaded and viewed by the superagents interrogating him.

***

Meanwhile, Khali managed to acquire access to the late Ravan's laptop, which had been in the EJFS archives for over a year.

Khali carried out a catalog search in the files for the terms "Vritra" and "Rebirth" to locate any data related to Final Wave's quest to revive the ancient dragon monster.

Khali found a password-protected file folder containing all the plans Ravan had stored on his computer, forcing Khali to hack into the folder to circumvent the password protection.

After a couple of minutes, Khali obtained access to the folder and found a treasure trove of data about Vritra. He scrolled down the file browser and noted familiar elements from Final Wave's abandoned site in Siberia, Russia. Khali examined the Gatekeeper's Blade photos that had since been housed and enshrined in the EJFS Atlanta Palace's dome top. He also located pictures and documents showing Vritra's seal before the dragon monster was released.

The results included a scanned document of the schematics of the underground ice cavern near the base.

Finally, after conducting some searching, Khali found a document and photo showing the ancient heirloom necklace that the late Ravan once wore to adorn around his neck. Khali enhanced the image and saw the familiar dragon shape resembling Vritra's seal pattern, forged and crafted many generations ago.

Khali also located a document file on Ravan's computer named "TSS_Proj_Vritra's Revenge."

Khali was mildly horrified that Ravan had a link to the Shadow State's development as the acronym listed in the filename had indicated.

Khali opened the file, and he found a scanned list of protected document files that described a potential backup plan in a case when Vritra was defeated and the plot to rule the world failed. An overabundance of data suggested that Vritra's remains could reform into another form of destructive energy that could tear the planet apart.

Khali promptly began downloading the files he viewed on an external hard drive and started copying files onto his portable data storage.

During the data transfer, Khali stumbled upon another file folder within the set of documents he had viewed. The name of the folder was labeled "TSS_12." He opened the folder that was not protected by a password.

Khali stumbled upon another hoard of data that pertained to the Shadow State while in its infancy stages.

He opened a file containing twelve public figures and six prominent persons who made up the Shadow State's core.

The people represented many different nations in Europe, Asia, Central and South America, and the United States.

Embodied in that list was Prime Minister Grigory Rostislav, and at the second tier of the list was the picture of the incumbent US President Kenneth Hill as one of the foremost leaders.

However, another profile was blacked out with no photo description except for a cryptic filename of "Black_Sparrow_FTR00."

Khali was stunned that President Hill was involved in the Shadow State's plans. The dots began to connect with why Hill suddenly became so uncooperative with the EJFS, hence forcing them to leave US airspace in less than three days.

Khali also tried to download the data he viewed regarding the Shadow State actors immediately after copying the first set of files. However, halfway through the data transfer, the computer suddenly shut down and the device became obsolete.

Khali scrambled to make sure that the data he obtained was still intact. After checking the storage drive on another computer, he learned that the files he recovered remained accessible.

Khali sighed with relief, but he was disappointed that he could not save all the data he sought.

In Interrogation Room One, Gyan was being questioned by Agents Raj and Singh while Khali returned to the observation room on the other side of the two-way mirror.

Gyan continued to be resistant to the agents, who were trying to break him down to cooperate.

"You two are wasting your time. My mind is like Fort Knox. You won't be able to break me down easily."

Raj scolded Gyan.

"I promise you, one way or another, you're going to give us the information we're seeking."

Gyan scoffed at Raj. "Don't count on it."

Raj fumed as Singh tried to help him keep his cool.

Singh spoke to Raj, trying to quell his anger.

"Easy, Raj, don't let him get to you. Everybody has a breaking point. We'll have to work harder to break Gyan down," Singh whispered calmly.

Suddenly, Khali paged both Raj and Singh.

"Agents, please report back to the observation room," Khali spoke on the intercom.

Gyan maintained his smug looks while it appeared that he might have temporarily bested the two agents working to interrogate him.

Raj briefly glared at Gyan before the two agents shuffled through the door to the other side of the observation room to speak with Khali.

Khali briefed both agents on his findings in the archives.

"I think I may have found some critical information regarding the Shadow State's plans. I reviewed data on Ravan's laptop, and he was sitting on a collection of data regarding Vritra, Final Wave, and the beginning stages of the Shadow State. I was able to save most of the data on a storage drive, but my connection was severed after Ravan's laptop shut down permanently," Khali explained.

"What were you able to find out?" Singh inquired.

Khali explained further, "Among other things: President Hill is an active member of the Shadow State network. There are twelve of them in a core group of elite members. Six of them were lower-tier members. This could explain why the President changed his tone to be unwilling to allow us in the US much longer."

Raj and Singh were both stunned and horrified by the revelation that Khali discovered in his investigation.

Raj spoke with a grave tone in his voice.

"That makes the President a traitor, and now we know he is an occupier in the White House. He should be impeached and executed for treason," Raj added.

Khali interjected. "That is undoubtedly true. Unfortunately, he has an underground network covering his assets. If we were to remove President Hill from office, it would reflect poorly on us because the Presidential Election is only days away. Nonetheless, it would take a herculean effort to remove a corrupt President. We must find a way to make use of all the time we have left before we must disperse from US airspace."

Singh had a pensive look on his face as he scratched his beard with his large fingers.

"We need to ramp up the heat on Gyan if we want to stay ahead of the deadline. I think it is time we begin the enhanced interrogation phase. Surely, Gyan will not handle it, and he should break," Singh recommended.

"You have the green light to proceed. Tell Devdas to start the injections," Khali instructed.

Soon after, Devdas loaded a syringe of pain-stimulating chemicals to increase agitation and discomfort in Gyan's neck.

Raj and Singh returned to the interrogation room where Gyan sat waiting while hooked up to the vital-reading equipment and a widescreen HDTV exhibiting his current thoughts.

Gyan continued to mock both agents.

"You two are wasting your time with me. I have high pain tolerance," Gyan sneered at Raj and Singh.

"We fully intend to see how long you may last until, inevitably, you break down and comply. You are only making it worse for yourself," Raj responded harshly, having enough of Gyan's mind games.

Raj snapped his fingers to Devdas, cueing him to administer the first dose of pain stimulators.

"We'll start you off with 25 cubic centimeters. The rest is up to you," Raj spoke with contempt for Gyan.

Devdas carefully injected some chemicals that stimulated Gyan's pain receptors in his brain, increasing his agitation and discomfort exponentially.

"What is your role regarding the Shadow State?" Raj asked.

Gyan remained steadfast, but the crimson capsule device in his throat became more potent in its effects on top of the pain he was experiencing.

"I won't tell you anything," Gyan resisted.

Raj continued to ramp up the pressure on Gyan, hoping he would give up quickly.

"Give him the second dose, Devdas," Raj commanded.

"Very well, sir," Devdas replied as he loaded another syringe to inject more pain stimulators into Gyan's neck.

Devdas carefully injected the loaded syringe into Gyan, doubling Gyan's neck and shoulder pain intensity.

Gyan remained non-verbal and resilient to the enhanced interrogation.

"Gyan, I take no pleasure in seeing suspects as you suffer like this. It's better for everyone if you would comply," Raj tried to level with Gyan to coax him into cooperating.

"I'm not falling for your mental gymnastics. I'm far too sharp for that," Gyan spoke with a significant strain in his voice.

Raj flared his nostrils silently, becoming frustrated with Gyan's stubbornness.

"Give him the last dose," Raj ordered Devdas, who obeyed the command.

Devdas loaded the last syringe, which usually maximizes the pain to the allowed limit.

Gyan was overly confident in himself that he would be able to withstand all the enhanced interrogation tactics. Yet, he vastly underestimated the powers of both the crimson capsule device and the pain stimulators.

Gyan profusely sweated as he struggled to remain resilient. He broke.

"Wait, I give up. I'll tell you everything you need to know," Gyan surrendered.

"Devdas, stop. Gyan, start talking now!" Raj commanded.

"I was the one who they contracted to become their technical engineer, and I developed the geoengineering projects that are currently being employed against the US and the West," Gyan explained.

"Do you have a way to reverse the superstorm you created off the coast of Cape Verde?" Raj interrogated Gyan further.

"Ungh – I don't have that function enabled in my geoengineering systems. I can only shut the storm enhancers off and turn off the cloud machines. But the storm could still gather strength in the Atlantic Ocean. Your only hope is that it curves east and falls apart in the jet stream somehow," Gyan whined.

Khali issued a command to the Interrogation Techs, Kumar and Yukti.

"Scan his memory and see if it verifies," Khali directed.

"Yes, Master." Kumar complied.

Both Kumar and Yukti scanned Gyan's memory, which confirmed his testimony.

"He's telling the truth, Master," Yukti indicated.

Khali patched into Raj's Bluejaw earpiece.

"Ask him if he knows where Anastasia is headed," Khali communicated softly.

Raj obeyed Master Khali's command.

"Where is Anastasia headed?" Raj asked with a stern tone in his voice.

Gyan paused momentarily, almost in tears.

"Where is she?!" Raj reiterated his question louder.

"She's going to Budapest!" Gyan revealed.

"Where in Budapest?" Raj asked.

"The Russian Embassy! She's going to the embassy to seek asylum," Gyan cried out in pain.

"Kumar?" Khali nodded at Kumar to verify Gyan's testimony.

"I'm on it, Master Khali." Kumar scanned Gyan's thoughts through his tablet screen while working with Yukti in his on-the-job training.

The images in Gyan's memory streamed across the screen and confirmed his testimony.

"Confirmed," Yukti noted aloud.

Khali had seen enough and decided to take over for the remainder of the interrogation.

The Chief Commander stepped into the interrogation room and asked more questions.

"Gyan, my name is Khali. I am the Chief of Command for the EJFS, and I will be issuing your verdict momentarily. But first, I need more information from you. Does the codename "Black_Sparrow_FTR00" ring a bell to you? Does he run the Shadow State?" Master Khali asked sternly but calmly.

Gyan felt overwhelmed by the power of the crimson capsule device and could not hold back any more.

"Yes, that is Black Sparrow, or also known as Black Sparrow Zero. He's the top of the food chain in the order of the Shadow State," Gyan tiredly explained.

"Do you know his real name? Where does he operate?" Khali asked while speaking in a calm tone of voice to coax Gyan into giving up his testimony.

"I don't know his name, but I know he's operating in Brussels, Belgium. He works for the Belgian government, but that's all I know." Gyan weakly conceded and became drowsy.

Khali cued his interrogation techs, Kumar and Yukti, to confirm his testimony.

Kumar scanned Gyan's brain again, and all information was found accurate to the best of his knowledge.

Kumar buzzed in on the intercom.

"Everything he told us is true, Master. There's no more data left to examine," Kumar explained.

Khali showed Gyan mercy and helped Gyan receive the antidote to cease all his pain and discomfort.

"Devdas, give Gyan the antidote. We have all the information we need right now. I am convicting him of conspiracy and ecoterrorism. But I will proceed with sentencing later. For now, we will let him rest. Singh, you may escort him to his holding cell." Khali issued his verdict.

Khali used his sedation device to put Gyan in restful sleep.

Singh seated Gyan in a hovering wheelchair and placed him in handcuffs before pushing Gyan in the wheelchair, down the hall to Gyan's holding cell, and positioned him on a full bed frame.

After Singh laid Gyan down to rest, he removed Gyan's handcuffs, closed the holding cell door shut, and locked Gyan up to sleep for a while.

Once Singh returned to confer with Khali and Raj, they strategized their next phase in their action plan.

Khali began the discussion.

"In light of what Gyan revealed to us, I suggest we send a team of agents to the EJFS European Division to locate and stop Anastasia. Furthermore, we need to identify the real name of this Black Sparrow Zero individual operating in Brussels, Belgium," Khali spoke solemnly.

"What are we going to do about the superstorm headed for the US?" Singh raised a question.

"The TAC Team in Staten Island recovered some of Gyan's computer systems, and we're going to try remotely shutting down his geoengineering systems and possibly weaken the storm before it gets here. However, the jet stream will determine the absolute path it takes. If it makes landfall, the American public will have to take shelter and ride it out until it passes. Just pray that it will significantly weaken before it impacts the shores," Khali continued.

Raj added. "We'll need to send teams over to Brussels and Budapest to find both Anastasia and Black Sparrow Zero. However, there is also the matter of Kim's imposter, the corrupt President Hill, the CIRB, and the whereabouts of Judson Clayborn. We don't even know if Clayborn is still alive at this point."

Singh interjected. "We are going to need much more crew coverage to fix all of these crises. We must call on the New York Division to team up with us again. Perhaps we should assemble joint TAC Teams from both Atlanta and New York to search for Clayborn and Kim's doppelganger."

Khali responded to the ideas of Raj and Singh.

"I highly concur. Kim should be transferred to the New York EJFS Thunderhead Palace Base to keep her near the area, and she may be allowed to return after we have located her imposter and arrested her. Another TAC Team will retrace Clayborn's movements. We cannot leave him in the hands of the Shadow State or the CIRB. At this point, neither of them can be trusted. I will call a briefing in the auditorium at 4:00 p.m."

Khali addressed his adopted son and most stellar agent.

"Singh, I want you and Abhu to deploy to Europe and collaborate with EJFS Branches and Divisions in the area. I will be your point of contact. Let us head back to the base. We still have work yet to be done."

The five agents in the room gathered their equipment and prepared to return to the main Thunderhead palace.

***

Meanwhile, at John F. Kennedy Airport in Southeastern Manhattan, Anastasia Zima boarded a private flight bound for Budapest, Hungary. Zima got on the plane for the trip paid for by her Russian counterparts in Moscow, Russia, Prime Minister Grigory Rostislav and his assistant Petya Ivanoff.

Zima brought her carrying case containing the ancient heirloom necklace that once belonged to the late Ravan.

On the night Vritra was defeated, his spirit dispelled into an energy plume. Since that time, the remnants were encased into the dragon-shaped amulet on the necklace centerpiece. She put her carry-on item in the storage compartment in the overhead space above her airline seat and sat down.

An athletic man wearing an expensive suit sat in the seat next to her and introduced himself to Zima before beginning the takeoff procedure. Zima recognized him immediately.

"Hi, Ms. Zima, it's Grant Bradford from the CIRB. I remember you from last night. Matthews wants me to make sure you have protection during your trip to the Russian Embassy in Budapest. So, here I am."

Zima was semi-amused but not happy that Matthews posted a protective detail assigned to defend her.

"I don't need an escort, but I don't mind that you're here. I could use some company for the flight. Are you the only asset on board?" Zima asked.

"No. Agents Cortez and Meyers are on board as well," Bradford replied with a smile.

"I can't imagine Matthews would go through that much trouble in assigning a security detail for my flight," Zima pondered.

"Well, let us face it, you're headed to a nation where they don't necessarily want you around. So, we have been posted with you to come along for a safe handoff. Besides, the flight crew already closed the hatch door, so I guess you are stuck with us now," Bradford continued.

"Lucky me, I suppose," Zima muttered as she looked out the window while the plane began to make its way to the starting point for takeoff.

Five minutes later, the plane took off en route to the Budapest Ferenc Liszt International Airport, rerouting the flight track to maneuver away from the massive hurricane spinning towards the Eastern US.

As the flight continued, the necklace stored in the carrying case in the overhead storage space, containing Vritra's remnants, began to respond to the cyclonic energy emanating from the hurricane, bypassing it while flying to Budapest.

While Zima was in her seat as the others were sleeping for the overseas trip, her personality started to change in response to Vritra's remnants becoming awakened by the hurricane passing by. A sinister smile came across Zima's face as the skies outside began to darken.

"He's almost here," A spectral voice reverberated in Zima's mind.

Suddenly, Zima was startled by the nudging of Bradford's elbow. She came out of her trance while the nightlights in the cabin were illuminated.

"Hey, are you okay, Zima?" Bradford asked.

"Uh, yeah, I just zoned out. I need some vodka. Be a dear, call the flight attendant and ask for some Russian Iced Tea while I use the restroom. Thank you."

Zima stood up from her seat and made her way to the restroom. She started feeling nauseous. She slowly began experiencing a transformation of her character and started hearing a cacophony of voices again.

She washed her face in the lavatory sink, trying to pull herself back together.

When she turned away to grab a paper towel to wipe her face, she turned around to face the mirror, and a reflection of the late Ravan Kanda Ganesh appeared as a hallucination.

Zima gasped as she rubbed her eyes, and the illusion of Ravan was gone.

Zima felt airsick and started heaving in response to the environmental changes she experienced.

Later, Bradford received a drink he ordered for his seatmate, Zima, per her request and placed her vodka-laced iced tea in the cupholder in front of the tray.

Zima recovered from her disturbing moment, left the restroom, and returned to her seat while somewhat perturbed by her daze.

Bradford raised his hand to get Zima's attention. She returned to her seat, took a healthy sip of her iced tea, and started to relax. Simultaneously, the necklace of Vritra's remains reentered dormancy, and the apparitions and hallucinations stopped.

"Are you all right?" Bradford asked, concerned.

"I'm fine. It must be altitude sickness," Zima responded.

"Just hang in there. We will be there in less than nine hours," Bradford assured.

Zima continued to sip her vodka while Bradford drank some bottled water. Soon after she finished half of her drink, she fell asleep in her seat for the night.

14: Kim Learns of Caleb's Dual Identity: Alicia's Latest Sabotage

Kim's Guestroom Quarters

EJFS Atlanta Branch – Eastern US Division

Current Location: Staten Island, New York, USA

November 2, 2024

3:35 PM EDT, Saturday Afternoon

Kim rested in her guestroom and pondered her quandary. She recently was allowed to have her phone reactivated, which allowed her to catch up on the day's events in Washington, D.C.

However, she yearned to talk with her boyfriend, Logan Hastings, the son of Chief of Staff Nicolas Hastings.

Just as she contemplated contacting Logan, Durga buzzed the call button on Kim's door.

"Come in," Kim replied.

Durga slid the door open to enter Kim's room and conversed with her.

"Hi, Kim. How are you holding up?" Durga asked with genuine concern.

"I don't know. I want to talk to my boyfriend, but I am uneasy that whoever this saboteur is may have ruined my whole life. I want to see Caleb and find out what's going on," Kim lamented.

"I'm so sorry, Kim. I cannot imagine what you must be going through. We are doing everything we can to stop her. But unfortunately, we cannot let you contact your boyfriend yet. Not until we know what forms of sabotage this woman has done.

Caleb is coming to speak with you soon. He is also working to locate and stop her." Durga comforted Kim in her distress.

"You know, I keep telling myself that Caleb is in the right place and in competent hands. At some point, I wonder what I can do to help him. I do not like being a non-factor. He has been acting strangely ever since the year before. He's matured from years past, but there is something I notice that troubles me," Kim continued.

"How so, exactly?" Durga queried.

"I feel like he's living a double life. Everything about him is so different now. I barely recognize him with his new super-athletic figure. I still question to this day how he attained that physique. I also noticed how he looks at you like he is completely and helplessly in love with you. You two must be dating each other, am I right?" Kim continued.

"You are correct, Kim. I see something special in your brother and his caring personality. He is a sweet, charming, and loving young man. But I cannot go into too much detail about that right now. Aside from that, I wanted to let you know that Caleb will talk to you privately. He has something that he wishes to share with you regarding his job at the EJFS." Durga sat next to Kim on her bed, explaining Caleb's role.

"So, there is something that he is not telling me," Kim replied with dismay as she lay in bed and internalized her emotions.

"Caleb intends to explain everything to you. Regardless, considering all that he has endured, I think you should cut him some slack. He is only trying to protect the ones that he loves. Such as his family, his friends, and me," Durga encouraged.

"I know his job probably requires him to keep a tight lid on things. I wish that it weren't so complicated," Kim continued.

"Soon, it will all be clear. I'm sure of it," Durga reassured Kim.

Meanwhile, Caleb was in his original identity as he boarded an elevator to Level 12 of the EJFS Thunderhead Palace to visit his sister, Kim. He scanned in, entered the smaller unit, and made his way to Kim's guestroom.

In Kim's room, there was a knock on the door.

"Who is it?" Kim asked.

"It's Caleb."

Kim rushed out of her bed and slid the door open to let her brother inside.

"Sis, I need to talk to you privately," Caleb spoke.

Durga excused herself to leave the room.

"I'll give you both some time alone." Durga looked into Caleb's eyes lovingly as she departed the room.

Caleb asserted, "Have a seat, Kimberly."

Kim obediently sat at her bedside.

"I need you to understand some things. You see, I have been living a double life, to an extent. However, it is part of my job. I spoke to my close friend, Singh, and he recommended that I find the right time to reveal my alternate identity to you. The identity that I operate with in the field is under the alias Abhu Dhuval Sandeep. Khali granted me that name when I first started working for the EJFS," Caleb explained delicately.

"I don't understand. How are you able to do these things?" Kim asked.

"I intend to show you. I want you to meet the other half of my dual personality," Caleb explained as Kim looked at him in awe.

Caleb activated a function on his smartwatch on his left wrist.

Suddenly, his appearance started to change dramatically as his hair grew much longer and thicker. Caleb's skin pigmentation changed to dark brown, his mustache and beard grew out, and Abhu came about in his full form right in front of his awestruck sister.

Kim was speechless after Caleb's wild transformation in full display before her.

"This is my better half, EJFS Agent Abhu Dhuval Sandeep," The transformed super-agent revealed in a thunderously deep-pitched Indian voice.

Kim gasped in shock. "Oh, my God!"

Kim covered her mouth upon bearing witness to Caleb's identity change. She got up out of her bed and examined the metaphysical differences of her brother.

Kim touched Abhu's hair and face. She saw that he retained the same eyes as Caleb.

Abhu grinned at his sister while in his alternate identity.

"I'm still fully Caleb and Abhu while I'm in this form," Abhu explained.

"How could this be?" Kim asked while trying to recover from her shock, grasping to understand Abhu and Caleb's identity split.

"This is my field agent identity. You are the only person in the outside world that has witnessed my transformation. You must promise me that you don't tell another soul about this until I say so," Abhu explained further.

"I-I understand. What can you do while you are in this form?" Kim stuttered.

"I can blow wind, manipulate the weather, and I have super-strength," Abhu revealed to his sister.

"Don't tell me, show me, but gently," Kim insisted.

"Very well." Abhu displayed a sampling of his powers gently to his sister.

First, Abhu took a moderate inhalation of air and blew a stiff breeze on Kim's face. Her hair whipped around in a frenzy while Abhu demonstrated his supernatural powers.

Abhu stopped blowing wind and then used his supernatural powers to change the weather outside Kim's bedroom window.

While Abhu slowly flexed his biceps, a mild thunderstorm appeared outside Kim's window. As she turned, she saw the skies darken outside as cumulonimbus clouds formed in the distance.

Instantly, lightning flashed, and thunder rumbled as Kim was continuously stunned by Abhu's superpowers.

As Kim watched the summoned storm outside rage, she heard Abhu grunting as he lifted her dresser drawer above his cranium with both hands.

Kim turned around and saw Abhu's impressive display of superhuman strength as he continued to hold the dresser drawer in both hands. During this, lightning and thunder resumed outside.

Abhu placed the dresser back down in its original spot and caused the storm to dissipate within a minute.

Kim was, in a way, impressed but shocked by Abhu's supernatural and superhuman abilities.

"Now, you know my powers and seen them with your own eyes. I hold nothing back from you," Abhu proclaimed.

Kim was able to speak after her moment of shock and awe.

"But why and how?" Kim muttered quietly, still enthralled by the display of Abhu's mighty powers.

"I was infused with elemental powers and blessed with supernatural strength that every agent here has attained. If not all of them, most agents have alternate identities that they use to conceal their true selves to others. We are given these capabilities and a principle that stealthily removes corrupt leaders and corrects the wrongs in this world. These powers are to be used responsibly and safeguarded to prevent any misuse," Abhu digressed.

"So that bit you told the family last year about the clinical test formulas was just a front, so to speak?" Kim raised a question.

"Correct, the reason why I couldn't tell the truth back then was that the EJFS was not yet a public agency. But now, things are different. My superiors trust me to tell you the truth. They want to ensure that you understand why they assigned me to this alternate identity. I was to blend in with the other agents that are also undercover superagents disguised as taxi drivers. Ever since the EJFS went public last year, the modus operandi has remained mostly the same. We work undercover as a network of taxicab drivers working to fight for justice, peace, and prosperity over the nations of this world," Abhu elucidated.

"Well, I guess since you've explained it that way, it somehow makes sense, strangely enough," Kim spoke frankly.

"As I said before, it was not my time to reveal my alternate identity to you yet. But now, you know. Do you still accept me as your brother, dual identities and all?" Abhu asked.

"I suppose it wouldn't do any good to say no. I must admit I'm impressed by your transformation. The part you played here was instrumental. Everything that happened last year makes sense now. I admire that you are fighting to restore balance, integrity, and justice for this world. We need more of that nowadays. I'm proud of you, brother," Kim smiled and hugged her much taller brother in the form of Abhu.

"Thank you for understanding. I was so worried about how you would react," Abhu responded.

Kim ended the embrace and posed another question to her brother.

"How does one go about signing up for this place?" Kim asked.

Abhu laughed quietly and then realized she was serious by the look on her face.

"Well, we can talk about that soon. There is a briefing at 4:00 this afternoon. I intend to be there, and I will ask Khali if you may observe. We still need to find your imposter and stop her from doing any more damage to your reputation. I must return to work. I love you, Sis!" Abhu responded.

Abhu proceeded to take off to his quadrant unit to prepare for the briefing while Kim was left to contemplate a possible career change.

Abhu returned to the Sapphire Quadrant and entered his private quarters. He noticed that there was a text message from his closest friend, Agent Singh. It read as follows:

New unread message from Agent Singh Puneet Sherpa, received at 3:48 PM:

"My dear brother and friend, Abhu. How did it go with Kim? Call me on my smartphone if you want. Love you, ~Agent Singh."

Abhu called his best friend, Singh, who was in the command center preparing to clock off to head to the briefing at 4:00 p.m. After Singh used his fingerprint to clock out, he heard Abhu's ringtone on his smartphone and answered it while preparing to leave the command center.

"Hi, Abhu. How did it go?" Singh asked as he exited the command center.

"Much better than I expected. Initially, I thought Kim would stage a protest right in front of me, but she actually asked me how to sign up to work in the EJFS," Agent Abhu explained.

"Wow, that's unexpected. What did you tell her?" Agent Singh asked curiously.

"I informed her that I would speak to Khali about it," Agent Abhu replied.

"How do you feel about Kim working at the EJFS?"

"Honestly, I don't know. I was not expecting Kim to be so open to the idea of my split identity. I guess we will give it some more thought later. We have a bigger business to tackle."

"Well, speaking of which, we have a briefing at 4:00 p.m., as I'm sure you are already aware. I will meet up with you then. I need to have a conversation with you about something else. Meet me in the lobby in five minutes. We have an assignment that I need to talk to you about in person," Singh added.

"I'll be down there as soon as I can. See you soon," Abhu prepared to end the call.

Singh boarded an elevator after passing by other agents heading to the main floor lobby for a briefing update in less than ten minutes.

Abhu packed up his gear and headed to the first floor.

Once Abhu and Singh reunited in the lobby, they conducted a "walk and talk" conversation.

"I want to give you a rundown of what happened with Gyan and his interrogation. We discovered that he caused a superstorm to form off the West Coast of Africa near Cape Verde. It was meant to disrupt the election," Singh explained while both agents walked briskly.

"Why would he do that?" Agent Abhu inquired.

"There's more to it. Khali dug up Ravan's laptop from the year before, and he found some files that indicate Ravan knew about the Shadow State in its early stages. To sum things up, Gyan is trying to re-manifest Vritra's remnants into destructive energy that could destroy the world. The massive hurricane is rumored to be a form of energy needed to revive Vritra in some harnessable way. But we do not have confirmation on whether Vritra's remains could reconstitute into a form of destructive power. The command center is also researching whether Vritra could convert into his true form. However, so far, we do not have quantifiable answers yet. We do not have much time left to work with. President Hill has ordered the EJFS bases to disperse and cease operations in the US in less than 72 hours. We have been deemed an enemy of the state," Singh explained further as they transited the hallways passing by other agents on the same level.

"What? Why?" Abhu asked puzzlingly.

Both Singh and Abhu stopped walking, and Singh spoke quietly to Abhu in a bleak tone.

"According to what Khali found on Ravan's laptop, President Hill is one of the inner twelve members of the Shadow State," Singh clarified.

Abhu's jaw dropped in shock.

"This is a worst-case scenario gone awry," Abhu remarked quietly.

"I know. However, I am confident that Khali will formulate a plan. We will not let Hill get away with this. But it looks like there is someone he reports to for direction. There was a secret dossier file of someone named "Black Sparrow Zero" in some of the encrypted data that Khali discovered before the laptop shut down. Maybe we will uncover their identity," Singh speculated.

"I would hope so," Abhu surmised as the duo resumed their stroll.

***

Meanwhile, as the early evening hours began to wear on in Washington D.C., with the sun setting, Alicia, Kim's imposter, and imitator drove her car up to Logan's apartment.

She prepared to meet with Logan to sabotage Kim's relationship with him as CIRB Deputy Director James Matthews sanctioned.

Alicia retrieved her purse and exited the car while making sure her birthmark was concealed. She chirped her car alarm on her silver luxury vehicle and walked up to the front door of Logan's apartment suite.

Logan was pacing back and forth anxiously as he watched the recent happenings on the national news coverage. This included the discovery of an incredibly massive hurricane that had recently formed near Cape Verde and was shown barreling toward the Atlantic coastline in a northwestern clockwise spiral.

Logan was startled by a knock at his front door. He walked up to the peephole and saw that it appeared to be Kim Porter at the door. He frantically opened the door, overcome with relief to see his girlfriend, not knowing it was an imposter.

"Kim, where were you? I have been trying to reach you all day long," Logan whined.

"It's a long story. But, let me cut to the chase. I am sorry to have to tell you this, but I cannot continue to see you. It's too risky," The imposter Kim began bluntly.

"What?! What are you talking about?!" Logan protested.

"Logan, your father wants us to break up. He thinks our relationship will hurt the President's chances of reelection on Tuesday. I'm sorry, but this is how it has to be," The imposter continued to stand her ground.

Logan became emotionally distressed.

"Kim, you don't understand. I was going to propose to you tonight. I bought you an engagement ring and everything. This was supposed to be a special night for both of us!" Logan responded with tremendous heartache in his voice.

"Logan, I..." The imposter trailed off.

Suddenly, a smudge of makeup fell from Kim's face while she became flustered and emotional. Logan saw that he was not talking to the real Kim Porter.

"Wait a minute. You aren't Kim. Who are you?!" Logan asked angrily.

"Logan, please!" The imposter pleaded.

"What happened to my girlfriend?! Where is she?!" Logan demanded answers.

Alicia approached Logan and injected him with a tranquilizer, causing Logan's eyes to cross as he fell backward, hitting the floor, falling asleep.

Alicia, while visibly shaken, stormed out of the apartment, and returned to her car. She called her boss, Matthews, to give him a status report.

Matthews was in his office watching the entire exchange going down as Logan's home had been bugged for the event just days before. He heard Alicia calling his phone, and he answered the call.

"Yeah?" Matthews answered.

"It's Alicia. Logan didn't buy it. He saw my birthmark, and so I tranquilized him."

Matthews sighed with disappointment.

"Why didn't you page me for authorization to capture him?" Matthews asked.

"I don't think kidnapping the Chief of Staff's son is a particularly good idea. Nicolas would draw that line on that, and you know it," Alicia argued.

"Fine, this last act of sabotage will suffice for the night. Come back to Langley, and we will have a chat. It's time to prep you for your overseas mission," Matthews concluded.

"I'm on my way," Alicia responded, then hung up the phone.

Simultaneously, she backed her car out of the driveway and drove back to Langley, Virginia.

Logan lay on his apartment suite floor, out cold from the imposter's tranquilizer injection.

15: The Second Briefing: Kim Scorned by POTUS Hill's Duplicity

EJFS Briefing Auditorium – Level 1 – Main Building

EJFS Atlanta Branch – Eastern US Division

Current Location: Staten Island, New York, USA

November 2, 2024

4:00 PM EDT, Saturday Afternoon

The entire Atlanta-based EJFS roster gathered in the Briefing Auditorium in the EJFS Thunderhead Palace Base. Other EJFS Branch locations ranged from New York City, New York. Budapest, Hungary, and Brussels, Belgium in the EJFS European Division, also teleconferenced as they collaboratively strategized a joint effort to bring down the Shadow State.

All EJFS agents, including those in the Sapphire Unit, took their assigned seats in the auditorium to observe while Singh joined Raj's side of the curved table in the center stage.

Kim Porter watched the briefing at the behest of Khali per Abhu's request to let his sister remain informed of the developments taking place within her brother's superagency.

After four o'clock, the auditorium lights dimmed, and Master Khali and his entourage of elite agents took the stage while accompanied by Second-In-Command Agent Raj, Agent Devdas, Agent Singh, Agent Kumar, and Khali's Personal Advisor, Tanveer Bhattacharya.

Master Khali directed the briefing to commence.

"Good afternoon, my subordinates. This is a briefing update to follow up on our conference earlier this morning. My colleagues, alongside me, have been working tirelessly to search for answers regarding the Shadow State's sinister plans to disrupt the election on Tuesday. Agent Raj will elaborate on our findings," Khali began.

Agent Raj emerged from his seat and prepared to inform the agency network of his findings.

"Welcome fellow agency branches hailing from New York and parts of Europe. Today's briefing will detail the list of crises facing us in the next several days. Let me begin by saying that this election cycle has been and will continue to be a monumental challenge to the core infrastructure of the EJFS. At large, the Shadow State is a highly formidable network that has tested the EJFS in unforeseen ways. From infiltrating various government levels, militarizing branches of the CIRB, and contracting tech giants to geoengineer storms of apocalyptic magnitude. Therefore, we must learn to adapt quickly, or this nation and the world would be doomed."

Agent Raj's speech was sobering to all in attendance and the others watching, including Caleb's sister, Kim.

Agent Raj continued as Kumar readied the briefing presentation, "Our elite team of super-agents has worked extensively to obtain further intel on the myriad of crises surrounding the Shadow State. I will elaborate further."

The first slide appeared on the screens of all agents watching in the auditoriums showing President Kenneth Hill's dossier report.

The report indicated Hill's alignment with the Shadow State. Among other images were dossier reports for Russian Prime Minister Grigory Rostislav and his assistant Petya Ivanoff. Also included in the slide were the dossier files of Anastasia Zima, Jagmohan Gyan, and several CIRB members, including Deputy Director James Matthews and a handful of rogue agents under his authority.

"In a recent interrogation of Mr. Gyan, we have learned that the Shadow State is working together to orchestrate a cataclysmic demise of the Western world on the eve of Election Day. Our findings have implicated the current US President after Master Khali had pulled the late Ravan Kanda Ganesh's laptop from the Detention Center archives. We were able to identify a few people on the dossier. This includes CIRB Deputy Director James Matthews, Anastasia Zima, President Hill, Russian Prime Minister Rostislav, Jagmohan Gyan, and an unidentified person with the codename "Black Sparrow Zero," Raj continued.

Kim Porter watched from her quarters, following the briefing on the HDTV screen. She was shocked and horrified that she was working with a traitor to her country.

Everything Kim knew about the President was a lie.

Raj continued the briefing.

"Finally, we have learned that Vritra's remains have been stored in an ancient heirloom necklace, with dormant energies from the previous year. According to the Shadow State's manifesto obtained from Ravan's laptop, they believe that a geoengineered hurricane of extraordinary magnitude will give them a second opportunity at reawakening Vritra. The hope was to reconstitute his remnants into terrible and destructive energy that could imperil the entire world. Thus, we have learned vital intel on Anastasia's whereabouts and the possible whereabouts of this Shadow State leader under the codename "Black Sparrow Zero."

Raj changed the slide to the following high-resolution graphic in the presentation.

"In Gyan's interrogation, we have learned that Anastasia has fled to the Russian Embassy in Budapest, Hungary, where we believe she will seek haven until she can be scooped up by whom we suspect is the top leader of the Shadow State. In closing, our mission outline remains mostly the same. However, there is a critical changeup in our overall strategy. Due to ongoing searches for the first victim of the Shadow State, Judson Clayborn, who was captured and missing since last night, the search for a hidden agent impersonating an EJFS agent's sister, Kim Porter, we are forced to split off into teams. President Hill has also declared the EJFS a rogue enemy of the state, and we have been given less than 72 hours to disperse from US airspace. But we will continue to operate within the mandate issued to us by the President until the timeframe has expired."

Raj prepared to close out his portion of the briefing.

"We will be issuing assignments to two agents quarterbacking the operation in Europe. Agents Abhu and Singh will be the top two agents burdened with the task to collaborate with the EJFS European Division to track down Anastasia in Budapest and requisition her to lead us to the top of the Shadow State order in Brussels, Belgium. They will be tasked with assembling a joint TAC Team operation from our roster to depart to Budapest, Hungary, and work to identify and track down the Shadow State leader. The remaining agents and subdivisions in the region will locate and maintain a clampdown on Kim's imitator, The Hill Administration, and his staff. We must locate and rescue Judson Clayborn from capture. I will let Master Khali take it from here," Agent Raj concluded.

Master Khali took over for the remainder of the briefing.

Khali began. "At this time, I call upon Agent Abhu Sandeep to join Singh and I onstage."

Agent Abhu arose from his seat as his fellow residents glanced at him while he made his way down to the center stage, joining Khali and Singh on the dais.

Master Khali continued. "I have entrusted these two exceptional agents to manage the operation in Europe to locate and apprehend Anastasia and the Shadow State leader. They will select five agents from the EJFS roster and depart to Budapest, searching for Anastasia and the Shadow State leader. You will answer to these two, and they will lead the operation through our set of missions in the coming days. I will be Abhu and Singh's point of contact. Furthermore, any major decision will be subject to EJFS executive approval."

Master Khali addressed both his top agents, placing his large hands upon Abhu and Singh's shoulders as a sign of trust and respect.

"You two, I am laying tremendous confidence in you both. As the top two leaders in the urgent operations against the fallen Final Wave organization, I trust both of you with this delicate task. You have 48 hours from the overseas mission's outset to accomplish the objective I have assigned to you. Now, make your selections regarding which agents you want to accompany you on this mission," Master Khali took a step back and gave Agents Abhu and Singh the floor.

Agent Singh was the first to draft his TAC Team, Agents Anil, Baadal, Naveen, Nitin, and Gangi.

Agent Abhu was the second to draft his TAC Team consisting of Agents Chand, Vasu, Daarun, Garjan, and Durga.

Khali carried the meeting to a close before the EJFS began its large-scale operations against the Shadow State and its operatives.

"There you have it. These two TAC Teams will be deploying shortly en route to Budapest within the next hour. All agents drafted in both TAC Teams will confer and depart to meet with the EJFS European Division. They will be awaiting your arrival early tomorrow morning. I wish you both well and Godspeed. Come back alive. This briefing is adjourned," Khali gave both leading agents a comforting embrace before Agents Raj and Devdas escorted both teams to the Situation Room adjacent to the Briefing Auditorium. Khali headed for the elevators.

***

After the briefing ended, Kim lay in bed in her guestroom quarters, fuming that she unknowingly worked for a traitor in the White House and worked as Hill's campaign events liaison. She knew that her conscience would not allow her to continue associating herself with Hill's Re-election campaign any longer.

Regardless, Kim knew the only way to make an impactful and resounding mark on the battle was not just to quit her job or jump ship at a time when it would be an insignificant blow than to join her brother's agency to shut down President Hill and remove him from office.

Unfortunately, Khali already planned for Kim to be transferred to the EJFS New York Subdivision to keep her out of the limelight until her imposter can be stopped.

Kim wanted to consult with Khali about joining the EJFS to seek retribution against President Hill and the imposter working against her.

With this in mind, she scrolled through the list of contacts on the Smart HDTV screen and picked out Khali's number for an AERIAL VOIP call.

Khali was on his way to the elevators when he felt a ping and vibration on his smartphone. He noticed that his guest, Kim Porter, was contacting him. But Khali was puzzled as to why she was calling him.

"Hello, Kim. This is Khali. How may I help you?" Khali answered while he was preparing to board the elevator.

"Hi, Mr. Khali, can you come to my room? I want to speak to you about something," Kim spoke on the other side of the split-screen on her HDTV.

"What is this regarding? I am short on time, as you have seen in the briefing today. Our agency has missions to carry out and accomplish within a mandate in place," Khali replied.

"I feel betrayed by the President and whoever is controlling this imposter of me to ruin my life. I want to sign up for the EJFS and help put a stop to all of this chaos," Kim began.

"Kim, I know that you must feel quite upset about what was revealed of the President and his corrupt administration, but I am not about letting you join the EJFS on the pretense of revenge against your president. Aside from that, we do not have hardly anyone who can train you to become a superagent at this time," Khali argued.

"Mr. Khali, maybe you won't consider it now. But I want you to know that I finally see the need for this agency, and I could be an asset if given the opportunity. I can help track down whoever is currently making my life a living hell, and I have connections that can get us close to President Hill. Could you hear me out?" Kim insisted.

Khali paused before he answered as he began to consider Kim's request.

"All right, I'll be in your quarters in five minutes," Khali conceded to Kim and pushed number 12 on the list of levels in the main building of the EJFS Thunderhead Palace.

"Thank you so much. I'll see you again soon," Kim graciously responded.

"You're welcome. I'm on my way," Khali disconnected the mobile AERIAL VOIP call, and the elevator ascended to the 12th floor of the main building as Kim awaited Khali's arrival.

Khali entered the guestroom suites on Level 12 and came into Kim's quarters for a brief discussion to hear her out.

Khali knocked on Kim's guestroom door.

"Come in!" Kim permitted entry.

"All right, Kim. Here I am. Now, please explain to me why you would make a valuable agent in the EJFS. If you impress me, I will offer a position contingent on completing our comprehensive and intensive training programs. Think of this as a pitch to your new employer. Then, I will ask you a series of questions to vet you before considering a position for you in the agency. You have sixty seconds, starting now," Khali sat down in one of the oversized, sturdy chairs in Kim's room. He hoped to be impressed by Kim's aspirations.

"First off, I know my way around government and politics. You can use me as an insider to gather intel on Hill's connections. As I am sure you already know, my boyfriend is the son of Chief of Staff Nicolas Hastings. If you let me speak to Logan and explain to him in the entirety of what has been going on, he could be used to influence his dad and those he is in his immediate sphere to join me in trying to keep tabs on Hill," Kim began her pitch.

Khali was half-attentive to what Kim was proposing, thus not overly impressed yet.

Kim picked up on Khali's lack of interest and tried to grab his attention again.

"One more thing to consider, Logan and Hill's kids will be interns at the CIRB Headquarters in Langley tomorrow morning. Logan and Trevor are like brothers, exceptionally crafty and intelligent guys. Both know how to investigate internal affairs. The Head Director of the CIRB, Janice Ausburn, will not be too happy that her second-in-charge has militarized her agency against the American people. She is due to come into work after her vacation in Ibiza, Spain, with her husband, Gabriel. The CIRB Director would roll some heads if she found out what kind of operation Matthews has been running," Kim continued.

"How do you know all of these things?" Khali asked.

"Because I do my research, I majored in Political Science at my alma mater, the University of Georgia, and do you know what my minor was?" Kim asked.

"Spill it," Khali insisted.

"Computer Science, the category that my big brother couldn't finish. So, I did it, and he learns from me a great deal," Kim explained further.

"Well, Kim. You have got my interest. I will certainly consider you as a potential agent. You seem to have more usefulness than I initially thought. I am thoroughly impressed. Sit tight for a while, and I will consult with my team before moving forward with this. Before we proceed, I want to make sure that this is your final decision. Are you confident that you want to join the EJFS?" Khali asked as he prepared to exit Kim's quarters.

"Absolutely, my eyes have been opened to what the EJFS is truly about, and I want to be a part of it. Without a doubt in my mind," Kim assured Khali passionately.

"Very well, I admire your honesty and newfound passion. I will bring this forward to my team shortly. I'll get back to you soon," Master Khali shook Kim's smaller hand and exited her quarters to return to his office.

Kim remained somewhat restless and antsy regarding her pitch to Khali in her hope of joining the EJFS superagency. She interlaced her fingers, pressed against her lips, praying that she made a convincing appeal to join the ranks.

***

In the Situation Room on Level One, Agents Abhu and Singh became acting Captain and Commander in their joint TAC Team to strategize a plan of attack before they departed for Budapest. Simultaneously, the EJFS European Division watched on a split-screen on the high-resolution screens in the Situation Room.

Agent Raj led the meeting to open.

"All right, agents. Singh and Abhu will lead all of you on a series of missions in Budapest and, eventually, Brussels. The objective is to gain access to the Russian Embassy by any means necessary to capture Anastasia and offer her non-binding diplomatic immunity from all wrongdoing before she may lead us to her leader, Black Sparrow Zero. Once we locate him, we will capture and interrogate him at the European EJFS Thunderhead Base in Warsaw, Poland. Our method of capture will be the tried-and-true method of Storm Summoning and Abduction. However, it will not be long before the Russians figure out that we are onto their schemes. So, we must act fast within the allotted time we have been given," Agent Raj explained.

"Are there any questions before we deploy?" Agent Singh took the lead in addressing the teams.

"I have a concern: what do we do if the CIRB is accompanying Anastasia to the Russian Embassy? Do you think they won't see us coming and that she may be a target?" Agent Garjan asked.

Agent Raj addressed Garjan's question. "We will come prepared for any resistance from the Russians and the CIRB. But we do not wish to cause an international incident. We will exercise extreme care about extracting Anastasia from her hideout. She may put up a resistance herself, and we will work with our European friends to counteract."

Agent Abhu spoke to his team.

"Any other questions?" Abhu asked.

Agent Anil raised another question.

"What if Anastasia doesn't go along with us under duress?" Agent Anil asked.

"Then we take her immunity off the table and extract her thoughts in an interrogation," Raj answered.

"Any more questions?" Raj asked.

The room was silent, and therefore the TAC Teams dispersed and headed to the deployment bay to board a set of two large MICVs to depart for Budapest.

***

As the evening hours quickly loomed, Alicia Blaze, Kim's pretender, drove back into Langley, Virginia, to meet with the Deputy Director, James Matthews, to be prepped for overseas travel.

Alicia pulled into the parking garage and parked in her usual space. Then she chirped her alarm before heading back inside the CIRB Headquarters.

While on her way, Alicia peeled off her disguise that she had been wearing to impersonate Kim. The faker's natural hair was dyed crimson-colored, and she no longer concealed the distinguishing birthmark on her face.

Alicia tapped her smartphone on the reader device to unlock the doors inside the building.

James Matthews was calmly watching the news in his office. President Hill prepared to give an emergency address to the nation after relocating all White House residents to the bunker and war room underneath the Nation's Capital and the nearby Potomac River.

Alicia approached the double glass doors to his office and knocked gently.

"Come in, Alicia," Matthews permitted with a look of sadness written across his face.

"Well, here I am. What's with the long face?" Alicia playfully asked.

"The President moved into the bunkers and war room. He's going to give a national emergency address shortly," Matthews explained woefully.

Alicia's demeanor became a little more pressing.

"Why, are we at Defcon Four or something?" Alicia asked with some slight worry in her voice.

"He's getting ready to declare martial law. There is a superstorm barreling in the Atlantic toward the East Coast. It is already the size of three-quarters of the lower 48 states, rapidly expanding and strengthening," Matthews spoke with bleak concern.

"What?! That's terrible!" Alicia exclaimed in horror.

"Alicia, calm down. This was part of the plan. Unfortunately, the President has grounded all flights and closed all entry ports to brace for this storm. I have already requested a military flight for you as an exemption. But it will have to wait until the President and Secretary of Defense approves it. The problem is the Secretary of Defense does not know what is going on at the top. Hill planned this months ago before the election to retain his role as President," Matthews explained.

"That's going to be a hard sell," Alicia commented.

"No, kidding. But we will find a way. There's always a way," Matthews assured her.

"The President is speaking. Turn up your volume," Alicia insisted.

President Hill began his address from his bunker beneath the White House and spoke to the Nation.

"My fellow Americans: It is with deep regret and sadness that my administration has detected an abnormally and unnaturally expansive hurricane barreling toward the East Coast of the United States. The storm has been at a Category Five status since it formed earlier today off the coast of West Africa. It is already the size of over half of the lower 48 states and continues to strengthen. The Azores had already succumbed to the terrible destruction left in this superstorm's

wake. The path of the storm is expected to make a direct impact along the Eastern Seaboard. This is an extremely volatile and dangerous storm of the likes that humanity has never seen before. Therefore, I am ordering all state and federal agencies to initiate martial law effective immediately. All citizens must evacuate to underground tunnels and sewers to take refuge from the storm," President Hill began at his podium.

The EJFS agencies watched as the President addressed his citizens from their bases stationed in the US.

"Furthermore, I have been in contact with the EJFS Director Khali, based in Atlanta and now occupying our airspace in New York City. I have reason to believe that the EJFS, Elite Justice Force Squad, has been directly or indirectly responsible for the creation and human-made engineering of the climate to form this catastrophic hurricane. As such, a couple of hours ago, I have declared the EJFS superagency a rogue enemy of the state and ordered them to disperse and vacate US airspace in less than 72 hours, until approximately three o'clock Monday afternoon. Suppose they do not comply with my orders. In that case, we will engage in military action against the EJFS to protect our nation's sovereignty and America and her people's safety. Be safe, and May God Protect America in her time of need," President Hill wrapped up his address from the war room in the bunker, and the telecast ended.

Master Khali watched the national address from his office, exceedingly displeased with the public and wrongful accusation brought forth by President Hill. However, Khali remained steadfast in the adversarial relationship with Hill.

At the Nation's Capital, President Hill walked out of the War Room and passed by his running mate VP Peter Drake without saying a word to him even as Drake tried to make sense of what had just transpired.

Drake spoke to one of the staffers, Sedgwick Barnes, to give specific instructions for the Chief of Staff, Nicolas Hastings, and his lead staffer, Laura Matheson, upon returning to the White House.

"Barnes, when the Chief of Staff and his lead staffer return, make sure they are taken down here to the bunker and let me speak with Hastings first. Don't tell Hill that we're having this conversation," VP Drake instructed.

"Mr. Vice President, are you sure you want to do that?" Barnes asked.

"Yes, I insist. Do it."

"Very well, Mr. Vice President. I will direct them to you when they arrive."

Barnes walked away and called the Chief of Staff's Secret Service Detail as they began to pull up to the entrance to the White House and were escorted down the tunnels to the bunker. Night fell over the East Coast as the citizens of the US were forcibly evacuated from their homes.

16: Drake's Defection and Escape: POTUS Declares War on EJFS

Underground Bunker Facility

The White House

Washington D.C., USA

November 2, 2024

4:47 PM EDT, Saturday Evening

Chief of Staff Nicolas Hastings and his top staffer Laura Matheson entered the underground bunker and war room underneath the White House.

Sedgwick Barnes, the younger staffer, was the first to greet both Hastings and Matheson.

"Welcome back, Mr. Hastings. Vice President Drake wishes to speak with you privately." Barnes greeted them with a subdued look.

"Take me to his office," Hastings insisted.

"Right this way, sir." Barnes escorted Hastings to VP Drake's office while Matheson felt excluded from the discussion.

Matheson was curious about what Drake wanted to convey.

"Why am *I* not included in the conversation?" Matheson asked.

"I don't know, I'll brief you as necessary," Hastings responded before leaving her alone to mingle with other staff.

Vice President Drake was anxiously pacing back and forth in his office, waiting for Hastings' arrival.

Immediately, Hastings knocked on the office door and entered to greet Drake, who was relieved to see him return.

"Hastings, Thank God you're here. We need to talk," Drake began.

"What's going on, Peter?" Hastings asked with a worried expression on his face.

He did not know why Drake was suddenly so happy to see him again after being lambasted by Drake in a conference call earlier that morning.

"First of all, I need your assurance that what I am about to tell you stays between us. Not even Matheson can know about this right now," Drake requested.

"Peter, I need to know what this is about before I commit to anything," Hastings responded apprehensively.

"It's about the President. He's running a pilot program involving our staffers in a method of international espionage." Drake spoke grimly.

"That's inconceivable. Who's your source?" Hastings was astounded.

"The President told me in private. He asked me for confidentiality, but I can't stand by and let him continue with this egregious abuse of authority," Drake continued.

"You do realize that you are accusing the Commander-In-Chief of treason. It is only your word against his. How are you going to prove beyond all reasonable doubt that Hill is willfully violating the Oath of Office?" Hastings challenged.

"There is more to it. Your son, Logan's girlfriend, Kim Porter, has an imposter agent posing as her, and she's part of the pilot program of inserting spies into enemy nations. Are you aware of that?" Drake asked.

"I know Kim has a doppelganger, but I didn't realize that she was being used to this extent. Still, that is not enough to start any impeachment proceedings. I have to say that I am surprised and appalled that this is happening. But I am troubled by the fact that you broke his confidence. If Hill finds out that you are working against him, he will have you removed from office and imprisoned," Hastings warned.

"Nicolas, President Hill is coercing me to keep quiet about this. He is threatening to blackmail me by destroying my career. I cannot allow him to dangle me like this and destroy my life and my family's life. Please, I need you to trust me on this," Drake pleaded.

Hastings contemplated his response after hearing everything Drake revealed to him.

"All right, I'll give you a chance and hear you out. However, seeing as though you have betrayed the President in the last days of an election, you are treading a slippery slope. But I will try to keep Hill distracted and preoccupied while looking for the smoking gun to prove what you are saying is accurate. If you get caught, I will dissolve our partnership and disavow you before any impeachment proceedings that may arise," Hastings explained harshly.

"I understand. I'm willing to accept whatever may come," Drake affirmed.

"I sincerely hope you are. Because if you fail, your career and your life are ruined forever," Hastings warned firmly.

"Then so be it, I will risk everything to preserve my conscience," Drake concluded.

Hastings exited the office and returned to the rest of the bunker. He did everything he could not to tip off Hill that his authority was being usurped.

While Drake contemplated his plan to find the smoking gun, his first instinct was to call upon the EJFS, even though they had been declared an enemy of the state.

Ultimately, Drake did not share the same sentiments as Hill did with the EJFS as an enemy. It would be dangerous to defy Hill and consult with the EJFS, but there were minimal options.

Drake chose to make a bold and daring decision to search the contact information of the EJFS that the US government had on file prior to their rogue status designation.

Drake ran a search through the database for EJFS related documents and found the contact information for Khali, whose primary contact number was listed in his profile.

Drake made an untraceable call to Khali's cell phone and attempted to engage in contact.

***

Khali was preparing to address the Board of Directors regarding Kim's aspirations to become an EJFS Agent-In-Training when he received a call from an unknown caller with a D.C. area code.

Khali decided to accept the phone call.

"EJFS, this is Khali speaking."

"Mr. Khali, this is Vice President Peter Drake. I need your help," Drake began.

"Mr. Vice President, I don't know what your intentions are, but your Commander-In-Chief has declared our agency an enemy of the state. What do you want with us?" Khali pushed back with caution.

"I'm aware of that, but I do not share the same view as President Hill does. Among other things, I know Hill is actively involved in the illegal espionage of our enemies. Even worse, he is using his staffers as imposter secret operatives," Drake hinted.

"Mr. Vice President, you are aware that you are usurping your Commander-In-Chief by what you are doing. I do not want to engage in discussion with you, knowing the relationship between your President and my agency has been severed. Unless you are willing to jeopardize your government career, I assume no responsibility for the ramifications you face due to contacting me. Are you still sure you want to proceed?" Khali questioned.

"In my opinion, I'm well past the point of no return. I accept the risks. I am no longer aligned with Hill's re-election campaign," Drake affirmed.

"Very well. If that is your decision. Because you are defecting from your role, we need to take a different approach in your plea for help. What is it that you are after?" Khali asked.

"I'm going to seek the impeachment of President Hill. He is completely corrupt. I have information that may lead to his arrest and impeachment. But I need your resources to find the smoking gun to bring him down," Drake explained.

"All right, I accept your partnership. But we need to get you out of your current location. You must find a way out of the bunker to rendezvous with one of our agents. Agent Prabodhan will pick you up and take you away to join us. You will be considered a traitor committing dereliction of your duty if you do this. Again, I ask you once more: Do you want to proceed?" Khali asked yet again.

"Yes, I'm sure. Hill cannot be allowed to remain in office." Drake spoke very quietly.

"More than you probably know," Khali quipped.

"Come again?" Drake asked.

"Not now. I'll explain later. You must sneak out of the bunker, get to the National Mall, and wait for a summoned tornado to take you up to our base. You have one hour to get out of there."

"I understand. I hope to see you very soon."

"Godspeed, Mr. Drake."

Khali ended the call, and Drake had to find a way to escape the bunker without getting caught.

Drake had noticed that a clicking sound echoed in his room, which caused a sense of panic, knowing that a recording device may have incriminated him.

Drake acted by barricading the office door that was adjacent to his bedroom and bathroom.

In a frenzy, Drake began searching for a tool and a method to open the air ducts to crawl his way out to the White House interior and escape from imminent capture.

Drake rushed to his bedroom door and barricaded another sturdy dresser blocking the entrance, and frantically searched through some items in the bathroom to open the lock on the air duct grate.

Drake was rummaging quickly through his bathroom supplies as he heard secret servicemen starting to rush up to his door and began pounding their fists on the door after failing to open it.

Drake found a lock pick and a hairpin to try to pick at the lock.

He struggled mightily at first, but after a few failed attempts, he managed to force the lock to open and climbed into the grate, barring the vent behind him as he carefully crawled through the ventilation system to bypass the swarming security actively searching for him.

Drake encountered an intersection of the air duct and had to pick a path to follow to find his way to safety. Drake made a right turn and then took the passage to a dead end.

Meanwhile, secret members of the armed forces battered down the blocked door, knocking over the heavy dresser as they entered the room.

"Check everywhere. Drake couldn't have gone far!" President Hill announced on the intercom system, which Drake overheard from inside the ventilation system.

Drake frantically and fearfully turned around and crawled the other direction and took a different way, leading to a vertical shaft with rungs attached to the top from the bottom.

Drake quickly hurried up the rungs while the secret servicemen searched the bathroom and busted the lock open to enter the air ducts.

Drake overheard the secret servicemen rushing through the tunnel, and he knew he had to move swiftly and carefully.

The secret servicemen moved through the ducts and made their way to the end of the tunnel just as Drake climbed out the top escape hatch used for emergencies.

Drake exited the ventilation system and re-entered the White House interiors.

He dashed through the empty hallways to the front door and kept running while the secret servicemen were still in pursuit.

Drake climbed through the gate, and immediately, EJFS Agent Prabodhan pulled up his vehicle to take him away.

The secret servicemen rushed out the White House's front doors and stormed the gate to stop Drake from escaping the White House grounds.

Agent Prabodhan inhaled a substantial quantity of air and blew the secret servicemen away to hold them off.

"Let's get out of here!" Drake insisted.

Prabodhan drove quickly to the National Mall, heading toward the Lincoln Memorial to take off to the Thunderhead Base Palace, still stationed in New York.

Prabodhan careened down the empty streets to reach the Lincoln Memorial down the other end of the National Mall.

Suddenly, helicopters watching the area followed the EJFS vehicle in their getaway attempt to take Drake out of reach.

Prabodhan continued to speed through the National Mall and simultaneously summoned a supercell thunderstorm to prepare a tornado's formation to take them up in the air.

Out of view in the darkened side streets, a pair of armored CIRB vehicles showed up to try to block the path for the EJFS ICV to escape the area.

"Hold on tight!" Prabodhan pivoted around the roadblock, veering toward a side street through the Beltway, drifting around to get to the monument.

Helicopters gathered overhead as the dusk fell, and the city was deserted, with only CIRB agents roaming the streets at night.

CIRB vehicles scrambled to head off the EJFS ICV.

"Are you able to fly this thing?" Drake asked urgently.

"Not when there are helicopters overhead. We need to reach the monument," Prabodhan emphasized.

Prabodhan continued to focus on trying to avoid getting hit by the CIRB armored cars in pursuit.

The thunderstorm finished forming, and a funnel cloud had formed.

Lightning flashed, and thunder crackled overhead as potent, gusty winds began to blow down the helicopters.

The helicopter pilots were forced to retreat, and the armored vehicles belonging to the CIRB began to assemble near the Lincoln Memorial Monument.

Prabodhan pulled up the ICV to the escape site and noticed the array of CIRB vans blocking the escape zone.

President Hill patched into the earpieces of the CIRB agents on location.

"ATTENTION ALL AGENTS, YOU ARE AUTHORIZED TO STOP THE EJFS ESCAPE CAR FROM TAKING OFF BY ANY MEANS NECESSARY!"

CIRB Corporal Commander Agent Landis acknowledged Hill's command and began a barrage of gunfire on the EJFS ICV to prevent their escape.

Drake cried out, "It's a trap!"

Prabodhan responded. "Don't worry. I got this!"

Prabodhan began twirling his finger wildly while blowing wind breath toward the CIRB blockade.

This impressive feat caused an EF-3 tornado to spawn, which blew all the CIRB vehicles away. The vortex provided a clear path for Prabodhan to pilot his ICV in flight mode, up toward the EJFS Thunderhead in New York.

Prabodhan flew quickly to New York to transport Drake to the Atlanta Branch EJFS Thunderhead Base.

"Well, there's no turning back now," Drake commented as he glanced at Prabodhan, who remained quiet but nodded at Drake in agreement.

***

Meanwhile, in the secure bunker underneath the White House, President Hill was fuming and panicking simultaneously upon discovering Drake's escape.

President Hill seethed at his staff.

"This is utterly unacceptable! How could you have lost him?!" Hill snapped at his Chief of Staff.

"Mr. President, all government agencies are working around the clock to locate Drake. It is highly likely that he fled and defected from our administration. He's now a known traitor." Hastings calmly spoke while trying to quell Hill's fury.

"Nicolas, you were the last person who spoke with Peter. I want to know what was discussed during the exchange. I think something must have triggered him in your conversation."

"Mr. President, this is an extraordinarily complex situation. I don't want to upset you further."

"Nicolas, as my Chief of Staff, you are obligated to fulfill your duties under my orders. So, I would think very carefully before you speak. Where is Peter Drake?" Hill interrogated.

Hastings began to sweat nervously.

"All right, I'll tell you everything: Drake told me about your foreign policy strategy to insert some duplicates of your staffers as incognito spies to perform espionage against our enemies. He also informed me that you are blackmailing him into cooperating with you. He was willing to risk his entire career to expose you for it," Hastings explained.

"What did you say to him in response?" President Hill asked.

"I told him it would be ill-advised to betray you. But he was undeterred. He was going to dig up records against you to have you impeached."

"I will not stand for this! He must be found!"

Suddenly, Barnes barged into the President's office to share obtained surveillance footage on his tablet device a short while ago.

"Mr. President, I apologize for intruding on your conversation. I pulled some surveillance video from outside the White House. It appears that Drake had a getaway driver waiting to take him away," Barnes spoke bleakly.

Hastings and Hill were shocked at the discovery.

Barnes explained. "The CIRB blockades could not successfully contain them. The EJFS agent summoned a tornado near the Lincoln Monument and abducted Drake upward into the sky while riding along with this unidentified EJFS agent. This agent blew all our CIRB patrol units away, allowing them to escape."

President Hill was outraged by Barnes's findings.

"That's the last straw! This means war! Call up a meeting with the Joint Chiefs. It's time to respond in force!" President Hill commanded forcefully.

"Right away, Sir!" Barnes used his smartphone to assemble all top military brass to draft a tactical response against the EJFS.

"As for you, Hastings. You are on a short leash. From now on, you do not so much as take a leak without my permission. I am not letting you out of my sight until we get Drake back. Do you understand?" President Hill warned.

"Yes, Mr. President," Hastings spoke with defeat written all over his face.

***

Meanwhile, Logan Hastings, the Chief of Staff's son, recovered from his tranquilizer injection from Kim's imposter earlier that evening. Logan arose from his tumble, right before a group of armed soldiers from the National Guard barged into Logan's home, startling him.

"Logan Hastings, we're relocating you to the White House bunker." The National Guardsman leader commanded. "Come with us now!"

"Wait, what's going on? Where's Kim?" Logan protested as the guards forcefully seized Logan from his home.

"Do not resist!" One of the guards shouted.

Logan was taken to an armored vehicle, and the driver sped away to the White House bunker to reunite Logan with his father as Logan cried out for Kim Porter.

17: Drake Meets Khali Under Ultimatum from POTUS: EJFS TAC Teams Deploy to Budapest

20,000 feet above sea level

Baltimore, Maryland, USA

November 2, 2024

5:13 PM EDT, Saturday Evening

EJFS Agent Prabodhan escorted Ex-Vice President Peter Drake, vacating his role and fleeing the Nation's Capital. The agent took him to the Atlanta Based EJFS Thunderhead Palace Base situated over New York City.

Numerous active deployments were occurring within the five o'clock hour on the US East Coast. Simultaneously, a mega hurricane continued to strengthen and churn toward the entirety of the Eastern Seaboard.

Drake was nervous about what strategy of military response President Hill would employ following his defection to meet with the Head of the EJFS, Master Khali, knowing that the EJFS had been declared an enemy of the state and might soon be met with military action.

Drake broke the silence.

"I'm so sorry what Hill is doing to your agency. Something must have gotten into him lately," Drake apologized.

"I'm not at liberty to discuss all the specifics, but you can rest assured that Hill is under ongoing investigation at this time. Apart from that, I appreciate your apology and your willingness to reach out to us."

Agent Prabodhan spoke kindly to Drake as he continued to pilot the ICV toward the upper troposphere over New York City.

Drake sighed nervously.

"I'm so worried about how Hill will respond. I hope he won't become so unglued as to start a military conflict with your agency in retaliation for my escape," Drake expressed with a tone of concern.

"In my honest opinion, I think that would be unwise of him. But, if he does, we will respond with the appropriate action," Agent Prabodhan assured him.

"What are you going to do if he decides to declare war on all of you?" Drake asked.

"That I do not know. But we will take a peaceful and diplomatic approach, first and foremost. We do not want to go to war with the United States, especially because they are under the threat of the approaching superstorm created by Gyan today," Agent Prabodhan continued.

Drake craned his neck in surprise at Prabodhan's explanation.

"Wait, Gyan is in on this?" Drake reacted dumbfoundedly.

"Evidently, the President has been keeping secrets from you. But I cannot say much more until I hand you over to Master Khali. He will explain everything to you. We'll be there soon," Agent Prabodhan explained as the ICV sped through the night skies over the East Coast while crossing over New Jersey airspace.

***

Meanwhile, at the EJFS Atlanta Branch, currently stationed over New York City, Agents Abhu and Singh and their outbound TAC Team deployment was underway departing for Budapest, Hungary.

Abhu, also known as Caleb Porter, Kim Porter's older brother, loaded their equipment and gear onto a fleet of MICVs in the mass deployment bay at the Thunderhead Palace base.

Abhu and Singh gathered their joint TAC Team deployments before they boarded the MICVs as Master Khali entered the deployment bay, accompanied by Kim Porter.

"Ladies and Gentlemen, I pray that you have a blessed journey to Budapest and Brussels, and all points between. May your team succeed in neutralizing the Shadow State leader." Khali bid his farewells to his departing TAC Team.

Agent Abhu became somewhat emotional seeing his sister, Kim, seeing him off.

Abhu approached Kim and hugged her goodbye before speaking to her one last time before his departure.

"Kim, stay strong for the family and me. They must be terrified for you, knowing that you are not with them right now. I love you so much, and I pray that we see each other again soon," Abhu spoke comfortingly while holding Kim's arms and embracing her gently.

"I will, my brother. I am going to be a part of this battle too. Maybe not now, but soon," Kim gleamed with overwhelming emotions.

"You're going through with this?" Abhu asked with awe.

Khali interjected. "Indeed, she is. Kim made her pitch to me earlier. I am pleased to say that the Board of Directors has offered her a chance to shadow our lead analyst before she begins training tomorrow. Kim will make an excellent addition to the EJFS."

Abhu was pleasantly surprised to witness the dramatic turnaround of Kim's maturity and personal growth.

"Wow, Sis. I am so happy for you. I wish you the best in your training. I'm sorry that I won't be here to support you, but know that you have my backing," Abhu continued.

Singh hastened Abhu as the touching moment became too lengthy.

"Abhu, we should get going soon," Singh urged.

Kim gave Abhu one last hug.

"You should go with them. We must not delay. I will be fine here. I love you, my big brother." Kim concluded the meeting.

"Take good care of her, d'ya hear?" Abhu demanded of Khali.

"You have my word. Your sister will be well looked after." Khali smiled.

Abhu rushed back to rejoin his TAC Team and boarded the massive transformative vehicles while Kim and Khali observed.

"Let's roll out!" Singh directed as he tapped his massive palm on the aircraft.

Both TAC Teams boarded the fleet of MICVs and activated the takeoff process. The pair of aircraft launched from the deployment bay in a sonic boom that jolted the structure.

Khali watched the fleet depart with a hopeful smile on his face as he gave a loving gaze while the TAC Teams flew toward Europe at warp velocity.

As Khali and Kim observed the TAC Team off in the distance, second-in-command Agent Raj convened with Khali to notify him of new developments regarding Drake's arrival.

"Master Khali, Agent Prabodhan and Drake are less than five minutes from reaching the base. Where do you want us to keep him?" Raj queried.

"Escort Drake to my office. Nobody except you and I are to have access to him once he arrives," Khali commanded.

"Yes, Sir!" Agent Raj complied with Khali's orders.

Kim overheard the conversation and was stunned that Drake had vacated his role in the Hill administration.

"Vice President Drake is coming here?" Kim asked with shock.

"Yes, but he's going to be isolated from the others until we can confirm his testimony. Regardless, I need you to follow me to the Command Center to begin your orientation and job shadowing. Let us get going," Khali insisted.

The Chief Commander and his newest recruit departed the deployment bay, leading the way to the elevators to ascend to the top floor of the Thunderhead Base Palace.

Roughly five minutes later, Agent Prabodhan and Ex-Vice President Peter Drake began their final approach over the EJFS Thunderhead Base Palace.

Prabodhan navigated the ICV over one of the helipads attached along the front courtyard to the palace's main entrance.

Drake was amazed at the sheer size of the Thunderhead Base Palace belonging to the EJFS superagency.

"Wow, that place looks so incredibly vast and yet so beautiful." Drake spoke in awe and wonder.

"Indeed, it does," Agent Prabodhan agreed as he initiated the landing sequence.

Prabodhan popped out the chopper wings above the ICV and started to land on the central helipad facing south. The ICV gently landed on the helipad. Prabodhan escorted Drake out of the vehicle and took him inside after he activated automatic parking on his key ring. The ICV drove itself down to the parking garage within the sublevels of the massive Thunderhead base.

Agent Raj, the second-in-command, served as the reception committee for the US's former vice president, Peter Drake.

Raj stood waiting at the palace's immense and tall front doors to accompany Drake to Khali's office for a private interview.

Drake was astounded by the imposing and well-rounded physique that Raj possessed.

"Who is that big man?" Drake asked.

"That is our second-in-command, Agent Raj. He will be escorting you to meet with our leader, Khali. He may seem threatening, but don't worry. His bark is worse than his bite," Agent Prabodhan assured him.

Agent Raj approached the duo and welcomed Drake into the agency.

"Welcome, Mr. Drake. My name is Agent Raj. We have arranged a private interview with the Head of the EJFS, Master Khali. Let us escort you to Khali's office. Please come with me." Agent Raj beckoned to Drake, and he nervously followed them inside.

Agents Raj and Prabodhan pushed the massive front doors open to the ornate interior of the palace. Drake admired the highly detailed lobby. He was stunned to see the well-maintained, beautiful, and high-tech appearance.

"This is quite a nice place so high in the sky," Drake said.

Drake noticed some glances and double-takes from other EJFS agents in the room and felt somewhat out of place among the giant agents traversing the hallways.

Raj reassured Drake. "Don't mind all the attention. You are an outsider, and these agents do not yet know what your intentions are. Let us head to the elevators."

Upon Raj's insistence, Drake followed Raj to the elevators, enjoying the palace interior's majestic beauty while passing by many EJFS superagents dwarfing Drake in size.

Raj summoned an elevator to bring them to the 13th floor, where the executive suites were located.

Raj spoke to Drake quietly as they boarded an elevator, making their ascension to the executive level suites.

"Mr. Drake, because you are an outsider, we will need to keep you isolated in Khali's office for some time. We need to make sure you remain protected from potential retaliation from your former administration," Raj explained solemnly.

"I understand, Agent Raj. I appreciate your efforts to protect me." Drake graciously accepted.

"These are unusual circumstances. We seldom have outside government officials seeking asylum with our agency network. Nevertheless, rest assured that we will do all we can to keep you safe here."

"Would you be able to protect yourselves in the event of a military strike from my pursuers?" Drake asked nervously.

Raj paused before he spoke again.

"We will find ways to protect our network from any such attack. But know that we do not desire to go to war with the US. Please trust us. We will keep you safe from harm and take all appropriate action for you to remain under protection," Raj continued calmly.

Suddenly, a digital voice chimed on the elevator PA system announcing their arrival on the 13th floor.

"Come with me," Raj beckoned Drake.

Drake followed Raj to the restricted access door to the executive suites to their left.

Raj scanned his badge on the reader device, unlocking the double diamond-studded doors with golden detailing and purple-tinted windows with lotus patterns etched in the unbreakable glass.

Drake continued to follow Raj to Khali's quarters, where the chief commander was waiting to speak with Drake in a private meeting.

Raj pressed the call button next to Khali's door.

"Please, come in," Khali said.

Raj opened the door to Khali's executive quarters to find Khali sitting at his desk. Drake was impressed by how massive Khali was in size.

"Welcome aboard, Mr. Drake. Please have a seat on the lounge chair and make yourself comfortable," Khali greeted him warmly.

"Thank you, Mr. Khali," Drake took a seat in the comfortable chair and rested while facing Khali and Raj.

"Would you like me to offer you something to drink?" Khali asked.

"Maybe some warm tea would be nice," Drake suggested.

"Raj can make some for you. We will serve you dinner shortly. We have lamb shanks with curry potato stew tonight," Khali offered.

"That sounds delicious," Drake commented, feeling like a special guest in a high place.

Raj prepared some hot tea for Drake before Khali joined Drake on a sofa across from him.

Khali began to question Drake on the extent of his knowledge of corruption and wrongdoing President Hill had been committing during Drake's term as vice president.

"Now, let us get down to business. I want you to tell me what you know about Hill's acts of treason." Khali expressed concern in his thick, hyper-masculine, soothing tone of voice.

"Absolutely, Sir. Hill has been inserting his staffers' duplicates into enemy nations to spy on them, as I have already told you. He has used the CIRB as a militarized armed force to deploy them overseas. Hill tried to coerce me into doing his bidding, threatening me with a military tribunal hearing and removing me from office," Drake explained.

"Why would he threaten you with a tribunal?" Khali inquired of Drake's elaboration.

"Hill is using my medical deferment as a counteractive measure to keep me from reporting him for congressional impeachment hearings. He claims that I am not a natural-born citizen although I explained to him that I have flat feet and couldn't enlist into the military because of that condition," Drake continued.

"I see. Is the President's claim true?" Khali asked with curiosity.

"To some extent, yes. I was born and raised in Guam during peak tensions with North Korea. I hated communism and dictatorial leaders ever since I was a young boy. But I migrated to Florida in the 1990s. Now, I am saddened to see a tyrannical leader in the making in Hill. I fear there are things he's hiding from me during my tenure as Vice President, and that was only the tip of the iceberg of my concerns about Hill's presidency," Drake elaborated.

"That is a terrifying ordeal, and I sympathize with your grief. I see the direction America is headed, and your president is taking the country in a further downward spiral. I fear what will become of the country should Hill be re-elected." Khali spoke gently in his thick and powerful voice.

"That's why I couldn't burden myself to remain associated with Hill anymore. He is putting the lives of our citizens in mortal danger. With the superstorm barreling towards the East Coast, I am worried about what destruction will bring to my beloved country. I do not know if America will survive. This deeply saddens me."

Drake lamentably spoke while he rested his head in his hands, feeling overwhelmed with tremendous grief.

Khali felt exceedingly pained upon witnessing Drake's sorrow and felt the urge to tell him everything that the EJFS investigations had revealed about Hill and the Shadow State. Drake had minimal awareness of the evil network.

Khali sat next to Drake and comforted him as they felt great anguish for America, stifling his emotions but shedding a few tears before he regained his composure.

Khali gave Drake a healing and comforting embrace before he spoke again.

"I need to show you the whole story about Hill and the extent of his corrupt administration. Come with me, and I'll show you our findings," Khali said.

Drake recovered from his emotional turmoil and followed Khali to his desk. Khali shared information about the Shadow State with him to give clarity and insight into Hill's intentions as President of the United States.

"I know that this is unthinkable, but President Hill is part of an organized, secret, dark network of a seditious and treasonous cabal called the Shadow State. However, he is not the top leader of the vast network. Right now, there are outbound deployments of TAC Teams consisting of my most trusted and distinguished agents quarterbacking an overseas mission to locate their leader and bring them all to justice," Khali explained passionately.

Khali showed Drake a series of images showing multiple bad state actors in numerous governments across the world. The first image was a scanned copy of Anastasia Zima's dossier report in the EJFS Intelligence Department system.

"Do you know who this woman is?" Khali questioned Drake.

"I believe that is Anastasia Zima, a former biotech engineer for the fallen Final Wave Terrorist Organization. Last I heard about her, President Hill was on an overseas trip to Moscow to meet with officials from the Kremlin regarding a partnership formed between two former enemy nations during the Cold War era. President Hill informed me that he established a connection with a foreign asset from Russia for reasons that he would not disclose to me." Drake answered.

"You're correct. Zima is also a member of the Shadow State, but not of the inner twelve prominent global leaders orchestrating a new world order. However, there is more..."

Khali trailed off before he changed the image on his computer screen.

The image displayed was the lost necklace containing Vritra's remnants stored in the centerpiece's dragon-shaped amulet.

"I'm certain you know what this object is, correct?" Khali asked Drake.

Drake was nearly breathless upon seeing the photo on the screen.

"That's the necklace of Vritra, the one that Ravan once wore before he died." Drake spoke with a strain in his voice.

"That's right. According to our findings on Ravan's laptop, he knew about the Shadow State's development in its infancy stages. Also, he had a document file outlining how to reconstitute Vritra's remains in a catastrophic fashion that would lead to the world's demise. The Shadow State leader with an unknown alias of "Black Sparrow Zero" has been theorized to be working in Belgium as part of their government working in tandem with Anastasia Zima. Their objective is to bring Vritra back to life using the geoengineered hurricane to accomplish this disastrous goal. However, as far as the method of implementing the final act of their evil plan, it is still unclear how they hope to use the storm to reconstitute the remnants of Vritra to destroy the Earth," Khali elaborated.

Drake was even more horrified than before this startling revelation.

"Now you know what we are up against. This shadow network needs to be stopped at all costs. Because of your defection from the Hill administration, you must remain with us until the threat is mitigated and Hill is removed from office. You cannot return to the US under these circumstances. Otherwise, they would surely arrest you and execute you for your knowledge of the Shadow State," Khali concluded bleakly.

"I don't know what else to say...other than you need to be careful of what Hill may do in response to my escape. If I know him, for one thing, he will not go down without a fight, even if it means starting a war. We have to be careful about this," Drake warned.

"We have less than 60 hours remaining on our deadline to disperse from US airspace. I intend to stay for that duration, barring any military response to you being here. In such an event, we will take all measures to protect you and our people. Pray that it doesn't escalate to that extreme level," Khali added.

Drake rubbed his hands on his head in great distress in response to what he had just learned.

***

Meanwhile, Logan Hastings, the Chief of Staff's son (and Kim Porter's love interest), rode along with the National Guard, relocating Logan to the White House Bunker complex.

Logan had his phone confiscated to keep him from contacting his girlfriend. However, the team leader sent a high-priority flash message to the Chief of Staff, Nicolas Hastings, on Logan's status, informing Hastings that his son was en route to the White House Bunker.

Hastings read his message out of view from President Hill, who had lost trust in his Chief of Staff.

President Hill saw Hastings looking at his phone and called him out on it.

"Who are you texting?" Hill asked abruptly.

"My son. He's being transported to the bunker. I just got a flash alert from the National Guard leader. Are you going to interrogate my son when he gets here as well?" Hastings talked back to his Commander-In-Chief.

Hill's face soured, and his eyes narrowed to slits.

"You better be careful how you talk to me. Your career is in danger of ending very soon," Hill threatened while clutching Hastings's expensive suit.

"Easy, this suit cost me a fortune!" Hastings retorted.

"Trust me, that's the least of your worries," Hill warned after he let go of Hastings's suit and continued to wait for the joint chiefs to assemble in the war room.

Barnes approached Hastings with information.

"Sir, your son has just arrived at the White House. He's being brought downstairs to the bunker now," Barnes informed him.

"Bring him to me," Hastings insisted.

"Yes, sir!" Barnes complied and informed the lead guardsman of the National Guard of Hastings's instructions.

Logan was escorted down the secret hallways to the White House's bunker and taken to Hill's office, where Hastings was being kept clamped down under tight watch by President Hill.

Barnes brought Logan into Hill's office and reunited Logan with his father, Nicolas Hastings.

"Dad!" Logan exclaimed.

"Logan, my son," Hastings greeted him warmly.

"Who was that woman that came to my apartment impersonating Kim? Do you want my relationship with Kim to end?" Logan asked with an emotional strain in his voice.

"Logan, I can explain, but not now," Hastings replied while trying to remain calm.

President Hill interjected himself into the conversation.

"Tell him the truth. I insist," Hill dictated.

"This doesn't concern you!" Hastings barked back.

"Oh, I think it does. Tell him!" Hill continued to press Hastings.

Hastings watched his son on the verge of tears, causing him to feel guilty about getting involved in his son's relationship.

"Logan, I'm sorry. I instructed Matthews to send a disguised agent to break off your relationship with Kim because she is a liability to the re-election campaign of President Hill," Hastings admitted regrettably.

"How dare you?! How could you do this to me?! I never want to speak to you again!" Logan cried out.

Logan stormed out of the room angrily, went into a private room, let off some steam, and then wept out of rage.

"Well, you ruined my relationship with my son. Are you happy now?" Hastings asked somberly.

"It serves you right. You have meddled in my affairs twice today, and this is what you get for it."

The corrupt president unapologetically explained while sitting in his chair with his feet up on the desk in an overt display of arrogance.

Hill's pompous action provoked Hastings's disdain for the President's self-righteous attitude.

"You should be ashamed of yourself! Drake was right to vacate his position. You are a national embarrassment!" Hastings snapped vehemently at President Hill.

"That's it! You are fired! Put Hastings and his son in a cell together. Then, you are both out of here!" Hill reacted angrily and ordered secret service agents to take Hastings away to a holding cell.

Another pair of secret service agents brought Hastings's son, Logan, out of his room and put both father and son in the same holding cell. At the same time, Logan remained non-verbal and kept his distance from his father, still heartbroken by Hastings' betrayal to protect Hill, a move that he now regretted.

***

At the EJFS Detention Center, top floor, Gyan woke up from his sedation in his prison cell and abruptly got out of bed while he was behind bars.

Gyan was still awaiting sentencing after his interrogation with Khali and Raj's interrogation team. Yet, Khali forewent the sentencing until a time when the action had settled down.

However, Gyan was up for a challenge to break out of his imprisonment. Gyan decided to get the attention of one of the guards patrolling the hallways, self-inflicting a bloodied nose after clawing his nostrils, penetrating a vein.

"Guard, help me! I'm bleeding!" Gyan pleaded.

One of the EJFS guards noticed Gyan bleeding and requesting medical attention.

The guard apprehensively approached the cell with his keys on his waist and his access card attached to a retractable keychain. The guard tried to calm Gyan down.

"Gyan, relax. You are going to make your situation worse. I'll give you a tissue to stop the bleeding." The corrections officer addressed the prisoner as he carefully approached the cell.

When the guard got close to the cell, he offered Gyan a tissue.

Opportunistically, Gyan abruptly shoved the tissue down the guard's throat.

Gyan jerked the key card from the guard's keychain and yanked his keyring, scouring for his cell number on the keyring before using the corresponding key to unlock the door to escape his cell.

The choking corrections officer called for help as other guards activated the security breach alarm and pursued Gyan as he tried to escape from the Detention Center.

Khali was with Drake when they heard an alert bulletin resonate from Khali's phone.

Khali glanced at his smartwatch and noticed an alert notification that a prisoner had escaped from his cell.

"What's going on?!" Drake asked with worry.

"It's Gyan. He escaped! Stay here, and don't leave my office for your safety," Khali instructed Drake.

Khali and Raj quickly slipped into their flannel jackets and raced down the stairwell to the Thunderhead Base's parking garage to stop Gyan from escaping.

18: Gyan's Escape: Nicolas and Logan Make Amends

EJFS Detention Center – Top Floor

EJFS Thunderhead Base Palace – Atlanta Branch – Eastern US Division

Current Location: New York, New York, USA

November 2, 2024

5:51 PM EDT, Saturday Evening

The escaped inmate, Jagmohan Gyan, carried out an attempt to break out of the EJFS Detention Center. Simultaneously, dozens of guards and EJFS agents stormed to the facility to prevent Gyan from escaping.

Khali and Raj took a fast-moving ICV to the Detention Center to stop Gyan, while both leading agents left former Vice President Peter Drake to be supervised and protected by Agent Kumar.

Gyan used his martial arts skills and sharp wit to avoid capture. He stole a gun and an access card from the guard that he manipulated into getting close enough to harm before breaking out of his cell.

Gyan shot and killed numerous guards and used the stolen access card to make his way down the stairwell to an emergency exit, which was heavily armored against prison escapees.

Gyan tried to kick the door open, but it was too heavy to open. Gyan grabbed a fire extinguisher from a wall-mount and tried to break off the latch to counteract this obstacle.

Guards and agents swarmed the stairwell as Gyan broke the latch open and escaped to the prison's front parking lot.

As soon as he stepped out of the emergency exit, several MICV aerials hovered over the Detention Center like helicopters, shining their spotlights on Gyan as he tried to escape from the lofty prison facility.

Khali and Raj arrived at the scene.

"Gyan, freeze! Drop your weapon and get on the ground, face down!" Khali commanded in a thunderous tone of voice.

Gyan held up his hands but maintained his grip on the stolen handgun.

"There's nowhere else to run, Gyan! Surrender now!" Raj demanded with a loud, authoritative voice.

"Never!" Gyan resisted, pointing his gun toward Khali and Raj.

Khali shot Gyan in the arm, and he fell to the pavement.

The guards and agents surrounded Gyan as he lay in agony.

Khali and Raj approached the fallen Gyan as he lay on the ground, writhing and howling in pain.

Khali addressed Gyan. "Do you have any more information that will lead us to the Shadow State leader?"

Gyan answered weakly. "Yes, I-I do."

Gyan trailed off before trying to reach for the handgun that had fallen out of his hand.

Khali and Raj observed Gyan straining to reach the weapon, prompting Raj to kick the gun out of Gyan's reach.

"No, you don't. You are finished. Guards, take him to the vaporization chamber immediately. I'm sentencing him to death," Khali ordered.

Gyan was placed in handcuffs by Raj. Many agents and guards escorted a pained Gyan to the elevators.

Gyan was defiant as he passed by other prisoners mocking him. At the same time, he was escorted to the elevator to be brought down to the Detention Center's Thunderhead's bottom sub-level floor.

Khali and Raj unlocked the vaporization chamber and powered it on. Agents locked Gyan into the cylindrical space and held him in place with restraints.

Khali and Raj activated the vaporizer, simultaneously inserting their action keys, and rotated them after the count of three.

The red lever emerged from the vaporization module as the vaporizer powered on entirely.

Khali prayed silently before pulling the lever towards himself.

The vaporization rays shot forth and zapped Gyan into precipitable rainwater. This incredible act left his clothes and a powerless crimson capsule device behind.

Khali issued follow-up orders to his agents in the room.

"Seal Gyan's remains and log the action report into the VAR system logs at once," Khali commanded.

"Yes, Master!" Agent Devdas complied.

Devdas extracted the clothes left behind after the vaporization module completed its cycle.

"Raj, we must return to the palace. We need to guarantee Drake's safety," Khali insisted.

"Acknowledged!" Raj assented.

Khali and Raj departed from the Detention Center and returned to their ICV to return to the palace.

***

Meanwhile, in Khali's quarters on the EJFS main building's executive level, Kumar and Drake sat in Khali's quarters. Drake was eating some lamb shanks, and curried potato stew served as a distinguished guest for dinner.

After Drake finished his meal, Kumar received a flash message from Khali, informing him of Gyan's fate and inquiring about Drake's status.

Unread flash message sent from Master Khali at 5:58 PM EDT:

"Gyan has been vaporized. His escape was foiled. What is the status of Drake?"

Kumar excused himself to reply to Khali's message.

"Mr. Drake, please excuse me for a minute. I need to respond to a message from our leader, Master Khali," Kumar left Drake momentarily and texted Khali in private.

Kumar sent his reply to the message from Khali. It read as follows:

"Drake has finished eating dinner. We're waiting for your return."

About a minute later, Khali texted Kumar back.

"We're on our way back to the palace. Please keep Drake occupied as much as possible."

Kumar rejoined Drake to ease his mind about the situation at the Detention Center.

"Mr. Drake, Khali, and Raj are on their way back. They have the situation with Gyan handled," Kumar spoke softly.

"What happened to Gyan? Is he dead?" Drake asked.

"I'll let Khali explain when he returns," Kumar assured Drake.

"Why is everything being kept so contained here? It's obvious that Gyan is dead," Drake stated.

"Mr. Drake, please remain calm. We must maintain order and stick to our protocol. As long as you are a guest here, we need you to respect our ways," Kumar calmly spoke.

Drake quietly sat and waited while both he and Kumar anxiously anticipated Khali's return.

Moments later, Khali and Raj returned to the palace and boarded an elevator to the main building's top floor. Once Khali and Raj returned to the executive level suites, Khali addressed Drake to calm his nerves.

Khali opened the door to his quarters. "Mr. Drake, Gyan tried to break out of the Detention Center. Gyan attempted to kill us both, so we subdued him and executed him by vaporizing him. He's gone for good now."

Drake was stunned.

"Where does that leave us then? How are we going to stop the superstorm from impacting the US now that Gyan is gone?" Drake asked in horror.

"All hope is not lost. Our TAC Teams have shut down Gyan's network of geoengineering experiments earlier this evening. The storm may not have the same influx of energy. However, we must continue to pray that the storm may avoid a direct impact on the continent," Khali explained.

"What do we do if it doesn't change course? What about the necklace of Vritra?" Drake asked passionately.

"We need to do everything we can to keep it away from the storm. If it comes in direct contact with the hurricane, the remains of Vritra could reconstitute devastatingly," Khali elaborated.

Raj interjected. "We are working on finding the necklace and bringing an end to the Shadow State. We have our elite team of superagents working tirelessly around the clock in the Command Center and abroad to fight this."

Drake felt overwhelmed with anxiety, but he could not let himself break down. There was nothing he could do but let the situation play out. The corrupted President Hill could be threatening a war with the EJFS.

"May God help us all," Drake muttered out of desperation.

***

At the White House Bunker detainment area, recently terminated Chief of Staff Nicolas Hastings and his son Logan Hastings were imprisoned in a holding cell together in awkward tension.

Unresolved anger from Logan was directed against his father.

Nicolas broke the ice and attempted to make amends with his son.

"Son, you can't keep up the silent treatment with me forever," Nicolas began.

Logan said nothing. He kept his back turned while standing facing the outside of the cell. Nicolas sat on the cold, metal bed.

"Logan, I'm sorry for everything. I shouldn't have had that woman interfere with your relationship with Kim," Nicolas apologized.

"You have always disapproved of my relationship with Kim. Why would you change your tune now?" Logan heatedly asked as he turned to face his father.

"I was thinking of what was best for the Hill Administration. However, now I know that my allegiance to the President was misplaced. I was looking out for Hill to make sure that he would be re-elected," Nicolas explained.

"That's convenient." Logan remained guarded against his father.

"Oh, Logan. I should have never accepted this position as chief of staff. You must realize that what I did at the time was for the good of the country. I was wrong. I shouldn't have sided with Hill over you," Nicolas spoke lamentably.

"Okay, if you genuinely feel that way, then at least tell me where the real Kim Porter is right now," Logan relented.

"Kim was detained by the EJFS earlier this morning. She was taken into custody because there was alleged involvement with a political extremist group. However, she was not involved in the group. Kim's doppelganger was complicit in the staged incident, the same lady who came to your apartment. As far as the real Kim's whereabouts, she is most likely still with the EJFS until they can locate her imposter and stop her," Nicolas continued.

"What is the imposter's real name?" Logan asked.

"Alicia Blaze, that's her alias," Nicolas elaborated.

"We have to do something. How can we stop Alicia?" Logan asked urgently.

"I suppose I could reach out to the deputy director of the CIRB, James Matthews, and demand that he stops all sabotage from Alicia," Nicolas explained further.

"How are you going to do that?" Logan questioned.

"As far as I know, I still have a security clearance at the CIRB, and I can influence Matthews to end his operation with Alicia. Hill will be releasing us soon. I have been fired as chief of staff. We will be on our own once Hill releases us," Nicolas continued bleakly.

"Considering what you've told me, I forgive you for this. But I need you to make this right. I want Kim's good name cleared, and I want Alicia to be held accountable," Logan responded.

"Thank you, my son. I promise you that I will make sure of that," Nicolas vowed.

Logan embraced his father. Nicolas comforted his son as they waited in their shared prison cell together to be released from detainment.

***

Barnes received a text message in President Hill's office notifying him of the joint chiefs' status.

"The joint chiefs are ready for you now. They're gathered in the war room waiting for you," Barnes informed the President.

"Take me to them," Hill insisted.

"Yes, Mr. President," Barnes complied.

President Hill followed Barnes to the war room to convene with the armed forces' joint chiefs to draw up a military response against the EJFS in retaliation for Drake's defection earlier that evening.

The joint chiefs arose from their seats and stood in salute to the President.

"Be at ease," Hill spoke as the joint chiefs sat back down in their seats.

"Tell me what kind of organization we are up against, and how are we going to stop them?" Hill began the conference.

The Secretary of Defense, Frank Clements, addressed President Hill regarding the military action drafted by the joint chiefs' assembly.

"Mr. President, we're dealing with a highly advanced group of vigilantes. But we have conducted lengthy research on their network. It seems that the Atlanta-based headquarters of the Elite Justice Force Squad and their network of floating bases known as the Thunderheads can manipulate weather patterns. They methodically dispatch their agents to engage in covert ops against anyone they deem a potential threat to the free world," Clements began.

"Do they have any vulnerabilities we can exploit?" Hill asked.

"The Department of Defense is conducting ongoing research to establish what their weaknesses are. It has been discovered that they have a reliable defense system, making them more formidable than they appear. But they are not entirely immune to cyberattacks. Any successful attempt to disable their systems will make them vulnerable to targeted military strikes," Clements continued.

One of the other joint chiefs, the Head of the US Air Force, Marshall Collins, interjected.

"Mr. President, the Air Force can send stealth bombers and fighter jets to multiple targets against the EJFS once their defense systems can be shut down. However, they have multiple bases stationed worldwide to aid them in their distress," Collins warned.

Clements continued. "Yet, it would be advisable that any military action would be swift and pre-emptive. If we delay, it will allow them to prepare a response of their own."

President Hill pondered momentarily before deciding.

"Call their leader, Khali. I'm giving them one last chance to surrender Drake to me," Hill commanded.

"Sir, are you sure you want to tip them off? It might cost us any military advantage we have on them," Clements warned.

"Drake must be returned to us. If they refuse and if Drake remains resistant, we will take them all down, and the world will know that Drake is a traitor," Hill insisted.

"Very well, Mr. President. I will connect you to their leader shortly. I will have the Air Force squadrons scramble within the next hour at your command," Clements advised.

The joint chiefs adjourned from the war room, and President Hill was given a landline phone to contact Khali in one last attempt to force the EJFS to surrender Drake.

***

At the EJFS base, in Khali's office: Drake, Raj, Kumar, and Master Khali were gathered in Khali's quarters while Drake was battling his internal fears that President Hill could authorize a military strike against the EJFS at any moment.

Khali sensed Drake's anxiety and tried to ease Drake's fears.

"It's going to be okay, Mr. Drake. Just relax," Khali spoke soothingly.

Suddenly, Khali's smartphone ringer sounded, startling Drake slightly.

Khali noticed the call was coming from Washington, D.C., and paused before answering it.

"EJFS, this is Khali."

President Hill spoke on the landline phone from the White House bunker.

"Hello, again. Mister Khali," President Hill greeted condescendingly.

"Mr. President, why are you calling me? You have declared my agency as an enemy of the state," Khali answered.

"You know why I'm calling you. I know you have an expatriate of ours. I demand that you return Drake to me, or you will experience the full might of my military against you and your organization," President Hill threatened.

"Mr. President, we do not respond well to threats. We know that you are an elite member of the Shadow State. It is only a matter of time before we expose you for who you truly are." Khali pushed back, protecting Drake.

"Your accusations are baseless and absurd. What proof do you have that would implicate me as a member of this "Shadow State" you speak of?" Hill asked.

"Stop deflecting. We have proof from Ravan's laptop that you have been involved with the Shadow State since its inception. You are merely an occupier of office with a harmful agenda against Western principles and freedom. As far as Drake goes, we will never surrender him to you, knowing that your administration may execute him." Khali continued to resist President Hill's ultimatum.

"You know nothing! This is your final chance: Hand over Drake to me, or there will be grave consequences against you and your network of agencies!" Hill demanded angrily.

"I refuse to be intimidated and bullied by you, Mr. President. We will not hand over Drake to you. We will instead honor your request to vacate US airspace per your earlier demands. If you engage in conflict with the EJFS, it will be a miscalculated error on your part. We have many effective defensive mechanisms at our disposal. Now, do not contact us again if you intend to continue to threaten Drake or us. Have I made myself clear?" Khali admonished Hill.

"Very well, your organization is about to pay a steep price for your resistance. You have been warned," Hill concluded in a haunting tone of voice.

Hill slammed the landline phone back in its cradle and stormed out of the war room in anger.

***

Drake was visibly shaken after the heated phone conversation between Khali and Hill. Khali made an executive decision based on the increasing danger with Drake's presence at the EJFS.

"Mr. Drake, I am going to be relocating you to an EJFS ghost site far away from Hill's reach. It is no longer safe with you here. I will instruct Agent Prabodhan to take you to our ghost site in Zurich, Switzerland. You'll be safe there," Khali informed him.

"Okay. I pray that you nail Hill to the wall. He must be stopped," Drake added.

"It will be done," Khali assured Drake.

Khali dispatched Prabodhan to take Drake out of harm's way as the ever-growing threat of war between President Hill and the EJFS continued to increase.

19: Drake Departs for EJFS Zurich Ghost Site: EJFS Vacates US Airspace

Master Khali's Headquarters – EJFS Executive Level Suites

EJFS Thunderhead Base Palace – Atlanta Branch – Eastern US Division

Current Location: New York, New York, USA

November 2, 2024

6:23 PM EDT, Saturday Evening

Moments after Khali's heated verbal exchange by phone with President Hill, Khali issued an executive command to all US-based Thunderhead bases to vacate US airspace immediately.

Within the hour, all EJFS Thunderhead bases hovering over the US mainland prepared to relocate to neighboring countries, such as Canada and Mexico, for an indefinite amount of time.

Former Vice President Drake was escorted to the deployment bay by Agents Raj and Prabodhan.

Agent Raj spoke to Drake before Prabodhan took Drake to his vehicle.

"Mr. Drake, I want to extend our gratitude on behalf of the EJFS for your willingness to reach out to us. I promise you that you will be well taken care of by our ghost agents in Zurich. They will offer you better protection than we can provide at this time."

Drake replied. "Thank you for taking care of me and your willingness to save me from Hill's reach. I am forever grateful. I hope that in the future, we may be able to heal the division between the EJFS and The United States."

"I'm sure that can be possible with time. But not until Hill has been removed from power, at least," Agent Raj suggested.

"If anyone could take down a corrupt president, it would be you people. You must stop Hill before he drags the country through a very dark path, one that the world cannot afford," Drake continued.

Raj smiled at Drake and spoke again.

"We will give it our all. Our agency means no harm to America, and we wish to keep it that way. Nevertheless, we must pray that Hill will soon face justice," Raj insisted passionately.

Prabodhan interrupted. "Mr. Drake, we must go."

Drake gave his last goodbye to Raj.

"May we meet again someday. Thank you, Raj!" Drake shook Raj's hand.

"Thank you, as well. Godspeed on your journey."

Agent Raj shook Drake's hand and gave a soothing embrace to Drake, which settled Drake in a full sensation of comfortable nirvana.

"I give you the gift of complete personal peace and comfort. You must not worry," Raj continued.

Raj ended the embrace as Drake felt fully relaxed, with his eyes half-open.

Drake quietly thanked Raj and boarded Prabodhan's vehicle as Prabodhan escorted him inside for takeoff.

In the front passenger seat, Drake was buckled in by Prabodhan as Agent Prabodhan gave Raj a quick salute before he boarded his ICV in preparation for departure.

Prabodhan powered on the ICV and drove it toward the launch zone.

The navigation screen counted from five to zero, and the ICV zoomed out of the deployment bay in a quick motion.

Drake and Prabodhan would arrive in Zurich within the next two hours at the current speed rate.

Drake fell asleep while still smiling as his blissful peace overtook him while Prabodhan piloted the vehicle towards the EJFS ghost site in Zurich, Switzerland.

*** *

Agent Raj returned to the Command Center, where Khali, Lochan, Darsh, Pranay, and Basu ran logistics for the entire EJFS network of bases.

Khali commanded, "Move all US-based EJFS Thunderhead Bases to neighboring countries immediately."

Basu complied. "Yes, Sir!"

Pranay relayed Khali's orders to all US-based Thunderheads to different site coordinates: latitude and longitude.

"Seattle and New York EJFS, relocate your bases to the coordinates I'm sending you. You'll be residing in Canada for the time being," Pranay transmitted the destination coordinates to both headquarters.

"Acknowledged." EJFS Director Jitender of the Seattle Subdivision complied.

"Orders received. We're relocating now," EJFS Director Vijay of the New York Subdivision acknowledged.

Both bases rumbled deeply as the Thunderhead bases moved out of the country toward Canadian provinces in Alberta and Ontario.

Basu relayed Khali's orders to the southern EJFS Thunderhead headquarters.

"Los Angeles and Houston EJFS, relocate your headquarters to the coordinates that I am transmitting to you now. You'll be relocating to Mexico for some time."

"Understood. We're moving out now," EJFS Director Indra of the Los Angeles Subdivision announced.

"Yes, Sir! Let's roll!" EJFS Director Krish of the Houston EJFS Subdivision exclaimed.

Within minutes, the EJFS Thunderheads stationed in both locations moved their headquarters to Cabo San Lucas and Mexico City.

Khali called engineering, where Agent Devdas was awaiting relocation orders.

"EJFS, this is Tandon," Devdas answered.

"Devdas, advance the Atlanta Thunderhead to Montreal. We will be staying there for the next few days," Khali commanded.

"Right away, Master!" Devdas complied.

Thus, all US-located EJFS bases vacated the airspace over America and took refuge in areas in Canada and Mexico.

***

At the White House Bunker war room, President Hill was joined by Secretary of Defense Frank Clements. They observed movements on the satellite and radar monitoring the EJFS Thunderheads relocating to neighboring Canada and Mexico.

"What are they doing, Mr. President?" Clements pondered.

"They are honoring my original request to vacate our airspace. Can we still engage in military conflict with the EJFS?" Hill asked.

"Negative, that would be inadvisable at this point. Any attack on their forces would risk casualties and collateral damage in Canada and Mexico," Clements explained.

"We have to take them out somehow," Hill spoke urgently.

"If you order a military strike while they are out of our airspace, you may as well declare World War Three with our neighbors. You need to take a different approach," Clements gravely insisted.

"Okay, fine. See if you can call a video conference with the Mexican President and the Canadian Prime Minister. I'll convince them that the EJFS are their enemies," Hill ordered.

"Very well, Mr. President. I'll see what I can do."

Clements excused himself to contact the leaders of Canada and Mexico in an impromptu video conference call.

Barnes approached President Hill.

"Mr. President, Laura Matheson wishes to speak with you regarding Hastings. She wants to know why he was fired," Barnes informed him.

"Tell her I'm unavailable to speak about that at the moment," President Hill responded.

"Very well, Mr. President. What do you want to do with Hastings and his kid?" Barnes inquired.

"Get them out of here," President Hill ordered.

"Right away, Sir!" Barnes complied.

Hill returned to his desk and awaited further development regarding the EJFS presence in Canada and Mexico.

***

At the Shadow State Black Site in Albany, Upstate New York, Clyde Patton and his team of specialists, Lukas Hightower and Alec Hawthorne, had nearly finished the dramatic transformation of Judson Clayborn into a deadly superagent-in-training.

Clayborn had been reprogrammed all day long with Clyde's re-education indoctrination designed to turn anyone into a freedom-hating, anti-American soldier of chaos.

Clayborn became a physical powerhouse after a harsh regimen of combat training, weapons training, and psychological warfare training.

Clayborn was furiously punching and kicking the stuffing out of many punching bags with pictures on them.

Now, Clayborn was about to be unleashed onto the rest of the world.

Clyde Patton congratulated his men on the excellent job they had accomplished.

"You two are amazing. Well done on yet another successful participant reprogramming." Patton congratulated them.

Lukas Hightower and Alec Hawthorne patted each other on the back in self-adulation while they smiled wickedly.

"Yes, Clayborn will be an excellent addition to the Shadow State," Hawthorne proclaimed.

"Indeed, he will," Hightower concurred.

Judson Clayborn continued kicking and punching the sandbag with pictures of patriotic images and influential, famous politicians who had positively impacted peace and prosperity over the nations.

Eventually, Clayborn punched the bags into oblivion, and the sand spewed out of the bags after Clayborn's power had substantially increased.

The complete transformation of Clayborn into a superhuman monster highly enthused Patton.

"Well done, Clayborn. You have passed all your training. It is time for your final infusion."

Clyde Patton snapped his fingers, and both brutes retrieved a large syringe of chemicals and synthetics to complete the transformation process.

Hawthorne injected the syringe into the left buttock of Clayborn. After the final injection, Clayborn's body swelled up to a massive superhuman physique, as most EJFS superagents possessed.

"He's ready. Let us give him his first assignment. Don't forget his cache of inhalers," Clyde Patton insisted.

Hightower retrieved a refrigerated case of inhalants from Gyan's farm to help equip Clayborn for his mission.

Clayborn was given his smartphone and all his belongings back to him. Subsequently, Clyde gave Clayborn his first assignment wrapped in a leather packet envelope.

Clayborn was given a new alias for his job within the Shadow State, TSS Agent Midnight Thunder.

Clyde Patton explained, "For all intents and purposes, Judson Clayborn is dead. From now on, your name is Midnight Thunder. You will be the one to shut down the US power grid for the next two days. This mission is part of the grand scheme to keep President Hill in office indefinitely. You must go and rendezvous with another operative named Alicia Blaze. She will take you to the Central Tower power grid center. Afterward, you will head to Brussels, Belgium, to meet with our dear leader,

Black Sparrow Zero. He will initiate you inside the Shadow State headquarters at the Rumbeke Castle in the West Flanders region. Do you understand your mission?"

"I understand, sir," Clayborn affirmed in a deep-pitched, hypermasculine voice.

"Good, now get going," Clyde Patton ordered.

Immediately, Clayborn was given the keys to his vehicle, a revamped and futuristic European car.

Clayborn turned over the ignition and drove out of the Black Site to rendezvous with Alicia Blaze at Joint Base Andrews in Maryland.

***

Around 6:48 p.m., at the CIRB Headquarters in Langley, Deputy Director James Matthews received an alert notification on his phone, which also showed up on Alicia's phone.

The message read as follows:

"Shadow State Advisory Bulletin:

"Agent Midnight Thunder has been activated. He has been dispatched to JBA, awaiting rendezvous with Agent Alicia Blaze. Project: Vritra's Revenge is now underway. Send all TSS Agents in the bureau to the Rumbeke Castle in Belgium for reinforcement.

~Shadow Falcon Five, CP."

Matthews reacted swiftly upon reading the message.

"Alicia, get to your car. We need to go now!" Matthews explained with utmost urgency.

Alicia Blaze quickly grabbed her keys and rushed with Matthews to the parking garage.

"Where are we going?" Alicia queried.

"Joint Base Andrews," Matthews replied quickly.

Matthews and Blaze entered their vehicles, turning over their ignition regulators.

Their tires squealed upon their exit from the parking garage to head to the military base.

***

Meanwhile, at the detainment cell under the White House Bunker, several guards escorted former Chief of Staff Nicolas Hastings and his son Logan out of the bunker and kicked them out of the White House on the darkened streets outside. They were left to fend for themselves.

"What do we do now?" Logan asked, stricken with fear.

"There's only one person left that could help us," Hastings replied while he speed-dialed a number to Janice Ausburn's phone, the Head Director of the CIRB.

Janice Ausburn's private jet landed in Washington D.C. when she received a call from Hastings.

"This is Janice Ausburn speaking."

"Janice, it's Hastings. I need your help. The President has fired me as his chief of staff, and I have no way of knowing what kind of madness is coming upon our nation now. You must reel in Matthews. He is a loose cannon. I can't get to him without your help," Hastings explained.

"Mr. Hastings, I need more details than that. We should not talk by phone. Meet me at the CIRB Headquarters. I can track Matthews down and keep him contained. I'll be there in 20 minutes," Ausburn insisted.

"I'll be there soon," Hastings replied.

Ausburn ended the call and directed her driver to Langley.

Hastings flagged down a taxi, and both father and son got inside the cab.

"To the CIRB Headquarters in Langley, please!" Nicolas urged the driver.

"You got it, sir!" The driver complied and sped away from the White House gates.

20: Midnight Thunder Activated: Nationwide Blackout

Main Entrance

Joint Base Andrews

Prince George County, Maryland

November 2, 2024

6:50 PM EDT, Saturday Evening

Shadow State Agent Midnight Thunder, formerly known as Judson Clayborn, took the interstate down to Maryland to rendezvous with fellow Shadow State Agent Alicia Blaze, the former doppelganger of Kim Porter, Caleb Porter's sister.

CIRB Deputy Director James Matthews and Alicia Blaze drove separate cars from Langley bound for Joint Base Andrews to bring Midnight Thunder into the plot to take down America.

Once Matthews and Blaze arrived at the base, they pulled their vehicles up to the entrance gate to validate their entry credentials.

A guard verified both operatives, and both drove their cars inside the base.

Matthews and Blaze exited their cars and met with the base's leader, Director Patrick Kelley, a hardened man with a slight Irish accent.

Kelley greeted Matthews and Blaze with their palms raised, bearing the Shadow State tattoo emblazoned on their hands.

"Welcome to Joint Base Andrews, Mr. Matthews and Miss Blaze. I am Commander Patrick Kelley. What business do you have that requires your presence here?"

Matthews answered promptly.

"We're here to arrange a military flight for two of our agents to Belgium for an international operation. Our newest superagent will soon join agent Alicia Blaze to accompany her on the plane. We recruited this agent late last night, and now he needs safe transport to the Rumbeke Castle in Belgium for his proper initiation into the Shadow State."

"I see. We will direct the new operative inside when they arrive. What is this superagent's codename?" Kelley asked.

"His name is Midnight Thunder. He's coming to shut down the nation's power grid for the next two days during the onslaught of the hurricane coming our way." Matthews continued. "We need the power to shut down to make sure the citizens do not see what will happen. Is your base well-stocked and prepared for a blackout?"

"Indeed, we are. President Hill ordered us to stockpile weapons and rations in preparation for this event. We expect to be back online on Election Day. All citizenries have been evacuated and are currently under martial law. However, we do expect some extreme destruction from the approaching storm," Kelley explained.

"There will still be massive casualties from the storm, and our goal will increase the death toll exponentially," Matthews continued.

"Vritra's Revenge?" Kelley hinted.

"Precisely. You will see soon enough," Matthews concluded.

Alicia Blaze grew impatient.

"Let's head inside. It's getting cold," Blaze insisted.

"Yes, let us bring you both inside. We will wait for Midnight Thunder in my office. Come with me," Commander Kelley directed.

The three Shadow State agents entered the interior of Joint Base Andrews and waited for Agent Midnight Thunder's arrival.

***

Shortly after seven o'clock in the evening, the cab driver transported both Nicolas and Logan Hastings to the Langley CIRB Headquarters.

The cab driver that drove both father and son to the headquarters was an undercover EJFS agent named Jaswinder Brahma, one of Agent Abhu's former enemies turned friend.

While Jaswinder drove the cab to Langley, he sent a text message to Master Khali, informing him of the development with Hastings and his son Logan.

Master Khali received the text message from Agent Jaswinder while he was in the Command Center with EJFS superagents Lochan, Raj, Darsh, Pranay, Basu, and Kumar. EJFS Trainee Kim Porter observed alongside Agent Basu during her job shadowing.

The text message read as follows:

New Unread Message from Jaswinder Brahma received at 7:01 PM:

"Master Khali, this is Agent Jaswinder reporting within the EJFS New York Subdivision. I have former Chief of Staff Nicolas Hastings and his son Logan. They are being transported to the CIRB Headquarters in Langley. Awaiting orders on potential assignments, please advise. ~JB."

Khali conferred with his team to formulate a strategic response regarding Jaswinder's message.

"Agent Jaswinder of the New York subdivision has texted me of the happenings of the now-former chief of staff and his son. They are being taken to the CIRB Headquarters. I am inclined to assign Jaswinder to stay on top of this situation," Khali explained.

"I would recommend that he remains in close contact as the situation unfolds," Raj suggested.

Khali replied to Jaswinder's message.

"Maintain your course and continue to monitor the developing situation. It might help us regarding the potential removal of Hill. ~Master Khali."

Jaswinder received the response from Khali and heeded his instructions.

***

Meanwhile, the Head Director of the CIRB, Janice Ausburn, arrived at the Langley Headquarters and made her way to her office suite near Matthews's office. She logged into the system to find out where Matthews was located.

Ausburn accessed the GPS tracking devices in Matthews's vehicle and discovered that Matthews and Blaze were located at Joint Base Andrews in Maryland.

All non-essential staff at the CIRB office went home for the evening. But that did not stop Ausburn from contacting Erika Cole, Matthews's secretary, to inquire of Matthews' intentions at the base.

Erika Cole was home preparing dinner for her family at her cozy home in Norfolk when she received Ausburn's call.

Erika cried out to her husband, Dan Cole, who tended to his kids while waiting for dinner to be served.

"Honey, please watch the stove. Janice is calling me," Erika insisted.

Erika's husband, Dan, finished cooking dinner for Erika while she answered Ausburn's call on her smartphone.

"Hello, Janice?" Erika answered while walking to a secluded room.

"Good evening, Erika. Did you happen to know that Matthews went on an excursion to Joint Base Andrews with one of our incognito agents without my prior authorization?" Ausburn began.

"No, I did not. I clocked off from my shift around five 'o'clock in the evening. Why would Matthews go there?" Erika asked curiously.

"I don't know, but this reeks of foul play, and I don't like it. I need to contact the Secretary of Defense to have a closer look at why he's at Joint Base Andrews," Ausburn answered while frowning.

"Well, I think I recall hearing Matthews mention that he was going to speak to Defense Secretary Clements about getting an exemption for Agent Alicia Blaze to take a military flight to Europe for some stealth operation," Erika hinted.

"Where in Europe?" Ausburn asked.

"Brussels, Belgium," Erika answered.

"Okay, I'm going to shut down this operation. You and your family should find shelter from the storm coming down on us," Ausburn suggested.

"We will soon, Janice. Thank you," Erika concluded.

"Thank you, too. Bye!" Ausburn ended the call and dialed Secretary of Defense Frank Clements' number.

Clements was in President Hill's bunker office while President Hill spoke with other staff and his family.

Clements saw that Ausburn was calling him on his smartphone and excused himself to a private room.

"Forgive me, but I need to take this call," Clements walked out of the President's office and answered the call from Ausburn.

"Hello, Janice. How may I help you?" Clements greeted.

"Mr. Clements, I'm calling you because my deputy director, James Matthews and another CIRB agent are at Joint Base Andrews. His secretary told me he is arranging a military flight overseas to Brussels, Belgium, for an operation. Have you authorized this exemption?" Ausburn inquired.

Clements was caught off-guard and nearly speechless.

"I wasn't aware of such exemption being proposed to me. Let me confer with the President about this. Please hold."

Clements muted his call and returned to President Hill's office.

"Mr. President, I need to speak with you privately," Clements insisted grimly.

President Hill arose from his desk and met with Clements outside the bunker office.

"The CIRB Director, Janice Ausburn, asks me why her deputy is at JBA with another CIRB agent. She claims that they are trying to arrange an exempted military flight to Brussels for an operation. Did you know about this?" Clements asked.

"Yes, Frank. It is a complicated matter, but it was planned many months ago. I need you to sign off on this and get Janice off my case," Hill dictated strongly.

"Why didn't you run this by me earlier before you declared martial law?" Clements asked puzzlingly.

"Frank, I'll explain later, but I need you to trust me on this. Now, tell Janice that you are signing off on this. That is a direct order," Hill commanded sharply.

Clements paused momentarily before unmuting his phone and spoke to Ausburn.

"Janice, thanks for your patience. I have spoken to the President, and we agreed to authorize the exemption. Now, I need you to stand down from any attempts to block my command. Let the situation play out," Clements insisted.

"But Mr. Clements –," Ausburn protested.

"No, buts, Janice. Goodbye!" Clements ended the call.

President Hill smiled in a slightly menacing manner.

"Thank you, Frank," Hill spoke before returning to his office.

Clements was still bothered inside that Hill did not inform him of the pre-planned mission. However, he maintained his loyalty to the President.

***

As Ausburn was frustrated and at a loss for a solution, Nicolas Hastings and his son Logan arrived at the CIRB office and met with Ausburn.

"Janice, I'm so glad you're here. Any updates?" Hastings asked.

"I got off the phone with the Secretary of Defense. He has just approved the exemption. I've been ordered to stand down from stopping them," Ausburn spoke solemnly.

Logan interjected. "But can you still track them?"

Janice had a contemplative look on her face.

"I suppose I could, but again, I can't stop them," Ausburn replied.

"Do what you can," Hastings encouraged while nodding.

Ausburn continued to monitor the situation at Joint Base Andrews as all three of them were stumped as to how to solve the problem.

***

Moments later, at JBA, Agent Midnight Thunder's upgraded European car pulled up to the base entrance, where the guard permitted Thunder's entry into the military complex.

The gates slid wide open, and Thunder pulled his car inside the base as the military officials were astounded by Thunder's enormously powerful physique.

The receiving guard called Matthews to inform him of Thunder's arrival.

"Mr. Matthews, Agent Midnight Thunder has arrived at the base," The reporting soldier announced.

"Bring him inside and load his vehicle on the military plane. We're deploying within the hour," Matthews spoke on the other end.

"Acknowledged! Agent Thunder, please follow me."

The receiving soldier escorted the incredibly massive superagent inside the base to meet with his superior and his partner agent, Alicia Blaze.

Each time Thunder took a step down the corridor, the floor shook mildly under the weight of Thunder's powerful physique.

The soldier bringing Thunder inside was somewhat intimidated by him, yet curious about how Thunder attained his monstrously powerful physique.

Matthews and Blaze were waiting in a private room when the escorting military official brought Agent Midnight Thunder into the workroom to rendezvous with his new team.

"Ah, Agent Thunder, welcome aboard," Matthews shook Thunder's heavy hand, which was rather painful to grasp before Thunder loosened Matthew's smaller hand.

"Ouch, you have such a strong handshake," Matthews winced slightly in pain.

"Sorry, boss, I'll be more careful next time," Agent Thunder spoke as powerfully as his name.

"Don't worry, it's okay. You will be a highly-valued agent in the Shadow State. Now, we need you to shut down the US's power grid for a couple of days. Agent Alicia Blaze will escort you to the Central Tower onsite. Then, you two will take a military flight to Brussels for your initiation into the Shadow State," Matthews explained.

"I'm looking forward to working with you, Thunder," Alicia Blaze smirked as she hugged the gigantic new agent.

"Well, what are we waiting for? Let us get this party started," Agent Thunder boomed.

Agents Blaze and Thunder were escorted to the Central Tower elevator in a restricted base area to the power grid center. A computer terminal faced the windowed glass pane of many electric turbines powering the US electrical grid.

The escorting soldier spoke to Thunder before he began the shutdown.

"I trust that you know what you are doing, Thunder," The high-ranking military official spoke bleakly before retrieving a battery-powered lantern in preparation for the blackout.

"Don't worry. I've been trained for this," Agent Midnight Thunder assured.

"I will make sure this goes through smoothly," Agent Alicia Blaze ensured.

"Very well. Proceed with caution," the high-ranking official advised.

Thunder and Blaze logged into the computer terminal under Blaze's CIRB credentials and accessed the power grid module settings.

Alicia Blaze instructed Midnight Thunder through the process.

"Access the power shut down settings and initiate the shut down for two days," Blaze directed.

Thunder did as instructed, and he was prompted to input the authorization codes for shut down.

"Today's authorization codes are Yankee-Oscar-Foxtrot-Nine-Seven-Zero," Blaze explained slowly.

Thunder typed in the phonetic military alphabet codes and the numbers in order. Then, the grid shut down function was enabled, and Thunder set a timeframe for 48 hours. A pop-up window appeared on the screen, prompting Thunder to execute to proceed with the shutdown.

"Set the timer for six minutes to begin the power down phase, then tap 'Execute,'" Blaze instructed.

Thunder followed his partner's commands, and a countdown was displayed on the monitor screens, and then the shutdown process commenced from six minutes and counting.

Alicia Blaze speed-dialed Matthews's number and alerted him of the imminent shutdown.

"It's done. The power will shut off nationwide in the next six minutes," Alicia informed him.

"Excellent work, you two. Both of you hurry back here and get ready to board your flight," Matthews urged.

"We'll be there shortly." Alicia Blaze ended the call and spoke to Agent Thunder.

"Agent Thunder, we're done here. We need to board our flight to Brussels now. Come with me to the airfield," Alicia instructed.

"Yes, ma'am." Thunder spoke deeply and powerfully before rising from his seat to follow Alicia to the tarmac.

The timer on the screens continued to count down from less than five minutes until the power grid shut down.

Agents Thunder and Blaze raced outside to the airfield to meet with James Matthews once more before their flight overseas.

"Good luck, you two. Keep your eyes peeled for the EJFS if they try to intervene," Matthews warned.

"Don't worry, boss. We'll take care of them," Agent Thunder spoke assuringly.

The two agents boarded the military plane, which included Agent Thunder's and Blaze's cars, and the hatch closed in preparation for takeoff.

Matthews scampered back inside the base as the military officials prepared their lanterns for the two-day blackout.

***

Meanwhile, at the CIRB Headquarters in Langley, Virginia: Janice Ausburn and the Hastings continued to monitor the developments at JBA. Ausburn watched with displeasure as the military flight began its takeoff process as viewed from the satellite imagery.

"This can't be good," she moaned.

"What are we going to do about this?" Hastings asked.

"I don't know. President Hill and Defense Secretary Clements tied my hands. It's out of my control now," Ausburn spoke bleakly.

"That tyrant. I know Hill is up to no good. We have to do something!" Nicolas fumed with frustration.

"I can't supersede the President's orders, Nicolas!" Ausburn argued.

"Maybe you cannot, but I don't work for him anymore. Perhaps it is time to call upon some outside help," Hastings hinted.

"Like whom?" Ausburn asked.

"The EJFS," Hastings answered.

Suddenly, the lights began to flicker and buzz as the blackout started to take hold of the grid.

"What's going on?" Logan asked with worry.

Ausburn checked her computer and logged onto the power grid module. She was shocked and horrified that a shutdown sequence had been initiated at Joint Base Andrews.

"Oh, my God! That is why those three were there! Matthews is trying to cover his tracks by shutting off the power grid!" Ausburn spoke with panic in her voice.

"Wait, the power grid is about to shut off?!" Hastings asked with tremendous concern.

"I can't override it from here. I have to call Clements while I still can!" Ausburn spoke urgently.

She speed-dialed Clements, but the call could not connect due to the power grid's shutting down. The cell towers began to power off in response.

"Damn it! The calls are not going through!" She cursed.

"We're screwed!" Logan exclaimed.

***

Outside the CIRB Headquarters, EJFS Agent Jaswinder observed the lights flickering outside the building, and the streetlights began to flicker as well.

"Dear God! The power grid!" Jaswinder exclaimed in horror.

Jaswinder immediately called Khali, but his call could not connect, and he struggled to remain calm.

Suddenly, the entire power grid shut down as the lights across America turned off from coast to coast, leaving America in the dark except for the underground bunker complex underneath the White House.

***

Master Khali observed the lights shutting down on the satellite feed over the US Mainland and grew fearful of its occurrence.

Khali and Raj stood grimly at the EJFS Command Center screens as they glanced at each other in mutual grave concern written all over their faces.

Kim Porter watched with tremendous distress as tears welled up in her eyes.

"Those poor people are in so much danger now," Raj spoke solemnly.

"May God be with them. We must remain undeterred but be mindful of the US citizens' plight. We'll have to improvise from here on out," Khali added somberly.

A noticeable soundlessness was observed in the command center and across the continental United States.

21: POTUS Hill's Video Conference with Canada and Mexico: Drake Arrives at Zurich EJFS Ghost Site

EJFS Logistical Command Center – Main Building

EJFS Thunderhead Palace Base – Atlanta Branch, Eastern US Division

Current Location: 1.4 km outside of Montreal, Quebec, Canada

November 2, 2024

7:29 PM EDT, Saturday Evening

The military leaders lit lanterns and torches from their survival kits to prepare for the approaching blackout.

After the nationwide blackout occurred, many US citizens were horrified as the grid network shut down while huddled together in groups.

***

At the EJFS Thunderhead Base Command Center, stationed over Montreal, Canada, Master Khali, Agents Raj, Darsh, Lochan, Basu, Nirav, Pranay, and trainee Kim looked at the giant screens in horror. They feared for the safety and well-being of the US and its citizens.

Kim became distraught by the developments she witnessed on the screen.

"We have to do something about this. Those poor people are in danger!" Kim cried out.

Master Khali tried to comfort Kim in her anguish.

"We'll do everything we can to protect them, but now we need to focus our efforts on taking down President Hill and the Shadow State." Khali softly spoke as he held a tearful Kim in his powerful arms.

Kim wept as Khali tried to provide solace to her.

She could not help but worry about the people, especially her family and friends, in the midst of the blackout.

Raj interjected. "Kim, I'm so sorry that you're distressed. But there is not much we can do at this point. Unless you know how to hack into the power grid remotely and reactivate it, then we must continually pray for the people."

Suddenly, Basu had an idea.

"Wait, what if we try to pinpoint the source location of the blackout, and we can try to reverse it?" Basu suggested.

Khali, while still embracing Kim in his arms, responded with a glimmer of hope.

"Do you have a way to accomplish that with the power already shut down?" Khali asked as Kim turned her face toward Basu, hoping for a sound resolution.

"We can try using a backdoor method by using neighboring satellites in Canada. But the difficult part will be accessing the portal for the US power grid system. However, I am willing to give it a shot," Basu explained.

"You have my permission. We have nothing left to lose now," Khali permitted.

Basu, Pranay, and Nirav accessed their computer stations and logged into the satellite navigation program.

"Pranay, reposition Satellite CAN-B 542 to the outer perimeter of the Eastern Seaboard," Basu instructed.

"Yes, sir! I'm repositioning the satellite now," Pranay affirmed.

Basu gave further instructions to his other subordinates.

"Nirav, try to establish a list of activities in the grid system and narrow down the list to the most recent major events," Basu ordered.

"Acknowledged!" Nirav complied.

The satellite scanned the area with its proximity sensors to detect any changes to the Northeastern US power centers.

The EJFS tech analysts discovered that Joint Base Andrews was the point of origin.

"Master Khali, the shutdown originated from the central tower in Joint Base Andrews in Maryland. Requesting permission to attempt an override," Basu expressed.

"Permission granted," Khali spoke optimistically.

Basu attempted to link the power grid module to the EJFS Command Center. Basu entered his credentials bestowed in conjunction with his high-ranking position in the Command Center's Intel Department.

After Basu entered the passcode, he was blocked by a warning prompt that his credentials were deemed invalid.

"Oh no! I'm being blocked!" Basu exclaimed.

"Could you try to bypass it?" Khali questioned.

"I would have to run a sequence analyzer. But, if I cannot pick out the code in time before we are discovered, the connection could be terminated," Basu warned grimly.

"Keep trying! Don't give up!" Kim pleaded passionately.

"Do it, Basu!" Khali insisted.

Basu continued his attempt to override the blackout, launching the sequence analysis application in a new dialog box on his screen.

There were six codes, three alphabetical and three numerical.

***

Meanwhile, at Joint Base Andrews central tower room, a technician observed the grid maintenance program to ensure the shutdown remained intact and discovered a flagged connection tapping into their system.

Military Officer Gregory Lewis contacted Matthews and notified him of the unauthorized access.

Matthews was still on location at Joint Base Andrews when he was dispatched via radio from Officer Lewis.

"Deputy Matthews, the grid portal is being intruded upon by a signal originating from Montreal, Quebec," Lewis informed him.

Matthews was somewhat unnerved by the news until he realized what entity might be trying to save the US from the blackout.

"The EJFS is at it again. How long can you hold them off?" Matthews asked.

"I don't know, maybe five minutes. I'm trying to block them," Lewis answered frantically.

"You better stop them if you want to keep your job! Do you understand me?!" Matthews barked forcefully.

"Yes, Sir! I understand, Sir!" Lewis affirmed and went to work in securing the grid from outside hackers from the EJFS.

Lewis accessed the credentials management system to prevent the EJFS from reactivating the power grid. He was prompted to add another security layer by entering another officer's credentials to stop the breach.

"Matthews, Sir! I need your passcode to enforce the blackout and secure the system from outside intruders!" Lewis exclaimed urgently.

"My passcode is 512JWM," Matthews explained quickly but clearly.

Lewis entered the codes and tapped the "Enter" key to send the command.

***

At the EJFS Command Center, the EJFS and Joint Base Andrews link was blocked, and the sequence could not complete itself.

Basu exclaimed, "They got us!"

Pranay sprang into action. "Hold on! Switch to the second satellite and keep going!"

"Acknowledged!" Basu complied.

Kim and Khali watched with extreme urgency, hoping and praying that the EJFS would reactivate the power grid.

Basu changed his hacking origin to the backup satellite and maintained the breach on the grid system.

***

Officer Lewis noted the continuous hacking performed by a different satellite and struggled to remain composed. He radioed Matthews again.

"Sir, the EJFS is not backing down! What are we going to do?" Lewis asked urgently.

"I'm calling the President. Stand by!" Matthews spoke heatedly.

Matthews rushed to the red landline phone to contact President Hill for assistance.

***

At the White House Bunker, President Hill was at his desk with his senior staffer, Barnes, and Secretary of Defense, Clements. The President's emergency landline phone rang, and he was alarmed to hear its ringing. He answered the call.

"This is President Hill."

"President Hill, it's Matthews! The EJFS is trying to undo the blackout. We need you to override the process and seal off the breach from the EJFS intrusion!" Matthews spoke urgently.

"Matthews, I thought you had this handled!" Hill fumed.

"Mr. President, EJFS is more persistent than we thought. We have to act fast before they restore power," Matthews pleaded with utmost urgency.

Hill motioned for Barnes's assistance.

"Barnes, get your tablet!" President Hill ordered.

"Yes, Mr. President!" Barnes complied.

President Hill quickly accessed the grid settings for the Joint Base Andrews central tower. Hill noticed that the EJFS was only one digit away from completing the reactivation code.

Hill struggled to maintain his composure as he searched his desk for the executive codes to seal all access to the system.

"Get me my damn override codes, now!" Hill seethed angrily.

Suddenly, other breaches appeared in the system from the neighboring EJFS branches, assisting the Atlanta Branch to restore the power.

"We're being overwhelmed! My screen is locking up!" Hill panicked.

Soon after, the sequence analysis on the EJFS front completed its cycle, and the power grid turned back on, restoring light to the entire US.

***

At the EJFS Command Center, the combination of all four branches in Canada and Mexico managed to overwhelm the system. They collaboratively reversed the blackout while planting a stranglehold on the orders, preventing the President from blocking the EJFS's action.

The analysts and agents in the command center celebrated their victory over President Hill and his Shadow State operatives. For the time being, things began to work in the EJFS's favor.

"We did it!" Kim cried out in jubilation as all the analysts high-fived and hugged each other.

"Excellent work, all of you!" Khali congratulated. "We must not let up. President Hill must be fuming right now. Stay on task. Our mission is not over yet!"

The other four EJFS directors within their bases, stationed outside the US mainland, wished Khali well before they signed off as they were displayed on the giant screens.

"Good job, everyone! Godspeed and many blessings upon your mission!" EJFS New York Director Vijay spoke on behalf of the other EJFS Branches.

"Thank you for your collaborative efforts. The American people are surely grateful as well. Do what you can to continue to assist us," Khali spoke light-heartedly.

The four directors bowed and signed off.

Khali addressed Kim before the late hours approached.

"Kim, I think you have had a great first job shadow. But now I insist that we let you go back to your quarters and rest for the evening. I will pass on any vital information about your brother's venture into Europe as needed. For now, we must keep you refreshed. Tomorrow will be the start of your training," Khali spoke kindly.

"Okay, if you insist." Kim followed Raj out of the command center to take the elevator down to the 12th floor to her quadrant unit.

Kim rested calmly in bed for the night, pleased with the words of encouragement from her chief commander.

***

Meanwhile, in the White House bunker, President Hill was fuming and seething with fury against the EJFS, throwing a wrench in his plans. He paced back and forth, muttering almost every curse word known to man before Barnes approached him with some news.

"Mr. President, the Canadian Prime Minister, and the Mexican President wish to speak to you right away," Barnes informed.

"Take me to the War Room," Hill spoke seethingly.

Barnes escorted Hill to the War Room to confer with their neighbors to the north and south.

Hill took a seat at the end of the boardroom table before the video conference began.

"Canadian Prime Minister Jacques Pierre and Mexican President Julio Suarez, you are on a video teleconference call with President Hill," Barnes introduced.

Canadian PM Pierre addressed Hill first.

"President Hill, it is my understanding that you have requested this meeting to address your concerns about the EJFS presence

255

in our airspace. Well, please rest assured that we will keep them occupied as you go about your response to the hurricane spinning toward your country's eastern coastline. We will send any aid and reinforcements as you deem necessary," Pierre stated.

President Hill responded. "Thank you for your assistance, Prime Minister Pierre. We will accept any help you may offer us at this time."

Mexican President Suarez contributed to the conversation.

"Señor Hill, on behalf of my citizens, I extend our sympathy to your people in your trying time. We will assist you in any way you find acceptable. The EJFS intruders are a threat to our nation's sovereignty as well and will be dealt with accordingly," Suarez added.

President Hill replied, "Thank you, President Suarez. You have our sincere gratitude. These EJFS networks need to be shut down for society's good. They cannot be allowed to operate any longer. I propose that the three nations go to war with the EJFS and show them no mercy." Hill spoke with a grimace on his face.

Pierre objected, "President Hill, we kindly appreciate the offer, but we don't know what we're dealing with at this time. I will have to confer with my intelligence officials in that regard. But please understand that military action remains a possibility."

Suarez added, "Si, Si, I fully agree with Señor Pierre. We need more time to strategize any possible military front. I strongly advise that you not engage with them at this moment, not while there is a risk of civilian deaths."

Hill was frustrated with the lack of willingness to engage in warfare with the EJFS.

"Very well, I will delay any military action against the EJFS in respect to your countries' well-being. But know that every minute wasted is a minute that the EJFS may be used to capitalize on our unwillingness to respond. I urge you both to come to a mutual agreement with all three of our nations to counteract. Goodbye!"

Hill ended the video conference, grumbling about his inability to convince the neighboring countries to go to war against the EJFS.

Barnes tried to speak to Hill to gauge his emotional well-being.

"Mr. President, what do you want us to do now?" Barnes inquired.

"There's nothing that we can do at this time. We will pick up where we left off in the morning." Hill retired to his quarters and prepared to sleep, although his mind was racing tremendously.

***

Meanwhile, in Switzerland's Swiss Alps, in Zurich's countryside town, former Vice President Drake and EJFS Agent Prabodhan arrived in the mountainside facility embedded under the mountains.

Agent Prabodhan lowered his ICV onto a helipad partially covered in snow and ice as they made their descent for a rocky landing.

Drake felt very cold in the frigid temperatures, which prompted Prabodhan to wrap two thermal blankets around Drake to keep him comfortably warm for the handoff.

"Well, Drake. Let us get you settled in right away," Prabodhan insisted.

Prabodhan led the way for Drake as they trekked to the EJFS Ghost Site on a cold, windy night in the frigid peaks of Mt. Zurichberg. An obscured Thunderhead rested over the mountainside.

Both men bundled up in the brisk weather. They hiked the staircase from the elevated helipad down to the snowy terrain and along the ravine, crossing a series of metal bridges and walkways to reach the Ghost Site sanctioned by EJFS agents sworn to protect and give asylum to fleeing government officials willing to cooperate with their goals.

Once they made their way past the ravines, Agent Prabodhan and Drake arrived at the front entrance of the Thunderhead situated over the summit.

Prabodhan scanned his badge and handprint to enter the palace tucked away in Switzerland's mountain ranges.

EJFS Ghost Agent and the senior watchman, Rommel Klug, welcomed both men as they headed inside the base in an off-the-grid living situation to prevent discovery by local governments.

"Guten Abend und Herzlich Willkommen!" Rommel greeted them.

Drake appeared to be confused by the German greeting.

"Ah, my apologies. We do not get many visitors during these harsh seasons. Please, come in and make yourself at home. We'll take good care of you here." Rommel escorted Drake into the warm and cozy base that had decayed in the time after Vritra's Rebirth.

Drake sat down on one of the couches and was offered some warm tea to help soothe him.

Rommel addressed Prabodhan before he left.

"Does he have any trackers on him?" Rommel asked quietly.

"He's clean. We checked him before we came here," Agent Prabodhan affirmed.

"I'm so sorry that you have to be confined to this place. This base was one of the many casualties suffered at the hands of Vritra. But it still serves a purpose. You will be practically invisible here." Rommel assured him.

Rommel coughed before he drank his Macha green tea.

Drake was semi-comfortable while he sipped his tea little by little.

Agent Prabodhan bid farewell to Drake before leaving to return to the Atlanta EJFS Thunderhead Base.

"Mr. Drake, it's been a pleasure working with you. May we meet again someday under better circumstances. Farewell, with love."

Agent Prabodhan hugged Drake before patting him on the back and departing the fallen EJFS base.

Rommel spoke to Drake as they spent the evening together before going to bed that night.

"It always warms my soul to see the love and support that our finest agents in the network give to everyone. They treat all their friends with great tender, loving care," Rommel pontificated to Drake.

Drake decided to break the ice.

"How long have you been here, and how many others stay here?" Drake asked.

"Very quick to question, eh? Well, I am the lead Ghost Site watchman. There are nine other agents, but they have already gone to sleep for the night. You will get a chance to meet them in the morning. As I said before, we seldom have visitors during these times. So, pardon the cold reception," Rommel continued.

"Not a problem," Drake shrugged.

"May I ask how come you defected from your commander-in-chief?" Rommel asked, frankly.

Drake paused before answering.

"Hill is a very temperamental and manipulative man. He tried to con me into going along with his reckless agenda. Despite my objections, I felt obligated to stay true to him for the good of the country. However, he is part of an elaborate scheme to take over the world and bring Vritra back to life for a second time. I regret ever being his running mate, but now my eyes are opened," Drake explained.

Rommel nodded as he sipped on his green tea.

"The adage rings true: The truth shall set you free," Rommel smiled.

"I know it," Drake agreed.

Rommel continued the conversation. "I always sensed that Hill was bad news from the moment he was elected four years ago. I sensed something about him that seemed like a bad omen in your country. All he has done so far is prove me right."

Drake shook his head while frowning tiredly.

"If you only knew what he was like from behind the scenes. This past day feels like an emotional roller coaster, and I want to get off the ride," Drake spoke lamentably.

"I'm sure things will be set right. Our network won't allow Hill to retain his position to abuse his authority much longer," Rommel added while stirring his tea.

"One can only hope," Drake added before taking another sip of his warm drink.

Later in the evening, Rommel escorted Drake to a comfortable guest room to sleep for the night. Drake had a difficult time falling asleep, knowing that the world was in imminent danger.

***

In Budapest, Hungary, the MICV carrying the Atlanta EJFS TAC Teams led by Abhu and Singh arrived near the Russian Embassy for a stakeout.

Anastasia Zima's flight to Budapest was expected to land within the next hour.

Singh addressed his TAC Team within the invisible MICV before the surveillance on Zima and the Russian Embassy would commence.

"All right, ladies and gentlemen: EJFS Central Command has intercepted Anastasia's flight path. The target and a few CIRB agents are expected to touch down at Budapest International Airport within the next half-hour. We are going to stake out the premises until 0400 hours. We will be extracting Anastasia once we have final confirmation that Vritra's necklace is in her possession. The method of extraction will be via Tornadic Thunderstorm Abduction." Singh explained while the other EJFS agents onsite listened.

Abhu continued the address to the TAC Team. "Remember, we have to remain stealthy in this operation as we are operating in International Territories. If we tip off the Russian Embassy officials of our presence, it could trigger catastrophic consequences. So, stay sharp and on point for this mission."

Singh concluded the address. "Are we all clear on that?"

"Affirmative!" The group responded.

"Good, now stay alert and wait for the authorization to advance on the embassy," Singh ordered sharply.

"Yes, Sir!" The group dispersed from the huddle inside the vehicle and remained cloaked under stealth mode vehicle settings.

As Singh and Abhu led the operation, both co-captains conferred with one another before the stakeout commenced.

"Is there any feasible possibility that Anastasia might not have the necklace?" Abhu pondered to Singh quietly as they kept watch.

"Why would you ask that?" Singh answered.

"Because if I were her and I knew I had you guys on my tail, I would probably consider the same strategy, hypothetically speaking," Abhu explained.

"If that is indeed the case, we'll have to change our strategy accordingly. Hopefully, we will adapt quickly enough, or this mission will be practically futile," Singh replied quietly.

"Let's hope it all goes according to plan," Abhu added.

"Exactly," Singh concluded.

22: Anastasia Zima Arrives in Budapest: EJFS TAC Team Stakeout at Russian Embassy

Gate N19

Budapest Ferenc Liszt International Airport

Budapest, Ferihegy, Hungary

November 3, 2024

2:18 AM Budapest Time, Sunday Morning

Later in the night during the early hours in the Hungarian Time Zone, Anastasia Zima's private flight with her entourage of CIRB agents on loan, courtesy of CIRB Deputy Director James Matthews, arrived at Budapest Airport.

Zima, accompanied by CIRB Agents Bradford, Cortez, and Meyers, disembarked from the plane in Budapest, Hungary.

After clearing through Customs and Immigration, with the CIRB's assistance fast-tracking Zima's passport credentials, Zima and her entourage boarded a black SUV with a chauffeur waiting in the arrival bay to take a half-hour drive to the Russian Embassy in the Terézváros region of Budapest. The destination was not far from the Millennium Monument and Heroes' Square.

The SUV drove down Route Four Northwest into Central Budapest. The streets at night were hushed, with little action.

Meanwhile, the EJFS TAC Teams led by Agents Abhu and Singh were staked out in an invisible MICV across the street from the Russian Embassy building along Bajza Street in District Six.

Abhu and Singh watched for the vehicle carrying Zima and her CIRB escort to arrive at the embassy.

Several EJFS agents hid in secluded areas near the route to the embassy. Each agent posted on the watch team reported to the TAC Team Captains: Abhu and Singh.

Agents Daarun, Garjan, and Durga maintained watch of one portion of the embassy from the west.

Agents Anil, Baadal, and Gangi kept surveillance of the embassy from the east.

Agents Chand, Vasu, Naveen, and Nitin, comprised of the "Grab Team" in the other MICV aerial overhead, circled the area in a complete orbit, in waiting, like birds preparing to attack.

The leaders checked in on the radio dispatch system.

Singh dispatched a message. "This is Alpha Leader requesting Sitrep for all teams. I want a status report of your surroundings. Please check in."

Durga radioed Singh in response. "Durga from West Tower, negative on the target so far."

Baadal radioed his status to Singh. "Baadal from East Tower, no sign of the target."

Chand radioed the status report from above the embassy.

"Chand, reporting from The Nest. I have a possible visual sighting of the target in the vehicle. It is heading northeast on Andrássy Road."

Suddenly, an SUV emerged from the main road and turned left to pull up to the embassy's front gate.

Durga noted the arrival of the vehicle over the EJFS radio dispatch system.

"Alpha Leader, this is Durga. I have visual confirmation of the SUV. It is pulling up to the embassy now."

Singh radioed the overhead surveillance team, also known as "The Nest."

"Nest Agents, engage your voice detection and software hacking capabilities on the SUV," Singh commanded.

Nitin and Naveen hacked into the vehicle's voice detection system to eavesdrop on the exchange at the gate.

"Hello, this is Sergei. What business do you have at the Russian Embassy?"

"My name is Agent Bradford from the CIRB in Langley. We have a Russian National seeking asylum at your embassy. I have documentation releasing her to your care."

"Hand over your papers, please," Sergei demanded.

The EJFS agents surveilling the area listened very carefully to the audio recon.

"Miss Anastasia Zima?" Sergei asked.

"Yes, we have her," Bradford affirmed.

Chand radioed Singh. "Target confirmed. Anastasia is in the vehicle."

"Very well, you agents may bring her in, but you're not allowed inside the building. This is Russia-controlled territory," Sergei advised sharply.

"We understand. We don't want to cause any international incident," CIRB Agent Meyers interjected.

"Open the gates!" Sergei commanded in Russian.

The gatekeeper opened the front gate, allowing the SUV to enter the premises.

Zima sat in the backseat with a carrying case that she traveled with, containing her carry-on item from the plane.

Russian soldiers, armed with AK-47s, stood by to receive their asylum seeker, Anastasia Zima, from the CIRB and the Shadow State by proxy.

Singh issued further commands: "All teams: maintain visual of the target and locate the possible carrier case for Vritra's necklace."

"Acknowledged!" Chand responded.

Zima exited the vehicle along with CIRB Agents Bradford, Cortez, and Meyers. This action led to the Russian soldiers drawing their weapons at the CIRB agents.

CIRB Agent Bradford responded with hesitation.

"Whoa, guys! We're only here to ensure the handoff is complete." Bradford tried to end the standoff.

"Do not take another step forward! Get back in your vehicle and leave the woman with us!" Sergei demanded.

Zima turned toward Bradford and spoke to him briskly.

"You should go. I need you to take your men to Brussels and stay there for a while. I need you to give something to Black Sparrow. Now, take the SUV and drive to Rumbeke Castle to meet with him. He will know what to do," Zima instructed.

"Anastasia, this wasn't part of the plan," Bradford murmured.

"Trust me. I know what I'm doing. Just do as I say," Zima insisted passionately.

Unexpectedly, something within Zima prompted her to kiss Bradford passionately on his lips in front of the Russians.

Bradford held her close in his arms and returned the kiss intimately. Bradford caressed Zima softly on her cheek with his left thumb before ending the overt display of affection.

"May we see each other again," Zima winked with a hint of a smile.

Bradford, while emotionally embattled, led his team back into the SUV.

"Guys, get back in the car. We're going to Belgium. Let's move!" Bradford ordered his men.

The CIRB agents returned to their vehicle and left Zima alone with her Russian counterparts at the embassy.

Sergei smiled at Zima as the CIRB vehicle made its exit.

"Welcome aboard, Miss Zima," Sergei greeted her.

As Russian officials escorted Zima inside the embassy, the soldiers lowered their rifles to settle her in under political asylum.

Zima was not fully aware that the EJFS was in the vicinity, hoping to scoop her up and take her into EJFS custody.

***

Amid the activity of the handoff, the EJFS TAC Team, in surveillance mode, witnessed the exchange that took place as Zima was brought inside the embassy to rest for the remainder of the night.

Captain Singh addressed his team with a measure of caution.

"Agents, we have visual confirmation of Anastasia's handoff to the Russians. Be advised: There is still no sign of the necklace at this time. We will proceed with the abduction in less than one hour. You are all now ordered to summon the storm to blow into the area before the abduction occurs," Singh commanded sternly.

Agent Abhu became wary after seeing how the handoff took place. He voiced his concerns to Agent Singh.

"Singh, I have a feeling that things are not as they appear," Abhu suggested.

"Explain," Singh insisted.

"I mean, you saw how Anastasia planted a sensual kiss on that Bradford guy. That did not seem like a natural response. Maybe Anastasia was trying to divert the necklace to Brussels. I'm not fully psychologically trained, but I think she has some tricks up her sleeve," Abhu theorized.

"If that is the case, we will find a way to have her lead us to it. But we need to stick to the plan until we know for sure that the necklace is not in Anastasia's possession," Singh redirected.

"Okay, Singh. If you have a plan, I will stick with it. I'm just saying we should consider altering our strategy if the necklace isn't with Anastasia," Abhu continued.

"Duly noted, now let's stop talking and start summoning the storm with everybody else on the team," Singh ordered.

"Yes, my friend," Abhu conceded.

Abhu and Singh began to swirl their index fingers in a circular motion while they blew forceful air out of their mouths, causing the wind to become stiff and gusty outside the MICVs.

Storm clouds billowed under the night sky, and thunder began to rumble faintly in the distance.

All EJFS agents on location continued blowing high winds out of their lips with their cheeks fully swollen and their eyes closed.

A severe thunderstorm formed north of the embassy, moving south in the direction of the structure.

***

Inside the Russian Embassy, Zima heard thunder rumbling and a strong wind howling outside. She knew, without batting an eye, that the EJFS was onto her, and it was only a matter of time before she would be taken upward into EJFS custody.

To counteract, Zima retrieved her handgun from her luggage and placed it under her pillow as she rested in bed, listening to the storm advance on the building.

The lights occasionally flickered each time lightning struck nearby, coupled with the gentle rumbles of thunder in the distance.

For a moment, Zima's heightened awareness caused her to hallucinate again. She closed her eyes, almost as if she were trying to inhibit the coming apparitions and delusions.

A hauntingly deep-pitched voice resounded in her mind.

"You are my chosen vessel. I shall take residence within you."

"Huh?!" Zima jumped out of bed as the storm continued to intensify in its approach.

Suddenly, there was a knock on Zima's door, and she was startled.

"Who is it?" Zima asked.

"It's Sergei. I need you to take cover in the bathroom. There is a storm coming our way."

Zima picked up her handgun from the backside of her pillow, and then she grabbed a lantern to take with her before the power would shut off. She raced to the bathroom as the wind continued to howl and intensify.

Zima felt the walls shake as a tornado began to form in the night sky in Budapest.

Meanwhile, all EJFS agents continued blowing strong winds to intensify the cyclone, quickly forming overhead as they continued to swirl their fingers in an entire loop.

Zima's bathroom lights shut off as a power transformer exploded in the high winds and heavy rains.

The backup generator kicked in, and the bathroom became poorly illuminated while the lightning flashes increased in frequency.

Zima's hallucinations became even more intense as she started to hyperventilate in extreme panic.

The handgun in her grip shook while she struggled to remain calm.

Suddenly, an apparition of the late Ravan appeared before Zima and seemed to sit alongside her, shushing her, and temporarily easing her fears.

"Anastasia, you must surrender to them," The voice growled softly.

"Who speaks to me?" She asked in a false sense of security.

All the chaos around her became an insignificant and surreal blur of nothingness.

The apparition spoke through Zima's mind.

"Shh! Do not be afraid. Vritra will show you the way. Surrender yourself to them and lead them westward. They will unknowingly do my bidding through you. You will be instrumental in my return!"

"But-I!" Zima resisted.

"Shh, all will be well. Surrender..."

The voice trailed off as the apparition faded away.

Zima fearfully returned to reality as she willfully gave herself up to who she thought the spirit of Ravan was referencing: the EJFS.

Suddenly, a powerful tornado tore through the roof of the Russian Embassy, and Zima opened her arms wide. She was taken into the custody of the EJFS when she briefly fell unconscious.

Inside the MICV above the embassy, the EJFS superagents shackled and chained the captured Anastasia Zima by her wrists and ankles.

Singh contacted Khali on his smartphone, informing him of Zima's capture.

"Dad, we have captured Anastasia. She didn't put up much of a resistance," Singh informed him.

"That is excellent to hear, my son! Did you confiscate the necklace of Vritra as well?" Khali asked anxiously.

Singh ordered. "Abhu, see if she has the necklace!"

Abhu searched Zima's belongings and found a carrying case Zima brought to Budapest as her carry-on item.

Abhu opened the carry-on case, but the necklace was gone, much to all the agents' horror.

"No!" Abhu cried out in disbelief.

"It's not there. Anastasia must have switched it out of the case earlier," Singh spoke grimly.

"Blast it!" Khali exclaimed over the phone.

"Now, what do we do?!" Abhu asked frantically.

"We have Anastasia, and we can give her diplomatic immunity if we can convince her to take us to the Shadow State leader," Singh tried to reassure Abhu.

"What if this is a trap? Remember, this is Anastasia Zima we are talking about here. Why would she resist us in New York but so easily give in while we are in Eastern Europe?" Abhu pondered.

"I don't know, maybe you're right. But we need to question Anastasia to find out what she knows," Singh insisted passionately.

Singh returned to his call with Khali.

"Did you hear all of that?" Singh asked.

"Indeed, I have," Khali answered.

"What do you want us to do? Where do you want us to go to interrogate Anastasia?" Singh asked with utmost urgency.

"Take her to the European Division EJFS, in Warsaw. They'll have the tools to break her down to cooperate," Khali directed.

"Very well. We'll be on our way shortly," Singh said.

"Keep me informed of any developments," Khali insisted strongly.

"I certainly will, Dad," Singh obliged.

"Godspeed!" Khali bid his farewell over the phone before disconnecting the call.

"Secure Anastasia in the brig, then set a course for Warsaw, Poland," Singh commanded his pilot, Nitin.

"Affirmative, Captain!" Nitin replied.

Zima, while still out cold, was taken to the brig.

They used their advanced technology to sedate Zima for five hours and chained her down to the rigid metal bed to rest.

***

Meanwhile, both CIRB Operatives, Alicia Blaze and Midnight Thunder, arrived in Brussels, Belgium, at a nearby base known as OTAN to board a military jeep and head toward Rumbeke Castle.

All the while, CIRB Agents Bradford, Cortez, and Meyers continued to drive westward toward the Rumbeke Castle as well.

Little did they know, the CIRB agents held a crucial key artifact stored underneath the seat that Zima once sat on, the necklace of Vritra. It was stored in the original shipping container that held it while stored in New York's subway system's depths.

The looming hurricane continued to churn westward toward the US East Coast, while America's citizens did not know that the worst was yet to come.

23: Abhu's Ominous Dream: Black Sparrow Zero's Identity Revealed

Deck One

EJFS MICV Squadron

En route to Warsaw, Poland

November 3, 2024

2:41 AM Budapest Time, Sunday Morning

Zima was fully secured in her holding cell aboard the MICVs. While en route to Warsaw, Poland, both Abhu's and Singh's TAC Teams retired to their joint quarters within the compacted space onboard the flying aircraft.

Even though the TAC Team agents lived in shared rooms, they made the best of it and spent time socializing together before sleeping.

Durga and Gangi were paired up in one shared room. Abhu and Singh, Baadal and Anil, Daarun and Nitin, Chand and Naveen, and Vasu and Garjan paired up in separate rooms in the aircraft.

The EJFS agents rested easy, knowing that the automated autopilot system guided its way to their next destination with the highly advanced technology under the superagency's control.

Soon after the team members retired to their quarters that night, all agents aboard the MICVs fell asleep while feeling a distinct sense of uneasiness about the next few days leading up to Election Day in the US.

***

In Abhu and Singh's shared quarters, Singh slept soundly through the night in his full-sized bed. While resting on the other mattress, Abhu was experiencing some mild insomnia confounded by Abhu's tendency to have vivid and eerily prophetic dreams and nightmares of the future.

Abhu thought back to the previous night while he was on vacation cut short by the current crisis events, fearing the likelihood of another ominous dream in the cards that night.

Hoping that the night would be restful, Abhu listened to the rather deep-pitched snoring emitting from Singh. The sound of Singh's snoring strangely comforted Abhu, knowing that Singh loved and cared for him tremendously. Singh would protect his best friend from death.

Eventually, Abhu blissfully fell asleep with the comforting sound of Singh's powerfully deep-pitched snores. Abhu fell into a restful slumber.

***

While Abhu was asleep, he dreamt of a stunningly beautiful wedding scene on a warm, sunny day in Savannah Beach, Georgia.

Durga and Abhu were getting married with Khali officiating the wedding ceremony, and the outside decor was beautiful and serene with the backdrop views of the Atlantic Ocean. Abhu was joined by his best man, Singh. His blood brother, Chris Porter. Abhu's father, Roger Porter, and Abhu's mentor, Darsh. Abhu's boss, Lochan, rounded out his best men.

The bride, Durga, was joined by her father, who flew in from Mumbai. Jindal Govind Deshmukh escorted Durga, adorned with many jewels and a fancy Indian-style wedding dress.

Among the attendees at the wedding, Abhu's mother, Donna, and his sister, Kim, sat in the pews recording the wedding ceremony on their smartphones.

Many of the EJFS superagents were in attendance to witness the marital union between Abhu and Durga.

Abhu was smiling, gleaning from ear to ear, with his silky long black hair wrapped into a large bun. He wore an expensive custom-tailored suit designed by Pranay, who oversaw the wardrobe preparations for the ceremony.

Durga walked down the aisle and up to the altar, joining her bridesmaids, including Gangi and Seva.

Once the couple united at the altar, Khali, the master of ceremonies, wore a brilliant white suit. Khali officiated the wedding and began by introducing the bride and groom.

Khali began the wedding festivities. "We are gathered here today, in the sight of God, to join this couple in holy matrimony. It is my honor and privilege to introduce to all of you, Abhu Dhuval Sandeep and Durga Gopal Deshmukh, as they carve a new chapter in their lives, to live as one couple caring for and loving one another."

While the ceremony continued, two figures dressed in black robes observed the wedding at a distance on a nearby boardwalk overlooking the venue.

The two dark-clad figures had their heads covered in cloaks while they watched the wedding from the boardwalk. Soon after, they were joined by two other shadowy hooded figures. One of them was wearing an ancient necklace that appeared to resemble the necklace of Vritra.

Abhu noticed the hooded figures lining up on the boardwalk. Abhu's facial expression turned from joy to concern as everyone else was oblivious to what Abhu saw in the dream.

Amid Abhu's worry, Khali began to read the wedding vows to the bride and groom.

"Durga, do you take your wedded husband to have and to hold. To love and cherish. In sickness and in health. For as long you both shall live?" Khali continued.

Durga spoke soothingly. "I do."

Abhu felt a tug on his ankle and felt a stiff breeze pick up. He noticed a ball and chain shackled to his ankle as if he were a prisoner.

Khali turned to face Abhu while Abhu felt a sense of doom overwhelm him.

Khali's voice started to distort as he spoke to Abhu.

"Abhu, do you take your lovely, wedded wife...as a prisoner of war, to weep and mourn, to grieve and to regret..." Khali's voice continued to change.

Abhu rebuked him. "Khali, stop it."

Khali's voice no longer sounded like his own but resembled Ravan.

"To bereave and bemoan, in hopelessness and despair, to devote your entire life as a slave for The Shadow State, and an eternal devotee to your overlord and master, Vritra?"

Suddenly, Khali transformed into Ravan, and the party ended as the others in the dream, which then became a nightmare, vanished from sight. Ravan turned into a plume of black smoke and disappeared, cackling maniacally.

Abhu was left alone on the altar as a monstrously powerful hurricane made landfall on the Savannah coastline while the wedding altar setup began to blow away. Scaffolding towers fell over in the powerful winds.

Abhu remained shackled to his ball and chain on an empty altar as the terrible hurricane raged around him during the chaos.

Rain began to pour in a deluge while the hooded figures, who were watching from the boardwalk, approached Abhu and surrounded him as the tide continued to rise with the storm surge rushing up to the shoreline.

Abhu cried out for help in his desperation.

"Somebody help me! EJFS, Khali, Singh, where is everyone?!"

The tall, feminine-looking hooded figure opened her robe from the top. Vritra's necklace was adorned on her neck. The dragon-shaped necklace was glowing bright red and orange. The clouds in the sky turned bright crimson and fire red in response to the necklace.

"No! You'll destroy the whole world!" Abhu cried out in terror.

The four hooded figures outstretched their palms, bearing the Shadow State tattoos emblazoned on their palms. The robed female character removed her cloak, and it was none other than Zima.

She unclasped the necklace of Vritra and held it up skyward while the amulet glowed brightly. The talisman burst into a bright red plume of smoke and ash, filling the skies with Vritra's remnants.

Darkness overtook the earth, as Zima declared ominously. "Vritra is reborn!"

***

Abhu was horrified in his nightmare, twitching and turning in his bed.

Singh overheard the noise coming from Abhu's night terror and rushed to his bedside.

"Abhu, Abhu! Wake up! You're having a nightmare!" Singh spoke loudly.

Abhu opened his eyes in sheer terror from the horrible nightmare he had experienced.

"Abhu, you're going to be okay. You had a nightmare." Singh calmed Abhu down, placing his hand around Abhu's shoulder, trying to comfort his best friend.

"Anastasia, she-she, the necklace. It's her," Abhu stuttered unintelligibly.

"Shh, it's going to be all right."

Singh held Abhu in his massive and powerful arms, holding Abhu's head against Singh's mighty chest as Abhu started to cry quietly.

"It's okay. I'm here for you. Everything is okay."

Singh held Abhu and did everything he could to comfort his best friend in his troublesome moment.

Abhu wept quietly in Singh's embrace, trying to articulate the horrible visions he had witnessed in his dream. But he was unable to form a complete sentence due to his night terror.

Durga entered the room to check on what had happened.

"What's going on?" Durga asked.

"Abhu had another nightmare. I can't understand what exactly he saw. He's so shaken up," Singh explained.

"Would it help if I admit that I had a horrible dream too?" Durga tried to help the situation.

"About what?" Singh asked.

"I was at a wedding, and Abhu and I were getting married. You were there, and everyone we work with was there. Abhu's biological family was there, and so was my father," Durga explained.

Abhu was able to recover from his night terror.

"That's what I dreamt, too," Abhu interjected.

Singh and Durga were in disbelief about what they learned in the shared nightmare vision both seemed to experience.

"That's remarkable. I can't quite understand how you both had the same nightmare." Singh was at a loss as the three sat on a bed together.

"I'm not completely sure, but I might be experiencing premonitions again. You know, as I had last year?" Abhu suggested in a slightly calmer state of mind.

"I believe you, Abhu. We can scan your device to help bring clarity to what you saw that scared you so badly. But I do not think we can scan your device until we get to the Warsaw EJFS Base. Maybe Durga should be scanned too," Singh added.

"I'm okay with that if Abhu agrees to it," Durga said.

"Yes, I agree," Abhu continued in a calmer tone.

"All right, I'll notify Khali and have him arrange for two device scans." Singh spoke quietly, trying not to disturb the others.

"You'll be fine, Abhu. Just remember that dreams cannot harm you." Durga rubbed Abhu's shoulders to reassure him.

"Thank you, Durga," Abhu smiled.

Singh walked back to his bed to access his tablet.

"I'm going to type up an email to Khali. He'll get the scan ordered right away."

Singh got out of Abhu's bed and returned to his own. He sat across from Abhu while Durga went back to the quarters she shared with Gangi.

Later in the night, Abhu fell back to sleep and did not experience any new dreams.

Meanwhile, Singh sent out the email to Master Khali detailing the incident in full.

Once Singh finished using his tablet, he turned off the lamp hanging over his bed. He rubbed his eyes with fatigue and went back to sleep until the rise of dawn.

***

In the Canadian airspace where the EJFS Atlanta Base resided, Master Khali read an urgent email from his adopted son, Agent Singh.

Master Khali reviewed the email on his tablet before adjourning to bed that night.

***

From: Agent Singh Puneet Sherpa

To: Master Khali

Cc: Agent Abhu Dhuval Sandeep; Agent Durga Gopal Deshmukh

Subject: STATUS REPORT – Abhu's and Durga's Nightmare Visions (Device Scan Order Requested)

Priority: High

Date: 11/03/2024 02:51 CEDT

***

Dear Dad,

I apologize for the late hour of this email transmittance.

I am contacting you to request an immediate dual device scan for Agents Abhu and Durga.

281

During tonight's rest period, I witnessed Abhu experience a dramatic nightmare and night terror. He was so distraught and disturbed that he had difficulty forming a complete articulation of what he saw in his dream vision.

Interestingly enough, Durga came into the room after hearing Abhu's distressing cries. She revealed to us similar elements in both agents' dreams that depicted a wedding between the two.

Beyond that, the rest of the details were unclear. However, both Abhu and Durga were considerably distressed about what they dreamt.

When Abhu awoke, he uttered vague references to our SIC (Ref: SUSPECT IN CUSTODY) Anastasia Zima and the IOI (ref: ITEM OF INTEREST) Vritra's necklace were somehow correlated in the nightmare. I responded to the incident by consoling Abhu and reassuring him that he was safe.

Upon recollection of past events from September 8-11, 2023, I feel that it would be wise at this juncture to expedite a DDS (Ref: DUAL DEVICE SCAN) to gain further insight and clarity regarding the similar elements of nightmares that Abhu and Durga experienced tonight.

Please attach this email to your request addressed to the WARSAW, POLAND - EJFS Subdivision. I believe that time is of the essence and that we need to process and execute this order swiftly and promptly.

Love,

Your son,

~Agent Singh P. Sherpa - EJFS TAC TEAM SPECIALIST - ATLANTA SUBDIVISION of the Elite Justice Force Squad

***

Master Khali typed up his report and attached the email he received from his adopted son, Singh, then expedited the email directly to the Director of the Warsaw EJFS Subdivision in Poland for immediate processing before the TAC Team would arrive later that morning.

Kumar, Khali's assistant, checked on him to learn about the Mobile TAC Team's status away in Europe. Kumar buzzed the call button outside Khali's private quarters.

"Please, come in," Khali insisted.

Kumar slid open the large doors leading to Khali's quarters.

"Master Khali, how is everything going with the TAC Teams?" Kumar inquired.

"They have captured Anastasia, but the necklace wasn't there. Singh emailed me a status report about Abhu's nightmares returning. I'm concerned about Abhu's mental state and what impact it could have on the mission as a whole," Khali explained.

"Do you feel that sending Abhu might have been a miscalculated risk?" Kumar asked.

"No, of course not. I am saying that I am worried about Abhu and how these dreams are affecting him. I am fully aware that Abhu's premonitions last year helped us save the world from Vritra's first rebirth. But it seems that his response to the intensifying nightmares warrants concern. I care for him and love him like a son as I do for Singh," Khali added.

"I understand that. We all love Abhu very much, and I shudder at the thought of what state the world would be in if we had not recruited him last year," Kumar responded.

"There's another piece of the puzzle: Durga had experienced a remarkably similar dream that Abhu had. They were getting married, and beyond that, the dream spiraled into a horrible nightmare. Abhu was so distraught that he could not articulate what he saw. They might be connected somehow, but Abhu and Durga will have their capsule devices scanned tomorrow morning when they arrive at the Warsaw Branch," Khali continued.

"I pray that those scans are conclusive. We don't have much time before the Shadow State implements its endgame strategy. The hurricane in the Atlantic has been exceptionally massive and destructive. Even the storm-enhancing technology that we have disabled at Gyan's compound has not made much difference. We need to stop the Shadow State soon before much more extreme destruction could occur," Kumar urged Khali.

"I understand. That is a very valid concern. But we do not quite know what kind of danger we are dealing with yet. At the very least, we might be able to gain further insight if both dreams are prophetic. I believe in symbolism, and that I believe that both the dreams Abhu and Durga experienced may have been a sign from God. We'll have to see it for ourselves," Khali continued grimly.

"It's a possibility, but what if we're wrong?" Kumar asked calmly.

"If we are wrong, then we may have just done a great disservice for the world by not sticking with our plan. But we must not lose hope as so long Vritra remains dormant," Khali answered.

"I'll be praying that this detour will pay off. In the meantime, you should get some rest. tomorrow is poised to be a long day."

Kumar smiled as he left and returned to his quarters while Khali reflected on the previous day before adjourning for bedtime.

***

Meanwhile, in Brussels, Belgium, Shadow State operatives Midnight Thunder and Alicia Blaze were on board a military jeep originating from the OTAN US Base en route to Rumbeke Castle in the West Flanders region of Belgium.

It was just after 3:00 a.m. in Belgium, and both Blaze and Thunder were still awake as they were driven to Rumbeke Castle to meet the top leader of The Shadow State, codenamed Black Sparrow Zero.

Blaze rested her head on Thunder's massive shoulders as she was beginning to feel exhausted. Thunder helped to keep Blaze comfortable as he allowed her to rest her head while they were less than a few kilometers away from the castle.

The driver noticed the duo was getting sleepy, and he spoke up to inform them of their arrival time.

"We'll arrive at Rumbeke Castle in three minutes. Hang in there, you two." The driver encouraged the duo to stay awake a bit longer.

Midnight Thunder spoke to Alicia Blaze quietly.

"Who is this Black Sparrow Zero guy? Does he look reptilian?" Thunder asked Blaze.

Blaze laughed tiredly. "Heh, I guess you could say that. But do not tell him you asked me that question. He would not be impressed by your demeanor."

Thunder smirked and shrugged his shoulders.

"It was only a joke. Are we not allowed to joke around in the Shadow State?" Thunder asked.

"Maybe not around our dear leader, but I don't mind if you joke around with me, Thunder," Blaze smiled while trying to stay alert.

"Sounds like this guy could use a sense of humor," Thunder added.

"Don't worry. I'm sure you'll fit in well with him." Blaze yawned as she spoke.

Soon after the brief banter concluded between Blaze and Thunder, the jeep drove up to Rumbeke Castle's entrance, where two armed guards stood watch to grant entry to the automobile.

One of the armed guards spoke to the driver.

"Do you have our newest member of the Shadow State?" The guard asked the driver of the jeep.

"Yes, Midnight Thunder is on board along with Alicia Blaze," The jeep driver confirmed.

"Excellent, come in. Black Sparrow will be pleased to see him."

The armed guard spoke in French to the other armed guard, instructing him to open the gates to the private road to the castle entrance.

"Ouvrez les portes!" The armed guard commanded.

The second armed guard opened the gate for the jeep to pass through and drive along the winding road to the castle entrance.

"Welcome. Enjoy your stay." The guard waved the jeep off as they drove past the opened gate.

The guards closed the gates and maintained a watch of the front entrance.

Rumbeke Castle was enormous and eerie-looking with the illuminated exterior from the outdoor lighting late at night.

Both Blaze and Thunder were relieved to be at the castle. They were ready to sleep for the night.

Augustus, the castle butler, welcomed the duo upon their arrival at the front entrance of Rumbeke Castle.

"Ah, yes! You must be the Shadow State's newest enrollee. Welcome! I am sure both of you are tired, but our dear leader has insisted upon both of you meeting with him before you go to bed for the night. Let the porters bring in your luggage and come with me," Augustus insisted.

Augustus escorted both Blaze and Thunder to the inside of Rumbeke Castle. The interior was slightly creepy and spooky, but neither Blaze nor Thunder seemed to mind at all. Sleep was the only thing they were worried about now.

Augustus, Blaze, and Thunder staggered up the spiral staircase to the top floor, where they would sleep for the night after meeting with Black Sparrow Zero.

Blaze enjoyed the decor of the castle. It matched her crazy personality and style.

"This place is incredible. You'll love it, Thunder," Blaze fawned over the interior of the Victorian castle.

Thunder looked at all the decor and the castle's design in awe and wonder, but his fear subsided as he quickly became acclimated to the surroundings.

"I like the interior of this place. The feel of it is so sexy," Thunder remarked unapologetically.

"Oh, my," Augustus blushed at Thunder's comment, although flattered by the compliment of the castle.

Blaze chuckled lightly but was nervous inside as to whether Black Sparrow would appreciate Thunder's sick humor.

Eventually, after ascending the tall flight of stairs, Blaze and Thunder were escorted to the master suite occupied by Black Sparrow Zero.

Augustus opened the tall double doors to Black Sparrow's room. Both Blaze and Thunder entered the room alone, as Augustus did not accompany them.

Now Thunder was slightly intimidated by the situation as they entered the poorly-lit master bedroom.

Black Sparrow was sitting in a tall chair at his desk facing the duo. His head's silhouette appeared ominous. He sat with his fingers touching each other menacingly.

"Approach," Black Sparrow commanded.

Both Blaze and Thunder approached the executive desk where Black Sparrow was seated. The rookie operative was nervous by the room's foreboding feel. There were bookcases and exceedingly high ceilings with a fireplace burning firewood behind the desk.

Blaze and Thunder reached the front of the desk, facing the darkened face of Black Sparrow Zero. The feel from the room was increasingly menacing as they stood before their leader.

"Welcome to your new home," Black Sparrow Zero hissed as he flipped a switch under his desk, turning on the lights in the room.

Black Sparrow Zero revealed his face, and he looked old and wrinkly. His eyes were buried behind the bags beneath his eyes. There was a distinct look of evil on his face as he evaluated his recruit, Midnight Thunder.

"State your entry codes!" Black Sparrow demanded.

Alicia was the first to lead by example.

"SP6AHB, Shadow Phoenix Six, Alpha Hotel Bravo. Alias: Alicia Harlequin Blaze."

"Excellent, you are cleared to go to bed for the night. Leave the newest recruit with me," Black Sparrow ordered Alicia Blaze.

Blaze and Thunder gazed at each other nervously as Blaze followed the command of their leader.

Alicia Blaze exited the room, leaving Midnight Thunder alone with Black Sparrow.

Black Sparrow began the initiation. "State your alias!"

Midnight Thunder gulped before answering.

"My alias is Midnight Thunder."

Black Sparrow chuckled evilly.

"Yes, that is a fine alias," Black Sparrow spoke ominously. "I see that your palm is bare. We will fix that soon. But first, I will grant you your entry codes. Do not forget them!"

Midnight Thunder listened intently, albeit nervously.

"Your entry code is SS10MT, Shadow Stingray Ten, Midnight Thunder. Recite the entry code that I have given you." Black Sparrow's voice rumbled authoritatively.

"Shadow Stingray Ten, Midnight Thunder."

"Well done!" Black Sparrow smiled, then he snapped the fingers of his left hand.

Suddenly, two humongous Shadow State agents appeared from behind, grabbed Midnight Thunder by the arms, and placed him in a chair in front of Black Sparrow.

"It's time to mark you as a Shadow State devotee. Get the branding iron, and you know what you have to do," Black Sparrow instructed.

One of the Shadow State agents took out an inhaler and inhaled three puffs of a blue inhalant solution.

The other agent grabbed the branding iron next to the fireplace and held it close to the flames, lighting up the metal branding piece that resembled the Shadow State tattoo design.

"Give him the fire and ice," Black Sparrow commanded his fellow agents.

"Yes, dear leader," One agent acknowledged.

"Midnight Thunder, if you wince in pain, you fail the initiation. Proceed!" Black Sparrow ordered.

The agent that inhaled the solvent blew freezing ice breath on Thunder's palm, numbing it up and preparing him to be marked.

Thunder maintained his composure and did not wince in pain, as much as his tolerance of pain withstood the initiation.

"Phase One complete, begin Phase Two," Black Sparrow directed.

Thunder took a deep breath, knowing he was about to be scarred for life.

The other agent took the branding iron and pressed it into the palm of Thunder's hand.

Thunder breathed quietly without whimpering or wincing.

The agent removed the branding iron.

"Well done, Midnight Thunder. You have completed your initiation. Now, I will reveal more about myself to you. My real name is Francois Tomas Richer. I am a member of the Belgian Parliament, and I am the Shadow State founder. I am also a former business partner with the defunct Final Wave Organization. Ravan was a close friend of mine, but I believe his legacy will continue through our institution," Richer began.

Midnight Thunder remained quiet as he listened to Richer speak for a moment.

"The hurricane spinning toward the US was done at my behest. I have an artifact that you may have been seeking before your initiation to the Shadow State. I am referring to the necklace of Vritra. Anastasia Zima brought you into our group. She knew you would be a resourceful asset to the Shadow State. But now, you are the final piece of the puzzle to reconstitute Vritra and bring him back from the dead. You must go to Atlanta to bring about Vritra's return and complete the legacy of Ravan. Do you understand your mission?" Richer asked.

"Yes, I do. I accept the mission you have given me," Thunder obliged.

"Excellent, you will depart for Atlanta in 36 hours. Now, get some rest. You'll need plenty of it," Richer grimaced wickedly.

24: A New Day Dawns: EJFS TAC Team Arrives in Warsaw, Poland

Deck One

EJFS MICV Squadron

Warsaw, Poland

November 3, 2024

7:57 AM Warsaw Time, Sunday Morning

At the dawn of the next day, the EJFS TAC Team led by Agents Abhu and Singh had arrived in Warsaw.

The MICVs had made their approach to land their aircraft inside the Warsaw EJFS Thunderhead Base's arrival bay. The TAC Teams would stay there to refuel their MICVs while they had Zima interrogated.

Abhu and Singh led their teams off the aircraft to stay in the Warsaw Thunderhead Base's guestroom quadrant units for a brief time.

Abhu and Durga felt a strange omen lingering from their nightmares in which both seemed to have experienced similar elements.

Abhu and Singh issued commands to their teams.

"Agents, the twelve of us will be staying at the Warsaw Base until further notice. You are ordered to assist the EJFS Warsaw Branch in every way possible. All agents will report to the Command Center or the Detention Center to assist with Anastasia's interrogation and continue to monitor the Shadow State's large-scale operations. Are we clear?" Agent Singh spoke strongly.

"Yes, Sir!" The other nine affirmed.

"Good. All of you except for Durga and Abhu are dismissed. I suggest that everyone nourish themselves with some breakfast in the cafeteria." Singh finished addressing the troops before they left to eat breakfast.

Abhu, Singh, and Durga stayed behind to discuss their plan of scanning their capsule devices to examine their dreamscapes from the previous night.

"Abhu and Durga, I sent an email to Khali last night to fast-track the Dual Device Scan order for both of you to help us see your nightmare visions. The Warsaw EJFS Director, Ikshan Choudhuri, should approve it soon. You'll both need to be ready to report to Ikshan at any moment to begin your dual device scans," Singh informed the dating couple.

"Who is going to be the one to evaluate us during our scans?" Durga asked.

"I will. Khali was adamant that I should analyze the dreamscapes in your scans. We will need to see them while we interrogate Anastasia this morning," Singh added.

"You'll keep these dream visions confidential between all of us, right?" Abhu asked.

"Certainly. You both can trust me. I will keep the results confidential. However, we will use these scans to see how they line up with Anastasia's testimony. It might help us in our search for the necklace of Vritra," Singh assured.

Abhu and Durga glanced at each other briefly.

"Do what you have to do. But please do not share our dream visions with anyone outside our circle," Durga insisted.

"I second that," Abhu added.

"Very well. Keep an eye on your messages. Both of you will be notified within the next hour or so," Singh said.

The three entered the base's interior, which looked like an upgraded and technologically advanced cathedral. The ceiling was beautifully ornate, and the floors were sturdy to withstand all the gigantic superagents traversing the hallways.

Abhu, Durga, and Singh joined the other nine TAC team members to enjoy a Polish-Indian fusion breakfast as a welcoming meal for the visiting superagents.

The twelve of them were served a hearty meal of potato pancakes with rice crisp on top spiced scrambled eggs alongside some Indian and Polish spiced breakfast sausage. Their morning meal included some warm Indian-brewed premium-roast coffee with some cream and sugar.

The twelve Atlanta-based superagents received welcoming greetings from numerous Polish EJFS super-agents who enjoyed their communal breakfast together.

Warsaw EJFS Agents Lars and Alexey introduced themselves to the visiting team.

"Welcome to the Warsaw EJFS. We are pleased to meet all of you. My name is Agent Lars, and this is my friend, Agent Alexey. We heard many wonderful things about your subdivision in Atlanta regarding the fall of Final Wave last year. It is truly inspirational and humbling to meet a few of you who helped defeat Vritra over 14 months ago."

Agent Alexey spoke kindly to all the Atlanta EJFS agents. "I wholeheartedly agree. You guys are awesome! Welcome aboard and make yourselves a home."

Singh smiled as his team enjoyed their meal. "Thank you for such kind words of accolades to our team. it is much appreciated."

Agent Lars wished the team well before both Lars and Alexey returned to their table. "May God bless you all in your quest to stop the coming superstorm from impacting American shores."

Agent Abhu spoke in response to the warm welcome they received.

"That was so thoughtful of them," Agent Abhu commented as he continued to eat his breakfast.

"Indeed," Nitin agreed while he sipped some coffee.

After the Atlanta-based EJFS TAC Team finished their breakfast, Singh explained the protocol for the day.

"Okay, everyone on my team will be taking a trip to the Detention Center to interrogate Anastasia. Abhu's team will be helping in the Command Center on the top floor of the main building. We will reconvene in a few hours to go over our next steps before departing for Brussels, Belgium. Let us get to work!" Singh commanded.

Both teams packed up their gear and made their way to their assigned Warsaw EJFS Thunderhead Base locations.

***

Meanwhile, Anastasia Zima was escorted from her holding cell in the Warsaw EJFS Thunderhead Detention Center to Interrogation Room Two.

A pair of Polish-Indian EJFS superagents connected Zima to some vital detection sensors and injected a crimson red capsule device down her throat to detect her subconscious thoughts. The capsule device also could dissolve her into precipitable rainwater.

However, the Interrogation Specialist named Marut Ketubah was under strict orders from the Head of the EJFS, Master Khali, not to vaporize Zima until all testimony and facts could be established and verified.

Agent Singh led his team of superagents to the observation room adjacent to the interrogation room, where Zima was prepped for questioning.

Warsaw EJFS Director Ikshan Choudhuri greeted Atlanta EJFS Agent Singh Puneet Sherpa in the observation room while Agent Marut accompanied Ikshan.

"Ah, you must be Agent Singh from the Atlanta Branch. I've heard many great things about you and the class of superagents in your division," Ikshan welcomed Singh.

"Well, I appreciate that, Sir. My team will be observing Anastasia's interrogation. They need to gather all data in relevance to the mission at hand," Singh informed them.

"Of course, and while your team is here observing, I need to speak with you in private regarding an email I received from Master Khali. Could you spare a few minutes?" Ikshan requested.

"Certainly," Singh addressed his TAC Team, "All right, all of you stay here and monitor Anastasia during her interrogation. I am needed elsewhere. The interrogation tech team will guide you for the time being."

Singh relinquished his command to the Warsaw Detention Center Interrogation Techs while making his exit with Ikshan.

Singh's team's remaining five members stayed behind as they observed Anastasia's demeanor and facial expressions.

The look on Zima's face sent chills down their spines.

Anil commented, "She looks so exhausted as if she had the life sucked out of her."

Naveen interjected, "She must be suffering from severe sleep deprivation."

Baadal added, "I don't know she managed to flee from our agency all this time. She looks like she hasn't gotten a decent night's rest for weeks."

Gangi chimed into the discussion, "Maybe she's burnt out and wanted us to end her misery."

Nitin contributed to the group conversation, "Whatever her reasons are for surrendering are about to be revealed to us. She had been avoiding capture for a very long time."

Zima continued her haunting glare at the two-way mirror while the interrogation team prepared enhanced interrogation elements.

***

Singh and Ikshan spoke privately outside the Observation Room before the start of Zima's interrogation.

"Agent Singh, I am aware that your boss in the Atlanta Branch has sent me a high-priority order, requesting that we allow you to scan the memory of two of your fellow EJFS agents," Ikshan began.

"Yes, that is correct. Two agents on the second team joining mine have experienced a disturbing nightmare that included similar elements in both nightmares," Singh affirmed.

"You are referring to Agents Abhu and Durga, the dating couple in your subdivision. I am fully aware of their romantic involvement with each other, as you implied in their dream that there was a wedding between the two of them included in the report," Ikshan continued.

Singh nodded with a grim look on his face.

Ikshan added, "I hope you share my concerns that this relationship has the potential to greatly and negatively impact the superagency's mission to neutralize the looming threat of the Shadow State. Wouldn't you agree with that overall assessment?"

"Director Ikshan, with all due respect, I know Abhu and Durga very well, and I know that they can set their relationship aside for the sake of the mission and the survival of the world. They are grown consenting adults. If that poses a conflict of interest, then maybe they will need to re-evaluate their priorities. However, I am in no position to forbid the couple from being romantically involved." Singh defended his closest friends, Abhu and Durga's relationship.

"I hope you're correct in that regard. However, I am not convinced that the couple will react appropriately to the device scan results. I fear what damage may occur to both Abhu and Durga's emotional wellbeing. In such a case, I am modifying the order to limit the results to only you and your adoptive father. You are forbidden from revealing the results of the dreamscape to the dating agents until Khali or I say so," Ikshan commanded.

"Ikshan, they're my closest friends. I would feel terrible if I were to withhold such results from them if it were to ease their minds," Singh rebutted.

"Dreams don't always come to fruition. Now, I am issuing you a direct order. Obey me," Ikshan warned.

Singh was internally upset, but he managed to keep his emotions checked for the mission's good.

"Fine, I won't tell them, and I hope both of them would not hold it against me for going against their wishes," Singh relented remorsefully.

"I'm sure they will understand. You cannot let them jeopardize the mission, the agency, or the world, for that matter. We cannot afford to have them compromise everything, not when there is too much at stake. But I will level with you on this: If and when the mission is successful, you can let them see the scan report," Ikshan stipulated.

"Okay, I can work with that," Singh said.

"Good, the device scan order will be approved. You are dismissed for conducting the scan after we've paged both agents to the exam room. The conditions of the order are in full effect, so take care to follow my commands," Ikshan concluded.

"I understand," Singh spoke solemnly before leaving his TAC Team under Ikshan's supervision.

***

Abhu and Durga were joined by the rest of Abhu's team of Chand, Vasu, Daarun, and Garjan as they assisted the Polish-Indian Tech Agents within the Warsaw EJFS Logistical Command Center.

All the tech agents and analysts spoke in Polish and English. They continued to monitor the Shadow State's worldwide developments and the mega-hurricane advancing toward the US East Coast.

At the same time, it rapidly strengthened into a monstrous and cataclysmic storm, expanding to the size of the entire span of the whole US mainland.

Abhu's team appeared horrified by the progress of the superstorm's movement and strength. The wind speeds on offshore buoys registered over 275 mph with gusts higher than 300 mph.

Abhu conferred with the lead tech analyst, Agent Kashi, for a status update on the hurricane's advancement and Europe's happenings.

"Agent Kashi, what is the status of the hurricane threatening the US mainland?" Abhu inquired.

"The hurricane has grown in size and power. It roughly measures as a Category Five hurricane, far exceeding the allotted wind speeds of the Sampson-Saffir scale of severity. This storm is not showing any signs of weakening or slowing. The hurricane's trajectory would directly impact the Florida coastline, advancing northward and up the Eastern Seaboard. The expected loss of life is astronomical at this rate," Kashi explained, sighing heavily at the grave potential of the loss of life projection displayed on the large screens.

The storm's depth and size were emulated in high-resolution and three-dimensional graphical formats displayed on the screens, with the strength of the wind velocity shown next to the vastly substantial rainfall rates that would inundate a large portion of the eastern seaboard.

"This is going to be the worst hurricane in modern history," Agent Garjan spoke grimly.

"No kidding," Agent Daarun added.

"Is there any way that we could mitigate this storm at this point?" Durga asked.

Kashi shook his head, "No, unfortunately, we're well past the point of no return. The only strategy that could be tangible would be for all local EJFS agents to form a wall boundary along the East Coast and try to blow the storm in a different direction. The best-case scenario would be for the storm to change direction and curve northeast, taking a path back into the Atlantic Ocean, which would spare the US. But therein lies another problem..."

Kashi loaded another simulated trajectory outcome on the big screens showing the storm taking a sharp curve eastward and impacting Western Europe.

"This is what could potentially happen to Europe if the storm is blown off the forecasted trajectory path. The storm could retain its power and size, demolishing the entire European continent within hours upon landfall," Kashi explained with great concern in his voice.

"It's a lose-lose situation for both outcomes," Chand spoke hauntingly.

"It gets even worse: If Vritra's remnants were to reconstitute within this hurricane, the world might be lost," Kashi explained further.

"Is there any possible strategy that we could use to spare any mass destruction and death?" Vasu asked, trying to find any glimmer of hope.

Kashi momentarily paused before he came up with a theory.

"There's a small probability that if the storm enters a cooler part of the ocean, the storm may fall apart. Thus, both continents and the world may escape an impending demise," Kashi theorized.

"How could we facilitate that outcome?" Abhu asked.

"Perhaps an arctic blast from the north would cause the storm to implode on itself. But the odds of that happening are less than 20 percent," Kashi suggested.

"Then maybe we can increase those odds by our agents performing arctic wind breath along the Eastern Seaboard," Chand interjected.

"That could be a possible solution, but the probability of success would only increase to 40 percent," Kashi warned.

"Forty percent is better than zero. We'll take those odds," Durga spoke encouragingly.

"We should inform Khali to mobilize all local EJFS agents on the surface to deploy to the coast. Then, the strategy may be implemented successfully," Abhu insisted.

"I will contact Khali right away!" Kashi exclaimed.

Suddenly, Abhu's and Durga's smartphones vibrated with a notification sound resembling an Indian musical instrument. Singh's text message informing them that their scan order request had been approved with Ikshan's conditions in place, and they were ordered to report to the first-floor exam room in the administrative offices.

"Durga, did you get this too?" Abhu asked, his brow arched in surprise.

"Yeah, I got it. I don't understand why this condition is being enforced. It must have been modified at the last minute," Durga suggested.

"Whatever it is, I hope Singh can explain it." Abhu turned to address his team.

"Chand: Durga and I need to report to the admin department. You are in charge until we return. Call me if you need me," Abhu ordered.

"Understood, Abhu Sir!" Chand replied.

Abhu addressed Durga, "We need to go downstairs now. Let us go!"

Abhu and Durga left the command center and took an elevator to the main building's first floor.

Singh was waiting in the foyer of the lobby to greet the couple.

Abhu appeared displeased with Singh after learning of the conditions he accepted as set forth by Director Ikshan.

"Singh, I hope you can explain this modification," Abhu asked with great dissatisfaction in his tone of voice.

"I can, but I need you both to come with me now," Singh directed.

Abhu and Durga accompanied Singh to the administrative offices' exam room on the department's second floor.

***

Early in the morning, at the White House Bunker in Washington D.C., President Hill woke up from a rough night with little sleep. He had tossed and turned all night long with a bout of fear-induced insomnia.

Barnes knocked on the door, requesting the President's attention.

"Mr. President, you have an international video call with the Russian Prime Minister, Grigory Rostislav, in the boardroom," Barnes spoke with utmost urgency.

"Give me ten minutes! I had a rough night," Hill barked in an irritable tone.

President Hill quickly dressed up in his suit, then left his quarters to join Barnes in the boardroom.

"Status update, now!" Hill dictated angrily.

"The Russian Prime Minister is calling you after one of their asylum seekers went missing in the dead of the night in Budapest," Barnes began.

"Budapest?" Hill craned his neck in response while he blew his nose in some rough tissue.

"The Russian Embassy, to be exact. The CIRB had delivered a woman named Anastasia Zima to the embassy late last night seeking asylum. She has since been abducted in a tornado and has been reported missing," Barnes continued grimly.

President Hill's face soured, and he furiously slammed his wadded tissue into a garbage can.

"I already know who is responsible," Hill spoke angrily.

"So do the Russians. They're not happy about it either. Let me get a hold of the Russian Interior Ministry," Barnes insisted.

Barnes brought Hill to the boardroom facing the video screen. Barnes's video device contacted the Russian PM Grigory Rostislav on the underground VOIP calling system.

Prime Minister Rostislav answered the video call and spoke with overtones of frustration with their American ally.

Barnes introduced the President to the Russian PM.

"Prime Minister Rostislav, you're on a video call with President Hill," Barnes spoke nervously.

Prime Minister Rostislav began with harsh words toward Hill.

"Mr. Hill, please pardon my hubris, but your country is in deep trouble with us. One of our nationals has gone missing during the night at our embassy in Budapest. Anastasia Zima, a comrade of ours, has disappeared. I think we all know which entity abducted her," Rostislav admonished.

"Mr. Prime Minister, we know the EJFS has a global influence, and therefore, we cannot make any promises that we can get her back. If my instincts serve me right, she may already be compromised. However, we will notify CIRB assets in the area to treat all EJFS entity personnel as enemy combatants. There will be a massive search to find Anastasia," Hill assured him.

"Mr. President, this mess will not be forgiven if you fail in finding Anastasia. She is a vital asset for the Kremlin, and if you do not fix this mess, our partnership will be over. Our nations will be at war. I hope you understand the grave consequences that your country has brought upon itself due to your lack of competence," Rostislav threatened.

President Hill was flabbergasted.

"Mr. Hill, we do not want to hear from you until Anastasia has been returned safe and sound. I hope I have made myself quite clear," Rostislav continued his harsh rhetoric.

"Prime Minister, we'll do all that we can. But please understand that we are already under an existential threat of the massive hurricane bearing down on our country." Hill became defensive.

"You have been warned, Mr. President. You have until midnight tonight, East Coast time, to produce, or there will be swift and steep punishment upon your country. Goodbye, Mr. President!" Rostislav disconnected the video call with impudence.

The video call ended abruptly. President Hill was sweating bullets, fearing that he may have bitten off more than he could swallow.

"What are you going to do about this, Mr. President?" Barnes spoke solemnly with a horrified look on his face.

"Give me the room, please. I need some privacy," Hill directed sharply.

"Very well," Barnes left President Hill alone in the boardroom.

President Hill calmly retrieved his scrambled smartphone and dialed an international number registered in a Belgium code.

***

Meanwhile, at Rumbeke Castle in West Flanders, Belgium, Francois Tomas Richer, also known as "Black Sparrow Zero," answered his scrambled smartphone. He recognized the call was from a Washington D.C. area code.

"Black Sparrow Zero," Richer's haunting voice sounded on the receiver.

"Shadow Eagle One," President Hill introduced himself with his Shadow State moniker.

"Mr. President, what can I do for you?" Richer asked.

"I need your help. Rostislav knows Anastasia was captured by the EJFS in Budapest last night. He threatens to go to war with the US if I do not rescue Anastasia from the EJFS by midnight. I need you to get him off my back, and I need you to help me find Anastasia while you buy us some time," Hill pleaded desperately.

"Relax, Mr. President, I will have this situation handled personally. You need not worry. I will send two of my agents to break her out before the deadline. Do not forget: This is all part of the master plan. You will get results, bank on it!" Richer exclaimed.

"Keep it down. The EJFS could tap this line. I have to go. Please don't disappoint me." Hill ended the call.

Richer shook his head in dismay before setting his phone down. He paged for Blaze and Thunder to enter his quarters.

"Shadow Stingray and Shadow Phoenix, please report to Black Sparrow's office, now!"

Both Shadow State operatives got out of their beds, dressed up in their overnight clothes, and headed to Black Sparrow's office.

Thunder spoke tiredly, "What's going on, Boss?"

Black Sparrow spoke with a distinct frown on his face.

"Both of you: pack up your gear and take one of my paramilitary aircraft machines to find Anastasia. She is being held captive: Her tracking signals have been parsed. She is somewhere in Warsaw. Find her and bring her to me," Black Sparrow commanded.

"Yes, Sir!" Thunder replied obediently.

Blaze led Thunder to the aircraft yard in the back of the castle, and she began the takeoff procedure after the pair boarded the paramilitary aircraft.

"You know how to fly this thing?" Thunder asked.

"Hey, they don't call me Shadow Phoenix for nothing," Blaze quipped.

25: Abhu's and Durga's Dual Device Scan: Zima Interrogated

Exam Room One

Cathedral Main Building – Level Two

EJFS – Warsaw Branch – Eastern European Division

November 3, 2024

8:23 AM Warsaw Time, Sunday Morning

Abhu and Durga joined Singh in the Warsaw EJFS Thunderhead Base Exam Room on the second level.

Abhu was rather displeased with Singh after learning that the Dual Device Scan order was modified to withhold the results from being viewed by both him and Durga.

Singh decided to explain the reasoning for the device scan order's stipulation to both Abhu and Durga.

"I know that you two are not happy about this modification that Ikshan enforced, but he is worried about the emotional impact the results would have once the scan results return. Please know that I am in no position to question Ikshan's or Khali's judgment. However, I was reassured by Ikshan that you might view the results after the mission is successful," Singh explained.

"Singh, if you felt that my emotional state would be an issue, then why didn't you consider this beforehand? You know my relationship with Durga wouldn't pose a conflict of interest as long as I wouldn't compromise the mission over my girlfriend," Abhu argued.

"I understand that, and I tried to explain it to Ikshan, but he wasn't having any of it. We can only go along with the stipulations and view the results after completing the mission. Please understand that this is a challenging position that I have been put in, and I do not relish it for anything. Now, we do not have time for this bickering. Are you going to accept the order or not?" Singh asked calmly.

"Fine, I accept. But, for the record, I am not happy about this change of plans," Abhu relented.

"Duly noted," Singh replied, then addressed Durga. "Durga, do you agree to the stipulations that Ikshan enforced?"

Durga felt conflicted inside upon seeing her close friends Abhu and Singh argue.

"I suppose so. I am sorry that this has put you in such a tough position, Singh. But I am grateful that at least you are the only one that has exclusive access to our scans," Durga said, then addressed her love interest, Abhu.

"Abhu, you know I love you very much, and I don't want this to stifle our relationship, your friendship with Singh, our careers, or the mission to stop this cataclysm for that matter. We can worry about the scan results later," Durga spoke lamentably.

Abhu and Durga took their positions in the exam chairs, sitting alongside each other. Abhu and Durga held hands as they prepared to undergo the procedure.

"I love you, Durga," Abhu proclaimed softly.

"I love you, too, Abhu," Durga expressed warmly.

Singh initiated the device scan to commence.

"All right, you two. I'm starting the scan now, so sit tight." Singh informed the couple as they continued holding hands while the halo-shaped headgear lowered past their heads in both exam chairs.

The scanning equipment began its loading sequence while both Abhu and Durga rested in their seats.

Singh evaluated both scans on two separate screens. The images became more evident during the set timeframe in which both Abhu and Durga were asleep the previous night.

The images appeared on a split-screen, indicating both dreams that Abhu and Durga experienced individually.

Both scans started identical to each other. The setting was on a beach in Savannah, Georgia, where a wedding ceremony occurred, as Abhu and Durga mentioned. Both were the couple to be wed together.

The dream sequence continued as Singh continued to evaluate the scans.

Singh viewed his father, Master Khali, officiating the wedding ceremony on the screen. He saw himself as Abhu's best man, along with members of both bride and groom's families, who were in attendance.

Soon after, in both dreamscapes, the mood started to change to become more ominous as four hooded individuals gathered on the boardwalk in both dreams. Khali's voice became distorted to match Ravan's tone. Soon after, the wedding scene disappeared in a highly stormy scenario, with only Abhu lingering in the dream with the hooded individuals approaching him.

Immediately, one of the figures uncloaked herself revealing Anastasia Zima. She unclasped the necklace of Vritra and hoisted it in the air, causing the amulet to burst into a red plume of ash to spew into the skies. At the same time, the clouds in the hurricane became red.

Then, the scan ended, Singh was visibly shaken after watching the dream play out on the screen.

After the scan completed its cycle, Singh generated a report from the scan and attached the visual imagery in an email to both Khali and Ikshan. He then printed both Abhu's and Durga's results to view later after the action settled down.

Singh sealed the report and images for Abhu and Durga in an envelope. He then stamped it with a "TOP SECRET MATERIAL" and "CONFIDENTIAL" imprint on the file with no specified date to be viewed by both participants.

After the scan results were analyzed, Abhu and Durga quietly exited the exam room with unspoken tension between Abhu and Singh as both leaders returned to their posts.

***

Later, Singh returned to the observation room attached to the Interrogation Room, where Zima was hooked up to vital-reading sensors.

Zima was shackled and chained to her seat. Her bound wrists rested upon the steel table in front of her.

Director Ikshan and Agent Marut were waiting with Singh's team's remaining members before Zima's enhanced interrogation would commence.

"Anastasia's vitals and readings are steady. She's ready for interrogation," Agent Marut indicated.

"Very well. Singh and I will conduct the interrogation," Director Ikshan insisted.

Ikshan and Singh entered the interrogation room where Zima sat waiting. Her face was hardened like stone. She glared at Singh when she recognized his face during the motorcycle chase in New York the previous day.

Ikshan led the interrogation to start. "Good morning, Anastasia. My name is Ikshan Choudhuri, and I know that you recognize this exceptional agent who worked to apprehend you. Our network has been searching for you for months. I'm glad that our associate agents based in Atlanta have located and arrested you."

Zima remained silent and motionless as she continually glared at both Singh and Ikshan.

Ikshan continued. "Now, this can go one of two ways: One would be that you tell us where Vritra's necklace is located, and you'll be given full diplomatic immunity for your share in the Shadow State's criminal activities. Or the second method would be much less pleasant for you and would test your pain threshold to the maximum, and you risk losing your diplomatic immunity. Thus, our agency cannot protect you from reprisal."

Zima remained non-verbal and despondent during Ikshan's introduction.

Singh picked up on Zima's veiled resistance and decided to speak up.

"Anastasia, I know you remember me from over a year ago. You evaded capture yesterday at Gyan's residence in New York. Gyan was subsequently captured after you fled the scene, and I have received word that he was vaporized last night after trying to break out of his imprisonment. If you are holding out because of Gyan, he is gone. Thus, there is no real reason to resist us. Now, tell us where the necklace is, and we will protect you from all legal recourse," Singh demanded.

Zima hissed angrily. "You can't protect me from them, and you won't be able to find the necklace in time. My allegiance is, has been, and always will be with Vritra. His return is inevitable, no matter how hard you deny him. His rulership will take hold of this world."

Ikshan and Singh exchanged glances.

Singh continued to work on breaking down Zima.

"Anastasia, trust me when I say that I do not wish to perform enhanced interrogation on you. We feel that your alignment with the Shadow State is misplaced, and you have been brainwashed into doing their bidding all along. If you cooperate with us, I will make sure they cannot touch you," Singh explained.

Zima felt conflicted inside as she felt the tugging of Vritra and Ravan trying to keep her from conceding to the EJFS.

Singh continued to coax Zima into giving up to free her from her misplaced alliance with the Shadow State.

"I can sense that there is something that is bothering you inside. You are fighting not only against us but against yourself. Vritra must have taken your spirit hostage. Do not let him consume you entirely. Stop fighting us and instead work with us," Singh offered.

Unexpectedly, Zima growled loudly like Vritra, startling both Singh and Ikshan as they took a step back.

Singh's team, viewing from the other side of the two-way mirror, was frightened by Zima's reaction to Singh's interrogative style.

Zima struggled with herself as Vritra took over her spirit.

Without hesitation, Singh retrieved his memory-resetting device to obliterate Zima's memory, and in the same act, wiped out the memory of her allegiance to Vritra.

Zima returned to her normal self and was seemingly lost and oblivious to what incredible action had just transpired.

"Where am I?" Zima asked.

"It seems that you were under Vritra's control during an extended time. You're in the EJFS Thunderhead Base in Warsaw, Poland," Singh explained as Zima experienced some minor amnesia.

"Poland? But how did I end up here?" Zima asked.

"We've captured and arrested you from the Russian Embassy in Budapest. You were staying there after fleeing from the EJFS in New York City. Does any of this sound familiar to you?" Singh crouched down and tried to help Zima's true self return.

"I vaguely remember something like that. Everything has been a blur for the past year," Zima emotionally responded.

"It's okay now. But you did many bad things, and the only thing we can do now is grant you immunity from your crimes. In return, we need you to tell us where the necklace of Vritra is located," Singh comforted Zima.

Zima stuttered and started to cry.

"I-I don't know," Zima wept.

Singh felt remorseful for Zima.

"Anastasia, we need to find that necklace and destroy it. If it is in the wrong hands, the world will continue to be in peril," Singh pleaded.

"I told you, I don't know! If I knew, I would have told you!" Zima shouted emotionally.

Singh looked into Zima's eyes as they were covered in tears amid her hopeless confusion and displacement.

"I believe you, but we don't have time to beat around the bush. We need you to recover from your memory loss," Singh rationalized.

"How are you going to do that?" Zima asked.

"We need to scan and recover your memory. Come with me," Singh insisted.

***

Meanwhile, Shadow State agents Midnight Thunder and Alicia Blaze seemed to have located Zima's tracking signal that Black Sparrow Zero parsed earlier.

Blaze spoke as she piloted their aircraft toward the signal originating from inside the Warsaw EJFS Thunderhead Base.

"I bet you anything that Anastasia is in that structure in the sky," Blaze suggested.

"I'm willing to take a gamble." Thunder accepted the wager.

The signal corresponding to Zima's tracking device became even more energetic, and the system in the paramilitary aircraft confirmed her presence.

"We got her! She's up ahead in that sky cathedral!" Blaze affirmed.

"Attack them! Fire at will!" Thunder ordered.

"Hang on tight. We're going in heavy!" Blaze warned.

***

While the visiting TAC Teams led by Agents Abhu and Singh were running the operation to help Zima regain her memory, suddenly, the base was hit by rocket fire from the paramilitary jet piloted by Blaze and Thunder.

Singh was with Zima while the base took a hit from the attackers.

"What's happening?!" Zima shouted while agents and specialists rushed to defend the Thunderhead Base.

"We're under attack. We need to keep you safe. Come with me quickly!" Singh tapped his badge on the reader device as Zima followed Singh out of the interrogation room.

Abhu and his team observed the base's attacks while the paramilitary jet fired rockets and lasers toward the EJFS Warsaw Base.

"All Agents, operate your stations for a battle defense! Go!" Director Ikshan announced on the system PA.

The entire base was in a frenzy of activity as the Thunderhead Base was under ongoing attack at the hands of Shadow State agents Blaze and Thunder.

***

At the Atlanta-based EJFS Thunderhead Base stationed in Montreal, Quebec, Canada, Khali received an emergency bulletin message from the EJFS Warsaw Branch.

EMERGENCY FLASH BULLETIN ISSUED BY EJFS WARSAW BRANCH:

S.O.S. WARSAW BRANCH REQUESTING IMMEDIATE REINFORCEMENTS TO BASE! WE ARE UNDER ATTACK BY TWO UNKNOWN ASSAILANTS. MAYDAY! MAYDAY!

Khali ordered all local European EJFS Branches to come to the aid of the Warsaw Branch under siege.

26: Warsaw EJFS Under Attack: Tragedy Strikes the EJFS

Command Center

Cathedral Main Building – Level 13

EJFS – Warsaw Branch – Eastern European Division

November 3, 2024

8:58 AM Warsaw Time, Sunday Morning

As agency personnel of the Warsaw EJFS Branch scrambled to defend their base, Shadow State agents Alicia Blaze and Midnight Thunder continued their aerial assault of the station in their plot to recapture Zima before she could defect from the Shadow State.

All the Atlanta-based EJFS agents led by Abhu and Singh raced up the emergency stairwell to the Warsaw EJFS Station command center to assist in the defensive strike.

Zima joined the group of EJFS superagents trying to protect their stronghold.

EJFS agents operated their battle stations, firing their turrets containing mounted heavy-artillery machine guns and laser guns.

Singh asked. "Anastasia, who are those attackers, and why are they attacking us?"

Zima watched closely at the visual footage of the paramilitary aircraft operated by Alicia Blaze with Midnight Thunder at the rear.

Zima explained urgently. "That's Alicia Blaze. But I don't recall seeing that brute riding behind her."

Kashi interjected. "Let me enhance the image."

The image of the Shadow State Agent, Midnight Thunder, was enhanced for clarity.

Zima's jaw dropped as she recognized the individual riding behind the pilot.

"My God, that's Judson Clayborn! He completed his transformation into a superagent and assassin!" Zima added.

Abhu grew incensed at Zima, knowing that she was responsible for the development of the newest Shadow State agent.

"That's Clayborn?! How did he get so big?" Abhu shouted deeply.

"Abhu, calm down," Singh commanded.

"Singh, whatever happens due to Clayborn's transformation, is her fault, and she knows it!" Abhu argued angrily.

Durga, Abhu's girlfriend, calmed Abhu, and he kept his emotions contained.

"Abhu, my dear, stop making her feel bad," Durga spoke calmly.

Zima felt her ears burning.

"He's right. This was my doing. I helped make this man into a monster," Zima spoke lamentably.

"Anastasia, we'll get through this together, okay?" Singh assured.

Suddenly, a powerful jolt struck the command center, and all the agents and analysts fell to the floor.

"What happened now?!" Abhu shouted.

"Their jet struck the cathedral building! We've been breached!" Kashi exclaimed.

The entire Warsaw EJFS klaxon blared overhead as the PA system sounded.

WARNING: STRUCTURAL INTEGRITY FAILURE REPORTED! EVACUATE ALL PERSONNEL IMMEDIATELY! STRUCTURAL COLLAPSE WILL OCCUR IN TEN MINUTES!

"We have to get out of here, now!" Agent Singh exclaimed.

"Everyone evacuate at once! The base is going down!" Kashi warned.

All the EJFS agents began emergency evacuation protocol, and everyone rushed to the escape pods in all the edges of the interior hallways.

"To the MICVs!" Abhu directed.

All TAC Team agents from the Atlanta Branch made their way to the bottom level, where the two MICVs were refueling.

Unbeknownst to the entire base full of superagents, Alicia Blaze and Midnight Thunder intruded upon the station. They exited the paramilitary jet with their handguns in a frenzy of activity.

Blaze and Thunder rushed up the stairs to locate Zima through the parsed tracking signal on Zima's body.

"She's here. Cover my flank," Blaze commanded.

Thunder went out ahead of Blaze as they rushed up the stairwell amid the base's structural collapse.

"Intruder!" An EJFS agent exclaimed.

Blaze raised her handgun, shooting and killing the warning agent.

After nearby EJFS agents heard the gunshot, other agents swarmed to eliminate the intruders.

Agents Abhu and Singh's TAC Team overheard the commotion as they raced down the stairwell. A gunfight ensued between the intruding duo and the other EJFS agents.

The PA system buzzed on again.

WARNING: STRUCTURAL COLLAPSE WILL OCCUR IN NINE MINUTES!

Agents Abhu and Singh led their teams down the stairwell as the structure continued to fall apart.

"Keep moving!" Agent Singh directed.

The TAC teams took a detour through the fourth-level quadrant of the cathedral building.

Blaze and Thunder maintained the pursuit of Zima, with the TAC Team protecting her.

The corridors and hallways were slowly collapsing while the gunfight continued.

Abhu and Singh led their teams down the alternate stairwell, passing by the remaining few fleeing EJFS agents heading toward the escape pods.

The TAC teams arrived at the MICVs docked at the Warsaw Thunderhead Base's bottom at the deployment bay.

WARNING: STRUCTURAL COLLAPSE WILL OCCUR IN EIGHT MINUTES!

Suddenly, a substantial chunk of the ceiling collapsed on top of Naveen, pinning him to the floor in excruciating pain.

"Naveen! Oh, no!" Singh exclaimed and rushed to his side.

"Guys, help me lift this debris off of Naveen!" Abhu cried out.

Abhu, Singh, Chand, Nitin, and Vasu successfully lifted the fallen debris from Naveen as he suffered life-threatening injuries resulting from the fall.

"Naveen, I'm so sorry!" Singh wept, watching a longtime friend suffering a devastating impact.

Naveen began to cough up blood as he struggled to speak.

"Singh, you must go on without me," Naveen spoke weakly.

"No, please!" Singh pleaded while in tears.

"You need to be strong for the superagency. The intruding assailants are coming. You must go!" Naveen warned while straining to speak.

Suddenly, Alicia Blaze and Midnight Thunder arrived on the scene.

"EJFS agents, you're not getting away!" Blaze shouted.

"Give us Anastasia, and this will end smoothly. Do it now!" Thunder demanded.

"No!" Zima resisted.

"We're not surrendering Anastasia to you!" Abhu shouted.

"Anastasia belongs to us. Release her!" Blaze dictated.

"That's not going to happen!" Singh insisted.

"Anastasia, you brought me to the Shadow State. I won't let you walk away from us!" Thunder growled.

"Anastasia, don't listen to him!" Abhu warned.

"You keep quiet, or you will get a bullet in your face!" Thunder threatened.

WARNING: STRUCTURAL COLLAPSE WILL OCCUR IN SEVEN MINUTES!

"Time is running out, people. Give Anastasia to us, and you will live to fight another day," Blaze spoke sternly.

"Forget it. We're leaving!" Abhu stated.

"Wait!" Zima shouted.

Everyone froze as the structure continued to shake and collapse.

"I will go with you. Just don't hurt anyone else," Zima conceded.

"Anastasia, don't do this!" Singh protested.

"I remember him, and I'm not on their side anymore. You must trust me on this. My tracking code is Alpha Hotel Zulu 293205. You know what you have to do," Zima whispered to Singh as she hugged him.

WARNING: STRUCTURAL COLLAPSE WILL OCCUR IN SIX MINUTES!

Singh looked at Zima's eyes intently.

"If that is your desired approach, then so be it. We will come back and rescue you, regardless of what happens." Singh assured Zima.

Zima glanced at Singh before walking away.

"I will hold you to that promise," Zima vowed.

Thunder spoke. "Enough of the games. Let her go!"

Zima looked at Thunder heatedly before approaching the duo.

"I'm coming...Judson Clayborn," Zima spoke with hostility.

"Clayborn is dead! My name is Midnight Thunder! Accept it!"

Zima joined Blaze and Thunder reluctantly. Both seized Zima and kept her restrained.

"If you or any of your partner agents follow us, she dies!" Thunder warned.

Both Blaze and Thunder dragged Zima down the hall to the paramilitary jet that plowed into the structure earlier.

"We have to go now!" Singh commanded.

Abhu experienced tremendous grief and sorrow as both TAC Teams loaded onto the MICVs and prepared to launch as the final five minutes approached before the structural integrity would give away.

All EJFS TAC Team agents boarded the MICVs as Naveen soon coughed up more blood and perished.

Both MICVs prepared the launch process and took off, speeding away from the crumbling EJFS Branch in Warsaw.

Blaze and Thunder forcefully escorted Zima to the paramilitary jet, boarded, and flew out of the breached hull, fleeing to the Rumbeke Castle.

All the EJFS agents solemnly watched as their Warsaw Base eventually imploded and crashed to the surface of the earth over the city of Warsaw.

Much shock and awe were apparent on the local bystanders watching the base crash to the ground.

***

Meanwhile, at the Rumbeke Castle, Richer contemplated his next move in neutralizing the EJFS after watching the morning news in Belgium of the fallen Warsaw EJFS base crashing to the ground.

Polish citizens were perplexed as to how the incident occurred.

Augustus, the castle butler, entered Richer's executive office on the top floor as Richer monitored the local news and tracking Shadow State agents Blaze and Thunder's return flight path.

"Richer, the aftermath of the base crash has arrived. The visiting Atlanta-based tactical team has fled the scene. There was at least one casualty," Augustus explained.

"Who was the casualty?" Richer inquired.

"It was an EJFS agent. The identity has yet to be released. But it appears that whoever it was, suffered blunt force trauma to the head and died of internal bleeding," Augustus explained.

Richer cracked a slightly wicked smile before regaining his composure.

"Is that all, Augustus?" Richer asked.

"Anastasia is on board the jet with Blaze and Thunder as you ordered. They are on their way back now," Augustus informed him.

"Very good, direct them inside when they return. When Anastasia returns, put her in the cellar, and do not let her out of the guards' sight," Richer ordered.

"Yes, my lord. I will keep you apprised of the latest developments." Augustus exited the large room and returned to the main floor of the castle.

Richer dialed Russian Prime Minister Grigory Rostislav's direct phone number to quell any concerns about Hill's role as POTUS.

At the Kremlin in Moscow, Rostislav answered the call on his smartphone.

"Shadow Bear Three," Rostislav answered in Russian.

"Rostislav, it's Richer. I have heard reports that you threaten to attack the United States after the abduction of one of your nationals. Miss Anastasia Zima will be returned to you in due time, but she may have been compromised. I am ordering my men to have her sequestered at my castle for the time being. Now, I insist that you restrain yourself from engaging in military conflict with the US," Richer demanded.

"Lord Richer, please forgive me if I sound doubtful, but what makes you so sure that she can be salvageable after being in EJFS custody?" Rostislav countered.

"If she cannot be salvaged, then we'll send her back on a one-way trip to Moscow and let you handle her. She's already a wanted international fugitive in Russia. I could easily dump data on her past, and the Interpol would have a field day tracking her down," Richer continued.

"I see. Very well, I'll hold off from any military action against the US at your behest. However, I need you to bring Anastasia back to the fold quickly. If not, then you know what must be done. I'll let you make the call," Rostislav responded.

"We'll be in touch," Richer concluded before ending the call.

Richer continued to monitor the developments out of Warsaw as he pressed his stubby little fingers against each other while smiling wickedly.

***

On the East Coast of the US, after 3:14 AM in Washington, D.C., President Hill received a briefing report about the developing events out of Warsaw, Poland.

As acting Chief of Staff, Barnes led the meeting to commence as the Joint Chiefs assembled before President Hill in the White House Bunker's Situation Room.

"Mr. President, we have received word from our friends in Poland that one of the EJFS bases stationed in Warsaw fell out of the sky and crashed to the surface. It is believed that a team of superagents, originating from Atlanta, were on board the hovering structure before the crash occurred," Barnes explained.

"Were there any casualties?" Hill asked.

Secretary of Defense, Frank Clements, added. "Only one known casualty, an EJFS agent yet to be identified. We are reviewing and monitoring the incident closely, Mr. President."

"What about Anastasia?" Hill inquired.

"As far as we know, she was on board the floating structure at the time of the collapse. But we have received intel reports that she escaped with two individuals. The duo responsible for destroying the EJFS base over Warsaw is currently en route to Brussels," Clements continued.

CIRB Deputy Director, James Matthews, was on a teleconference call during the meeting.

"Mr. President, I strongly insist that we let this situation play out without interference. These two individuals responsible for rescuing Anastasia were acting under my authority," Matthews spoke over the phone from his secure bunker bedroom.

"Mr. Matthews, are you suggesting that this situation does not warrant any further action on our side?" Clements asked.

"That is precisely what I am saying. These two agents were following orders, and they will soon return to the states in the next day or so. I insist that you let me handle this personally," Matthews urged.

"Very well, but you need to straighten out the situation with your superior, Janice Ausburn, and make sure she is aware of what operation you're running," Clements warned.

"Yes, Mr. Secretary, I understand," Matthews concluded.

"That will be all from you." Clements disconnected the speakerphone.

"Mr. Hill, how do you want to proceed?" Barnes asked.

"Let it play. I do not need any more additional headaches this morning," Hill decided.

Clements furrowed his brow in serious doubt of Hill's abilities to manage the situation.

"If there's nothing left to discuss, this meeting is adjourned," Hill concluded.

Clements began to question Hill's mental capacity to continue serving as the President of the United States.

However, Clements decided to continue his support of Hill, albeit hesitantly, knowing that two cabinet members had vacated their role or were terminated.

***

Later in the morning, at the Rumbeke Castle in Belgium, Shadow State agents: Blaze and Thunder touched down their damaged paramilitary jet loaned by Richer.

One of the agents on site observed the damage from the attack in Warsaw.

"Wow, you scratched Richer's best machine. He's going to chew you out for that," Agent Goff warned.

"Oh, what a tragedy," Thunder retorted as he escorted Zima off the jet.

"*Smartass...,*" Goff muttered under his breath.

"If you don't mind, I'll be taking our prize to Richer," Thunder added as he had the wrists of Zima bound and tied up with rope.

"Actually, he issued orders to have her brought down to the cellar," Goff countered.

"Fine, you take her there," Thunder continued to be ornery.

Goff was not amused, but he decided not to spar with Thunder knowing his size outmatched him.

Zima was taken to the cellar and was kept in indefinite confinement per Richer's orders.

***

Meanwhile, the fallen Warsaw EJFS Branch members emigrated to different European bases to join other agencies amid the tragedy in Warsaw's skies.

On the MICV operated by Atlanta-based superagents Nitin and Chand, they had no time to mourn the loss of fallen Agent Naveen Brahma Kamboja, a veteran agent who helped in the first operation against Final Wave during the previous year.

Agent Singh composed a casualty report for fallen Agent Naveen with severe emotional difficulty as he was killed in action. At the same time, they escaped from the Warsaw EJFS base that had since plunged to the surface.

Singh regrettably sent the casualty report to Master Khali's email for review while Singh wiped a few tears from his eyes.

Abhu stepped beside Singh and gave him a tender embrace.

"I'm so sorry, brother," Abhu consoled Singh.

Singh was rarely emotional in front of others, but he could barely contain his grief over Naveen's loss.

"He was my first partner in the field. He was such a great man," Singh spoke woefully.

Gangi and Durga joined Abhu and Singh's mourning, showing signs of great emotional distress.

"I know it's hard, but we can't afford to grieve right now. We have a vital mission still ahead of us. Naveen was a stellar agent, and I know one day we will reunite with him in Heaven," Gangi comforted her boyfriend, Singh.

"You're right. Naveen would rather see us mourn his death later. There is no time to grieve. We must press onward," Singh replied.

Singh addressed his logistical backup, Garjan.

"Garjan, did you find anything from the signal parsing?" Singh asked.

"Yes, I sourced the tracking codes, and the signal has been traced to the West Flanders region of Brussels, Belgium," Garjan explained.

Abhu interjected. "Anastasia is leading us to Black Sparrow Zero."

Singh let out a weak smile. His hope was not lost.

"Chart a course to the originating signal source location and inform the Brussels Branch to remain on high alert," Singh ordered.

The MICVs started advancing toward the Rumbeke Castle with the Brussels EJFS on standby to assist the TAC Teams.

27: CIRB Director Confronts Matthews: Vritra's Necklace Resurfaces

Janice Ausburn's Office

CIRB Headquarters

Langley, Virginia, USA

November 3, 2024

3:37 AM EDT, Sunday Morning

On the United States East Coast, CIRB Director Janice Ausburn was in her office suite while fighting off severe jet lag. Ausburn yearned to sleep, but she knew that the US was still in danger from the reckless actions that her subordinate, Matthews, had taken earlier in the night.

Ausburn called Matthews during the three o'clock hour in the early morning to rein him in.

Matthews, who was barely awake in bed in his underground bunker, heard his smartphone ringing. Matthews dreaded providing his superior with an account of his actions during Ausburn's vacation to Ibiza, Spain.

"Hello, Mrs. Ausburn," Matthews began.

"Matthews, we need to talk. I know what you have been up to during my vacation time. You owe me a serious explanation," Ausburn chided sternly.

"I can't talk about this over the phone. We'll have to meet in person," Matthews insisted.

"Matthews, don't jerk me around! I want answers for the operations you've been running!" Ausburn shouted angrily.

"Easy, easy! I'll meet you wherever you want me," Matthews said.

"I hope whatever you have to tell me will impress me. Otherwise, you should consider yourself dishonorably discharged, and you can fully expect to be brought up on conspiracy and treason charges," Ausburn warned.

Matthews paused at the sobering warning from his superior.

"Meet me alone at McLean Central Park at the Eastern Entrance in thirty minutes," Ausburn instructed.

"I'll be there." Matthews ended the call and prepared to leave for the meeting place.

At the CIRB Headquarters, Ausburn slipped into her winter coat and prepared to rendezvous with Matthews.

Hastings and his son, Logan, were still sleeping in a waiting room at the CIRB Headquarters after regular operating hours.

Ausburn snuck out of the office, took a black SUV with shaded windows, and drove off to McLean Central Park with a feeling of uneasiness for both the Hastings being left alone while she was by herself. Ausburn did not know what to expect.

***

Meanwhile, in Brussels, Belgium, the CIRB operatives team led by Agents Bradford, Cortez, and Meyers traveled with the necklace of Vritra toward the West Flanders Region of Brussels, where the Rumbeke Castle was located.

Not knowing that Zima was no longer aligned with the Shadow State, Bradford pulled up his SUV toward the front gates of the long, winding road to the castle. The castle guard approached the vehicle as it stopped at the checkpoint.

"What business do you have here?" The lead guard asked.

"We're from the CIRB. Anastasia told us to come here with the necklace of Vritra," Agent Bradford explained.

"Show me the necklace," The lead guard demanded.

Bradford retrieved the courier case underneath the middle backseat of the SUV and exited with it.

The lead guard approached Bradford to verify the authenticity of Vritra's necklace.

Bradford unlatched the case and revealed the haunting presence of the ancient necklace of Vritra.

"I need to confirm your entry with Black Sparrow before I allow you to pass through the gate. Please wait in your vehicle, and I will clear you through." The lead guard returned to the gate and called Richer on his smartphone.

Sitting at his desk, Richer heard his lead guardsman calling him. He paused before answering the phone.

"Yes?" Richer began.

"Black Sparrow, it's Sebastian. We have visitors from the CIRB. They have the necklace in their possession."

"Let them in, Sebastian," Richer insisted sharply.

"Right away, sir!" Sebastian exclaimed before ending the call.

The lead guardsman waved at Bradford as the front gate was opened.

Bradford turned over the ignition and drove past the opened gate toward the castle, going along the winding road to the front entrance of Rumbeke Castle.

Agent Meyers commented on the spooky architecture of the castle.

"This place looks like a scene out of a horror movie," Meyers remarked.

"You better not be getting the heebie-jeebies, Meyers," Bradford warned.

"No, not at all. It's a castle fit for a man that leads the Shadow State," Meyers retorted.

Bradford merely scoffed at Meyers as they reached the front entrance of Rumbeke Castle.

Augustus, the butler, welcomed the three agents into the castle as the porters carefully transported the courier case containing Vritra's necklace inside the structure.

"Is Anastasia here?" Bradford asked.

"Yes, she is here. But she has been isolated because the EJFS broke her. Thankfully, Agents Midnight Thunder and Alicia Blaze captured her in Warsaw, Poland," Augustus explained.

"Warsaw?" Bradford exclaimed with a puzzled look on his face.

"Indeed, it seems that the EJFS has far-reaching influence in Europe as well. The Warsaw base was destroyed by Thunder and Blaze earlier this morning," Augustus continued.

"Where is Anastasia being kept?" Cortez interjected.

"She's in the cellar. She will be confined there until she can be reinstated as a Shadow State agent. She is choosing not to cooperate with us. We may have to reprogram her mind to be one with us again," Augustus explained further.

"What did the EJFS do to her?" Bradford asked.

"I don't know. Perhaps it would be best to discuss this with Black Sparrow. I insist you follow me inside," Augustus concluded.

The group of CIRB agents joined Augustus and entered the creepy castle.

***

Meanwhile, Zima remained bound and tied up inside the castle cellar, all alone, watched by Richer on the surveillance feed.

Zima sat in her uncomfortable wooden chair, trying to conceive an escape plan to break free from her imprisonment.

Suddenly, Zima felt the pangs of Vritra's presence fill her thoughts in a highly unpleasant way. Vritra's spirit was angry that Zima had broken free from his stranglehold on her mind, thanks in part to EJFS Agent Singh Puneet Sherpa.

Zima felt increasingly troubled by the sensations permeating her mind. However, she remained resilient and resisted the advances of Vritra's angry spirit.

Suddenly, Goff entered the cellar holding a late breakfast meal tray to gesture goodwill to Zima.

"Hey, I know you probably haven't eaten in a long while. Richer wants me to serve you breakfast to keep your strength up." Goff spoke gently, trying to put Zima at ease.

"I don't want anything from Richer or you." Zima scowled.

"Why are you so oppositional? The EJFS must have done a great deal of damage to your mind," Goff implied.

"They opened my eyes, and I'm with them now," Zima spoke defiantly.

"You have been fooled. The EJFS are your enemies. They killed Ravan and dispelled Vritra into a dormant state. Why do you misplace your hope in the EJFS?" Goff asked.

"You can't manipulate me. They are coming to save me and destroy you all in one fell swoop." Zima continued to resist.

Goff's sense of hospitality began to fade away as his act of kindness was rejected. He slammed the tray of food on the table in front of Zima. Goff stormed out of the cellar in frustration.

334

Zima maintained her resiliency and refused to eat, knowing that the food presented to her might be laced with mind-control drugs.

***

Ausburn drove her SUV into the parking lot at McLean Central Park in upstate Virginia to rendezvous with her Deputy Director of the CIRB, James Matthews.

The park was eerily silent and dark. She held her handgun forward with a flashlight in her other hand.

Ausburn maintained her composure as she scanned all her surroundings for signs of Matthews.

"Hello, Janice!" Matthews's voice echoed in the distance.

Matthews appeared before Ausburn as she was slightly startled by his arrival.

"Matthews, why did you insist on meeting like this?" Ausburn lowered her pistol, placing it back inside her holster.

"You know me. I always like a dramatic entrance," Matthews quipped.

"Let us end the theatrics. What kind of operation are you running, and why are you keeping me out of the loop?"

"Janice, this was a pilot program that President Hill had appointed to have me as the point person," Matthews began.

"That doesn't make any sense. Why would Hill appoint you as the head of this operation and not me?" Ausburn queried.

"You don't understand. I was the one who drafted this proposal before Congress earlier this year. Since that time, Hill entrusted me as the point of contact for this operation. But now, our roles are about to change..." Matthews trailed off.

"Matthews, what are you telling me exactly?" Ausburn spoke with a sense of heightened danger.

"Hill has promoted me as the Head Director of the CIRB. Your role in the CIRB has ended, effective immediately," Matthews spoke with a condescending tone.

Ausburn was confounded.

"You are such a snake!" She exclaimed.

"That will be enough from you," Matthews spoke harshly.

Suddenly, Matthews gave a cueing hand gesture, and an incredibly robust Shadow State agent subdued Ausburn with an alcohol wipe, causing her to lose consciousness.

"Onyx, gag her and tie her up to the oak tree," Matthews ordered.

"Yes, sir!" The gruff shadowy operative named Onyx complied.

While out cold, Ausburn was bound, tied, and gagged against an oak tree before Matthews and Onyx fled the scene.

Ausburn was abandoned at the park in the early morning hours just before 4:00 a.m. Eastern Time.

***

At the EJFS Atlanta-based Branch currently hovering over Montreal, Quebec, Canada, Khali received a casualty report documenting veteran EJFS Agent Naveen Brahma Kamboja's death.

Khali felt grieved inside, learning that one of his star agents had been killed in action and that the Warsaw EJFS had been destroyed.

In response to the death of Naveen, Master Khali was forced to implement a plan that he did not relish in the least. He realized that he needed to send a replacement or perhaps some reinforcements to Brussels to assist the TAC teams.

Agents Devdas and Prabodhan were asleep in their quarters when they received an urgent flash message from Khali.

URGENT FLASH MESSAGE FROM THE HEAD OF THE EJFS: Your presence is required with the away TAC teams in Brussels. Please report to my office at 0415 hours for details and mission prep. ~Khali

Khali messaged his adopted son, Agent Singh Puneet Sherpa, offered his condolences to the team, and informed them that backup agents were on the way.

Unread message from Master Khali:

"Dear son,

I extend my profound condolences for the loss of Naveen. He was a terrific agent and an upstanding man. He will be greatly missed. Do not let Naveen's death be in vain. You must remain focused on the mission at hand. Do not lose hope and be resilient.

I am sending you two backup agents, Agents Devdas and Prabodhan, who will be joining you in battle in a short while.

Love you,

~Khali

***

On the MICV piloted by Agents Abhu and Singh's joint TAC team, Singh viewed the message with mixed emotions and a gleam of hope in his eyes.

Agent Chand spoke with encouragement. "Commander Singh, we'll be entering Belgian airspace in less than an hour."

"Full speed ahead!" Agent Singh ordered.

"Yes, sir!" Chand affirmed.

28: Zima and Bradford Face-Off: EJFS TAC Team Attacks Rumbeke Castle

Wine Cellar

Rumbeke Castle

West Flanders Region – Brussels, Belgium

November 3, 2024

10:02 AM Brussels Time, Sunday Morning

Zima continued her resistance against the Shadow State. She remained tied up and bound in the Rumbeke Castle cellar with a tray of food sitting on a wooden table, rapidly becoming cold and stale in Belgium's late autumn months.

Later that morning, CIRB Agents Bradford, Cortez, and Meyers met with the Head of the Shadow State, Francois Richer, to discuss the next steps of bringing Zima back into play.

Augustus, the castle butler, served breakfast to the visiting CIRB agents at the grand dining hall inside the Rumbeke Castle.

Richer opened the discussion:

"Gentlemen, I know that Augustus briefed the three of you on Anastasia's rogue state now. I am lost as to what to do with her since the EJFS extremists in Warsaw broke her. We have a mandate to meet, and we can't afford to let Anastasia put a wrinkle in our master plan." Richer spoke solemnly.

"Their agents must have brainwashed her with such persuasion," Cortez suggested.

"That much is obvious," Richer retorted.

Meyers added. "Maybe we need to reprogram her. She seems to have defected."

While experiencing emotions ranging from sorrow to guilt, Bradford decided to offer his opinion to the group meeting.

"I feel terrible. I was the one that let Anastasia slip out of my grasp. We turned her over to Budapest's Russian Embassy, yet she insisted upon the three of us letting her go. She told me that she had a plan, but I have difficulty accepting that this was her plan all along," Bradford spoke lamentably.

"So, you do share some of the blame for this conundrum," Richer replied with a harsh tone.

"I told her that what she was doing wasn't part of the scheme, but she insisted on this change of plans. I see that was clearly a ploy," Bradford added.

"Ploy or not, this defection was your doing. You need to see Anastasia and try to talk some sense into her," Richer admonished Bradford.

"Believe me, I intend to do so," Bradford spoke reassuringly as they ate their late breakfast.

***

Around 10:19 AM, Zima was visited by CIRB agents Bradford, Cortez, and Meyers. They hoped to bring Zima back to center with the Shadow State amid the approaching opportunity to revive Vritra in the superstorm bearing down on the US East Coastline.

Shadow State Agent Goff led the three men to the cellar, where Zima was isolated.

Goff warned the three before they entered.

"She's a resilient one. Don't say I didn't warn you," Goff unlocked the cellar door for the three agents to enter.

Zima, while bound and tied, laid eyes on her former associate, Bradford.

"Anastasia, what happened to you?" Bradford asked.

"I am awakened. That is what happened to me," Zima responded defiantly.

The three agents glanced at each other as Goff looked on with dismay.

"Leave the three of us with her," Bradford spoke to Goff with authority.

"Very well, then," Goff closed the door and stood to watch outside.

Bradford removed his suit coat and only wore his dark polo shirt with a red tie. He never thought that he would ever see the day where he would have to break down Zima, a woman who enticed him at the Russian Embassy in Budapest.

"I'm not going to hurt you," Bradford reassured Zima.

"Oh, that's comforting," Zima remarked with a continued aversion to Bradford's tactics.

"You're not making this easy for any of us, Anastasia," Bradford added with a stern tone of voice.

Bradford pulled up a wooden chair facing backward as he sat toward Zima with a look of concern on his face.

"What is this? Your sad puppy eyes aren't going to fool me." Zima continued to resist.

"Anastasia, you remember the night that I dropped you off at the Russian Embassy in Budapest. You kissed me passionately and sensually. Were you playing me like a patsy, or were the last ten months of our relationship just a fling?" Bradford questioned.

"Last night was the end of us and my affiliation with the Shadow State. That necklace had an incomprehensibly powerful effect on me. It harbored my spirit in a way that was beyond my control," Zima explained with an emotional zeal.

Bradford looked at Zima with a sense of disbelief.

"Is that what was making you sick on the plane to Budapest last night?" Bradford questioned further.

"It must have, but it doesn't matter any longer. The EJFS took me away and freed me from Vritra's grasp, and now I am entirely opposed to the Shadow State and its quest for world domination," Zima continued.

Suddenly, Bradford's phone rang. It was Richer calling him.

Bradford answered dryly. "Yeah?"

Richer spoke on the other end. "Bradford, I listened to everything she said. We can no longer count her as one of us. You know what you must do now. Send Goff back in to finish her." Richer commanded from his executive desk.

"Richer, please give me some more time. It doesn't need to end this way," Bradford pleaded.

Richer was somewhat hesitant to spare more time for Zima. However, he reluctantly relented ever so slightly.

"You have ten minutes. That is all Anastasia has left if you cannot rein her in. If you cannot finish the job, then her time is up." Richer spoke sternly, pressuring Bradford to come through.

"Yes, Boss, I understand," Bradford concluded.

Richer ended the call, and Bradford was forced to take extreme measures towards Zima for her resistance.

"You brought this upon yourself, Anastasia," Bradford sighed heavily as he prepared to begin enhanced interrogation tactics on her.

Zima felt threatened as she quickly formed a plan to stall Bradford further before the EJFS could rescue her.

She noticed a battle-ax on a wall mount that inspired an idea of how to break free from her bondage.

"Give us the room," Bradford commanded.

Agents Cortez and Meyers left the cellar, obeying their leader's orders.

Bradford rolled up his sleeves and regrettably prepared to inflict pain on Zima for her refusal to rejoin the Shadow State.

Bradford retrieved a syringe of pain stimulators from his case.

Once Bradford took away his watchful gaze, Zima took preventive action and thrust her knee into Bradford's groin. Then, Zima ran toward the wall-mounted battle-ax.

Bradford stopped Zima by grabbing her by the hair.

Zima thrust her elbow into Bradford's ribcage and kicked him to the ground with force. She kicked the syringe out of Bradford's reach. Richer noticed the struggle between the two on his surveillance feed.

"Goff, get in there, now!" Richer ordered loudly.

Goff kicked the door open as Zima jumped up to the ax on the wall to tear through the rope bound to her wrists.

Goff rushed to Bradford's aid as he tried to pull Zima down.

Zima tightened her legs around Goff's neck and twisted it, killing him as his eyes crossed.

Zima finally freed herself from the rope once binding her.

Bradford returned to his feet and faced off against Zima in hand-to-hand combat.

Zima readied to defend herself.

Bradford thrust himself toward the syringe. Zima stopped him in his tracks by swinging him into a wooden armoire, causing the glass to shatter into his flesh.

Bradford screamed in pain, and he was momentarily immobilized.

Zima stole one of Bradford's handguns and broke out of the cellar.

CIRB Agents Cortez and Meyers returned to the cellar, but Zima shot them both dead while escaping.

Richer's voice sounded on the castle loudspeaker.

"All Shadow State agents, be on the lookout for Anastasia Zima. She has escaped!" Richer shouted forcefully.

Zima heard footsteps rushing toward her as she tried to elude the Shadow State agents swarming to her location.

The agents spoke in French and English as they fanned out in search of Zima.

A team of Shadow State agents rushed past her as she hid behind a massive crate.

Alicia Blaze led one of the teams to search for Zima.

Zima rushed through the hallways and corridors of the massive castle grounds.

Alicia used Zima's tracking signal parsing to locate her.

While Zima was in pursuit, she noticed a vibration emitting from her side. It was a tracking node implanted inside her hip.

Zima knew she was being tracked and needed to counteract.

She searched for the castle armory as she hid from the rushing guards and agents.

Meanwhile, the EJFS TAC Teams crossed their MICVs into the airspace of Rumbeke Castle.

Zima's signal began to weaken as there was a tremendous deal of disruption from the MICVs flying overhead.

***

Meanwhile, EJFS TAC Team Commanders Abhu and Singh led the MICV to accelerate their attack on Rumbeke Castle as Agents Devdas and Prabodhan joined the fray.

Agent Singh noted the erratic movement of Zima's signal.

"Anastasia is on the loose! We need to assist her and keep an eye out for Vritra's necklace! We must locate both!" Singh warned urgently.

The MICV's hovered over Rumbeke Castle as the weather began to change in response to the EJFS superagents summoning a massive storm overhead.

***

Zima smiled as she heard the weather becoming stormy outside, knowing she was about to receive much-needed assistance from the EJFS in her aid against the Shadow State.

All EJFS Agents rappelled down their MICV's to locate Zima, search and destroy the necklace of Vritra, and apprehend the Shadow State leader, Richer.

Agents Abhu and Singh led their teams, joined by Agents Devdas and Prabodhan, as their backup agents stormed the castle.

Richer sensed the arrival of the EJFS superagents and chose to modify his strategy.

"Agents Thunder and Blaze, get the necklace, and let us get out of here right now! Get to the helicopter on the roof!" Richer commanded authoritatively.

"Yes, Master Richer, we're on our way now!" Agent Blaze affirmed.

"Thunder, come with me!" Agent Blaze instructed.

"Yes, Ma'am!" Thunder replied obediently.

Thunder and Blaze dashed to the castle's top floor as a loud rumbling sound from the storm shook the court. A funnel cloud began to form overhead.

Agents Abhu and Singh and the other EJFS TAC Team Agents entered the castle, shooting down Shadow State operatives one after another.

"Find Anastasia and get her out of here!" Agent Singh ordered.

"Yes, Sir!" Abhu complied.

***

Zima was on the other side of the castle, making her way to rejoin the EJFS TAC Team in the area.

Bradford recovered from Zima's attack and sought to kill her for her resistance.

"Anastasia!" Singh called out from the other end of a hallway.

Zima rushed to join Singh as she raced to reunite with him.

Suddenly, Bradford approached from where Zima once lingered and called out to her.

"Anastasia! Stop!" Bradford shouted. His handgun was trained in Zima's direction.

Zima stopped running and stood in the middle of the hallway between Bradford and the EJFS TAC Team.

"Anastasia, you're making a tremendous mistake by joining the EJFS and their kind. I could have given you the world, but you have betrayed me, and you have betrayed the Shadow State in the same manner. Now, you must choose between them or us." Bradford spoke with fierce anger.

Zima glanced at Bradford then back at the EJFS TAC Team, waiting in the wings.

"It's over, Bradford," Zima turned away from Bradford, and his heart sank. His heartache caused him to lose sight of his target.

Zima rushed into the arms of Singh, and he returned the embrace.

Bradford was furious with Zima and chased after them.

Abhu countered by blowing an intense burst of wind out of his mouth to slow Bradford down.

The wind coming from Abhu's mouth was strong enough to knock over a tall bookcase, crushing Bradford to death.

"Get Anastasia to safety! We're going to find the necklace!" Singh ordered his remaining agents: Anil, Baadal, Nitin, and Gangi.

"Acknowledged. I wish you good luck!" Nitin escorted Zima to one of the MICVs outside the castle while the skies' storm continued to rage.

Meanwhile, Alicia Blaze and Midnight Thunder escorted Richer to the castle's roof as a storm, summoned by the EJFS agents, continued to brew.

"Take us to Atlanta, Georgia, now!" Richer commanded.

"But, sir, the hurricane!" The helicopter pilot warned.

"I don't care! Get us to Atlanta right away!" Richer demanded strongly.

"Yes, Sir!" The pilot complied.

Richer, Thunder, and Blaze boarded the helicopter with the necklace in tow. They fled Rumbeke Castle inbound for the US East Coast.

Inside the castle, Singh and Abhu raced up the stairs to the Shadow State leader's vacant executive quarters, Richer, a.k.a. Black Sparrow Zero. The room was dark and empty.

"They've left. They must have the necklace too," Abhu noted grimly.

"We have to follow them," Durga added.

Singh directed. "Call the Brussels Branch and have them seal off this area for investigation. We'll track their flight path and follow them in stealth mode."

"I'm on it." Agent Chand complied as he retrieved his smartphone from his left cargo pants pocket.

Singh and the remaining team members rushed down the staircase to the MICVs to leave the area.

"We have to assume that Black Sparrow and his minions are heading to the US to begin the last phases of their schemes. We don't have much time before we could stop them," Singh continued.

"What do you suggest we do now?" Abhu asked.

"We need to bring the EJFS back into US airspace," Singh suggested.

"But that would mean the President would declare war on us," Abhu protested.

"I understand that, but we need to take the risk if we want to stop the Shadow State from completing their endgame. Let's get out of here and return home. I'll call Master Khali when we're inbound," Singh concluded.

The EJFS TAC Team, with the addition of Anastasia Zima, Agents Devdas, and Prabodhan, entered the MICVs and fled the scene, leaving Europe and departing for the US.

***

Meanwhile, at 4:45 AM at the EJFS Thunderhead Base over Montreal, Quebec, Canada, Khali received a call from his adopted son, Singh, with a status report.

"EJFS, Khali."

"Khali, it's Singh. We successfully rescued Anastasia, but unfortunately, Black Sparrow and his minions escaped with Vritra's necklace. They must be heading to the US East Coast at this moment," Singh spoke with regret while on speakerphone with Khali.

"That is terrible, but at least you have Anastasia back in custody. I have no other choice but to re-enter US airspace as President Hill will not like it. Do you know where Black Sparrow is headed?" Khali asked.

Chand triangulated the signal of the helicopter ahead of them.

"They're heading to Atlanta," Chand replied grimly.

Abhu felt his stomach turn.

"I see. Maintain your distance, and we will see you back in Atlanta. I'm returning the Thunderhead bases to their original posts," Khali added.

"I understand, Dad. We will see you soon," Singh concluded, thus ending the call.

Abhu experienced some anxiety as he felt a part of his nightmare was coming true.

Khali issued immediate orders to the US-based EJFS Thunderhead Bases to return to US airspace, a move that could prove to be costly.

***

Meanwhile, onboard the military helicopter, carrying Richer, Thunder, and Blaze: Richer developed an arrogant smirk on his face as he knew his plan was nearing completion.

29: EJFS Returns to Atlanta: Richer Makes His Move

Deck One

EJFS MICV TAC Team Squadron

19 miles East of Atlanta, Georgia, US

November 3, 2024

5:10 AM EDT, Sunday Morning

The sun crept above the horizon as the Atlanta-bound EJFS TAC Team squadron sped toward the US East Coast amid the approaching catastrophic hurricane bearing down on the country.

The MICVs operated by Agents Chand and Nitin safely piloted the aircraft away from the hurricane as they maintained their course to Atlanta. Captain Singh and Commander Abhu led the return.

The TAC Teams were continually tracking the military helicopter carrying the top leader of the Shadow State, Richer, along with Shadow State operatives Alicia Blaze and Midnight Thunder.

The EJFS TAC Teams bound for Atlanta hoped to reunite safely with the rest of the EJFS Atlanta Subdivision to prepare for the onslaught from the approaching hurricane.

***

Meanwhile, in Montreal: Master Khali issued the command to return all US-based EJFS Thunderhead Headquarters to their original posts in the US Mainland.

The other EJFS Thunderhead bases, temporarily residing in parts of neighboring Canada and Mexico, began their advancement in return to the original posts spanning from Seattle, New York City, Los Angeles, and Houston.

The EJFS leaders understood their return to US Airspace would arouse President Hill's anger once more. However, they were willing to risk an armed conflict with the Hill Administration to prevent the Shadow State from fulfilling their endgame strategy of bringing Vritra's remnants back to life.

Master Khali returned to the Command Center on the top floor to oversee their return passage's progress.

"Agent Basu, what is our ETA to Atlanta?" Khali inquired.

"We should reach Atlanta airspace within the next hour at our current speed and heading," Basu informed.

"Excellent. Maintain your velocity. I must consult with Agent Lochan." Khali spoke in his powerful voice.

Lochan was in his office, sipping his morning coffee before preparing to start work in the early part of dawn.

Khali gently tapped the glass door leading to Lochan's upper-level office overlooking the entire Command Center.

"Please, come in!" Lochan said.

Khali entered Agent-In-Charge Lochan's office.

"Agent Lochan, I have an update from last night. Agents Abhu and Singh are inbound to Atlanta to rendezvous at our original headquarters locality," Khali said.

"Did they accomplish the mission objective?" Lochan asked.

"Negative, but we have Anastasia, and she appears to have turned on the Shadow State. She is working with us to stop the Shadow State leader, Black Sparrow Zero, from achieving their final goal of reviving Vritra. However, that is not the end of the bad news from the overnight hours," Khali spoke solemnly.

"What happened?"

"Tragically, the Warsaw EJFS Thunderhead Base has been destroyed by two members of the Shadow State. Moreover, we lost one of our own: Agent Naveen Kamboja was killed in action as our visiting TAC Team escaped from the collapsing Thunderhead Base in Poland," Khali continued.

"That is heartbreaking and terrible news!" Lochan grieved. "How did he perish?"

"Naveen was crushed under a large piece of fallen debris. We have recovered his remains and have alerted his next of kin. Naveen's son, Amir Kamboja, has requested to collect Naveen's belongings before we arrange a memorial service in the coming days," Khali explained somberly.

"Such a casualty! Please extend my condolences to Amir and the rest of his family."

"Amir will be here later this morning after we reach Atlanta. His residence is in North Decatur, Georgia. We will send an EJFS vehicle to transport him here."

"What will we do in the meantime?" Lochan asked.

"I shall instruct Agent Amit to wake up our newest recruit, Kim Porter, to begin her training later this morning. He will be the one to conduct the training," Khali concluded.

"Very well, keep me updated on her progress," Lochan finished.

"I will," Khali exited the room to meet with his team in the top-level conference room on the same floor.

***

Meanwhile, in the mountainside of Mt. Zurichberg, Drake awoke from his slumber.

EJFS Ghost Agents were following the developments on the darknet regarding the events from the previous night.

Snow continued to fall outside the concealed Thunderhead Base atop the mountainside as Drake looked out the window before bundling up for the bracing chill coming upon them.

"Good morning, Mr. Drake," Agent Rommel greeted.

Drake was slightly startled by Rommel's visit.

"Oh, I'm so sorry that I frightened you. Breakfast is ready for you in the dining hall. You better come and eat before it gets too cold," Rommel added.

"What are we having?" Drake asked.

"Cinnamon oatmeal with some coffee and tea," Rommel answered.

Drake did not like the sound of what was on the menu, but he decided to show respect as a distinguished guest and reached the dining hall to join the others for breakfast.

Drake followed Rommel to the dining hall, where a few ghost agents were eating breakfast, viewing heavily encrypted and private news feeds while off-grid.

"I apologize that our menu isn't as exciting as the main Thunderhead Bases, but our meals will provide essential nutrients that we rely on to remain nourished," Rommel explained.

Drake merely smiled as he did not want to sour the mood because of the tasteless food.

A younger ghost agent was operating his tablet while hiding his IP address to retain anonymity. He sat next to Drake, sipping black coffee.

"Hi, Mr. Drake. I'm Agent Ariel. Rommel told us that you vacated your role as Vice President of the US. So, what is your story? Hill must have been an unbearable tyrant for you to abandon your government." The young agent spoke in a laid-back demeanor.

Drake clenched his jaw to keep his cool.

"It was a multitude of things. One of many reasons why I fled was because of Hill trying to blackmail me into retaining his presidency, or I would face a tribunal hearing if I didn't cooperate," Drake explained.

"I see. We have been following many developments on the darknet regarding the Shadow State. I am about to print an updated briefing report we have obtained from the Atlanta subdivision. Would you like to see it?" Ariel offered.

"Most certainly, if you don't mind," Drake answered.

Ariel transmitted his print request to the private network printing spooler inside the base. After the document finished printing from the machine, he bound the report inside a binder file.

Ariel provided a copy of the report to Drake for him to review.

Drake was stunned to learn of the Warsaw Branch's downfall in nearby Poland, along with the news that Zima had switched sides after her overnight capture in Budapest.

Another section of the report detailed Black Sparrow Zero's escape and the newest Shadow State operatives, Alicia Blaze and Midnight Thunder, from Rumbeke Castle:

"I'm so sorry about the loss of one of your headquarters in Poland. That is so tragic." Drake offered his condolences.

"Thank you for that. It's been a rough 24 hours. I dread what developments the next day will bring," Ariel commented.

Rommel interjected. "Have faith, my friend. Things will work out."

Ariel did not say another word and kept a stoic appearance.

Drake began to lose his appetite amid the growing tension in the room as he stared into his bowl of cold, bland oatmeal.

***

Janice Ausburn slowly regained consciousness in McLean Central Park's wooded area after being bound, gagged, and tied to an oak tree.

The sunrise was blinding her eyes. She winced in pain from her straining eyesight.

McLean Park was closed to the public due to President Hill's implementation of Martial Law during the previous night. Ausburn feared that nobody would rescue her in her distress.

Ausburn surveyed her surroundings to find a way to break free from her bondage. She noticed numerous twigs mixed in with some broken beer bottles and used syringes from the park's local transients.

Ausburn was horrified to see a nearby encampment of vagrants wandering the area in tents. She hoped a good-hearted soul would help free her from her plight.

Unfortunately, several of them just stared blankly at her without paying much regard.

Ausburn whined quietly, feeling forsaken.

Several wandering, unsavory characters walked by her as they were abusing substances for their pleasure.

Ausburn could not believe what a reckless and lawless society had pervaded her sight.

One of the vagrants mocked Ausburn in her distress.

"Do you need rescuing, young lady?" One of the loiterers mocked.

The others laughed at her and taunted her.

Another menacingly approached her as Ausburn looked for any object that could tear her away from her bindings.

She could only see a scattering of stones and heroin needles lying around. She shuddered at the thought of using violence on a civilian to escape or a contaminated needle to attempt her escape.

Ausburn was able to pull a stone nearer with the back of her heel just as the vagrant approached her.

She kicked the stone with one of her shoes, subduing the attacker.

Ausburn struggled to shred the rope on a needle from a nearby syringe. But the others prepared to pounce on her.

Suddenly, screeching tires sounded as Ex-Chief of Staff Hastings and his son Logan drove up to the scene to save Ausburn.

"Get away from her, right now!" Hastings barked.

The vagrants were motionless but undeterred.

Hastings drew his pistol, pointing it at Ausburn's attacker.

"I'm warning you! Leave her alone!" Hastings demanded.

"What is that, a revolver?" The vagrant asked mockingly.

Suddenly, the smug look on the vagrant's face faded away as he heard some thunder rumbling in the distance.

EJFS Agent Jaswinder arrived on the scene and began blasting intense wind breath onto the vagrants, which blew away all the tents and encampments.

The drifters were soon overcome by the powerful winds blowing out of Jaswinder's mouth, and they were blown far away from the park.

"Guys, help me free her!" Jaswinder ran to the oak tree, where Ausburn was tied up.

He used an EJFS-brand obsidian switchblade to cut through the thick rope quite easily.

"Oh, my God! Thank you so much for saving me!" Ausburn exclaimed after hugging the massively athletic EJFS Agent.

"It's no problem. Let us get you all out of here. Let me take you to the EJFS Headquarters in New York. You'll be protected there." Jaswinder smiled warmly.

"I'd thought you'd never ask," Ausburn retorted.

Hastings felt like Jaswinder was stealing his thunder, but he was thankful to have prevented a terrible outcome from occurring to Ausburn.

"My cab is parked by the entrance. Let's go!" Jaswinder led the way to the McLean Park parking lot, and they fled the scene.

Meanwhile, Director James Matthews monitored the situation in its entirety from his office and his associate Shadow State operative, Onyx, hulking and towering behind him.

"Get President Hill on the phone," Matthews ordered.

"Yes, Sir," Onyx complied while Matthews observed the interchangeable vehicle driven by Jaswinder change into a flying cab while en route to the sky.

***

President Hill and Defense Secretary Clements were holding a meeting when Barnes barged into Hill's office.

"Mr. President, Matthews is on the phone. He wishes to speak to you," Barnes informed him.

"We need to focus on the hurricane preparations," Clements interjected.

"It's okay. Let me take this private call for five minutes," Hill asserted.

Hill retreated to his private quarters to take the call from Matthews.

"Matthews, I hope you have a good reason why you keep calling me," Hill spoke impatiently.

"Mr. President, I wish there were something I could tell you to improve your mood. However, you will not like what I am about to tell you," Matthews began.

"That's not very promising, Matthews," Hill spoke with disappointment.

"Ausburn broke free, and she had help from Hastings and the EJFS."

Hill sighed sharply with increased dissatisfaction.

"I thought you told me you had this handled. I am running quite thin on patience and sleep. So, I suggest you get a handle on this quickly," Hill replied with fuming frustration.

"Yes, Sir! I will clean this mess up!" Matthews assured him.

Hill ended the call and returned to the meeting.

"I'm sorry. My Acting CIRB Director is giving me a headache right now. You were saying, Clements?" Hill spoke with mild irritability.

"The latest trajectory of the hurricane shows that the track of the storm is rapidly accelerating at an alarming speed. At this rate, the expected time of landfall has been moved up by a day earlier. We don't have the resources necessary to keep most citizens safe with this new forecasting projection," Clements added bleakly.

Hill's headache continued to worsen as his plot quickly began to unravel.

"What's the status of the EJFS bases?" Hill inquired.

"They have returned to US Airspace. They seem to be calling your bluff," Clements continued.

"Those fools!" Hill snapped.

"How are we going to proceed, Mr. President?" Clements asked.

Hill paused for a moment before responding.

"Put the fighter jets in the air, but do not engage until I give the strike authorization. I have one last Ace up my sleeve," Hill hinted subtly.

***

Meanwhile, the helicopter carrying Richer, Blaze, and Thunder sneaked out of the inbound EJFS MICV Squadrons' sight range returning to the US.

Richer felt his phone ping with a high-priority order from President Hill.

"EJFS Front has returned to US Airspace. Activate all Shadow State Sleeper Cells and give them hell!" ~SE1KEH.

Richer heeded President Hill's order, and he transmitted the command to activate all sleeper cells in the country to attack all EJFS personnel on sight.

30: Shadow State Sleeper Cells Activated: Kim Begins Training

Joint Base Andrews

3.5 miles Northeast of McLean, Virginia, US

November 3, 2024

6:19 AM EDT, Sunday Morning

Once the order from Richer was transmitted, two fighter pilots at Joint Base Andrews received commands to intercept Jaswinder's ICV located over Virginia airspace, on its way to New York City.

The two fighter pilots donned their gear and took flight, heading to Richer's target coordinates sent to them.

***

Meanwhile, former Director of the CIRB, Janice Ausburn, was joined by former Chief of Staff Nicolas Hastings and his son Logan onboard the ICV taxicab owned by the EJFS base in New York City.

Jaswinder continued to pilot the ICV into the air, heading to the EJFS Thunderhead Base in New York.

Ausburn spoke to Jaswinder while he maintained his course to the base.

"Thank you again for rescuing me. I shudder to think what could have happened to me had I been left tied to that oak tree," Ausburn spoke gratefully.

"You're very welcome, Ma'am. How did you end up in that situation anyway?" Jaswinder asked.

"It was Matthews. He usurped my authority with President Hill's backing. I have been relieved of duty as the Head Director of the CIRB," Ausburn explained.

"Those two are reprehensible," Jaswinder proclaimed.

"No arguments here," Nicolas concurred.

"It has become quite clear that the EJFS and the Shadow State by proxy of the US Government are on a collision course for war. I'm sorry that you have been dragged into all of this," Ausburn noted.

"Don't worry, Ma'am. This is our job. We will sort these crises out one way or another," Jaswinder spoke reassuringly.

Suddenly, a proximity alarm sounded in the cab. A couple of fighter jets had swarmed toward the EJFS ICV that Jaswinder piloted.

"Watch out!" Logan exclaimed.

The fighter jets flew dangerously close to the ICV, causing Jaswinder to initiate evasive maneuvers. Jaswinder prepared to engage the two fighter jets threatening the ICV.

"We've got company! Hold on tight while I try to fend these guys off!" Jaswinder insisted with urgency.

The fighter jets looped vertically to pursue the ICV.

Inside the military aircraft were two pilots from Joint Base Andrews. Both were Shadow State operatives enlisted in the US Air Force.

Both pilots fired from their gun turrets onto the ICV. Jaswinder, who piloted the ICV, continued to dodge and evade.

"Agent Jaswinder, shouldn't you request backup?" Logan suggested.

"Good idea, son," Jaswinder replied.

Jaswinder radioed his backup, Agent Bahadur, stationed near Washington D.C. Bahadur woke to answer the call.

"EJFS, Jain!" Bahadur used his last name for identification.

"Bahadur, my unit is under attack! Please come to assist me!" Jaswinder exclaimed.

"Don't worry. I'm on my way! Hold them off for a few more minutes!" Bahadur assured his friend before he sourced his signal.

Bahadur quickly activated flight mode before taking off to the sky to assist his friend in air defense.

Jaswinder kept his flight controls steady while defending the ICV from the attackers. He counterattacked by causing storm clouds to develop in the sky to obscure his ICV from enemy sight.

Clouds filled in thicker as thunder crackled and lightning flashed, and severe turbulent winds further hindered the fighter pilots as Jaswinder started to blow strong gusty winds out of his mouth, directed toward the fighter jets.

The storms continued to intensify as Jaswinder flexed his gigantic bicep to strengthen the turbulence.

The fighter pilots were quite overwhelmed by the onslaught of severe weather.

"Black Sparrow, we're being bombarded by the EJFS agent's superpowers. We can't maintain our assault!" One of the fighter pilots exclaimed.

Richer spoke on his Bluejaw earpiece as he was in contact with the two fighter pilots.

"Deploy your heat-seeking rockets and take them down!" Richer shouted.

"Acknowledged!" The fighter pilots engaged their rocket launchers to fire on the ICV.

In the ICV, another alarm sounded, indicating that rocket fire was imminent.

"Hold on tight. They're about to unleash rocket launchers on us!" Jaswinder warned.

Ausburn and the Hastings were increasingly terrified that their doom was near.

Suddenly, the ICV belonging to Bahadur appeared from the eastern horizon. He caused a cyclonic updraft to scatter the rocket fire to boomerang into the fighter jets, destroying them in one fell swoop.

"Good job, Bahadur, you saved our butts! Let us head to New York right away!" Jaswinder insisted.

Bahadur nodded while smiling.

He escorted Jaswinder to the New York EJFS Thunderhead Base as the storms kept the ICVs camouflaged from sight.

***

Richer was infuriated by the signal loss of two of his fighter jets.

"Damn it!" Richer cursed aloud.

"Don't worry, Boss! We'll get them soon enough!" Thunder comforted Richer.

"Yes, we'll bring them all down in due time, Black Sparrow," Alicia Blaze spoke reassuringly, parroting Thunder's comforting words.

Richer remembered that the massive hurricane barreling toward the US would all but ensure the country's destruction and perhaps the world once Vritra reconstituted himself in the storm.

The military helicopter continued its flight path toward Atlanta, which was less than six miles away.

***

The EJFS Thunderhead Base originating from Atlanta had returned to its original post in the sky over the city.

The EJFS TAC Team squadrons led by Agents Abhu and Singh made rendezvous with the returning base.

Agents Nitin and Chand landed the MICV in the return bay of the EJFS Thunderhead Base in Atlanta.

There was a somber tension aboard the aircraft as they counted a loss in personnel during their visit at the Warsaw EJFS before it plummeted to the surface in Poland.

Khali solemnly greeted the remaining eleven members of the TAC Team upon their return. Agents Abhu, Singh, Durga, Gangi, Garjan, Nitin, Chand, Vasu, Baadal, Anil, and Daarun disembarked from the aircraft with Zima in their custody.

Khali spoke with his booming thunderous voice. "Welcome back, and I extend my condolences to all of you. Naveen's loss will not be forgotten, but we must remain undeterred in our quest to destroy the Shadow State."

Khali turned his attention to Zima, a former member of the Shadow State. Khali was hesitant to trust Zima upon her return.

"Anastasia, I'm glad you have finally opened your eyes to the error of your ways. I sincerely hope you remain aligned with us in our newfound partnership in opposition to the Shadow State. We will prepare you a place to stay where you will be more comfortable and secure." Khali spoke with cautious optimism.

"Thank you, Sir. I appreciate your willingness to accommodate me. I want to start by apologizing to all of you for the trouble I have caused. I am at your mercy, and I have nowhere else to go.

I humbly ask for forgiveness and a chance to start anew." Zima spoke remorsefully.

"We will do what we can on our side to help you help us. But please understand that you are on a short leash. You will have to work hard to build our trust completely," Khali responded with caution.

"I understand, and I accept that. Thank you," Zima continued.

"Take her to the guestroom quadrant unit on Level 12 for the time being," Khali ordered.

"Yes, Master," Singh responded.

The remaining agents returned to Thunderhead Base's interior as the skies continued to brighten amid a gloomy backdrop during the massive hurricane's quickening approach to the mainland.

***

In Kim's guestroom quarters, Kim was resting in bed when she heard the intercom in her room emit a call sound from another agent standing outside her quarters.

"Who is it?" Kim asked.

"It's Darsh. May I enter?"

"Come in, Darsh," Kim said.

Kim was half-awake in her pajamas as Darsh walked into her quarters.

"Good morning, Kim! Rise and shine. It is time for breakfast. After we eat, we will begin your training. I'll meet you in the dining hall after you get dressed," Darsh spoke warmly to Kim before he left the room to give her privacy.

Kim took a hot shower and put on a training uniform that the EJFS had provided to her.

After Kim left her quarters, she walked to the dining hall to join Darsh at the table for breakfast.

Darsh explained in detail what Kim's training would involve.

"I hope you are well-rested, Kim. You have a long day ahead of you," Darsh explained.

"Let's start with extra-strong coffee, with cream and sugar, please," Kim requested, not wanting to hear anything more until she had her daily cup of morning coffee readily available.

"Right away, Kim." Darsh retrieved Kim's breakfast tray that contained plenty of prepared coffee.

Darsh uncovered the cloche to reveal a platter of Indori Poha, which was an Indian breakfast delicacy and a dietary staple at the EJFS.

"Nice," Kim commented, appearing to enjoy the thought of trying a new breakfast item she had never eaten before.

Kim enjoyed her breakfast while Darsh explained the training that she would undergo that morning.

"After you are finished eating, I will escort you downstairs to the Citadel Plaza Intake Center to begin your training. You will have shared control over three specific elements on earth: Rain, Wind, and Thunder. You will be trained to use these powers responsibly and to use them in combat. I will provide you with a comprehensive walkthrough as your trainer," Darsh explained as Kim ate her breakfast.

"How long will this training last?" Kim inquired.

"It could take up to a full day. But we will do everything in our ability to assist you in your mastery of our skill sets. All you need to do is follow instructions and let our powers infuse into you," Darsh elaborated.

"Wow, I'm intrigued," Kim quipped as she sipped her morning coffee.

Darsh was somewhat amused by Kim's frankness, as off-putting, it might be to others.

"There is another thing you should know: Anastasia is here, and she will be living on the same floor as you," Darsh informed her.

"Anastasia? Who is she?" Kim asked.

"She's an ex-member of the Shadow State. She disavowed them after one of our top agents repelled the spirit of Vritra consuming her soul. She will not be accessible to you for the time being as we will have agents guarding her room. She will be sequestered until we can properly vet her," Darsh continued.

"I'm not sure that I understand. I thought Anastasia was one of the people responsible for Vritra's rebirth. Why would you trust her?" Kim asked, with her eyes narrowed.

"I know it's hard to comprehend right now, but we are giving her a chance to prove her intentions are pure. Regardless, I would advise you to steer clear of her until we can verify that she is acting in good faith," Darsh cautioned further.

Kim was stunned at what she had learned. She had difficulty reconciling that she would share the same floor with a wanted international fugitive with a history of involvement in the fallen Final Wave Terrorist Organization at the hands of EJFS Agents Abhu and Singh and her role in the Shadow State cabal.

After breakfast was finished, Kim followed Darsh to the unit exit.

Suddenly, Agents Prabodhan and Devdas appeared, escorting Zima to her sequestered quarters for the remainder of the mission.

Kim and Zima briefly glanced at each other as they crossed paths.

"Keep walking, Kim. Don't mind her," Darsh advised.

Zima continued to be escorted by Devdas and Prabodhan to her temporary quarters for her sequestration.

Kim was somewhat rattled when she saw Anastasia Zima in person.

"It's going to be okay, Kim. Let us head downstairs to the outside plaza," Darsh instructed.

***

Around 7:22 AM Eastern Time, the military helicopter belonging to Black Sparrow Zero, a.k.a. Francois Tomas Richer, arrived in Atlanta, accompanied by Shadow State operatives Thunder and Blaze.

The deadly trio gazed into the sheer immensity of the mega-hurricane, quickly accelerating its approach to the US East Coast. They chuckled evilly as they knew their wicked plans were nearing completion.

Richer ordered. "Let's head to my mansion in Savannah. We'll operate from there for the next 36 hours."

The three of them took an upgraded European car to Richer's colonial mansion in Savannah as the skies continued to display an ominous hue of black and blue.

31: Kim's Transition into EJFS Superagency Begins: Richer Targets EJFS Atlanta Base

EJFS Palace - Atlanta Branch

20,000 feet over Atlanta, Georgia, US

November 3, 2024

7:35 AM EDT, Sunday Morning

Agent Darsh led Trainee Kim to the EJFS Citadel Plaza and Intake Center outside. Kim was nervous about undergoing a metaphysical change to become an EJFS superagent that could control and manipulate the weather.

While Darsh and Kim walked through the lobby and main foyer on the first floor, Kim passed by Agents Abhu, Singh, Durga, and Gangi while they made their way outside.

Abhu gave words of encouragement to his sister.

"It's going to be okay, Kim. You will do well in your training," Abhu exhorted.

"Thank you, Brother," Kim spoke quietly as she wrapped her arms around her much more massive brother, Abhu (a.k.a. Caleb Porter).

Darsh and Kim exited the tall front doors and walked outside, heading to the Thunderhead Base's eastern portion, where the Citadel Plaza was located.

Darsh escorted Kim to the Intake Center building that stood before the entrance to the plaza.

Darsh initiated intake and training. "First and foremost, we need you to go through our PAVATS module walkthrough. We will need you to develop a new identity for your job. As an EJFS senior agent, I have been given the authority to bestow upon you a new name for your alias. From now on, you shall be named Agent Indrina Kalyani Padmal."

Kim was astounded.

"You mean...I'm going to be part Indian?" Kim stuttered.

"That is correct. This is our standard procedure. Your brother underwent the same transformation as you have seen with your own eyes," Darsh affirmed.

"I'm not so sure about this. I don't know if I'm cut out for a double life," Kim spoke with nervous hesitation.

"Kim, you have already committed to our cause. Most of us have dual identities. This is how we retain our anonymity from the outside world," Darsh contested.

"Agent Darsh, I'm nervous. Will it hurt?" Kim inquired.

"Don't worry. It's completely painless. You will have the ability to switch identities as you see fit. However, as is the case with your brother, your physique will be retained throughout your time here," Darsh tried to console Kim while attempting to ensure Kim's commitment to the EJFS.

Kim sighed, "I can't believe I am going along with this. But I cannot let my brother down. I'll do it."

Darsh gently patted Kim on her back. "That's the spirit!"

Kim let out a weak grin.

"Follow me to the Intake Center. I'll be with you the whole way," Darsh comforted Kim.

Darsh and Kim began Kim's transformation procedure, much to the chagrin of Kim herself.

However, she sought to follow through on her end of the bargain.

***

Meanwhile, in Savannah, Georgia, the trio of two Shadow State operatives and the head of the Shadow State, Richer (a.k.a. Black Sparrow Zero), alongside Agents Blaze and Thunder, arrived at Richer's colonial mansion near the coastline.

The building overlooked the Atlantic Ocean as the billowing hurricane continued approaching the East Coast of the US.

Blaze and Thunder helped Richer out of the vehicle, and they entered the old mansion facing the coastline.

Richer clutched the necklace of Vritra in his wrinkly hands.

"Blaze, text Matthews, and request as many Atlanta-area CIRB assets available to protect us and the mansion. I want to make sure we have plenty of backup," Richer dictated.

"Yes, Sir," Blaze complied as she retrieved her smartphone.

She transmitted her request to Acting CIRB Director James Matthews' smartphone.

"Shadow Phoenix Six, requesting backup CIRB assets to the perimeter of BSZ's colonial mansion near Savannah. Phase III of Operation: Vritra's Revenge will soon commence! ~SP6AHB"

***

Matthews received the text from Agent Alicia Blaze while en route to the Atlanta CIRB Headquarters in a mobile unit van. He quickly approved the request.

Matthews issued an urgent flash bulletin across the CIRB airwaves.

"Attention all assets, Operation: VR Phase Three is about to begin. All Atlanta-area agents are to assemble a perimeter around BSZ's headquarters near Savannah. Send all available assets and agents to the area," Matthews spoke on speakerphone as he sent out the order.

While driving the mobile unit van, Agent Onyx maintained his course toward Atlanta with a breakaway of CIRB vehicles heading to Savannah to stage a perimeter boundary near the colonial mansion.

***

Blaze and Thunder unpacked all their gear at the colonial mansion they salvaged from Rumbeke Castle in Belgium.

Richer, clutching Vritra's necklace's carrying case, took a seat on the covered sofa in the living room. He unlocked the case and admired the amulet, which had a haunting effect on him.

Vritra's dormant powers remained encased inside the dragon-shaped talisman for fourteen months after the cataclysmic release from his imprisonment in Siberia, Russia.

Blaze and Thunder finished unpacking their gear and activated their satellite uplink to maintain comms throughout the region before the hurricane's landfall.

***

Meanwhile, at the EJFS Thunderhead Palace Base, Agents Abhu and Singh worked in the top-level command center under Agent-In-Charge Lochan's direction.

Singh and Abhu met with Lochan in his upper-level office to discuss the next plan of action.

"Agents, thank you for all the hard work you have put into arresting Anastasia. However, we still have not obtained the necklace of Vritra, and the world is still imperiled by the monstrous hurricane charging toward the East Coast. The good news is that we have tracked the three individuals that have escaped from Rumbeke Castle," Lochan began.

"Where are they?" Singh asked.

"They're located at a colonial mansion near Savannah. They activated a satellite uplink, which we have parsed the signal's origin. The leader of the Shadow State has dispatched the assistance of numerous CIRB assets and agents in the Atlanta area to protect the perimeter," Lochan explained.

Abhu felt a pang of nausea enter him.

"I have an awful feeling about this," Abhu spoke lamentably.

Singh interjected. "I know how you feel about the nightmare from last night, but maybe it won't turn out the way you think, Abhu."

Lochan was puzzled.

"Wait, Abhu had another nightmare? Am I missing something?" Lochan questioned.

Singh addressed. "Abhu had another vivid nightmare last night while we were away. There was a scan order carried out, but Khali has forbidden us from releasing the results to Abhu and Durga at this juncture. We are under strict orders to keep the results sealed until after the mission has concluded."

Abhu interjected. "It's a decision that I am not too thrilled about."

Lochan replied. "Abhu, we're aware of the fact that your vivid dreams from last year have helped us tremendously in the operation front against Final Wave. But Singh may be right. Not all dreams are equal."

Abhu clenched his jaw and restrained himself from speaking further on the issue.

Lochan continued. "Aside from that, Naveen's son, Amir, has been notified of his father's death. We're sending a pair of agents to pick him up so that he may collect Naveen's belongings."

Singh lamented. "God rest Naveen's soul."

Abhu asked. "Who is the team picking up Amir?"

"Raj and Devdas are heading to his home in North Decatur at this moment to transport him to the palace. Would you both please look after him when he gets here? His emotional state must be in turmoil," Lochan informed.

Singh commented. "Don't worry. We'll keep an eye on him. I am sure he remembers me well from earlier days. May I request to speak to him privately when he arrives?"

"I don't have a problem with that. I know you and Naveen were partners in the early years of the EJFS. You may spend some time with Amir," Lochan permitted.

"Thank you, Lochan," Singh responded.

"In the meantime, we need you both back downstairs to your stations. President Hill has threatened war against us, and he seems to be making good on his threat. We have received word from the New York EJFS Branch that one of their agent's ICV was attacked earlier this morning. Agent Jaswinder was transporting Janice Ausburn, Nicolas Hastings, and his son Logan. They have safely arrived at the EJFS Branch over Manhattan, where they are being interviewed," Lochan continued.

"What happened? I thought Ausburn was the Head of the CIRB, and Hastings was the Chief of Staff," Abhu wondered aloud.

"We hope to find out very soon. Regardless, we need to protect the base from any such attack by Hill's Command. Please report to your stations. We will reconvene later," Lochan commanded.

Agents Abhu and Singh left Lochan's office and operated their workstations for the time being.

***

Later that morning, Agent Raj drove his ICV while riding with fellow EJFS Agent Devdas en route to Amir's residence in North Decatur, Georgia.

Amir Kamboja looked outside from his living room while the ominous skies continued to thicken as the hurricane continued its path toward the US.

Amir was somewhat slender. He was 21 years old and in college. However, the University campus was closed for the weekend due to the advancing hurricane barreling towards the entire US east coastline.

Soon enough, EJFS Agents Raj pulled the ICV up to the curbside next to Amir's house.

Amir let out a profoundly pained sigh as he opened the front door to greet the approaching superhuman agents.

Raj and Devdas exited the vehicle with somber looks on their faces.

The duo approached the walkway to meet with Amir. They offered their consoling and comforting embraces for Amir.

"Amir, please accept our condolences to you and your family. Naveen was a terrific man and an excellent agent. He will be missed by many," Raj held Amir in an embrace as Amir wept in Raj's loving hugs, grieving for his late father, Naveen.

"Thank you," Amir spoke softly.

Raj ended the embrace, and Devdas gave Amir another comforting hug.

"Amir, your father loved you very much. I'm so sorry for your loss," Devdas consoled Naveen's son.

"Thank you both. Please take me to your headquarters now. I want to collect my beloved father's belongings," Amir insisted.

"Very well, let's go," Raj assented.

Raj and Devdas escorted Naveen's son, Amir, to their vehicle to return to the Atlanta-based EJFS Thunderhead Base Palace.

Little did they know, there were a couple of Shadow State operatives watching from an SUV out of the EJFS agents' line of sight.

The two Shadow State operatives Burke and Doherty observed from inside the SUV as they prepared to pursue them at a distance.

Shadow State and CIRB asset Burke radioed Black Sparrow Zero (a.k.a. Richer).

"Black Sparrow, this is Agent Burke. I have identified two EJFS agents in the North Decatur neighborhood, picking up a young man in his 20s. Requesting permission to engage," He spoke quietly.

"Permission granted, but exercise caution. These EJFS agents are a force to be reckoned with," Richer warned.

"Understood, boss," Burke acknowledged.

The SUV followed the ICV at a measurable distance on the quiet streets toward the EJFS-owned ICV in pursuit.

Soon enough, Agent Raj began to sense that they were being followed.

"We're not alone," Agent Raj rumbled grimly.

"I have that spectral feeling too," Agent Devdas noted.

"I'm activating Stealth Mode. I'm not risking another loss of life," Raj decided.

The pursuing SUV made a turn around the corner after the ICV veered down a fork into a back alley near an apartment building.

The SUV turned only to find no sign of the ICV.

"Damn it, they must have sensed we were following them!" Doherty cursed.

"Keep looking for them. They couldn't have gone far," Burke insisted.

Suddenly, a wind tunnel appeared and sucked up the ICV while it was invisible, and the SUV got sucked up into the wind vacuum.

Burke and Doherty were flung into the air, screaming before the car came plummeting down to the surface as it crash-landed while upside down into the alley.

Burke and Doherty were gravely injured. Both men died seconds later after they had crashed.

While accompanied by Amir, Raj and Devdas continued their ascent to the EJFS Thunderhead Base Palace as they heard a resounding thud from the crashed SUV.

"What was that?" Amir asked nervously.

"The pursuing vehicle crashed back down while caught in the updraft," Raj explained.

"A shadow government is targeting us. We'll explain more when we get to the base," Devdas added.

***

Meanwhile, in Zima's sequestered quarters in the guestroom quadrant unit: Zima continued to ward off any sinister advances from Vritra's evil spirit.

Zima decided to take a shower and change out of her dingy clothes.

While Zima was showering, she noticed the Shadow State tattoo emblazoned on her palm and frowned upon it. She was stuck with a constant reminder of her former allegiance to the Shadow State.

After she showered, she wore a change of clothes and wrapped her wet hair in a towel.

Zima decided to rest in bed as she endured a long 24 hours with little sleep.

While she was dreaming, she experienced a vivid nightmare of being in her darkened quarters while Vritra appeared over her bed while levitating.

"You betrayed me, Anastasia!" Vritra spoke with seething rage.

"No, leave me alone!" Zima spoke aloud while in her dream state.

"ANASTASIA! ANASTASIA!" The haunting voice of Vritra echoed loudly as he pressed his slit-patterned eye against Zima's face menacingly.

Suddenly, Zima woke up to the sound of a knocking on her door. It was Khali.

"Anastasia, are you awake?" Khali asked.

"I am now," Zima replied with a hint of annoyance.

Khali entered her quarters while Zima sat in bed, exhausted from her brief rest.

"Anastasia, I'm sorry that I woke you. I need to ask some questions to finish vetting you," Khali began.

"What is it?" Zima inquired while yawning.

"Has the spirit of Vritra been haunting you during the whole time you were working against us?" Khali asked.

"Yes, I believe so," Zima confirmed.

"Do you have any sense of being led by Vritra's spirit against your will?" Khali continued.

"In some aspects, yes," Zima retorted.

"Explain," Khali insisted.

"I have nightmares and sensations after Singh had cast away the spirit of Vritra. He's angry and tells me that I have betrayed him," Zima elaborated.

"It sounds like you're in the midst of a war for your mind and soul," Khali added.

"I guess you could say that," Zima remarked.

Khali felt bad for Zima and decided that there was only one thing he could do. He retrieved a Bible from the bookshelf.

"I think you need this. Let's spend some time reading it," Khali smiled lightly as he gave some scriptures for her to read.

Most of them were from Psalms and II Corinthians, involving strongholds. After spending some time reading, Zima felt fully liberated from the haunting spirit of Vritra.

"Thank you, Khali. You opened my eyes even further. I'm going to keep reading this," Zima spoke graciously.

"You're very welcome, and I pray that you become receptive to what the Lord wants you to understand. He loves you dearly, and He wants you to break free from this bondage," Khali spoke with his soft, booming voice.

Khali spoke to her before exiting her quarters.

"Your sequester is over. You may roam freely throughout the unit. I'll tell the guards to leave their post," Khali spoke comfortingly.

Zima had a wholesome smile on her face as she rested in bed with her Bible.

***

Richer lost contact with the two Shadow State operatives at Richer's colonial mansion that monitored EJFS Agents Raj and Devdas, which roused his anger further.

"No!" Richer shouted with fury.

"Again?" Blaze questioned.

"The EJFS took out another couple of my finest operatives. I will not stand for this! Get President Hill on the phone!" Richer demanded sharply.

President Hill was at his desk in the White House Bunker office when his burner phone vibrated. He was alone when Richer called him.

"Richer, please tell me you have good news," Hill pleaded.

"I'm afraid I do not. Another couple of my best operatives were killed by EJFS extremists this morning near North Decatur, Georgia. They are fearless. We need your assistance immediately!" Richer spoke with utmost urgency.

President Hill sighed with discontentment while wiping his eyelids and pinching the bridge of his nose.

"Fine, I'll send some F-18s to the Atlanta EJFS. It's time to fight fire with fire," Hill proclaimed.

"We'll be watching through our satellite uplink on location," Richer assured.

Hill hung up without saying goodbye. He was tired from sleep deprivation and was out of patience. He called up Defense Secretary Clements to issue the strike order.

"Clements, I am authorizing you to send a squadron of fighter jets to the EJFS Base over Atlanta. It's time to put an end to them," Hill ordered.

"Acknowledged, Mr. President. I will make the call immediately," Clements spoke.

"Clements, tell them to show no mercy," Hill spoke with repugnance.

"Understood, Mr. President!" Clements ended the call.

Clements dispatched a nearby squadron of F-18s to Atlanta for an aerial assault on the EJFS Atlanta Branch.

The EJFS were unwittingly endangered by the impending threat of attack at the behest of President Hill.

32: Atlanta-EJFS Thunderhead Base Defense from Hill's Wrath: Amir Laments Naveen's Death

EJFS Command Center – Level 13

Main Building

EJFS Atlanta Branch – Eastern US Division

20,000 feet over Atlanta, Georgia, US

November 3, 2024

8:16 AM EDT, Sunday Morning

EJFS Agents Abhu and Singh sat inside their workstations in the top-floor Command Center.

Both agents' mood was reasonably tense as they continued to operate within their stations amid the drama stemming from the overseas missions during the previous night.

Even though tensions were high between the two, Abhu and Singh maintained their focus on the mission.

An email notification sound emitted from Singh's computer.

Singh noticed that the message was from Khali regarding Abhu and Durga's dream scan.

***

From: Master Khali

To: Agent Singh Puneet Sherpa

Subject: RE: Abhu and Durga's Dream Scan Results Expedited

Priority: Normal

Date: 11/03/2024 08:18 EDT

***

My Dear Son,

I regret to inform you that earlier sealed results from the dual device scan have been lost in the EJFS Warsaw Base's fallen wreckage.

However, all hope is not lost: I had taken the initiative to back up the results to the EJFS server. I am in the process of downloading the report in its entirety.

I strongly urge you not to mention these developments to Abhu or Durga until the action has settled down. I will release the scan report to Abhu and Durga individually, in full disclosure, when I deem it necessary.

Do not let this mishap distract you from the high-priority mission.

Love you, Son!

~Master Khali

***

Singh briefly read the email while Abhu was not paying attention. Singh felt somewhat awkward for reading the email within such close proximity to Abhu.

Singh closed the email window as Agent Basu spoke with him regarding an Intel Report update passed down through Agent-In-Charge Lochan.

"Hey, Singh. Check this out: We have intercepted some radio chatter between CIRB Director Matthews and several of his assets. They're sending an envoy of assets to their headquarters in downtown Atlanta while a separate team of assets is heading to the Shadow State leader's mansion," Basu informed him.

"I already reviewed the intel from Lochan earlier this morning. Is there something new that hasn't been discovered yet?" Singh inquired.

"There is: The satellite uplink that we parsed earlier has transmitted immediate strike orders to F-18's to launch an aerial assault on our base within the hour. In response, I have been monitoring the flight radars over US airspace. There is a squadron of four fighter jets coming our way," Basu continued.

Abhu overheard Basu and Singh's conversation. He craned his head toward Singh.

"Where did they originate? What is their ETA?" Singh asked.

"They launched from Joint Base Andrews in Maryland. They're expected to reach us in about 25 minutes," Basu replied.

"This warrants an emergency response. I'm contacting Khali right away," Singh added.

Singh picked up his landline phone and promptly called Master Khali.

Khali was in his executive quarters monitoring the day's events. He also had a watchful eye on the flight radar over the US East Coast.

Khali's smartphone began to ring, and he noticed it was from Singh's workstation inside the Command Center. He answered the call.

"It's Khali."

"Master Khali, I have received word that the US military has scrambled fighter jets to our location under Hill's authority. Their estimated time of arrival is less than a half-hour. We need to respond quickly," Singh urged.

"I knew it was only a matter of time that this would happen. I will relay orders to all agents to their Battle stations straight away! Have everyone on the highest alert possible. We're in for a battle for our very survival!" Khali urged.

"Acknowledged, Master," Singh placed the phone back in its cradle.

Khali accessed the all-base overhead PA system for an emergency action announcement.

"Attention all EJFS personnel: Our base is under threat of imminent attack from a squadron of fighter jets heading to our location. I am issuing emergency orders for a base defense at the highest level of priority. Please operate your Battle stations immediately! We are on Red Alert!" Khali spoke loudly and clearly into the PA system.

Abruptly, the base Klaxon resounded throughout the Thunderhead Base Palace, prompting all agents to heed Khali's orders for a defensive battle to protect the palace.

***

Meanwhile, Kim (a.k.a. Agent Indrina) and Agent Darsh were about to proceed with the next training class.

The alarm sounded, and the security gates lowered, blocking all entrances to the training citadels, though Trainee Indrina had already finished the Wind Training Class.

Indrina was panicked amid the chaos.

"Darsh, what's happening?!" Indrina cried out.

"We're on Red Alert. We need to head back to the palace to get you to safety. Come with me!" Darsh exclaimed.

Indrina hurried behind Darsh as they rushed back to the Palace Base entrance, but the tall doors were sealed shut as the palace was on lockdown.

"Darsh, can you get us inside?" Indrina asked.

"I can't. The doors are sealed shut," Darsh answered.

"Then, what shall we do?!" Indrina cried out.

Darsh held Indrina by her shoulders to reassure her.

"Listen, Indrina. We need to stick together to survive this! You and I will use our powers to ward off the assailants coming for us all," Darsh insisted.

"But I only know the power of wind so far," Indrina whined.

"I will compensate with the powers that I have already mastered," Darsh added.

Indrina felt somewhat calmer, although her nerves were frayed amid the heightened alert level.

"Okay, promise me that you'll protect me," Indrina demanded.

"I promise I will keep you safe," Darsh continued. "Now, follow my cues: When you see the fighter jets approach the Thunderhead Base, start blowing wind as strongly as you can. I will help you with the manipulation of other weather elements," Darsh concluded.

***

Abhu and Singh positioned themselves at their Battle stations on the exterior of the palace turret alcoves facing outward from the inside.

Abhu was horrified to see Darsh and Kim, developing EJFS persona as Indrina, still outside atop the Thunderhead Base.

"Oh, my God! Kim and Darsh are still out there!" Abhu exclaimed, fearful at seeing Kim and Darsh in danger.

"Abhu, stay calm under pressure! Darsh will defend her along with the base as we are doing. Do not lose focus!" Singh exhorted him.

The other agents in the base maintained their positions at their battle stations, hoping to ward off the same terrible fate that befell the destroyed Warsaw EJFS base earlier.

***

Zima was in her quadrant having breakfast when she overheard the commotion outside the unit.

Suddenly, she overheard the sound of violent thunder and wind roaring outside as both Darsh and Indrina were summoning the forces of nature in a bid to save the EJFS headquarters.

Zima walked toward a window overlooking the palace's front courtyard. She observed Darsh and a female agent blowing and flexing their massive biceps as the skies continued to darken.

"Oh, no," Zima muttered.

Zima felt the collective doom of the EJFS was about to become her downfall. She could not do anything except watch as the sound of streaking fighter jets zoomed over the palace base generating a sonic boom.

Four F-18s split into two pairs as they arrived to begin the aerial assault on the base.

"Fire at will!" Khali announced on the intercom.

The darkened skies were peppered with artillery fire from the fighter jets. The EJFS agents responded in power. All agents fired their turret guns toward the fast-moving F-18s.

The heavy artillery rounds tore up the ground outside atop the Thunderheads, where Darsh and Indrina provided aid to the EJFS defensive front.

Darsh pulled Indrina behind the water fountain to take cover from the artillery fire.

Abhu fired his turret gun with force while he shouted, "Leave my sister alone!"

Abhu's turret fire inflicted significant damage to one of the fighter jets.

Singh blew an intense burst of winds out of his mouth, intensifying the turbulence overhead.

The fighter jet struggled to hold steady amid the violent winds.

Darsh flexed his enormously swollen bicep in a sharp motion, causing a mighty thunderbolt to strike the damaged fighter jet.

The military aircraft burst into flames and crashed down to the surface.

"One down, three to go!" Abhu noted loudly.

All other EJFS agents followed suit in modifying the weather to further increase the turbulence impacting the fighter jets.

The stormy weather above continued to intensify while the remaining three fighter jets broke off in different directions to evade the attacks of the EJFS.

The fighter jets looped around to conduct another massive attack on the base.

A trio of sentinel drones launched from the deployment bay to even the odds in their favor. The sentinels fired heavy artillery rounds, striking the three military aircraft.

"Keep fighting. Don't let up!" Khali shouted into the PA system.

Everyone heeded the encouragement from their leader as the sentinels managed to destroy another fighter jet.

"Two left!" Singh noted aloud.

The remaining two fighter jets went on the offensive and started to launch massive attacks on the base.

"Look out, Darsh!" Indrina exclaimed.

"I'm on them like a heavy torrent. Don't worry!" Darsh assured her.

The rain intensified over the skies as thunder crashed, and the wind howled, causing the fighter jet pilots to become very disoriented in the inclement weather.

Another sentinel fired a pair of rockets toward a fighter jet, destroying it instantly.

"One left to go!" Darsh exclaimed.

The last remaining fighter jet circled the Thunderhead Base's perimeter, firing its machine gun onto the palace building.

Some of the agents were struck by the spray of bullets, subduing them.

"Medical!" Singh shouted.

Abhu fired his turret gun toward the last fighter jet while Darsh prepared to summon a tornado to rip the aircraft into pieces.

Darsh blew boisterously as he swirled his index finger in a broad, circular motion.

This action caused a tornado to spawn upward from the clouds below, which caused the last fighter jet to be destroyed in midair.

"We did it!" Abhu shouted with exuberant jubilation.

"Excellent job, everyone!" Singh congratulated them.

"Great work! But do not think this is over yet! Hill will not let up until we are demolished. Keep your eyes wide open!" Khali gave accolades to his subordinates over the intercom.

The lockdown was temporarily lifted. Darsh and Indrina re-entered the base palace to reunite the sibling agents.

***

Amid the action over the EJFS Thunderhead base, Agents Raj and Devdas made their final approach toward one of the many helipads surrounding the damaged palace grounds.

"What the hell happened?" Amir asked in shock.

"I saw an alert on the manifest screen. There was an aerial assault on our base," Agent Raj noted.

"By whom?" Amir inquired.

"President Hill did this. We'll explain later," Raj concluded.

The ICV landed on the damaged helipad and drove into the parking garage within the Thunderheads.

During Amir's arrival at the base, Abhu and Indrina (a.k.a. Kim) reunited in the foyer.

Abhu was awestruck by Kim's new identity.

"Wow, Kim, is that you?" Abhu asked.

"Not anymore. I'm Agent Indrina now!"

"Agent-In-Training Indrina," Darsh corrected.

"Regardless, I'm so glad that you're okay. When I saw you and Darsh outside, I was distraught," Abhu added.

"It's okay, brother! We held them off," Indrina spoke confidently.

Agents Raj and Devdas escorted Naveen's son, Amir, inside the palace's foyer.

Amir looked at the surrounding agents with a solemn and subdued expression on his face as they made their way to the elevators.

"Who's that?" Indrina asked, puzzled.

"That is Amir, Naveen's beloved son. His father was killed in action during an attack at the Warsaw Branch," Singh explained woefully.

"Oh, I'm so sorry," Indrina said.

"So am I," Singh concluded with a darkened expression of sadness on his face.

***

Amir followed Agents Raj and Devdas to Naveen's quarters, where he once resided in Unit Seven.

"We will be outside if you need anything. Let us give you some privacy to grieve," Raj said as they closed the door to Naveen's quarters, leaving Amir alone in emotional anguish.

Amir gathered Naveen's belongings while viewing photos of the class of EJFS agents posing at different functions within the superagency.

Amir felt saddened to know his father was no longer in the world, although he felt his spirit all around him. He shed a few tears as he continued to survey his father's living quarters.

***

Meanwhile, at Richer's Colonial Mansion, Blaze and Thunder sat at their computers, monitoring the hurricane's advancement on the shores of the US East Coast.

Richer was troubled to learn that the F-18s that attacked the EJFS base were destroyed. He had minimal options left to eliminate the EJFS.

"Why the long face, Richer?" Blaze asked.

"The extremists destroyed them, the fighter jets. I should have expected no less." Richer spoke lamentably as his eyes sunk beneath the bags underneath them in despair.

"Do not fear, boss. The storm is accelerating faster than expected. It should be here ahead of schedule. By midnight tonight, everything will be destroyed," Thunder said.

"Oh, that warms my heart, but we must stay firm against the EJFS extremists. I don't expect them to go down without a last hurrah," Richer warned.

Outside the mansion, sirens and helicopters whirred around the area as the Shadow State CIRB assets' backup arrived to bolster security around the perimeter and surrounding areas.

"Ah, yes! We have company!" Richer exclaimed.

Richer looked outside the vastly darkened skies as the helicopters circled the region, and CIRB vehicles lined the streets around the mansion.

A plethora of CIRB brute assets patrolled the property. They were equipped with inhalant solutions to increase lung capacity and semi-automatic rifles, making rounds every hour.

Soon after, the whole area was swarming with Shadow State operatives and CIRB assets, protecting Richer's mansion.

The EJFS mission to put a halt to the Shadow State had just become much more complicated.

33: EJFS Strikes Back: POTUS Hill and Shadow State Exposed

EJFS Command Center – Level 13

Main Building

EJFS Atlanta Branch – Eastern US Division

20,000 feet over Atlanta, Georgia, US

November 3, 2024

9:32 AM EDT, Sunday Morning

After the recent aerial assault against the EJFS from the US Air Force, at the behest of President Hill and Black Sparrow Zero (a.k.a. Richer), Khali was mulling a response against the Shadow State.

Agent-In-Charge Lochan Nair oversaw his tech agents and analysts working on the Command Center's main floor from his upper-level office. He received a landline phone call to his smartphone from Master Khali to prepare a logistics package for the large-scale operation that had escalated against the Shadow State with the US Government as a proxy war between the two.

"EJFS Command Center. It's Lochan."

"Lochan, it's Khali. We need to strategize a response to Hill's corrupt acts in cooperation with the Shadow State," Khali urged emphatically.

"What shall we do?" Lochan inquired.

"We need to expose Hill and the Shadow State for who they indeed are. They are evil and rebellious traitors working against the American populace. I propose that we dump all our data on the internet for the world to see Hill's despotic actions for what they truly are," Khali elaborated.

"Where do you want to dump the data? Many of the US citizens have been evacuated in preparation for the hurricane," Lochan continued.

"We have to take over the airwaves for some time. We will also dump all relevant information regarding Hill's corruption and his alignment with the Shadow State all over the internet. Once we execute this method, Hill will presumably ramp up his offense against us. We may have no choice but to continue to defend ourselves while we attempt to mitigate the hurricane before it makes landfall," Khali continued.

"This is going to get ugly quite quickly if we do this. Are you sure that we should evoke the full might of the US Military under Hill's influence?" Lochan asked with heightened concern.

"I'm fully aware of the risks, but this might be our best shot at exposing Hill and the Shadow State. We must take decisive action now," Khali contended.

Lochan let out a heavy sigh of distress, trying to find any alternative strategies to employ, but there were minimal options.

"Okay, I will assemble all the intel we have on both Hill and the Shadow State, and I'll inform our press corps of this plan. They will need to seek protection until Hill can be removed from office," Lochan assented.

"Very well. I will issue urgent orders for all agents to remain on high alert. There is no telling how severe Hill's response will be. Keep your guard up. I will call upon the assistance from all local EJFS Divisions to aid us," Khali concluded.

"Affirmative, Master," Lochan ended the call.

Lochan carried his smartphone before heading downstairs to the Command Center Bullpen.

"Okay, people, listen up!" Lochan shouted as he rushed down the stairs, demanding every agent's attention.

"I just got off the phone with Khali. We are implementing a new strategy. We are setting forth full disclosure against Hill and his affiliation with the Shadow State. I will need everyone to compile all data pertinent against both and all those affiliated within their alliance. We will be seizing control of the airwaves before we dump all the data for the public to review. This will, without a doubt in my mind, cause further attacks from Hill. However, we are taking a calculated risk. Khali will be sending out orders to all Branches and Divisions to assist us in our goal. Maintain your focus on the overall objective at hand to stop the advancement of the hurricane, and above all else, prevent the Shadow State's endgame of releasing Vritra's remnants into the atmosphere," Lochan explained in a commanding tone of voice.

The tech analysts looked at each other with mutual concern written on their faces.

Lochan continued, "Therefore, all active field agents must remain vigilant against any such retaliatory strike from the Shadow State. I am using my authority to initiate a partial lockdown. We need to keep everyone in check during the height of these operations against the Shadow State. That means all essential staff on the roster are forbidden from leaving this room without my prior authorization. Are we clear on that?" Lochan continued.

"Yes, Sir!" The crowd in the room affirmed.

"Good, get to work!" Lochan asserted thunderously.

Lochan remained on the floor to supervise.

While he was with his department, which included Abhu and Singh, Basu observed the radar and satellite readings of the advancement of the expansive hurricane barreling toward the North American continent.

"Hey, guys. We have another problem." Basu spoke grimly.

Abhu and Singh wheeled their chairs next to Basu.

"Explain," Singh insisted.

"The hurricane we're closely monitoring – it's accelerating its approach rapidly. The forecasted landfall has been moved up to later this evening or sooner," Basu informed them with increased worry.

"That's terrible! We have to act now!" Abhu exclaimed.

"How? Lochan placed us all under a partial lockdown," Basu replied.

"Maybe we should propose our strategy to Lochan about attempting to blow the hurricane away from the continent," Abhu suggested.

"We would need a tremendous amount of wind breath even to attempt such an extraordinary feat. How are we going to go about doing this?" Singh argued.

"We should run it past Lochan. He might be convinced if we explain our theory. Time is not on our side. We can't afford to hold off much longer," Abhu urged.

Singh and Basu exchanged glances, knowing Abhu had a point.

"Lochan, could you please join us for a moment?" Singh asked.

Lochan approached the group.

"What is going on?" Lochan asked.

"The massive hurricane is gaining speed. The latest forecast bulletin indicates that it should make landfall before the end of the night," Singh explained.

Abhu interjected. "Lochan, I have a possible solution to this crisis: What if all local EJFS agents assemble near the coastline and make an effort to blow the storm off course and back into the Atlantic Ocean?"

Lochan answered. "That would hypothetically be a longshot. However, I cannot envision any alternative strategy. I will discuss this further with Khali. Nonetheless, at this moment, we need to focus all our time and energy on removing Hill from office. But rest assured that I will discuss this strategy with Khali in detail."

Abhu and Singh returned to their stations to resume the data dump on Hill and the Shadow State.

***

Meanwhile, Amir was sitting in the late Naveen's quarters, overcome with grief as he continued collecting all of Naveen's items that he left behind.

Amir came across a few pictures of Naveen with Amir as a young boy on Naveen's desk in a miniature framed portrait.

Agent Raj visited Amir while his heart was heavy with sorrow. Raj provided comfort to Amir.

Amir had always trusted Raj along with Singh. They were like second uncles to him.

"Do you need anything, Amir?" Raj asked with a somber expression on his face.

"I could use another bin. My dad has so many left-behinds," Amir said softly.

"Certainly, I'll retrieve another bin for you," Raj assured him.

"And Raj..." Amir added.

"Yes?"

"Could you ask for Agent Singh to visit with me as soon as he is available?" Amir requested.

"Yes, I will let him know that you have requested his presence. But please know that the Command Center is under a partial lockdown right now. I will ask for him to connect with you by phone until he is more accessible," Raj explained.

Amir stifled tears from welling up again.

Raj sensed Amir's great grief and gave him a soothing embrace.

"Hey, I know it's a tough time for you. But you are surrounded by people who loved your father, and we are here for you. I'm sure he is in a much better place," Raj consoled Amir.

Amir was experiencing so much emotional agony. He wept in Raj's embrace.

"I'll miss him so much," Amir lamented.

"We all will." Raj shed a tear, streaming down his right cheek as he comforted Amir in a tender moment between the two.

***

Lochan and Khali held an AERIAL video teleconference through their computer screens to discuss a new method to stop the hurricane from obliterating the US mainland.

"Khali, I have terrible news: The expansive hurricane heading toward us is rapidly accelerating its approach to the east coast. Agents Abhu and Singh have formulated a strategy to blow the storm back out to sea," Lochan began.

"How?" Khali inquired.

"They are suggesting that we should form an assembly of agents, lining up along the shoreline and use the maximum strength of our wind breath to blow it away," Lochan explained.

"I suppose that it would be worth a try," Khali added.

"How soon do you want us to assemble?" Lochan continued.

"As soon as you have dumped all intel on Hill and the Shadow State. We can't afford to allow Hill to continue abusing his Oath of Office," Khali insisted.

"I understand, Master," Lochan acknowledged Khali's instructions.

"That will be all," Khali disconnected the video call.

Lochan called Abhu's landline phone for a brief update following the teleconference.

"EJFS, Sandeep."

"Agent Abhu, the plan has been approved, but the priority continues to be exposing Hill. This will be a two-pronged attack against him and the Shadow State. Continue what you're doing to carry out the remaining mission objectives," Lochan instructed.

"Yes, sir, I understand," Abhu replied.

Singh spoke with Abhu regarding his call.

"What was decided?" Singh asked.

"We're sticking to the original plan as ordered. After we finish the data dump, we will all assemble by the shoreline to blow the hurricane away," Abhu informed him.

"All right, let's keep at it," Singh said nonchalantly.

Suddenly, Singh's smartphone rang. It was from Raj.

Singh excused himself in the lower-level hallway to receive the phone call.

"EJFS, Sherpa."

"Agent Singh, it's Raj."

"Yes, what is it?"

"Singh, I'm with Amir right now, and he is requesting your presence for solace."

"I would love to see him, but I am somewhat tied up at the moment," Singh spoke regrettably.

"Could you at least speak to him by phone to ease his mind?" Raj asked.

"Yes, give him your phone, but I must keep it brief," Singh said.

Raj handed his smartphone to Amir.

"Singh, I'm sorry to bug you at the wrong time," Amir began.

"No, Amir, it's okay, given the circumstances. How are you holding up?" Singh spoke with a faint smile.

"It's been hard being in Dad's room. I feel overwhelmed with sadness," Amir continued.

"I'm so sorry. I can only imagine what you must be going through. Please know that this has been a profoundly difficult day for all of us. I know your father loved you so very much, and I want you to know that I love you like a son. I will try to see you and help you through this. But I must remain focused on the task at hand, or billions of people could die, including us," Singh spoke with an ominous tone.

"Please be careful!" Amir spoke with intense emotion.

"We will persevere. Stay strong for me, okay?" Singh encouraged.

"I will," Amir concluded.

"Please give Raj his phone back," Singh requested.

Raj retrieved his phone from Amir. He spoke to Singh once more.

"Singh, I need you to promise me that you will come to see Amir as soon as you can. He needs your support," Raj spoke adamantly.

"I promise I will come to see him soon. Look after him as long as you can, please," Singh continued.

"I will stay with him as long as possible. Do everything you can to put an end to the Shadow State," Raj said passionately.

"You have my word. Goodbye," Singh ended the call while maintaining his composure before returning to his station.

***

Meanwhile, inside the White House bunker, President Hill monitored the hurricane's quick progression toward the US east coast.

Defense Secretary Frank Clements reviewed forecasting models with other staffers.

Amid the discussion, Laura Matheson, a lead staffer, became worried about Hastings.

Matheson spoke with the First Lady during breakfast, hoping to get a sense of where Hastings was located.

"Mrs. Hill, I'm wondering what is going on with the President. There's something he isn't telling me," Matheson began.

"Really? How so?" Mrs. Hill asked.

"I'm trying to get in touch with Hastings. I haven't seen him around here since last night. I know he was discussing something at Drake's request. Now, they are both gone. I'm just beside myself with worry," Matheson continued.

"Drake vacated his role as VP. He fled the White House last night with the help of the EJFS. As far as I know, Hastings was complicit with a plot to impeach my husband."

"What? You knew this whole time?" Matheson fumed.

"I'm sorry, Laura, but I need to go," The First Lady whisked herself away to be with her children, Trevor and Allison.

Matheson began to connect the dots. Hastings was gone and undoubtedly fired.

Barnes approached Matheson, checking on a potential conflict.

"Matheson, is there a problem?" Barnes asked.

"Yeah, there is a problem. Why hasn't the President informed me of a change in the Chief of Staff position? Who's the Chief of Staff now?" Matheson asked quietly.

"That would be me," Barnes informed her.

Matheson scoffed at Barnes.

"I can't believe this, Barnes. I thought you trusted me to tell me sooner," Matheson reacted.

"I'm sorry, Matheson. But things were unraveling quickly last night. I've been tending to an angry and irritable Commander-in-Chief." Barnes defended himself.

"That's not a valid excuse, and you know what?" Matheson continued to show hostility.

"What?" Barnes reacted.

"You can find yourself a new lead staffer. I'm done!"

Matheson gave up her White House credentials and left the bunker.

"Matheson!" Barnes shouted.

Matheson ignored him as she exited the bunker, yet another member repudiated the Hill administration.

Barnes returned to speak with President Hill.

Hill wrapped up his conversation with the Secretary of Defense. "We need those amended aerial attack strategies readily available, Clements!"

"Yes, Mr. President," Clements departed from him.

"Matheson resigned, Mr. President," Barnes informed him.

"That's fine. She was on borrowed time anyway," Hill sneered.

"Sir, with all due respect, our turnover rate is too high for the election season that we are currently..." Barnes cut off.

Clements interrupted. "Mr. President, the EJFS has seized control of the nation's airwaves! Turn on the TV!"

Khali appeared on television, delivering a scathing and damning exposé of President Hill.

"Citizens of America, we do not wish further conflict with your country. However, we have discovered critical information regarding your commander-in-chief that implicates him as a seditious traitor and a member of a secret society known as the Shadow State. His role and influence are far-reaching across the world..."

Hill seethed. "Somebody, shut him off the airwaves!"

Barnes spoke urgently. "We're working on it, Mr. President!"

"President Hill has been continuously partnering with enemy nations, providing aid to enemy combatants, international rogue fugitives, and aiding and abetting terrorists to strike the US in a recent false flag with his weaponized branch of the CIRB. Furthermore, he has planted spies in enemy nations to perform espionage, including the use of staffers as body doubles."

Matthews, the CIRB Director, slammed his fist against the car horn and dashboard in a fit of rage.

"We have gathered a high quantity of data regarding the Shadow State's top leader, a Belgian Parliament member named Francois Tomas Richer as their founder. Former Shadow State operative, Anastasia Zima, has defected after a long year of living in hiding. Richer has deployed many attacks against my European friends in Warsaw, Poland.

Richer, along with Shadow State operatives Blaze and Thunder, watched bitterly.

"Tais-le!" Richer cursed in French.

"Lastly, the hurricane formed off the coast of Cape Verde yesterday was done at the behest of President Hill, the Shadow State, by the hand of Jagmohan Gyan, a technological weather warfare mastermind who harnessed the weather in a highly chaotic way to wreak havoc on the planet. The goal of the Shadow State is to revive Vritra's remnants to destroy the whole world potentially. I have employed my subordinate agents to declassify and release all relevant data regarding the findings discussed in this broadcast. We implore you: Correct your government's errors, heal the Republic and the partnership that once flourished between the nations and the EJFS. Thank you!"

***

Hill was outraged upon the revelation of information about him that the EJFS brought forth to light.

"Clements, send the stealth bombers to annihilate them all!" Hill barked.

Clements froze, not wanting to comply after what was revealed of Hill.

"Did you not hear me, Clements? Send the stealth bombers, now!" Hill demanded.

After a brief pause, Clements picked up the landline phone.

"Send them in immediately!" Clements ordered.

Suddenly, a group of military brass entered the President's office and approached Hill.

"Mr. Hill, you need to come with us," Admiral Warren insisted.

"What is this?!" Hill exclaimed.

"You've been summoned by the Attorney General and Members of Congress. You are relieved of command. You have been deemed unfit to hold public office any longer," Admiral Warren decreed.

"I can't believe this! This is a direct usurpation of my authority!" Hill yelled.

Hill was placed in handcuffs and escorted out of the office to sequestration.

"Call EJFS, have them extradite Drake to the US. He's now the acting commander-in-chief," Admiral Warren ordered.

"Yes, Sir!" Clements assented.

***

In Mt. Zurichberg, Switzerland, a landline phone rang where Drake had rested in exile for less than half a day. EJFS Ghost Agent Rommel Klug answered the call.

"Hello?"

"Good morning, this is EJFS Atlanta-One. I am issuing orders to extradite Peter Drake to Washington, D.C. He has been summoned to take over as Commander-In-Chief." The deep-pitched, thundering voice spoke on the phone.

"Yes, this is EJFS White Dove from Zurichberg. We will send Mr. Drake on his way there now," Rommel spoke his cryptic name, acknowledging the EJFS orders at the behest of the US government.

The phone disconnected, and Khali placed his smartphone back inside his pants pocket to leave for the Nation's Capital to testify against Hill.

***

Drake received word of the latest happenings from D.C. and was equipped to return to the U.S. to rise to Commander-in-Chief.

34: EJFS Oversees Hill's Impeachment: Another Government Mole Operative Activated

Interrogation Room

White House Underground Bunker Complex

Washington D.C.

November 3, 2024

10:19 AM EDT, Sunday Morning

Military officials escorted Hill to an interrogation room within the White House Bunker complex.

The disgraced former president was fuming following his removal from office.

"You people are making a colossal mistake in impeaching me. You can't interfere with my agenda!" Hill resisted as he was forcibly handcuffed to the chair across from the lead interrogator.

US Attorney General Brian Geoffries, the former state attorney general for Georgia, oversaw Hill's resistive entry into the interrogation room.

Geoffries was accompanied by House Speaker Raymond Weiss in preparation to question Hill in a closed-door deposition.

Hill was strapped into his chair at the table, and his vitals were measured. Geoffries received a phone call from the Head of the EJFS, Khali. Geoffries accepted the phone call.

"US Attorney General Geoffries speaking."

"Hello, Geoffries! It's Khali of the EJFS."

"Good morning, Khali. I want to start by saying that I extend my sincere apologies for Hill's mistreatment of you in his incompetent leadership on behalf of the US Government. I fully expect that our partnership will heal with Hill out of play in the foreseeable future." Geoffries spoke warmly.

"What is the status of Hill at this moment?" Khali inquired.

"Hill is being held for questioning. We're about to interrogate him after your findings had been made public moments ago," Geoffries explained.

"I want to be available to testify against him at the soonest opportunity. I am departing from the EJFS base in the next thirty minutes to meet with the proper officials. There are additional witnesses we have at the New York Subdivision who may wish to testify as well," Khali continued.

"I will have to confer with House Speaker Weiss about that request. But I will give you a clearance to enter the halls of Congress shortly to speak with you in private," Geoffries responded.

"Very well. I shall see you soon."

Khali hung up before contacting Second-In-Command Agent Raj to relinquish authority to him for the chief commander's excursion duration.

Geoffries spoke with Weiss in preparation for Khali's arrival.

"Mr. Speaker, Khali is en route to Capitol Hill to testify. He has informed me that there are additional witnesses who may testify against the President."

"Very well, but I am concerned about this precedent we are setting forth. I suggest we keep Khali on a short leash for the time being," Weiss recommended.

"I will bear that in mind, Mr. Speaker. I realize that I am in a peculiar situation, considering my past involvement with the

EJFS. But please be aware that I will remain impartial and will see to it that justice is swiftly carried out for the good of the country," Geoffries assured him passionately.

The interrogation tech, Yasmin, finished calibrating the vitals of Hill.

"Mr. Attorney General, Mr. Speaker: Hill's baseline vitals are synced to the system. He's ready for interrogation," Yasmin informed.

"Thank you, Yasmin," Geoffries replied.

Geoffries and Weiss entered the interrogation room to question Hill.

"Mr. Hill, as the US Attorney General, I will be conducting your questioning. You have been accused of treason, sedition, and willful violation of your Oath of Office. The punishment carries a maximum sentence of execution by firing squad. Do you have anything to say for yourself?" Geoffries asked.

"I'm not saying anything until I have legal representation," Hill retorted.

Weiss spoke angrily to the President in a sharp rebuke.

"Mr. Hill, we don't have time for this. You have caused undue hardship across America with your gross abuse of executive powers. The country is under grave threat from the hurricane, in which you were accused of complicity. It was created at your behest. Who are your accomplices, and what benefit do they have in destroying the United States mere hours before the election?" Weiss interrogated.

"I already told you, I'm not saying anything until I have my attorney present!" Hill continued to resist.

Geoffries relented and gave into Hill's wishes.

"Fine, but the longer this goes on, the less we can do to protect you, especially if the man-made hurricane causes extreme death and destruction," Geoffries warned.

Hill remained silent as both Geoffries and Weiss left the room.

"Call his attorney, send an escort to bring him here," Weiss ordered.

Yasmin assented. "Yes, Mr. Speaker."

Yasmin called Hill's legal representative, Kevin Whittaker, who resided in Norfolk, Virginia.

***

Meanwhile, at the EJFS, Khali spoke with his second-in-command, Agent Raj, before he departed for Washington D.C. They walked to the outside helipads where Khali's transport vehicle was waiting.

"Agent Raj, I am giving you full command of the EJFS until I return. I am needed in D.C. to testify against Hill in front of Congress. Please exercise your best judgment in stopping the calamity in my absence," Khali requested as both superagents made their way outside in the windy skies, clutching their fleece coats.

"Master Khali, I will do my absolute best to maintain command while you are gone. But I must warn you to be incredibly careful. D.C. is swarming with anti-EJFS politicians in Congress. You will have little protection there," Raj cautioned.

"I fully understand, and I will do everything I can to protect myself. May God bestow great wisdom and blessings upon your leadership," Khali added.

Khali and Raj gave a proper salute before Khali entered his vehicle to descend upon D.C.

Raj continued to observe Khali's transport vehicle's takeoff process as the wind whipped his long hair around in a fury.

Khali's vehicle ascended and engaged its supersonic engines to travel long distances within minutes.

The car finished its transformation and whisked away with a sonic boom toward D.C.

Acting Commander Raj returned to the interior of the EJFS Base Palace. He took the elevator to the command center to address the latest developments to the entire superagency network.

Once Raj entered the command center, the tech analysts and agents stood at attention, offering their salutations to their new commander.

Raj addressed his subordinates.

"My fellow agents, I have been granted full command by Master Khali. He has left the palace, heading to Washington, D.C., to oversee the impeachment of Hill. During this time, I will be the acting Head of the EJFS until he returns. The mission at hand has not changed, but we will be sending local superagents all to the surface to blow the hurricane away from the US shores. Moreover, we will be assembling TAC Teams to storm the colonial mansion currently housing Black Sparrow Zero, along with his closest minions and weaponized CIRB assets on location," Raj began as the group of agents, including Abhu and Singh, observed.

"I will be sending out mission updates to all your tablets and phones. All Level Seven agents, and higher, are ordered to head to the shores to assemble a wall of arctic wind breath to blow the storm away and cool down the waters. The wall shall span the entire East Coast of the US. Abhu and Singh will be your points of contact. The partial lockdown issued by Agent Lochan has been lifted under my command. Good luck and Godspeed!" Raj spoke thunderously.

All EJFS Field Agents excused themselves from the command center to suit up for a joint tactical operation with all agents in the area from Atlanta and New York City.

Abhu and Singh led the remaining superagents that were fresh off a mission from Europe, and they headed to the mass deployment bay.

***

Amid the happenings at the EJFS Thunderhead Base, Agent-in-Training, Indrina Padmal (a.k.a. Kim Porter) continued her training at the gym after finishing the introductory training classes following the end of the partial lockdown.

Indrina possessed quite an upgrade in her physique as she built some healthy and lean muscle mass to accompany her acquisition of newly learned powers.

Darsh continued to train Indrina to become an up-and-coming EJFS field agent.

"You're coming along very nicely, Indrina. You are outpacing your brother at this rate," Darsh complimented her.

Indrina smiled while she continued to focus her energy on finishing the training by the day's end. Indrina was practicing mixed martial arts with Durga.

Indrina followed Durga's cues to strike her blows onto the padded combat equipment while dodging Durga's attacks to practice defending herself.

Darsh was pleased with what he saw.

Suddenly, Darsh's smartphone rang. It was Raj.

"Excuse me, ladies. I need to take this call," Darsh stepped out into the foyer of the palace gym.

"It's Darsh."

"Agent Darsh, it's Raj. How is Indrina progressing in her training?" Raj asked.

"Indrina is doing exceedingly well. She may even outpace her brother at this point," Darsh informed him.

"Outstanding! Those two siblings are very quick and adept learners," Raj continued.

"Indeed, Commander Raj," Darsh concurred.

"Please let me know once she has completed all phases of her training. I want her to be available in the Command Center or the field as soon as possible," Raj ordered.

"Very well, Sir, I will keep you apprised on her progress," Darsh said.

"Thank you, Darsh!" Raj ended the call.

Darsh returned to the gym to observe Indrina and Durga's combat practice.

While the practice continued, Indrina became oblivious to her smartphone vibrating in her purse, resting in a locker.

It was Logan Hastings who had tried to re-establish communication with Kim.

Yet, Logan did not know that Kim was no longer her primary identity.

***

"Hi, you've reached the voicemail for Kimberly Porter. I can't take your call right now. Please leave a message!"

Kim's voicemail sounded on the receiver, much to Logan's dismay while with his father, Nicolas, at the New York EJFS Thunderhead Base.

They had recently completed their debriefing interview with some agency officials, and they were notified of the latest development regarding Hill's impeachment.

Both former Chief of Staff Hastings and his son Logan were called to testify against the disgraced president.

"Son, I don't think you'll reach your girlfriend at this point," Hastings said.

"I don't understand. I thought you said Kim was cleared of all wrongdoing. Why else would she not be able to answer her phone?" Logan asked.

"It's possible that she is forbidden to communicate with her outside friends while she is in this situation. I'm sure that the EJFS is taking good care of her." Hastings encouraged him.

"Maybe she forgot about me," Logan moaned.

"Oh, don't worry, I don't think she would forget about you. You two have been nearly inseparable in your relationship despite my earlier meddling," Hastings grinned.

"I wonder if she knows that you aren't the chief of staff anymore," Logan pondered aloud.

"It's a possibility, but I don't know what information she is privy to while she is with this certain agency," Hastings continued.

"Dad, I'm sorry for everything that has happened to you. I share your regret in being involved in the Hill campaign. Now, I can't believe we have to testify against the President," Logan spoke lamentably.

"It's okay, son. We'll get through this together somehow and some way," Hastings assured him.

Logan was feeling tired and rested his head on Hastings's shoulder.

"Stay strong, son. We are in an uphill battle," Logan's Dad said.

"I know, Dad. I just want to go home," Logan muttered.

Suddenly, the Hastings was joined by EJFS Agents Jaswinder and Bahadur, accompanied by Janice Ausburn.

"Hello, you two. We need to take you both back to Washington, D.C., along with Mrs. Ausburn. You all will need to testify to Congress against Hill and his corrupt acts. Don't worry. We'll be with you the entire time," Jaswinder comforted the duo.

"Well, let's go, son," Hastings spurred.

"All right." Logan ascended from his seat with his father.

"Agent Jaswinder can take the Hastings. I'll escort Mrs. Ausburn along with you all," Bahadur informed them.

All five of them were taken to the downstairs parking garage built within the EJFS Thunderhead Base.

Both vehicles were armored for optimal protection to withstand most attacks.

"Let's head out," Jaswinder insisted.

"Yes, Sir!" Bahadur assented on the radio.

Both vehicles were driven out of their garage spaces. Both agents drove the ICVs to the exit ramp, heading to Washington, D.C.

***

In Savannah, Shadow State Leader Richer was seated at his mobile dispatching unit alongside Shadow State operatives Blaze and Thunder.

All three were incensed with the fact that they had been exposed by the Head of the EJFS, Khali.

Thunder was listening to the radio chatter on his headset while tuned to the frequency that the EJFS used in high altitudes. The satellite uplink assisted the three villains in that endeavor.

"Boss, I overheard some chatter on the radio waves. They are sending their leader to testify against Hill in Congress. Should we modify our strategy to capture the Head of the EJFS?" Thunder inquired.

Richer's frown started to weaken.

"Why, yes! I know who I can call on for help. Let me send a message to my mole operative in the State Department." Hill spoke with increased menacing excitement.

Richer typed a message on his phone addressed to a high-ranking government official in Washington, D.C. It was a short message.

"EJFS Head is in the field. Stay on top of him and prepare to scoop him up."

Meanwhile, a tall blonde lady in a red pantsuit received a message on her phone while at her desk at Capitol Hill. She heeded the message and typed a response.

"I copy, BSZ. I will notify my team to stay on top of the extremist leader. Awaiting permission for capture and imprison authorization."

Richer momentarily hesitated before he transmitted his response.

"Permission granted. You are authorized to capture and imprison Khali by any means necessary. Take him alive."

After receiving the response, the state official grabbed her purse and left her desk. The nameplate inscribed Pamela Harsh's name, US Secretary of State.

Harsh texted her partners to notify them that their plan to capture Khali was activated.

35: Khali Arrives in D.C.: Drake Assumes Command

30,000 feet over US Airspace

Washington D.C.

November 3, 2024

11:05 AM EDT, Sunday Morning

Khali's transport vehicle continued its flight path to D.C. as the immensely vast hurricane approached the US East Coast. The ICV hovered over Washington, D.C., when Khali made his descent to the surface.

Khali's visit caught the mainstream media's attention with a large gathering of press members and journalists covering a large swath of the D.C. area leading up to Capitol Hill.

Groups of local EJFS agents wearing custom-fitted suits. Their attire made them appear as an elite team of Secret Servicemembers also piloted a few ICVs to provide a layer of added protection for the Head of the illustrious super-agency.

The skies maintained their dark silver and blue hue as the massive hurricane threatened from the southeast.

Khali's ICV landed near the Washington Monument and proceeded to drive north to Capitol Hill. His purpose was to testify against disgraced President Hill to ensure his impeachment and conviction.

As Khali continued his progress toward the Nation's Capital, Secretary of State Pamela Harsh observed the incoming fleet of EJFS superagents driving their ICVs along the road's main drag.

Harsh was standing outside with several members of Congress and the US Attorney General Brian Geoffries.

A sense of malice stirred within Pamela as she witnessed Khali's arrival.

Little did Khali know, Harsh was a mole for the Shadow State. She intended to capture Khali alive during his visit.

Meanwhile, another trio of ICVs traversed the street. Former CIRB Director Janice Ausburn, along with the Hastings, were on board the transformational aircraft.

The large gathering of press corps members made the goal of capturing Khali impossible for Harsh to accomplish without arousing a mass frenzy in public.

Khali disembarked the ICV, escorted by an entourage of elite EJFS superagents from the D.C. subdivision. He greeted the government officials who served as a reception committee.

Geoffries spoke first to him. "Mister Khali, welcome to Washington D.C. It is an honor and privilege to see you again."

Geoffries and Khali exchanged handshakes.

"Likewise, Mister Attorney General. What made you decide to return to politics?" Khali inquired.

"The President nominated me earlier this year after my predecessor stepped down. I could not pass up the opportunity to serve again. Rest assured that this process will be fair and without bias. However, your being here sets a precedent in our Nation's history that could be seen as a rebellion in the eyes of other countries. I need your assurance that you won't overstep the sovereignty of our nation," Geoffries continued.

"I promise I will abide by your methods," Khali assured him.

"Excellent," Geoffries spoke, relieved by the knowledge of Khali's intentions.

Suddenly, the second fleet of ICVs arrived near the entrance to Capitol Hill.

"Ah, the other witnesses are here as well," Khali announced.

Agents Jaswinder and Bahadur exited the transformative vehicle and escorted the Hastings' and Ausburn up the front steps.

Initially, the trio of witnesses was startled by Khali's incredibly massive stature.

Geoffries welcomed the three additional witnesses.

"Welcome, Mr. Hastings, Logan, and Mrs. Ausburn," Geoffries greeted them warmly.

"Thank you for the massive reception party, Mister Khali," Ausburn greeted him while subtly criticizing him for the extra publicity.

"Mrs. Ausburn, please rest assured that I mean no harm to the US. My goal is to shed light on Hill's misdeeds while serving as President. I alerted the media to ensure transparency before the public," Khali explained.

Ausburn whispered to Khali. "I suppose I'll take your word for it. But, let me offer you words of advice: This place is a corrupt swamp. Watch your back."

"Duly noted, Mrs. Ausburn," Khali replied.

Geoffries spoke up to the foursome.

"Well, let's head inside and begin the proceedings."

The government officials entered the interior hallways of Congress escorted by the Sergeants-In-Arms, some of whom kept their distance from Khali.

***

Amid the happenings in D.C., the EJFS superagents within the Atlanta Thunderhead Base followed the national news coverage events displayed on the big screens in the command center.

Simultaneously, Richer of the Shadow State watched the televised media event from his colonial mansion in Savannah with Midnight Thunder and Alicia Blaze. CIRB Director Matthews, who had arrived at the CIRB satellite office in Atlanta, also monitored the proceedings.

A national news outlet was covering the developments of the Hill impeachment hearings.

"We are following continuing breaking news coverage of the impeachment proceedings against former president Kenneth Hill at the Nation's Capital. We have witnessed live footage of the Head of the EJFS, named Khali, make his first public appearance as his transformative vehicle touched down and drove to the front steps of Capitol Hill. Sources from the EJFS Press Corps have indicated that Khali will join former Chief of Staff Nicolas Hastings and his son Logan. Both will testify against the president in Congress this morning. Also joining them is Former CIRB Director Janice Ausburn, who was forced out of her position by the new Director James Matthews at Hill's behest. The proceedings are expected to last throughout the day as the massive hurricane continues its approach along the Southeastern US Coastline. We also have received word that former Vice President Peter Drake will be the acting Commander-In-Chief throughout the remainder of Hill's first term in office. We will continue to monitor these unprecedented events as they develop."

***

Meanwhile, at the White House Bunker Interrogation Room, President Hill's attorney, Kevin Whittaker, was joined by Admiral Warren and Secretary of Defense Clements.

After being briefed by both Warren and Clements about Hill's charges, Whittaker was brought into the Interrogation Room.

House Speaker Weiss entered the interrogation room facing Hill and Whittaker. Both Hill and Whittaker had hostile looks on their faces remaining defiant and insolent.

Weiss addressed the disgraced President. "Mr. Hill, we have brought your attorney here to be present at your interrogation per your request. Now, let us begin the questioning: Have you been implicitly acting against the American people with regards to Khali's allegations?"

Whittaker interjected on Hill's behalf. "Mr. Speaker, with all due respect: I think you are overreaching."

Weiss was unamused by Whittaker's response.

"Mr. Whittaker, this is not a time for triviality. Hill needs to answer for his role in the events of the past couple of days," Weiss admonished.

The room remained silent as both Hill and Whittaker refused to cooperate.

Weiss tapped his wrist to cue Yasmin to check the status of Hill's vitals.

Yasmin spoke. "Hill's vitals are stable, Mr. Speaker."

Weiss turned up the pressure on Hill.

"Mr. Hill, does the name Francois Tomas Richer ring a bell to you?" Weiss asked.

Suddenly, Hill's vitals began to spike as Weiss struck a nerve with his line of questioning.

Yasmin paged into Weiss's earpiece again. "Hill's blood pressure just increased by 20 points."

Weiss studied the expression on Hill's face as the disgraced president began to sweat.

"Mr. Hill, my interrogation technician, has indicated to me that my question caused your vitals to heighten in reaction. The more you resist, the less I can do to ensure leniency," Weiss warned.

Hill shouted angrily. "You think you can undo everything that my administration has done over the past four years by this overthrowing of my presidency?! You have no idea what kind of mess you are getting on your hands. I am only a cog in this vast machine that you can't control!"

"Mr. Hill, your overly emotional reaction tells me that you know this Richer person very well. I suggest you start telling me everything you know if you want to avoid death by firing squad," Weiss countered.

"You are not going to break me!" Hill seethed.

"Guard, sedate him, and take him back to the Holding Room," Weiss instructed.

"Yes, Sir," The guard complied and injected a sedative fluid into Hill, causing him to fall asleep.

"Sit tight, Mr. Whittaker. This isn't over," Weiss pointed at Hill's attorney before exiting the room.

Weiss rejoined Yasmin in the observation room.

"Where do we stand on Hill's vital readings?" Weiss inquired.

"Mr. Speaker, Hill's vitals spiked tremendously during the tail end of this portion of interrogation. But his vitals alone are not going to be enough to convict him," Yasmin indicated.

"This isn't working, and we don't have time to beat around the bush. Perhaps we should begin enhanced interrogation," Weiss suggested.

"Are you sure?" Yasmin asked with her brow raised.

"I'm afraid that we don't have any other choice. Call Warren and have the black room ready to go," Weiss ordered.

"All right, Sir," Yasmin complied nervously as she picked up the landline phone and dialed Admiral Warren's extension to relay the Speaker's orders.

***

EJFS Ghost Agent Ariel and Former Vice President Peter Drake had reached Washington D.C. in a secluded area near the White House where a gathering of top military brass served as the reception committee for the Acting President.

EJFS Ghost Agent Ariel spoke to Drake before dropping him off.

"Mr. Drake, or should I say, President Drake, I wish you the best of luck and Godspeed!" Ariel spoke kindly.

"Thank you, Agent Ariel. May we meet again someday!" Drake smiled at his escort.

Ariel flew back into the stratosphere and returned to stealth mode to maintain the EJFS Ghost Agency's anonymity.

The military officials escorted President Drake inside the White House to assume command over the troubled US.

Admiral Warren briefed Drake upon his return.

"Mr. President, Hill has been placed under arrest, and he's being interrogated. House Speaker Raymond Weiss has ordered the enhanced interrogation to proceed. Are you willing to sign off on this order?" Warren asked.

"Is Hill refusing to cooperate?" Drake queried.

"He hasn't given us much information as we hoped. We don't have much time now that the hurricane has accelerated its advancement toward the continent," Warren informed him.

"You have my permission. Do what is necessary," Drake replied.

"Yes, Mr. President," Warren said.

"Take me directly to the Bunker," Drake ordered.

"Yes, Sir!" Warren complied as the winds began to increase upon the massive storm's approach. Acting President Drake was escorted inside the White House bunker complex to be officially sworn in as President.

***

Meanwhile, a massive TAC Team MICV aircraft flew over the coastline near the colonial mansion belonging to the Shadow State leader Richer over Savannah's tropospheric region.

Agents Abhu and Singh observed the incoming storm as they intruded upon the large mansion's airspace near the coast.

In Savannah, Georgia, the Shadow State leader, Richer, and his two subordinates, Agents Alicia Blaze and Midnight Thunder, maintained their satellite uplink to monitor the comms of the incoming EJFS TAC Team's arrival.

While he was wearing his headset, Thunder overheard some rumbling sounds of the MICV flying over the mansion. Then, the signal became static, and the power turned off.

"They're here!" Thunder shouted.

"Let us give them a proper welcome. Go join the others and blow their ship down," Richer dictated while winking.

Thunder and Blaze nodded at each other. They retrieved their lung-expansion inhalers, rushed outside of the manor, and instructed the other CIRB assets to equip their inhalers.

"Well, well, well! If it is not the EJFS yet again," Blaze retorted.

"Let us give them a windy welcome. Everyone, blow the intruders a kiss goodbye!" Thunder suggested.

Both Blaze and Thunder took three puffs of their inhalers and watched their bosoms expand. Blaze and Thunder blew a burst of mighty wind breath toward the MICV in the overcast skies over Savannah.

The other CIRB assets followed Blaze and Thunder's example, inhaling three puffs of their inhalers and blew a massive wall of wind breath toward the MICV.

Onboard the MICV, the EJFS TAC Team Agents spotted the Shadow State operatives' gathering similarly expelling wind breath that the EJFS superagents could do.

Abhu and Singh took notice of the gathering's activities below.

"Are they blowing wind as we do?" Abhu questioned.

Suddenly, a surge of wind struck the MICV, causing it to veer away from the target site.

"There's the answer to your question, Abhu," Singh replied.

The MICV began to veer sharply toward the northern shores of Savannah Beach as the wind breath of all Shadow State operatives overwhelmed the MICV's flight capabilities.

"Hang on, we're in for a rough landing!" Agent Nitin warned.

The EJFS agents braced for an impactful landing near the beach, several miles away from Richer's mansion.

A resounding thud struck the northern shores of Savannah Beach, which was heard from the mansion's exterior.

The Shadow State operatives laughed out loud menacingly while the rapid acceleration of the massive hurricane continued.

Off in the distance, the emergency hatch popped open, and all the EJFS agents aboard safely disembarked the crashed aircraft.

Singh radioed the EJFS Thunderhead Base, but the signal was weakened by the increasing turbulence above.

"Raj, come in, please!" Singh cried out.

The static continued to increase.

"Send a distress signal. They'll call for more backup!" Singh ordered.

"Yes, sir!" Abhu complied.

36: Khali Testifies in Congress: EJFS TAC Team Forms Boundary Along US East Coast

Richer's Manor

1.8 miles east of Savannah Beach, Georgia, USA

November 3, 2024

11:55 AM EDT, Sunday Morning

The EJFS TAC Team's crashed MICV aircraft transmitted a distress signal at Agent Abhu's command, summoning most of the fleet of EJFS MICV's to be dispatched toward the US East Coast.

Commander Singh gathered his TAC Team of superagents to assemble near the shorelines as the massively monstrous hurricane drew near the continent.

"Agents, we'll be joined by our partners soon. We must be ready for them before we can blow away the hurricane," Singh said.

"What is their ETA?" Agent Garjan asked.

"Fifteen to 20 minutes. We need to keep watch of any Shadow State operatives combing the area. Stay alert and look sharp!" Singh commanded.

Abhu and Singh noted that they were not far from Singh's Beach Villa in Savannah, but the team could not risk going inside because of the growing Shadow State presence due South to their location.

Abhu started ruminating about his nightmare from the previous night. He almost lost himself in a daze as he envisioned the wedding taking place at Singh's backyard from his vantage point.

Singh snapped Abhu out of it. "Abhu, are you okay?"

"Yeah, I'm fine," Abhu affirmed with a slight hesitative look toward Singh's back deck.

"Are you sure?" Singh continued.

"Yes, I'm sure. Don't worry about me," Abhu assured him.

"All right, then let's get back on task," Singh insisted.

Abhu carried his gear as they traveled farther up the beach, close to the boardwalk.

***

Meanwhile, at Capitol Hill, in Washington, D.C.: The Head of the EJFS, Khali, was led inside the enormous foyer of Congress as he was brought inside the House Intelligence Committee room where the proceedings against former President Hill would soon commence.

Members of the Press took photographic and video footage of Khali as he entered the chamber. He was joined alongside the Hastings father and son duo and former CIRB Director Janice Ausburn.

Additional state officials and distinguished members of the public arrived inside the chamber. Among them was Secretary of State Pamela Harsh. She sat across the left side of the seating area aisle to observe. She wanted to remain within grasping distance of Khali so that she could prepare to seize him at the most opportune moment.

Khali and the three witnesses stood at attention as the House Intelligence Committee members filed into the room.

The Chairman of the committee, House Representative Paul Erickson, opened the impeachment proceedings.

"Everyone, please be seated," Erickson insisted.

All in attendance took a seat in the public chamber as the hearings commenced.

Erickson spoke sternly in his address to Khali.

"Mr. Khali, you have opted to appear before this committee at your own risk. Our nation is only days away from the Presidential Election. You are accusing President Kenneth Hill of treason, sedition, and willful violation of his Oath of Office. Do you have any additional testimony to submit in your opening deposition?"

"Mr. Chairman, I am here in good faith to extend an olive branch between the EJFS and the United States of America, and I do not wish to trample over your constitutional republic. However, as I have observed and experienced the brunt of Hill's malicious acts, I have no choice but to call him out in these proceedings. I shall submit my video message to the committee as my sworn statement. I have already produced all relevant records about Hill's mischief, and I have documented every instance in which I had firsthand knowledge of his misdeeds," Khali stated for the record.

"The witness's opening deposition has been entered. The clerk will receive the witness's records as evidence," Chairman Erickson continued.

Representative Sandy Becker interjected. "Point of Clarification!"

"The congresswoman from Virginia has been recognized," Chairman Erickson consented.

"Thank you, Mister Chairman. Mr. Khali, you do realize that our country is facing an existential crisis by the hurricane created, as you alleged in your report? What can you offer for our time to ensure this process is speedy and fair for the good of the country and your organization?" Becker asked.

"I can only present the firsthand knowledge of what the fellow agents in my organization, along with the other three witnesses joining me today, and I am aware. I leave the outcome up to the proper procedures directed by US law," Khali replied clearly.

"I yield back to the Chairman." Becker relinquished the floor.

"Ladies and gentlemen, as stated by the congresswoman from Virginia, we are under an active extreme weather threat poised to strike the continent as early as tonight. That notwithstanding, we have a sworn duty to ensure that this process is fair and speedy, considering the revelations made public by Mister Khali. Therefore, we will conduct a day's worth of hearings until the time shall pass when we will need to adjourn the proceedings until after the storm passes," Chairman Erickson explained.

Khali remained silent, unwilling to divulge that the storm might be blown off the forecasted trajectory.

***

Meanwhile, at the EJFS Thunderhead Palace over Atlanta, Anastasia Zima watched the impeachment trial on the Smart HDTV in her quarters, mounted near the kitchen entryway.

Zima was agonizing at not being able to involve herself in the proceedings or the away mission in Savannah. She wanted to finagle a place into fighting against the Shadow State with Acting Commander Raj's approval.

She decided to check the directory of extensions to reach Raj's AERIAL video teleconferencing line. She went down the list of EJFS personnel and found Raj's contact information.

In his executive quarters, Raj heard his AERIAL VOIP calling app ringtone resonating in his room. He took a seat in front of the screen and accepted the call from Zima.

"Hello, Miss Zima. How may I help you?" Raj spoke cordially.

"Agent Raj, I wish to become more involved in your operation against the Shadow State. May I ask you if I can be of further assistance?" Zima queried.

"Miss Zima, I'm not sure if that we can guarantee your safety with the majority of superagents on an away mission in the TAC Team operations in Savannah. You would be putting yourself in harm's way." Raj rebuffed Zima's request.

"Agent Raj, trust me, I know this impending catastrophe was partially my fault. All I ask is for two agents to back me up. I can manage the rest on my end. Please, let me join the fray. Could you at least trust me and hear me out?" Zima pleaded.

Commander Raj ruminated on Zima's request, knowing that Khali would have his enormous posterior on a platter should she fail.

"All right, if you insist on being involved, I will grant you your request. You will be accompanied by Agents Prabodhan, Durga, Gangi, and our newest Agent, Indrina. You must promise me to be careful out there," Raj insisted.

"I promise I will do everything I can out there. Thank you for allowing me to redeem myself." Zima spoke with gratitude.

"You're welcome. Please meet us in the lobby before you deploy." Raj ended the call and took an elevator to the main floor.

Zima left her guestroom quarters to join her team bound for Savannah.

***

Around the end of the midday hour, Agent Indrina mastered her training as she exceeded her brother Abhu's ascension as a new agent.

Darsh and Indrina sat in the cafeteria, eating lunch with the inactive agents who were not partaking in field operations.

Darsh received a text message that Indrina had been summoned to her first mission.

"What is it, Darsh?" Indrina inquired with concern.

"You have been summoned for your first mission at Raj's behest. Let's finish up and follow me," Darsh insisted.

Indrina, while somewhat caught off-guard by her quick mission call, grabbed her lunch tray to return it to the kitchen return system in the rear of the cafeteria.

As Indrina passed through the entrance with Darsh, Pranay gave her a thumbs-up.

Indrina smiled back at him while nodding.

Commander Raj and Agents Prabodhan, Durga, and Gangi, along with Anastasia Zima, met with Darsh and Indrina in the main palace's foyer.

"What is she doing here?" Indrina whispered to Darsh.

"Indrina, it's okay. Let Raj explain," Darsh responded quietly in his soothing hypermasculine voice.

Agent Raj addressed Indrina. "Welcome aboard, Indrina! I am astonished by your rapid ascension as a new agent. I cannot help but wonder if our training is too easy for recruits. But enough of that, you and these exceptional agents will join with Anastasia to put a stop to the Shadow State. Your goal is to assist with the TAC Teams already on location in Savannah to stop the hurricane and neutralize Black Sparrow Zero and his minions," Raj explained.

"Anastasia is the one who used to be with Final Wave, right?" Indrina questioned.

Zima responded. "Yes, but not anymore, and I am certainly no longer affiliated with the Shadow State. Singh opened my eyes today, and now I want to redeem my past with all of you."

Indrina paused momentarily. She was very hesitant to trust Zima, given her history.

Raj interjected. "It's okay, Indrina. We've vetted her. She's clear to perform field operations on our behalf for the time being."

"All right, if you say so," Indrina relented.

"There is a MICV aircraft in the deployment bay waiting for you. Please suit up and head to the surface. Time is of the essence!" Raj commanded.

The female agents led by Agent Prabodhan made their way to the locker room to suit up before heading to the deployment bay.

While that was happening, Raj and Darsh spoke with each other candidly.

"I pray that Indrina will be safe in her first mission. Abhu would be furious with us if anything happened to her. I feel compelled to join her for Indrina's safety," Darsh remarked.

"Darsh, you haven't been involved with field operations for several years. Do you still think you can be of use to them in terms of physical aptitude?" Raj questioned.

"Yes, I'm sure. I feel that Indrina may fare better with me by her side. She trusts me, and I would never forgive myself if anything tragic happened to her," Darsh implored.

"Very well, you may go with them. But do not go overboard," Raj warned.

"Yes, Commander," Darsh saluted before leaving for the deployment bay.

Raj briefly sighed as he felt like the situation was spiraling out of his control.

***

Meanwhile, in Savannah Beach, Georgia: Agents Abhu and Singh rendezvoused with fellow EJFS agents from New York and Houston. They formed a line, spanning up along the coastline, and prepared to blow the hurricane back out to sea.

All agents glanced at each other semi-confidently as they felt the tide increasing in strength.

"We've only got one shot, people! Let us do this right!" Agent Singh rallied the troops as the winds began to intensify.

"On the count of three, we'll blow!" Abhu shouted.

"Inhale!" Singh commanded.

All agents on the eastern coastline of Savannah took a massive quantity of wind energy from the approaching storm. One after another, every super-agent from Savannah, Georgia to Long Island, New York, expelled powerful wind breath toward the hurricane as it began to react to the blowback from the super-agents on location.

The hurricane began to curve northeastward toward the Nova Scotia region in Newfoundland. The storm curled farther eastward as the skies started to clear slightly.

The superagents continued to blow the hurricane away from the shoreline, and their efforts successfully changed the storm's trajectory.

Soon after, the Shadow State operatives at Richer's Manor noticed the weather conditions changing.

Midnight Thunder tracked the changed trajectory of the storm on the satellite and radar through the battery-powered computers.

"Mr. Richer, the hurricane! It changed course!" Thunder exclaimed.

"No! *No!* ***NOOOO!***" Richer shouted with terror.

"What do we do now?" Alicia Blaze asked frantically.

"Get to the motorboat and head to the oil rig up north. We are going to initiate Plan B. Take the necklace and head to the docks!" Richer shouted.

"What about you?!" Thunder yelled.

"I'm staying put. This will be my last stand while you carry out the plan. Get the necklace to the oil rig and empty the contents into it. The retreating storm will take care of the rest. Now, go!" Richer insisted.

Shadow State operatives Blaze and Thunder took the necklace of Vritra and fled the manor to the back trail, rushing to the motorboat at the dock.

Richer uncovered a plethora of C-4 explosives to destroy his mansion to sacrifice himself and decimate EJFS forces while he equipped his handgun to further stall the EJFS front en route to his location.

37: EJFS Strikes Richer Manor: Shadow State Seizes Offshore Oil Rig

Richer's Manor

1.8 miles east of Savannah Beach, Georgia, USA

November 3, 2024

12:32 PM EDT, Sunday Afternoon

Many people witnessed the quick exit of the massive hurricane blown off the course trajectory and back out to sea across the US East Coast. The skies cleared out as sunshine and a few clouds lingered following the storm's exit.

Many along the East Coast were relieved that the storm had moved away from the coastline. Thus, the looming threat of the hurricane's impact appeared to be over.

The EJFS agents lining the coast were exuberant with glee, not knowing that Vritra's Revival was not yet thwarted.

Agents Abhu and Singh and their team of agents were stricken with fear as they noticed a motorboat with Shadow State operatives, Blaze and Thunder, at the helm. The two were speeding toward the outer waters of the Atlantic Ocean.

"Oh, no," Abhu said grimly.

"Everybody, the threat is not over yet! Richer's minions must be taking the necklace out of reach!" Singh shouted.

Singh retrieved his smartphone, which had regained a service signal. He immediately called Agent Lochan at EJFS Central Command.

"EJFS, Lochan."

"Lochan, it's Singh. I need you to lock onto the GPS transponder of the motorboat that just left the Shadow State manor. We have reason to believe that the Shadow State leader is initiating a contingency plan if the storm is mitigated," Singh urged emphatically.

Lochan reacted with utmost urgency. "I'll put Basu to work on tracking them to their destination. Do you have any ideas where they might be heading?" Lochan asked.

"I don't know. Where is the storm's current location?" Singh inquired.

"The storm moved northeast and is advancing near Edisto's outer reaches, near the Carolinas," Lochan informed.

Singh quickly pondered to himself before he suddenly realized the intended endgame of the Shadow State.

"Oh, my God! Lochan, I need you to run a search for all offshore oil drilling rigs near the area and send them to my phone right away. I have a theory that we have not considered. They might intend to dispense Vritra's remnants into the oil rig to reconstitute them," Singh spoke with urgency and fear.

"Oil rigs? Those had to have been shut down during the storm's approach. They closed all their points of entry last night," Lochan responded in bewilderment.

"Exactly, they know that the oil rigs would be a high-probability and high-value target. If they manage to access the drilling equipment, it will spell catastrophe for all of us," Singh answered with increasing urgency.

"Okay, I'll compile the list of oil rigs and put the GPS tracking ping on the motorboat. You have backup coming your way. Agent Durga and Gangi are leading a team to Savannah to run point against Richer in his manor, and I will reroute all other TAC Teams to wherever the GPS tracking hit takes us. I'll send another MICV. Both you and Abhu need to stop the two

439

operatives on the motorboat by any means necessary," Lochan emphasized.

"Acknowledged," Singh affirmed.

Singh addressed his partner. "Abhu, we need to follow that motorboat. They may be headed to an oil rig to accomplish their goal. The MICV is en route to pick us up," Singh spoke to Abhu calmly.

"What about Richer?" Abhu asked.

"There's another team on the way. Other groups will divert to the manor for backup. This is it, Abhu. We have to stop those two!" Singh exclaimed.

Singh commanded the remaining agents on the beach.

"Attention, all agents: Abhu and I must head out to stop the two operatives from releasing the remnants of Vritra into the oil rigging sites. I am ordering the rest of you to storm Richer's manor and take him out. This is our last stand, so let's make it count!" Singh rallied the troops.

Suddenly, the MICV dispatched from the Atlanta EJFS arrived on the beach. Abhu and Singh boarded the transformative aircraft piloted by Agent Pranay, much to both agents' surprise.

"Pranay?!" Singh shouted.

"Yes, that's me. We don't have time to chat. We must go now!" Pranay exclaimed.

The MICV locked onto the motorboat's GPS transponder location, and they pursued the watercraft.

***

Meanwhile, the MICV carrying the backup TAC Team of Agents Prabodhan, Darsh, Durga, Gangi, Indrina, and Anastasia Zima, arrived over the Shadow State manor.

The MICV fired their machine guns over the property and neutralized most enemies guarding the property while landing their aircraft several miles away from the manor.

Agents Prabodhan and Darsh led the team into action. They exited the MICV and began storming the premises, killing CIRB hostile targets.

Richer, watching from his seaside manor's attic, peeked out the window as the gunfight ensued. He knew that he had nowhere else to run.

Agents Prabodhan and Darsh fired a barrage of gunfire toward every hostile target.

Suddenly, another black armored Hummer showed up on the scene.

Agent Onyx, a fierce brute representing the Shadow State through the CIRB's weaponized arm, joined the fray. Onyx outmatched the leaner, female agents as they shifted their focus to attack him.

"I'm here to crush, kill, and destroy the lot of you!" Onyx rumbled thunderously.

Onyx delivered a devastating left hook slugger punch to Prabodhan, who had the wind knocked out of him.

The other agents, including Darsh, Durga, Gangi, Indrina, and Zima, maintained their distance from the oversized brute.

Prabodhan recovered from the attack while Onyx wrapped an extensive line of chains around his fists as weapons.

"Durga and Gangi, take Indrina and Anastasia inside the manor to find Richer. Darsh and I will take this guy down," Prabodhan spoke intently and quietly even though his lip was partially lacerated.

"You heard him. More backup will come soon. Now, go!" Darsh insisted.

"Come on, let's go find Richer," Durga directed.

The women agents rushed to the front doors of the manor, which were locked. Durga used all her might to kick open the doors, and the four women entered the spacious house.

All four agents drew their weapons and pointed them forward, searching every space and room for Richer.

"The first floor is clear. Heading upstairs," Durga announced to her team as they ascended the stairs to the second level.

Prabodhan and Darsh attempted to engage the gigantic supervillain, Onyx, as he wrapped his line of chains around his fists with a vicious look of rage on his face.

Darsh summoned a thunderstorm to use the lightning against Onyx in the EJFS's favor.

"Oh, what a clever man you are!" Onyx quipped.

The storm continued to intensify overhead as lightning and thunder crashed in the skies above.

Prabodhan kicked Onyx in the stomach, but the attacks seemed to have little impact.

Onyx smiled wickedly as he equipped his lung-expanding inhaler solution, taking three puffs and blowing Prabodhan into the front window of the house, shattering the glass to pieces.

"NO!" Darsh cried out.

"It looks like it is down to you and me, comrade!" Onyx mocked.

Suddenly, backup arrived and fired a barrage of gunfire onto Onyx as rainfall began to intensify.

Darsh kept his distance and flexed both of his enormous biceps in a sharp motion, causing a mighty thunderbolt to strike Onyx's chain-wrapped fists and electrocuting Onyx.

Onyx fell to the ground, unconscious.

Darsh sprinted inside the manor to revive Prabodhan and rejoined the female agents hunting down Richer while backup agents swarmed the area.

***

Meanwhile, Shadow State operatives Alicia Blaze and Midnight Thunder approached the nearest oil rig off the Eastern Seaboard. They were five nautical miles east of Charleston when they found an evacuated oil rig.

"We have to find a way inside, Thunder," Blaze urged.

"Grab the grappling hook gun. We'll climb our way inside," Thunder instructed.

Blaze retrieved the grappling hook gun and shot the hook onto the lower platform ten feet above them.

"Hold on tight," Thunder insisted in his deep voice.

Blaze wrapped her arms around Thunder's massive torso as the grappling gun hoisted them both to the lower platform while they clutched the carrying case of Vritra's necklace.

"Where's the drilling room?" Thunder asked.

"It must be on the sublevel floor. Let's head downstairs," Blaze suggested.

Both operatives traveled down three flights of stairs to the platform's bottom. The drilling room was located on the lower level.

"There it is," Thunder indicated.

"Open the drilling port," Blaze directed.

"Yes, ma'am!" Thunder obliged.

While Thunder attempted to unseal the drilling equipment, Pranay piloted the MICV with EJFS Agents Abhu and Singh. They soon made their presence known.

"We've got company!" Blaze exclaimed.

"I'll keep working on this. You fend off the EJFS agents," Thunder insisted.

Blaze readied her handgun as she stayed within earshot of the MICV humming over the area.

Blaze kept her weapon drawn as she peered through the corridors.

The MICV descended upon the helipad on the top of the oil rig. Pranay identified both Blaze and Thunder's heat signatures in two separate locations.

"Singh, I have detected both hostiles inside the rig, and one of them is in the drilling room on the bottom level," Pranay explained.

"All right, let's go, Abhu. There's no time to waste," Singh commanded.

"Yes, my friend," Abhu complied.

"I'll stay here to run logistics," Pranay announced.

"Very well, keep out of sight," Singh accepted.

Both agents exited the MICV and entered the rig's top level, descending the stairs to locate Blaze and Thunder.

The massive hurricane maintained its changed trajectory, but it was still in the oil rig's vicinity and gradually weakening.

Thunder unsealed the drilling floor. He rushed to the control room to power the oil cylinders to begin the thermalization process.

Meanwhile, Pranay monitored all activity on the oil rig platform when he noticed that one of the cylinders was activating.

"Agents, be warned. Cylinder D6 has initiated a process. You must hurry and stop them from pouring the remnants into the pipes!" Pranay urged.

"We copy," Singh answered.

Suddenly, Blaze appeared out of cover and fired a round of gunfire toward both agents, causing Abhu and Singh to take shelter behind a corner room.

Blaze approached the corner office room's shattered windows, pointing her gun toward the open segment of glass.

Abhu and Singh took cover behind the desk inside the corner room.

Singh instructed Abhu, "On the count of three, we'll blow her away."

Both Abhu and Singh began to inhale large quantities of air in their chest, causing their massive pectorals to expand.

"One, two, three," Singh counted.

Both agents rose from the floor and blew Blaze down the stairway. She tumbled down the stairs and fell, hitting her head on a steam pipe.

"Pranay! Kim's imposter is down. I repeat, Kim's imposter is subdued," Singh announced on his comm mic.

Abhu and Singh held Alicia Blaze at gunpoint, hoping to extract crucial information on the whereabouts of her accomplice, Midnight Thunder.

"Where is your accomplice?" Singh asked.

"I'm not afraid to die," Blaze remained defiant while gritting her teeth.

Singh cocked his handgun and pointed it at Blaze's head.

"Last chance, or I'll make sure you go down with this rig," Singh warned.

Blaze remained silent while straining to control her anguish.

Abhu kept sight of his surroundings while keeping a close eye on Blaze.

"Thunder! They are here! Empty the –" Blaze was interrupted by a gunshot to the head by Singh and was killed.

"Go now!" Singh commanded urgently.

Midnight Thunder overheard the commotion upstairs. He quickly responded by retrieving the metal case carrying Vritra's necklace.

The thermalization process was 45% complete and accelerating, but not yet at the prime percentage to perform the deed, which was at least 75%.

Thunder heard a metal clang from the floor above him. He stopped what he was doing, pointed his gun upward, and maintained control of the drilling room.

Abhu and Singh rushed down the stairs and tried to rotate the sealed door to enter the drilling room floor.

"Thunder, we have you cornered! Come out with the necklace, and we can end this without you getting hurt," Singh ordered.

"The only way this will end is with you coming out with the necklace with your hands in the air now!" Abhu added forcefully.

Thunder was sitting on the sealing floor while the heating indicator displayed 60%.

Soon enough, Vritra's necklace started to respond to the thermal energy emanating from the cylinder, and the dragon-shaped amulet began to glow faintly.

A shroud of darkness filled the oil rig's interior as the lights dimmed, and the room became darkened.

"You're out of time! It's over!" Thunder shouted and began to cackle like a maniac.

Suddenly, the oil rig platform began to tremble and shake as Vritra's remnants became more active.

Darkness overtook the world along the east coast, and the daylight began to fade away and changed into an ominous red hue.

In Washington D.C., as the impeachment proceedings resumed, the view outside became rather dark, and a sharp tremor shook the Capitol Building.

Khali was horrified as he knew what was happening, and he had no control over the imminent apocalyptic return of Vritra.

At the Shadow State Manor in Savannah, the backup TAC Team reached the attic where Richer was waiting with the detonator device in his hands. He cackled like an evil madman.

"It's too late. Vritra is about to return once more. HA-HA-HA-HA-HA!" Richer chuckled menacingly.

"Dear God," Darsh exclaimed in horror as the team witnessed the skies turning crimson. It seemed that all hope was lost.

38: The Last Hurrah over the Southeast Atlantic: Vritra's Cataclysmic Return

Richer's Manor

1.8 miles east of Savannah Beach, Georgia, USA

November 3, 2024

1:07 PM EDT, Sunday Afternoon

The skies over the US East Coast darkened over Vritra's imminent return, and the darkness spread vastly to all areas around the world.

Darsh and his TAC Team of agents stood in the attic at the Shadow State Manor as the darkness overtook the world. Richer maintained a watchful gaze on his detonator device. He was on the verge of sacrificing himself explosively to hamper further the EJFS efforts to prevent the total return of Vritra.

Indrina grew increasingly fearful that she was not going to make it out of the mansion alive.

Richer taunted. "It won't be long now. All of you are about to witness the return of Vritra and experience his terrible wrath."

Darsh attempted to reason with Richer.

"Richer, you don't have to do this. When we entered the attic, you hesitated to blow yourself up. That must mean you are trying to bide your time until you destroy us all. But it doesn't need to end like this." Darsh spoke calmly.

"You can't undo what is about to happen, and I hold all the power. There's no getting out of here alive now. Even if I were to let you all go, you have little time to stop what is coming," Richer retorted unapologetically.

Darsh continued. "I am starting to doubt that you are not afraid to die. If so, you would have detonated yourself by now."

Richer mocked, "You know nothing, fool! I have already fulfilled my goal, and now all of you will watch the world end with me."

Zima was observing the exchange. "I have a proposition for you: Why don't you let my friends leave alive. I will stay here. Please, let my friends go!" She implored. Zima felt a sick pang in the pit of her stomach.

Darsh rebuffed Zima's proposal. "Anastasia, no! We came in together, and we leave or die here together!"

Richer decided to entertain Zima's plea.

"I see, you have dedicated yourself to your newfound cause to protect your friends. So, you desire to fall on the sword for them," Richer chuckled malevolently.

Prabodhan interjected and drew his gun and pointed it at Richer. "I won't let you take this woman down with you!"

Darsh redirected. "Prabodhan, holster your weapon!"

"Not until he tells us where the necklace is located!" Prabodhan shouted.

"Don't do this, Prabodhan!" Durga pleaded.

Richer continued. "Very well, shoot me! You know your only way out of this is to leave Anastasia with me. Otherwise, I will detonate the explosives, and nobody gets out of here alive."

Prabodhan pointed his handgun toward Richer intently and angrily. He disengaged the safety lock.

Richer hovered his thumb on the detonator in response to Prabodhan.

"I would urge you to think this through, agent. Do you truly value this woman's life over eight billion people living on this planet?" Richer added while smiling deviously.

Prabodhan grunted, lowered his handgun, and returned it safely to his holster.

Zima continued. "He's right. My life doesn't take priority over the lives of everyone else. I wish there were another way, but there is not. I will take the fall for everything that has happened."

Thunder started rumbling outside as the dark energy continued to accelerate its growth and influence over the world.

"I'm sorry that it has come to this, Anastasia," Darsh spoke somberly.

"Don't be sorry, Darsh. If this is how my life is meant to end, then I know that I have died for your network's noble cause." Zima smiled.

Darsh nodded before giving Zima one final comforting embrace goodbye.

"Thank you for everything," Zima sighed.

Richer shouted. "That was very touching. Now, everyone except Anastasia needs to get out of my house! Go!"

Darsh looked at Richer with contempt, but Darsh chose to honor both Zima's and Richer's final wishes.

"Let's get out of here," Darsh commanded.

The TAC Team's remaining members left Zima alone with Richer as the window to stop Vritra's return continued to narrow.

"How does it feel, knowing that everyone on this planet is about to die for everything you've done in the past two days, hmm?" Richer mocked Zima in her moments of profound regret.

"Please, spare me the mind games, Richer. You got your wish. Now, be quiet and let me be," Zima responded with disgust.

Richer smiled wickedly as the hour of doom continued to draw near.

Darsh, Durga, Indrina, and Prabodhan fled the manor and encountered Onyx, who had recovered from his electrocution.

"Unh-unh-uh! You four aren't going anywhere!" Onyx taunted.

The four agents stood nervously while Indrina gulped in fear.

***

Meanwhile, inside the oil drilling rig platform, Abhu and Singh continued their standoff against the remaining Shadow State devotee, Midnight Thunder (formerly known as Judson Clayborn).

Knowing that Vritra's necklace contents have begun to resonate, jeopardizing the survival of humankind, Abhu and Singh were forced to break into the drilling room.

Abhu used all his strength to pry open the sealed door, allowing EJFS Agents Abhu and Singh to enter the room.

Both agents pointed their guns forward and performed a grid search of every cylinder on the drilling room floor. They attempted to locate the column identified as D6, which had an active drilling process launched by Thunder.

Thunder heard the approaching agents and acted by pre-emptively trying to unscrew the dragon-shaped talisman that was faintly glowing red and orange.

Abhu located Thunder. He signaled Singh of Thunder's location.

"Thunder, put down the talisman! Then get on the ground facedown!" Singh commanded.

Thunder maintained his stance as he held the talisman of Vritra, now detached from the necklace.

"I said, put the talisman down, *now!*" Singh reiterated his order.

Thunder remained defiant of the EJFS agents engaging him.

"You're too late. There's no going back now." Thunder laughed.

Abhu and Singh continued to stand off against Thunder.

"Thunder, you are outnumbered. The EJFS has this oil rigging platform locked on target for an aerial assault. The only guarantee that will keep you from going down with this platform will be your surrender of the talisman, and you will walk away from here without anyone else getting hurt," Abhu added.

Thunder looked at both Abhu and Singh intently and proceeded to comply with the order.

"That's it. Get on the floor, spread-eagle position. Set the talisman down gently," Singh continued.

Thunder slowly lay down on the darkened drilling room floor as he continued his grip on the talisman.

"Slowly place the talisman down and put your hands behind your waist," Singh ordered.

Thunder set down the talisman. However, he still maintained a grip on the dragon-shaped vessel.

"Let go of the vessel!" Singh shouted.

Thunder sneered at both Abhu and Singh in defiance.

"Obey my command, Thunder! Release your grip of the vessel immediately!" Singh demanded.

Abhu noted Thunder's subversive actions, just as Thunder appeared to make his move.

Thunder prepared to shove the vessel into the open port, but Abhu stopped him cold with a gunshot to his hand.

The vessel containing the essence of Vritra continued to glow with powerful energy.

Abhu radioed the EJFS Command Center. "Thunder is down! I repeat: Thunder is down!"

Abhu and Singh held Thunder in place before placing him in handcuffs and isolating him from the vessel. Thus, the threat of Vritra's Revenge had seemingly passed.

Suddenly, the D6 cylinder's thermalization reached 75%, and the vessel containing Vritra's remnants caused the oil rig platform to quake.

The vessel tipped over, and the contents drained into the drilling port.

"NO!" Abhu shouted in horror.

Singh frantically radioed the command center without hesitation.

"The vessel has drained into the oil rig! I repeat: The remnants of Vritra are inside the port!" Singh spoke into his comm mic with tremendous fear.

"Basu, access the Atlantic Drilling Management System! We need to force a shutdown of the platform before Vritra is reborn!" Abhu ordered on the EJFS comm system.

Basu reacted quickly from the command center. "I'm on it, Abhu!"

"To the control room!" Singh shouted.

Both Abhu and Singh dragged Thunder to the control room at the rear of the drilling floor.

Thunder mocked both agents defiantly. "You can't stop what's coming! You're too late!"

"Shut up, and keep walking," Abhu nudged Thunder as the darkened corridors became illuminated in a red hue.

Abruptly, the drilling floor started to shake again.

"Basu, you must hurry! We're out of time!" Singh spoke into his comm mic.

"We're doing the best we can on our end, Singh! The system manifest is going haywire. You need to attempt a manual override to shut down the rig! We can only do so much to control the thermalization process," Basu urged before there was sharp feedback on the audio.

Suddenly, the audio system disconnected, and EJFS lost contact with Abhu and Singh.

"Singh? Singh?!" Basu tried to reconnect the comms.

Lochan and Raj noticed the lost connection signal from the giant screens.

"What's going on?" Raj inquired.

"The thermalization process, coupled with Vritra's energy, knocked out our audio connection. All we can do now is try to regain control of the rig." Basu spoke grimly.

Raj and Lochan watched the video footage of the action, horrified that Vritra's rebirth was near.

***

Meanwhile, the interior of the oil drilling platform continued to shake and collapse amid the process of Vritra's return, which grew increasingly imminent.

Singh and Abhu reached the control room, and they frantically locked Thunder in place while both agents tried to attempt a manual override to shut down the platform.

Amid the chaos, the retreating storm that the EJFS agents managed to blow away earlier regained strength while hovering over the Atlantic Ocean. Frequent lightning and thunder blasted throughout the darkened crimson skies as remnants of Vritra began to reconstitute.

"Open the manual shutdown latch, now!" Singh commanded.

Abhu ripped the manual override panel out from its hinges and pulled the lever, but it was locked under the growing pressure that continued to build underneath the drilling floor.

Abhu kept trying to pull the latch, but the pressure was far too intense.

"It's stuck!" Abhu exclaimed.

Singh and Abhu tried a cohesive effort to pull the lever, but it would barely budge.

Both agents heard the explosively loud thunder rumbles outside the platform as it continued quaking.

Singh and Abhu pulled with all their might, and the lever strained to lower.

Suddenly the lights shut off, leaving the three agents in the dark with only the glowing red energy from the active cylinder emanating Vritra's evil power.

A deeply sinister laugh emitted from inside the drilling room floor.

"Oh, no!" Abhu muttered in horror.

"He's back!" Thunder declared while laughing maniacally.

39: Vritra Consumes Midnight Thunder

Control Room

Edisto Oil Rig Platform – Drilling Room Floor

3.5 miles east of Edisto, South Carolina, USA

November 3, 2024

1:43 PM EDT, Sunday Afternoon

The residents of the world were fear-stricken as a shroud of darkness covered the entirety of the planet.

The endgame of resurrecting Vritra had succeeded despite all EJFS efforts to prevent the event.

Raj and Lochan watched in terror from the EJFS Command Center, knowing that Vritra had completed his second rebirth.

***

In Savannah, Georgia, all EJFS agents on location against the evil pairing of Onyx, Richer, with Zima (who was held captive by Richer in exchange for the survival of the four EJFS agents trapped in place by Onyx). They could only observe the glowing bright red, orange hue faintly emanating north, off the coast of Edisto, South Carolina. The oil rig was radiating energy from Vritra's awakening.

Onyx mocked the agents. "The end is here, you meddling fools!"

***

In Washington D.C., the Head of the EJFS, Master Khali, quickly exited the Capitol to see the terrible sight off the East Coast of the US.

The public officials were in mass hysteria amid the chaos.

Khali addressed the visiting superagents from the New York and Washington D.C. EJFS subdivisions.

"Jaswinder and Bahadur, do what you can to maintain order," Khali commanded. "I must return to the palace!"

Jaswinder replied. "But, Master, what about your testimony?"

"It'll have to wait. I am needed elsewhere," Khali concluded before rushing back inside his ICV and quickly launched in return to the EJFS Atlanta Base.

***

Raj remembered the Gatekeeper's Blade was stored inside the palace's upper dome and could be the last hope to destroy Vritra again.

Without hesitation, Raj rushed out of the command center to Khali's office. He inputted his entry code to enter the suite. He inserted his golden key card to access the hidden elevator door inconspicuously placed behind Khali's office.

Raj boarded the elevator and used his handprint to gain access to the inside of the sealed dome top where the Gatekeeper's Blade was stored.

***

Inside the drilling floor's control room, both Abhu and Singh's efforts to stop Vritra's return proved futile.

Abhu and Singh rushed up the stairs to return to the MICV parked on the helipad, where Pranay was waiting with tremendous anxiety.

Pranay pulled himself together upon seeing Abhu and Singh.

"Hurry, get inside! We have to get airborne!" Pranay urged emphatically.

***

Midnight Thunder remained inside the control room while still shackled to the pipes, witnessing Vritra's return coming to completion.

Thunder remained fearless as he longed to see Vritra in his complete form.

Vritra's chillingly ominous voice called out to Thunder.

"You, my liberator! Approach me!" Vritra's booming voice echoed powerfully within the confines of the drilling platform floor.

Suddenly, Thunder's handcuffs, while attached to a pipe, magically released themselves. He was free.

Thunder was now in a calm trance under Vritra's control.

Vritra caused the control room door to unlock and open as Thunder entered the drilling floor, and the door shut by itself.

Thunder remained under Vritra's influence. The dragon's presence entranced him, rendering him helpless.

Vritra's voice rumbled in a deep tone.

"I know who you truly are. You have been transformed into your current form to bring about my return to reign over the world. Yes, you have been instrumental in my reawakening. You have always pursued my power for months, and now..." Vritra trailed off.

Suddenly, an explosion of oil and fire emerged from the drilling floor.

Vritra's humanoid form emerged from the depths of the drilling floor in all his massive size, and he smiled upon his liberator wickedly.

"You and I will be one, and you will do my bidding," Vritra concluded.

Thunder (a.k.a. Judson Clayborn) fawned over the dragon's immense power, intoxicated with an affinity for the monstrous humanoid dragon.

"Take me now," Thunder spoke in a moment of reckless abandon.

"As you wish!" Vritra answered.

Vritra transformed into a red cloud and entirely entered Thunder's body, and Vritra's power was absorbed into him.

The influx of Vritra's power entering Thunder's body caused a series of pleasurable sensations all around him as there was a booming and rumbling sound emitting from within him.

Thunder was overcome with a potent force that was the evil essence of Vritra. The feeling felt so incredibly enjoyable to Thunder's body, and it caused him to grow in size and strength.

Midnight Thunder's body continued to grow like an enormous giant, and Thunder enjoyed every moment of it as the fantastic feelings intensified. He moaned as the power of Vritra swelled Thunder up into an enormously towering figure.

Soon after, the massively expanding body of Midnight Thunder outgrew the oil rig, and it burst into flames.

Midnight Thunder resumed his growing into a supermassive giant of epic proportions.

***

Abhu, Singh, and Pranay observed the happenings from the destroyed oil rig near the Atlantic Ocean from above the stratosphere.

"Oh, my goodness! Is that who I think it is?" Pranay asked, horrified.

"It's Midnight Thunder. Vritra must have housed his power in him. He's an enormous giant now!" Singh marveled.

Thunder stopped growing and was now well over 150 feet tall. He towered high above the sky as the chaotic storm in the troposphere continued to rage.

"Whoo! What a rush!" Thunder shouted, and his voice reached far and wide around the world.

"What are we going to do now?" Abhu asked in desperation.

"We need the sword you used last year to defeat Vritra. That could be our only hope!" Singh suggested.

The AERIAL VOIP calling system aboard the MICV sounded as Raj and Khali called in a video teleconference call. Singh swiped the green button to answer it.

"It's Singh. Are you two seeing what we're seeing?"

Raj explained grimly. "Yes, unfortunately. Thunder's body has been used to house Vritra's power. We have no choice but to destroy him to dispel Vritra once again."

Abhu urged. "Khali, we're going to need all the help we can summon to defeat this monstrosity. We'll need every base in the vicinity to attack Thunder before he crushes the country!"

Khali replied while nodding. "It will be done."

Raj informed them. "Agents, I have the Gatekeeper's Blade. We must find a way to use it to draw Vritra out of Thunder and dispel Vritra. You must exploit a weak spot to bring Vritra out of the host body of Thunder."

"We understand, Raj. We will surround Thunder to subdue him," Singh affirmed.

Khali implored the star agents. "Agents, I don't know if this will be our last battle, but you must succeed! The world is counting on you!"

Singh continued. "Acknowledged, I hope we live to survive this day!"

"Godspeed, Agents!" Khali disconnected from the call.

"Raj, how do you want to proceed?" Singh asked.

"I am on my way to you shortly. I will join the battle against Vritra," Raj explained.

"Understood, we will see you soon. Good luck!" Singh concluded.

The call ended, and all MICV's gathered in a circle while the nearby Thunderhead bases encircled Midnight Thunder thoroughly under Vritra's power and influence.

***

In Savannah, the TAC Team of Darsh, Durga, Gangi, Indrina, and Prabodhan faced off against the towering and massive Shadow State operative, Agent Onyx.

Onyx smirked arrogantly. "Give it up. You can't win."

Darsh challenged Onyx. "Let's put that to the test."

Onyx's smirk turned into a scowl as he prepared to engage in combat with five agents.

Darsh delivered a hard slugger punch to the face of Onyx. It had minimal impact.

Prabodhan fired his handgun into Onyx's powerful chest, but the bullets did not wound him and seemed to have bounced off his massive chest.

With a forceful swing, Onyx's backhand slapped the handgun out of Prabodhan's hands.

From inside the manor, Zima saw that her friends were in danger. She decided to act.

"Where do you think you're going?!" Richer asked angrily.

"I'm not letting my friends die for your cause!" Zima barked.

"They'll die anyway by the day's end!" Richer shouted.

"You don't know that!" Zima responded defiantly.

"Anastasia, stop!" Richer demanded, but Zima quickly drew her concealed pistol and shot Richer dead, which caught the EJFS agents' attention outside the manor.

"Anastasia?" Darsh muttered.

Suddenly, Richer's body was tossed out of the attic window.

"Richer!" Onyx shouted remorsefully.

Onyx rushed to the front of the manor, where Richer lay dead. He tried to resuscitate him.

"Oh, Onyx?" Zima coyly taunted.

Onyx looked upward and saw that Zima held the detonator in her hands.

"You wouldn't!" Onyx baited her.

"Think again!" Zima pressed the detonator, and the manor burst into flames, killing Onyx in the blast with Zima still inside. The mansion was completely leveled.

"Oh, my God!" Indrina's mouth was agape with shock.

"Oh, Anastasia!" Darsh fell to his knees and wept quietly.

The other agents were at a loss. They could not believe what had happened.

"Oh, Anastasia, *NO!*" Darsh continued to cry for Zima's death, taking her own life to eliminate Onyx.

Prabodhan tried to console Darsh as rain began to fall in response to Darsh's emotional anguish.

The fires in the house became doused out by the heavy rains, and the agents saw the wrecked estate of Richer's manor.

Zima was seen face up with her clothes, hair, and face burnt and disfigured with third-degree burns.

"Darsh, we need to leave. There's nothing more we can do!" Durga insisted sympathetically.

Darsh stood up while in continued emotional pain, and he left with the remaining EJFS agents to return to the Thunderhead Base.

***

Agents Abhu, Singh, and Pranay rendezvoused with Raj, who held the key to the destruction of Vritra: The Gatekeeper's Blade. They rushed to Atlanta in aid of the US.

They all watched in horror as the gigantic Midnight Thunder walked toward Atlanta and began shooting out lightning on everyone below. He crushed many buildings in his wake.

Thunder laughed evilly in Vritra's voice.

The National Guard, and Army Reserves summoned by Acting President Drake's command, assembled and attempted to take down the giant.

"Fire at will!" Drake ordered.

"Locked on target! Ready to engage!" Several fighter pilots spoke into their comm mics.

The fighter jets fired their rockets, but with the help of Vritra, Thunder shot down all the rocket fire with thunderbolts, obliterating them.

Thunder shot out more thunderbolts from his palms, destroying all aircraft attacking him.

Drake was undeterred in trying to stop the giant brute from destroying the country.

"Don't give up, people!" Drake commanded. "Hit him with everything we've got!"

All the fighter jets and stealth bombers prepared to drop their most powerful non-nuclear explosives.

However, Thunder utilized the help of Vritra's fiery breath to incinerate all the military aircraft trying to destroy him.

Air Force General Marshall Collins informed Drake.

"Mr. Drake, he just took all of our army reserves. We don't have anything left to strike the target," Collins spoke frantically.

Suddenly, many EJFS MICVs in the vicinity swarmed toward Atlanta, along with the force of EJFS Thunderhead Bases. The Elite Justice Force Squad came to the aid of the American Armed Forces.

"Help is on the way!" EJFS Agent Raj hailed the President's radio frequency before the fleet of EJFS MICVs sped toward the action.

"This is our moment. Let us give it our all!" Agent Abhu encouraged the rest of the superagency near the city as the final showdown began.

40: The Final Battle in The Atlanta Skies

EJFS Command Center – Level 13

EJFS Thunderhead Base – Atlanta Branch

Main Building

Current Location: 10,000 feet above Atlanta, Georgia

November 3, 2024

2:19 PM EDT, Sunday Afternoon

The EJFS fleet had reached the Atlanta city limits and prepared a methodical aerial assault. The target was Midnight Thunder, who was under the control of Vritra.

"Fire everything at him!" Khali ordered from the Command Center.

"Yes, Master!" Raj responded to the command of Khali.

All the MICV's attacked Midnight Thunder with everything they had.

Many EJFS paramilitary aircraft kept their distance while they fired their attacks on Thunder.

Thunder attempted to counteract by striking lightning bolts against the EJFS fleet, and a few New York EJFS MICV's suffered critical hits, forcing them to retreat.

"Find a weak spot to exploit!" Raj commanded his entire fleet in conjunction with all neighboring EJFS Branches.

Agent Abhu remembered that Thunder was shot in the left hand earlier, so he attempted a precision laser fire to attack Thunder's left hand.

Abhu's laser shot struck Thunder's left palm. It effectively brought the menacing giant to one knee.

"He's down. Fire at will!" Raj ordered.

All EJFS military aircraft fired a barrage of rockets toward Thunder, and all missiles struck the target. Thunder was momentarily immobilized, but he recovered after the power of Vritra restored him to full health.

Thunder laughed in his gigantic and powerful voice.

Vritra spoke through Thunder. "Your weapons are no good against this vessel as long as I have control over him," Vritra mocked the fleet loudly.

"Raj, we need to use the Gatekeeper's Blade to bring him down!" Singh insisted.

"Acknowledged. Bring me close to Thunder's left palm. Everyone else: cover me!" Raj directed.

"You've got one shot at him, Raj! Make it count!" Abhu urged.

All EJFS military aircraft fired multiple laser attacks and missile strikes.

Raj sped toward the giant attacking them. He held the Gatekeeper's Blade in both hands and struck Thunder's left palm.

The sword strike was highly effective in reducing Thunder's health, and Vritra's influence over Thunder was weakened.

Raj maintained his aerial assault on Vritra. He fired his machine gun mounted on the MICV hood. The barrage of artillery rounds weakened Vritra's health slightly before he resumed control over Thunder as his vessel.

"Keep fighting, everyone! He's not done yet!" Khali encouraged on the comms.

Vritra's spirit became angrier, with Thunder rampaging throughout the city in response.

Thunder started firing many thunderbolts from his hands, and a quarter of EJFS fleets were struck down. Most of the New York EJFS MICV's were destroyed. But the remainder of the fleet was undeterred in its quest to save America and the world.

"Cover me! I am going back in with the blade!" Raj commanded.

Abhu and Singh, along with the rest of the EJFS aircraft, laid down cover fire for Raj's safe passage to strike Thunder's left palm once again.

Raj struck the left palm of Thunder with the Gatekeeper's Blade, and once again, Thunder was immobilized. Vritra's evil spirit emerged from Thunder, and Raj fired another barrage of heavy artillery fire from his machine gun.

Vritra suffered critical damage and lost control of the vessel of Midnight Thunder.

It was only Vritra's spirit that was left to be dispelled by the Gatekeeper's Blade.

Raj pointed the Gatekeeper's Blade toward the spirit of Vritra, and the sword shot out a golden, bright light that completely annihilated Vritra.

Vritra's remnants were turned back into the dragon-shaped amulet initially attached to the heirloom necklace that once adorned Ravan's neck.

The threat of Vritra's Revenge had ceased.

Soon after, the skies cleared out, and the sunshine returned to illuminate the country that afternoon.

The EJFS was ecstatic in defeating Vritra yet again.

However, there was still a crucial task of keeping Vritra's remnant in its dormant form away from the wrong hands.

The EJFS fleet retreated, except for Agents Raj, Abhu, and Singh. They landed safely in Atlanta after searching for Vritra's remains, which were found near Georgia's state capital.

Abhu, Singh, and Raj glanced at each other before they safely contained the remnant and placed it in a sealed waterproof container.

Raj ordered. "Take this container and dump it in the ocean. We can't allow this terrible power to befall the world ever again."

"Yes, Sir!" Singh complied.

Abhu and Singh handed off the sealed container to another group of local EJFS agents entrusted to dump the remnant in the sea, far out of enemy reach.

Suddenly, the three heroic EJFS agents were stunned to see Judson Clayborn in his former self.

"Clayborn!" Raj exclaimed.

"Yes, Mister. I want to say thank you for all that you have done. You saved me from the beast that I had become." Clayborn spoke humbly.

Singh interjected. "Mr. Clayborn, you have caused a great deal of trouble over the world. I hope what you have endured over the past few days has taught you a lesson not to covet wicked powers that have no business in human hands."

Clayborn looked down in shame. "I realize that a great deal of what happened the past few days has been partially my fault. But I have learned my lesson. I am going to fold my company to ensure that I won't have the same encounter with that dark power ever again."

Raj smiled at Clayborn. "You're a good man, Clayborn."

Clayborn added. "Please send my regards to your agency for keeping me alive while I was under the control of a darkened mindset."

"I will pass on your gratitude to all our active agents. Is there anything else I can do for you?" Raj offered.

"Yes, could you tell me what happened to Miss Zima?" Clayborn asked.

Raj paused awkwardly before showing a sad look on his face.

Clayborn picked up on Raj's facial expression, and his heart sank.

Singh spoke up. "She gave up her life to save our agents, and in doing so, she took out the persons responsible for everything that happened today. Unfortunately, that is not the only loss of life that we counted among us. One of those casualties was our own, a fine man and father, Agent Naveen Kamboja. He left behind a son named Amir."

"I'm terribly sorry to hear this," Clayborn said woefully.

"I'm sure you could have handled things differently, but this is your opportunity to learn from your misdeeds. All you can do is pick up the pieces and try to move on with your life. You have been given another chance to go on living. Forgive yourself," Raj comforted Clayborn.

"Thank you for your kind words, Mr. Raj," Clayborn continued.

Raj hugged Clayborn before they parted ways.

"Well, I need to get back to Manhattan. Could any of you fine agents get me a flight home?"

"Done. I'll set you up with a ride to the airport and book you on the quickest flight." Raj smiled.

Soon after, Clayborn took a cab ride to the airport and took a standby flight to return to New York.

Raj, Abhu, and Singh returned to the EJFS Thunderhead Base to tie off some unfinished business regarding the ex-President Hill's corrupt administration.

***

Later that afternoon, Abhu and Singh returned alongside Raj at the Thunderhead Base over Atlanta.

Agents Abhu and Singh were greeted by their girlfriends, Durga and Gangi, respectively. The remaining agents in the lobby applauded Abhu's, Singh's, and Raj's return.

"Congratulations, and well done to all of you!" Khali paid a hero's tribute to the returning agents.

All three agents smiled exuberantly with glee.

The agents gathered in the foyer and gave a round of applause to the heroes.

"This country, and the world for that matter, continue to owe you a debt of gratitude. Now, we need to debrief all of you soon. I must return to D.C. to conclude the proceedings against Kenneth Hill," Khali ended the tribute.

The group returned to settle back in after the crises of the past few days had ended. Khali headed back outside to the front courtyard of the palace.

Khali contacted US Attorney General, Brian Geoffries, to reconvene the proceedings against Hill.

Unbeknownst to Khali, a stealth military drone was performing recon on Khali. A few holdovers from the Shadow State influenced the CIRB to observe Khali's transport vehicle departure to Washington, D.C.

One of the CIRB assets contacted James Matthews, the Head Director of the CIRB.

"Mr. Matthews, It's Agent Stevens. Khali is on his way down now."

"Acknowledged, I'll notify Pamela Harsh to take action," Matthews said on the other end of the phone conversation.

***

Meanwhile, Secretary of State Pamela Harsh was driving her government-issued SUV when her phone rang.

She connected her Bluejaw device and accepted the call while driving.

"Hello?" Harsh answered.

"Miss Harsh, it's Matthews. Khali is en route to Capitol Hill. You know what you have to do."

"I understand. I'll let you know as soon as it's done."

Pamela quickly disconnected the call as she donned her sunglasses and continued her drive from Virginia to Washington, D.C.

41: Hill Learns His Fate: Khali in Dire Straits

Khali returned to the Nation's Capital to resume Hill's proceedings and see it through the culmination.

Hill's impeachment was fast-tracked after the day's events stemming from the Shadow State's scheme to revive Vritra was stopped earlier in the afternoon.

The vote to remove and convict President Hill was expected to have support from enough of the Senate majority to remove Hill from office officially. The question remained whether the disgraced President's actions would meet the criteria for execution by firing squad.

Khali sat in the upper gallery to observe the final vote to convict and remove Hill.

The Secretary of State, Pamela Harsh, sat behind Khali during the proceedings.

Also in attendance was CIRB Director James Matthews, who observed from across the gallery.

Several covert CIRB assets stood watch, trying to keep Khali contained until after the vote was held.

Chief Justice of the Supreme Court, John Buchanan, addressed the gathering.

"My fellow Americans, it is with great sadness that we have come to this dark moment in our nation's history. The past few days have been a sobering reminder that the electoral process is not always picture-perfect and that our democracy can be used against us in such trying times that our people had the misfortune of enduring."

While the presiding Chief Justice addressed the country before the voting commenced, Matthews texted his assets to ensure that the plan to capture Khali was perfectly executed.

Buchanan continued. "I will submit for the record that this day marks the end of a dark time in our nation's history. However, there is the hope of a new tomorrow. With this vote, we may witness the restoration of the American Dream and become a leading example to all nations that tyranny will not be tolerated in any chamber in any state or federal government."

Amid the happenings in D.C., the EJFS was glued to the impeachment proceedings taking place on Capitol Hill. The agents watched as the vote was soon to commence.

Chief Justice Buchanan finished his address. "It is with a heavy heart that I now open the floor vote by roll call. Remember, it takes two-thirds of a majority to convict the President. If any impeachment articles receive the majority needed to convict, the President will be considered removed from office and, therefore, ineligible to hold public office again. Let us begin."

As the votes were being counted, the covertly placed CIRB assets within the gallery began to move into the final position before they attempted to capture Khali.

Matthews spoke to the camera operations office in the Senate wearing a wired mic.

"Pan all the camera angles away from the target's view, please," Matthews ordered.

"Yes, Sir," The operator of the cameras in the Senate heeded the order.

Furtively, all cameras in the chamber changed angles to keep the gallery's section where Khali was seated out of view.

Khali noticed the change in his surroundings as he saw several people in the upper sections of the gallery move around toward him. Khali felt somewhat threatened.

The vote was completed, and the results were 94-6 to convict Hill. Thus, Hill was officially removed from office, and Drake was named the new President for the remainder of Hill's term in office.

As the events in Congress ended, Khali made his exit from the gallery.

Once Khali excused himself from the Senate gallery, a government official approached him.

"Excuse me, Mister Khali?"

"Yes, and you are?" Khali answered.

"My name is Robert Manning. I'm working with the State Department. The Secretary of State wants to ask you some questions following your congressional testimony."

"I assume this is only a formality," Khali said.

"Yes, Sir. It won't take long, follow me," Manning insisted.

"Very well," Khali followed Manning down the hall to the right.

Khali and Manning wound up at the building's darkened corner, where nobody else was in the vicinity.

Suddenly, another CIRB asset peered out of the corridor to muzzle Khali and subdue him with a fast-acting sedative.

Khali tried to resist the attack, but he was overwhelmed by both operatives.

Manning and the other brute CIRB agent checked Khali's vitals. His pulse was weak.

"Clear!" The CIRB agent announced.

"Thank you, Agents Manning and Robinson. Shackle him, and plant the microchip into his arm," Secretary of State Pamela Harsh spoke assertively.

Manning and Robinson rolled up their sleeves and dragged Khali out of view before the deed was done.

***

Meanwhile, at the EJFS Thunderhead Base, the mood was somewhat upbeat after Hill's impeachment trial concluded. Now, the agents waited for the return of Khali.

Agents Abhu and Singh and their girlfriends, Durga and Gangi, spoke in the Sapphire Quadrant Unit's commons area following the trial. They were due to be debriefed by Agent Darsh in the coming days.

"Well, that's the end of the Hill administration," Durga declared.

"It wasn't even a close vote," Abhu noted.

"At least we can count that as a wrap," Gangi added.

"Maybe when Khali returns, he can shed some light on what will happen next to Hill," Singh suggested.

"Do you think they'll go through with executing him?" Abhu asked.

Singh shrugged, "It could happen."

Abhu thought out loud. "I would be surprised if they go through with it, especially if there are any Shadow State holdovers in the government."

"Only time will tell, Abhu," Agent Singh smiled before leaving the room to return to his quarters.

Singh entered his room to settle back into a somewhat calmer time at the superagency. He was exhausted from the crises of the past few days, and he wanted to decompress.

Suddenly, his smartphone rang, and Singh reluctantly answered it.

"EJFS, this is Singh."

A slight staticky delay in the reception sounded on Singh's phone.

"Hello?!" Singh raised his voice.

Hill's voice sounded on the other end.

"Hello, Agent Singh. I suppose that you weren't expecting to hear from me. Did you honestly think I would be executed by firing squad?" Hill asked patronizingly.

"Mr. Hill, why are you contacting me, and how did you get my number?!" Singh asked frantically.

Hill spoke passive-aggressively. "That's not important right now. You should know that your adoptive father is in our custody. He's unharmed, but that could change if you try to find me."

Singh felt a sinking feeling in his abdomen.

"By 'our,' I assume you mean what's left of the Shadow State," Singh said.

Hill chuckled. "Please, that was only a means to the end. All you need to know is that if you attempt to track me down, Khali won't be returned to you in the same condition he is in now."

Singh was horrified by the change of developments.

"Let me see my father," Singh demanded.

"Fine," Hill took a picture on his phone and transmitted it to Singh.

Singh was petrified after seeing his adoptive father, Khali, bound by his wrists and gagged. He was dangling on a chain attached to the ceiling of a large cargo ship, moving with a faint light shining on him.

"You worm! Why are you doing this to him?" Singh asked furiously.

"It's a little thing that I like to call a bargaining chip. He is going somewhere far away, where not even crows can land their poop on him. If you genuinely want to see your father again, you will call me back at this number within 72 hours. Do not tell anyone else that we had this conversation, or your father dies."

Hill taunted the alarmed agent then disconnected the call, leaving Singh noticeably distraught.

Singh lay in his bed under heightened emotional distress. He began to cry after the disturbing discovery of his father's capture.

Abhu overheard Singh crying and knocked on his door to check on him.

"Singh? Singh? Are you all right in there?" Abhu spoke with concern.

Singh was unresponsive and too upset to utter a single word.

"Singh, what's going on?"

"My dad is gone! Khali is gone!" Singh wept.

Abhu was stunned and felt utterly helpless to comfort Singh in his suffering.

Singh continued to spiral downward emotionally and mentally. His distress level was increasing dramatically.

***

Inside a large cargo ship named the Siberia King, Khali was strung up by a thick chain keeping his large feet from touching the ground as he was unconscious but alive.

"What is our ETA?" Hill asked.

"The ship captain estimates that we will dock in Belfast by tomorrow evening," CIRB Asset Manning answered.

"Good, we're right on schedule," Hill smiled menacingly.

The cargo ship crossed the Atlantic Ocean, heading to Northern Ireland.

While Khali was in a dire predicament, the rest of the EJFS superagency was in a state of serendipitous delight. They did not know that the chief commander was captured and held prisoner by the disgraced ex-president Kenneth Hill.

Khali's adoptive son continued to spiral downward into a state of extreme emotional distress.

Nobody in the EJFS could have known such a terrible fate had befallen them.

Epilogue: Three Days Later

Three days after the end of Hill's trial, the EJFS was alerted of Khali's disappearance, following the disgraced ex-President's proper removal from office.

Khali's adopted son, Singh, has not been the same since Khali was captured by Hill and a select number of associates.

Singh made it his top priority to locate and liberate his father with the help of the EJFS, now under the permanent leadership of Raj.

Abhu, Singh's best friend, became worried for Singh as he dedicated his focus to finding clues leading to the conspiracy of Khali's capture and his quest to bring his adoptive father back home safely.

After the 2024 Presidential Election occurred, President Drake lost his election bid against Republican Challenger Wes Grisham after the exit polls showed a lack of public trust for the Hill Administration's remaining holdovers.

The President-Elect, Wes Grisham, vowed in his victory speech to launch full investigations into Hill's corruption and his administration and whether Drake was complicit with Hill's schemes.

While he assumed the top leadership of the EJFS, Agent Raj remained determined, along with Singh, to locate and rescue Khali from his abductors.

Singh's mental state became a growing concern for the leadership of the EJFS as he became mentally unstable in the absence of Khali.

Zima and Naveen's remains were recovered, and both were given memorial services at the top of the EJFS Thunderhead Base's front courtyard.

Both individuals' remains were dissolved into purified rainwater and became a part of the evaporation cycle forever.

Naveen's beloved son, Amir Kamboja, decided to enlist in the EJFS due to Raj's influence, to become a Tech Analyst in Training. The transition was somewhat difficult under Singh's mentorship as the forlorn agent became increasingly preoccupied with Khali's disappearance.

Darsh maintained his role as a backup to Agent Lochan as the Agent-In-Charge in the EJFS Command Center, and he was also the next in line for the Second-In-Command designation after the disappearance of Khali.

Lochan retained his role as Agent-In-Charge of the EJFS Command Center and was appointed one of Raj's advisors.

Abhu and Durga were permitted to view the Dream Scan Results Report, but both declined to see them after the dream did not come to fruition.

After the recent events stemming from the Shadow State and Vritra's Revenge attacks, Judson Clayborn sold his expedition business as promised.

Gangi continued to support Singh in every way possible, although their romantic relationship was on hold due to Singh's deteriorated mental state.

Indrina (a.k.a. Kim) decided she was not cut out for field operations and decided to stay involved in the Command Center.

After the second return and defeat of Vritra, his remnants were buried at sea at an undisclosed location.

The intricately sealed container was tagged with a GPS transponder to track any relic changes or detect any attempts to intercept the container, thus risking world annihilation yet again.

Khali's disappearance largely confounded the overall focus points to rid the world of corruption, terrorism, and tyranny. The unspoken mantra for the EJFS is never to leave another brother behind, and for both Abhu and Singh, it was vital to save Khali.

With Hill and his new team of associates, Manning and Robinson, and their involvement in Khali's abduction, the overall mission at hand shifted to save Khali while holding those responsible for his capture accountable.

After-Story

1: Khali Missing: Singh Overcome with Grief

Unit 11 - Singh's Quarters

Level Five – Sapphire Quadrant

Main Building

EJFS Thunderhead Palace Complex – Atlanta Branch – Eastern US Division

November 3, 2024

4:14 PM EDT, Sunday Afternoon

Singh remained in his quarters, visibly upset after his distressing phone conversation with Kenneth Hill had concluded, Singh was stricken with overwhelming grief and unease.

Agent Abhu tried to calm Singh down, but nothing could console his best friend with the unsettling knowledge that Khali, Singh's adoptive father, was taken away and his whereabouts unknown.

"Singh, please let me in and help you," Abhu pleaded.

Singh wept. "I don't know if I can take this much loss in one day, Abhu! Hill threatened to maim my dad beyond recognition if we pursue them."

Abhu never felt so helpless in his attempt to calm Singh down.

"Singh, I know it's been a hellacious two days, but I am here for you. You are my best friend. We can work through this together," Abhu continued.

Singh momentarily stopped crying as now the entire Sapphire Quadrant was outside his door, concerned for Singh's emotional wellbeing.

Singh slid open the door to his quarters, and Abhu came into support a tearful Singh. Abhu did everything he could to comfort his best friend enough so he could discuss the incident.

"My Dad is gone, Abhu. My heart feels like it has been ripped out of me," Singh lamented.

Abhu's heart broke upon hearing Singh's plight for his dad.

"I'm so sorry, Singh. I wish I could take away your anguish," Abhu empathized with his best friend.

"This is beyond what I can handle, Abhu. Naveen and Anastasia have died today, and I would be damned if I let my dad suffer the same fate without me trying to rescue him. I don't know what to do, especially if Hill finds out that the EJFS is aware of my dad's disappearance," Singh raised his voice.

Abhu was at a loss for words.

Singh continued but in a slightly calmer tone. "Hill has given me a choice to call him if I ever wanted to see my dad again. Beyond that, I don't know what he plans on doing to him. He referred to my father as a bargaining chip."

"A bargaining chip?" Abhu asked.

"I don't know what he wants, maybe power or money. My guess is he wants to disappear from the limelight after the US Government clearly dropped the ball in the post-impeachment process. I don't understand how he slipped away from custody," Singh said.

"I think you should call him back within the next three days. We can try to locate him and your father," Abhu said reassuringly.

Singh held his head in his hands, overwhelmed with tremendous worry and heartache.

"I'm deeply sorry, Singh. But we need to take this to Agent Raj. He is the second-in-command. He must take the reins of the EJFS during this time," Abhu urged.

"What if Raj decides to intervene? Do you think he would take Khali's capture lying down? He's going to involve himself, and it could end very badly for my dad," Singh theorized.

"You never know for sure, but this is not up for debate. The EJFS lacks a director. You need to give Raj a chance to lead us," Abhu suggested calmly.

Singh felt utterly lost.

"This is the worst day of my life. I will never forgive myself for letting my dad go to the nation's capital without protection." Singh sighed in distress.

"I promise you that I will do everything I can to support you, and I will help you find your father," Abhu vowed passionately.

Singh paused before answering. "I will talk to Raj. I want to be the one to explain it to him."

Abhu gave Singh another brief hug, hoping that it would provide some solace to Singh's immense emotional pain.

"I must ask that you accompany me in this meeting," Singh imposed.

"Of course, you're my brother and friend. I am here for you," Abhu spoke softly as they hugged it out.

Both Abhu and Singh left the unit as the others inside noticed Singh's tear-stained eyes as they made their exit from the quadrant.

***

Meanwhile, Raj experienced a much different emotion than Singh's. His mood was upbeat as the superagency learned that Hill's removal from office was finalized.

It seemed that all was right in the world.

Raj enjoyed some chamomile tea in his quarters to soothe his nerves following the end of the mission against the Shadow State.

Raj was oblivious that Khali was no longer in the US and that he was not coming back.

Suddenly, Agent Singh texted Raj, marked with high importance, that something was wrong and needed to speak with him.

Raj felt a sudden knot form in his gut. He did not want to hear any more bad news from the mission's end. However, he could not disregard the urgent message. Raj replied to Singh's text message.

"Meet me in my office. We can talk in private."

Raj was not looking forward to hearing what Singh needed to convey, but he allowed himself to be a sounding board for Singh to communicate what was wrong.

Abhu and Singh reached the top floor. They veered down the hall to Raj's quarters and buzzed the call button.

"Come in," Raj permitted entry.

Both Singh and Abhu entered Raj's quarters, and Raj became increasingly concerned that something was horribly wrong when Singh brought Abhu along with him.

Singh's eyes were still red and puffy from his emotional meltdown.

"Oh, my God! Singh, what's wrong?" Raj asked in a worried tone of voice.

"I received a disturbing phone call about thirty minutes ago, and it requires your attention," Singh began.

"What is it, Singh?" Raj asked.

Singh was barely able to maintain composure to articulate his response.

"It was Hill. He informed me that he had captured Khali, and he's using him as a bargaining chip," Singh answered.

Raj was horrified to learn the terrible news. The emotional highpoint Raj had just experienced faded away rapidly.

"Oh, Singh, I'm so sorry to hear this," Raj hugged Singh upon hearing about Khali's disappearance.

"We must find him, Raj," Singh felt almost numbed by the emotional outburst he experienced earlier in the afternoon.

"We'll find him, Singh. I'll make it the top priority of the agency to track them down and bring Khali back home," Raj consoled Singh.

Abhu interjected. "Hill instructed Singh to call him in 72 hours if he wants to see his father again, and we can't pursue them. If we do, he'll mutilate Khali to the point where Singh won't recognize him anymore."

Raj was breathless and mortified. His face became slightly pale. "This is so unfortunate," Raj replied as he sat down, feeling faint.

Singh spoke. "You must take the reins over the EJFS now that Khali is missing. But I need you to know that I am not willing to treat my father as an acceptable loss in any shape or form. We have to rescue him somehow."

Raj replied. "I understand, Singh. This is an extraordinarily complex and delicate crisis. But we will exercise great caution in tracking them down to ensure your father's safe return."

Abhu asked. "What are you going to do?"

Raj answered. "I must notify the EJFS Board of Directors. I now have to take over as the acting head director during Khali's absence."

Raj trudged to his desk and accessed his computer to reach out to the EJFS Board of Directors to share the terrible news that necessitated Raj's rise to the headship of the superagency.

***

Aboard the Siberia King cargo ship (eight hours away from the Port of Victoria in Belfast, Northern Ireland), Khali was still strung up by his wrists and feet above his captors: Ex-POTUS Kenneth Hill and CIRB Asset Robert Manning.

Khali regained consciousness while bound and gagged in the high ceiling inside the cargo ship's lower deck. His vision was exceedingly clouded. He could barely make out his surroundings. He faintly heard a voice saying, "He's awake. Lower him."

Hill's henchmen lowered Khali in a sudden drop to just above the floor space.

Khali cried out in pain as he was jolted out of his unconsciousness.

Hill was sitting before Khali in the shadows. He was smoking a cigar in a celebratory moment of his escape from the US and of Khali's capture.

"Welcome to your imprisonment, Khali," Hill mocked.

Khali was too weak and pained to respond.

Hill chuckled malevolently as he rose from his seat, emerging from the shadows. He approached Khali and joined Manning to torment their captive.

"I have spoken to your adopted son. Singh, is it?" Hill spoke condescendingly.

Khali appeared to be emotionally embattled inside, not able to speak a word to his enemy. He grunted in pain with the wet cloth tied around his mouth.

"I thought you should know that I relish the opportunity to hold you as a political prisoner. The damage you have done to my image and my family will be remembered forever," Hill declared while in Khali's personal space.

Hill stepped away from Khali so Manning could land some punishing fist blows to Khali's torso.

Khali groaned in pain. The blows inflicted upon his body made him wince.

Hill turned back around and taunted Khali some more.

"Your son knows that you are being held captive, and he also is aware that if he tries to find you, I will make sure the pain and suffering will be much worse. Your beautiful face will be long gone," Hill informed him.

Khali's face turned red in rage.

"If your son doesn't call me in the next 72 hours, I will make sure you will never see him again for the rest of your life," Hill vowed vehemently.

Khali grunted angrily. His eyes were widened with fury.

Hill cackled menacingly as Khali struggled.

"Give him another beta-blocker and tranquilizer combo," Hill instructed.

"Yes, Sir." Manning complied. He jammed a full syringe into Khali's back, putting Khali back into a further weakened state.

Khali fell asleep while strung up and bound.

"Raise him to the ceiling again," Hill commanded.

Manning pulled a lever to hoist Khali back into the air while out cold yet again.

The sun began to set as the Siberia King crossed into another time zone.

Khali's dilemma continued to worsen.

2: Abhu Debriefed: Singh Seeks Sharma's Counsel

Abhu's Quarters, Unit 12

Sapphire Quadrant – Level Five

Main Building

EJFS Thunderhead Palace Complex – Atlanta Branch – Eastern US Division

November 4, 2024

8:36 AM EDT, Monday Morning

Agent Abhu was scheduled to undergo his post-mission debrief with Darsh following the significant operations against the Shadow State at the subsequent dawn. Abhu was increasingly concerned about the deteriorated emotional condition of his best friend, Agent Singh.

Still, Abhu acknowledged that he needed to fulfill the obligations necessary to bring the active protocol to a close.

Before Abhu departed from the unit, he checked on Singh one more time before his extensive debriefing that morning.

Abhu gathered his tablet and notes from the past week and exited his quarters, approaching Singh's door.

Singh was inside his room, watching the post-impeachment news recap on his HDTV, linked to all local and national news.

Abhu buzzed the call button by Singh's quarters.

"Who is it?" Singh inquired.

"It's Abhu."

Singh turned off his TV and changed it back to his schedule screen.

"Come in, Abhu," Singh responded.

Abhu slid open the door to Singh's room. Singh was still in his pajamas, lying in bed.

"Good morning, Singh. How are you holding up?" Abhu asked.

Singh sighed heavily in distress.

"I don't know, Abhu. I feel so distraught that my dad has been captured by Hill. I wish I had done things differently," Singh answered somberly.

"You should strongly consider talking with Sharma. He might be better at providing adequate counsel than I can," Abhu suggested.

"I don't think it is as simple as counseling, Abhu. My father has been captured, and I don't know what sort of approach I should take to ensure that he is safe," Singh argued.

"Give Sharma a chance. He might be an excellent resource to reach out for help," Abhu continued.

Singh did not respond and stifled himself from crying.

"I can't imagine how much pain you must be going through, Singh. But I want you to know that I love you and care about you very much and that I am here for you, no matter what happens," Abhu assured.

"Thank you, Abhu. I appreciate your continued loyalty," Singh replied in a subdued tone.

"Well, I need to meet with Darsh for my debrief. If there is anything I can do for you to help you, please let me know," Abhu said as he prepared to leave.

"Thank you, Abhu. All I ask from you is your prayers and support," Singh responded.

"You got it," Abhu affirmed.

Singh rustled out of bed and gave Abhu a quick embrace. Abhu reciprocated the hug and held him in his powerful arms.

"Abhu, thank you so much for everything. You're a true friend," Singh commended softly as a single tear ran down his cheek.

Abhu wiped away Singh's tear from his eyes.

"We'll get through this together, Singh," Abhu spoke soothingly.

Abhu patted Singh on his back before ending the hug.

"Forgive me, Singh, but I must go. Darsh is waiting," Abhu concluded.

Singh smiled at his best friend. "It's okay. We'll talk later."

Abhu left Singh's quarters as Singh remained in his room, contemplating an AERIAL VOIP call to the resident doctor and psychiatrist, Sharma Ahsan Rishi.

The more Singh considered it, the more practical it became to him.

Singh sat in his armchair facing the HDTV and electric fireplace. He accessed the all-agency call directory within the quadrant.

He initiated an audio call to Sharma, and the HDTV speakers emitted a ringtone.

EJFS Agent and Doctor Sharma Ahsan Rishi

Sharma was preparing for duty in the Level Three Infirmary when he heard Singh's call.

He saw on his HD screen in his room that Singh was calling him. Sharma quickly retrieved his smartphone to answer.

"Hello, Singh. It's Sharma. how may I help you?"

"Good morning, Sharma. I need to set aside some time today to speak with you. It's about something important," Singh responded.

"Of course, I can make time for you. But I need to report to the infirmary for duty. I will meet with you after my shift ends at 3:00 PM. Does that work for you?" Sharma asked.

"Yes, that is fine with me," Singh confirmed.

"Excellent, I'll add you to my schedule for this afternoon. Hang in there, my friend. We'll talk soon." Sharma spoke assuringly.

"Thank you." Singh accepted graciously.

"Mm'bye," Sharma ended the call. He entered his new appointment with Singh in his phone, and he left the unit to descend to the third floor.

Singh was semi-catatonic as he lay in bed while doing his best to hold himself together. He had taken some off-time to rest and grieve for Khali's kidnapping.

The unpleasant thoughts of Hill's evil laughter invaded his mind. There were only two more days until he must call Hill back, and every moment with this thought in Singh's mind was like an empty void in his soul.

***

Darsh was sitting in his office suite, reviewing field reports and other documents filed after the recent operations against the Shadow State.

Abhu arrived at the admin offices to consult with Darsh for his debrief.

"Good morning, Abhu: Are you ready?" Darsh asked.

"Yes, I am," Abhu smiled as he brought his tablet and notes.

"Excellent, let me take you to the debriefing room. Come with me." Darsh stood and beckoned.

Darsh delegated his filing duties to Agent Durga, Abhu's girlfriend. She spent some time working in the admin offices to keep her mind occupied after the missions concluded.

Durga glanced at Abhu momentarily and smiled weakly. She was concealing the pain of all the loss she endured with the casualties of Agent Naveen, Anastasia Zima, and the capture of Khali.

"This way, Abhu," Darsh redirected Abhu as his smile faded away upon seeing Durga's saddened facial expression.

Darsh led Abhu upstairs to the debriefing room he booked for their appointment that morning.

"After you," Darsh gestured for Abhu to enter the room before he activated the 'Active Session' sign above the doorway.

"All right, Abhu, try to recollect all the events that occurred the past few days during the operations against the Shadow State," Darsh began.

Darsh prepared the equipment in the room to assist in the debriefing of EJFS Agent Abhu.

Abhu sat in the seat to detect and retrieve all thoughts and memories related to the operations conducted during the last few days from his implanted capsule device in his sternum.

"As is the case with every debriefing, we must record this session for our internal recordkeeping purposes."

Darsh started the recording and began fetching all data from Abhu's capsule device planted inside his body.

"This is the debriefing of Abhu Dhuval Sandeep. Today's date is Monday, November 4th, 2024, and the approximate start time of this session is 9:00 AM. This is Agent Amit Darshan Vivek, and I am the conductor of this debriefing session. Abhu, please state your name, age, badge number, rank, and hire date for the record," Darsh stated on video.

"My name is Abhu Dhuval Sandeep, aged 23. My badge number is 2031586, I'm a Level Eight Field Specialist, and my hire date is September 8th, 2023."

"Let's start from the beginning: When you were called back to the Thunderhead Base and learned about the disappearance of Judson Clayborn and the New York City train derailment, what was your assignment concerning the largescale operations against the Shadow State?" Darsh inquired.

Abhu began his recollection. "Initially, my role was to assemble a logistics package against Anastasia Zima when she was still affiliated with the Shadow State. However, before the agency briefing, I was informed that my sister, Kimberly Porter, was implicated in political extremism."

"I see, and what was your reaction to that finding?" Darsh asked.

"I did not react to the news very well. I didn't believe my sister would be engaged in the extremist group in question, Upheave Fascism. Something wasn't adding up," Abhu explained.

"Please explain your reservations and what happened henceforth for the record," Darsh directed.

"I was highly doubtful of my sister's alleged affiliation with Upheave Fascism because I know my sister wouldn't pivot that far left on the political spectrum. My reservations were proved correct when it was later determined that Kim's imposter was the woman in the photo. The person in the photo was, in actuality, a CIRB asset named Alicia Blaze, working for a rogue faction of the government in the alignment of the Shadow State," Abhu elaborated.

"Moving on to the following events that occurred last Friday, what was the danger you discovered that posed a threat to America?" Darsh queried.

"The threat that the agency uncovered was that there was a massive geoengineered hurricane barreling toward the US East Coast, and it was created at the hands of Jagmohan Gyan. His goal, along with the entire Shadow State order, was to resurrect Vritra's remains into destructive energy and manifest itself into some form to obliterate the world," Abhu continued.

"Upon this revelation, how did the EJFS proceed in its mission to stop the catastrophe?" Darsh asked.

"Fellow Agent Singh and I were burdened with the task of finding Anastasia, the Necklace of Vritra, and the leader of the Shadow State. The mission led us through parts of Europe: Hungary, Poland, and Belgium. First, we captured Anastasia at the Russian Embassy in Budapest, and she surrendered to us willingly. Secondly, our TAC Team traveled to Warsaw to utilize their interrogation room, command center, and capsule device scanning equipment," Abhu explained further.

"What significant events played out during your overseas mission deployment?" Darsh posed a follow-up question.

"There was a multitude of significant events that happened during my deployment. Firstly, two intruders seized Anastasia Zima, Alicia Blaze, and Midnight Thunder, alternatively known as Judson Clayborn. He was radically transformed into a superhuman brute by the Shadow State. Secondly, one of our agents was killed. Agent Naveen Brahma Kamboja was crushed to death by a collapsed chunk of debris from the ceiling at the Warsaw EJFS base. Lastly, our TAC Team located the Shadow State leader codenamed Black Sparrow Zero, also known as Richer. We managed to rescue Anastasia after Singh reset her memory. Anastasia became one of us," Abhu elaborated.

Darsh noted all the input Abhu had given him and continued with the debriefing questions.

"During the last few hours of the operation against the Shadow State, how did the final objective of dispelling the hurricane succeed, and how did you defeat Vritra a second time?" Darsh asked his last question before the debriefing concluded.

"Raj, Singh, and I used the Gatekeeper's Blade to attack the wounded palm of Midnight Thunder after he had metastasized into a 150-foot giant since Vritra consumed his spirit after being reborn at the Edisto Bay Oil Rig near the Carolinas. It took a couple strikes to defeat Vritra and return Thunder to his original self. After the battle concluded, Vritra's remains returned to a solidified form, and Midnight Thunder reverted to his original identity of Judson Clayborn," Abhu concluded.

"Well done, Abhu! I am so proud of you for your recall of the events that took place. I will submit your recollection as part of the final mission report in the next few days. You are free to go now." Darsh finished the debriefing, and Abhu returned to his unit.

***

Later that afternoon, Singh met with Sharma to seek his professional advice on how to handle the situation of Khali's kidnapping. Sharma approached Singh's quarters to visit with him.

Sharma buzzed the call button near Singh's door, and Singh permitted entry.

"Hello, Singh, I'm so sorry about your father," Sharma wrapped his massive arms around Singh for a hug.

"Thank you, Sharma," Singh spoke weakly. He had been tired yet restless the entire day.

Sharma took a seat next to Singh's chair as Singh explained the crisis to the resident psychiatrist.

"Tell me how I can help you through this," Sharma urged.

"My father is being held captive by ex-President Hill. They were on board a boat. Hill sent me a photo message of my dad being strung up to the ceiling inside a darkened ship," Singh explained.

"I'm terribly sorry for your plight, Singh. What did Hill tell you before your conversation with him ended?" Sharma inquired.

"Hill told me to call him back in the next three days if I ever wanted to see my father again. I only have two days left, and I am terrified of what state my father is in at this moment," Singh continued.

"This is such an ordeal for both of you. I know you must be heart-wrenched by these troubling developments. However, I believe you should allow the agency to intervene," Sharma suggested.

"And to what end? So, Hill and his men can kill my father?" Singh balked at Sharma's idea.

"Singh, I'm only trying to help you. You've sought my assistance, and I am giving it to you directly," Sharma countered.

"I'm sorry, Sharma. I shouldn't be so hostile. These past few days have been an absolute nightmare," Singh spoke tiredly.

"I'm genuinely sorry, Singh, but I need to know why you won't allow the EJFS to help locate your father, who also happens to be the Head of the superagency," Sharma continued.

"Hill warned me implicitly not to let our agency interfere with his schemes, or I would never see my father again," Singh spoke with raw emotion.

"How else should you approach this issue? Are you sure you have the resources to seek out Khali before much worse things could happen?" Sharma tried to reason with Singh.

"Believe me, I wish I had never allowed him to travel to D.C. alone, but I don't want to risk any more harm that could be wrought upon my father," Singh spoke lamentably.

"You shouldn't blame yourself. It will erode you from the inside out. The only way we can handle this is to call Hill's bluff. The Command Center is equipped to handle ghost calls, and they can take action without Hill knowing about it," Sharma suggested further.

"Don't you think he might see that coming? I am sorry, but I do not want to risk losing my father. He means the world to me. I will never forgive myself if he dies," Singh spoke passionately.

"Give your employer a chance to make this right. You alone cannot change the situation. But, if the collective of EJFS branches and divisions can find him, then it would be a risk worth taking," Sharma continued.

"I don't know what to do anymore." Singh was on the verge of an emotional breakdown.

"Let us help you," Sharma implored.

Singh was feeling defeated and utterly spent.

"All right, we'll do this together. But if my father dies, I will hold everyone involved responsible for it," Singh defended his stance.

"I understand, Singh," Sharma responded solemnly.

Singh sighed heavily. "I never thought I'd see the day where I would have to save my adoptive father after he saved me from my situation."

Sharma empathized with Singh, "My heart aches for you, my friend. But we are here for you no matter what happens."

Singh remained strong after Sharma's encouraging words, and he did everything he could to not lose hope.

"I'll tell Raj and Lochan to strategize the next steps tomorrow," Singh declared decisively.

"Thank you for giving us a chance to help you," Sharma spoke comfortingly.

Sharma realized he was being summoned to the infirmary for another scheduled appointment after receiving a notification from his smartwatch.

"I have to go, Singh. If you need anything, please do not hesitate to contact me again," Sharma said before exiting.

"Certainly, and thank you for your counsel," Singh concluded.

Sharma smiled, "It's my pleasure, my friend."

Sharma left Singh's room while Singh continued to pray and lament Khali's capture.

3: Singh Debriefed: Khali Bound for Siberian Prison

Singh's Quarters, Unit 11

Sapphire Quadrant – Level Five

Main Building

EJFS Thunderhead Palace Complex – Atlanta Branch – Eastern US Division

November 5, 2024

10:19 AM EDT, Tuesday Morning (Election Day)

Two days after the end of the operations against the Shadow State, EJFS Agent Singh Puneet Sherpa was due to appear in his post-mission debrief with Agent Darsh at 10:45 AM that morning.

Singh had difficulty sleeping during the previous night. He mourned his father, Khali's capture.

Abhu would periodically check in on Singh to encourage and comfort him whenever possible. But it seemed that nothing could console Singh without his adoptive father present.

Singh only managed to sleep for two hours before his phone alarm sounded to wake him up for the day.

He half-attentively tapped the snooze button on his phone and fell back into bed to catch as many extra ten-minute increments of sleep that seemed to be an illusion.

Three snoozes later, Singh received a call from Darsh, telling him that he was late for his debrief appointment.

"Crap!" Singh cursed under his breath before answering his smartphone.

"Hello, Darsh," Singh greeted him.

"Singh, this is unacceptable. You are late for your debriefing. I insist you come downstairs to my office immediately!" Darsh admonished Singh.

"Yes, Sir! I apologize. I'll be there shortly," Singh responded with shame.

Darsh abruptly ended the call while Singh hastily gathered his tablet and notes for his appointment.

Singh hurried out of the quadrant and rushed to the elevator, descending to the lobby.

Once Singh reached the main floor, he briskly walked to the admin offices where Darsh was waiting.

"Darsh, I'm so sorry I'm late. I won't allow it to happen again," Singh assured him.

Darsh was perplexed by Singh's sudden unprofessionalism.

"Singh, this is so unlike you. You're one of the most punctual agents in the EJFS. I hope nothing is troubling you." Darsh spoke with grave concern.

"Honestly, I am not doing too well. I'll explain more in my debrief," Singh replied with a distinct frown.

"Very well, Singh. Let us head upstairs," Darsh asserted.

Darsh led Singh upstairs to Debriefing Room Two to conduct Singh's session.

After Darsh beckoned Singh to come inside the room, he allowed the heavy door to close by itself, and he illuminated the 'Active Session' sign above the doorway.

"All right, Singh. Per the EJFS guidelines under your rank level, you must undergo a monitored and recorded debriefing every three years. Your capsule device within you will download all data relevant to the missions of the past week," Darsh reminded him.

"I understand. Let us get this over and done with," Singh said tiredly.

Darsh initiated the data download from Singh's capsule device, and he began the recording.

"This is Agent Amit Darshan Vivek, and this is the post-operations debriefing of Agent Singh Puneet Sherpa. Today's date is November 5th, 2024, and the start time is 10:53 AM," Darsh began.

"Singh, please state your name, age, rank, and hire date for the record," Darsh directed.

"My name is Agent Singh Puneet Sherpa. I am 32 years old. I am a Level 10 Field Ops Manager, and my hire date is August 18th, 2015," Singh stated.

"Excellent. Let us revisit the morning of this past Saturday, November 2nd. After the initial agency briefing early that day, what was your role in the beginning phases of large-scale operations against the Shadow State?" Darsh inquired.

Singh answered. "My role after the first briefing was to join Agent Raj with the assigned task of taking Kim Porter up to the EJFS Thunderhead Base for questioning at Abhu's request. Abhu was dumbstruck when he heard that his sister, Kim, had alleged ties to a known political extremist group named Upheave Fascism."

Darsh recorded Singh's answers on his tablet.

"Did you believe the intel we had received that Kim was actively engaged in political extremism?" Darsh asked.

"I had my doubts at first, knowing Abhu was adamant that Kim had no affiliation with that group. However, I know from the past year that Kim had a rebellious streak within her. She disagreed with how the EJFS operated when we first became introduced," Singh continued.

"I see, and how did Kim's ordeal conclude?" Darsh queried.

"Kim's good name was cleared after it was later discovered that she had an imposter posing as her and sabotaging her life. Personally, I was relieved to know that Kim was not involved with any extremist groups," Singh added.

"Very good, moving on," Darsh changed the topic.

"What was the overall threat facing the world as the day progressed?" Darsh questioned.

"The EJFS learned that there was a seedy, underground, and evil cabal known as the Shadow State working against the West to topple the free world. Their method of doing so was to attempt to locate and revive the ancient remnant of Vritra, whom we defeated and dispelled into dark matter encased inside of the necklace that the late Ravan Kanda Ganesh once wore," Singh explained.

Darsh continued to jot down the responses from Singh during the debrief.

Singh explained further. "To facilitate that outcome, the Shadow State had sourced their contractor, Jagmohan Gyan of the Phoenix Tech Enterprises, to geoengineer a massive hurricane to bring Vritra back to life."

Darsh continued his line of questioning toward Singh.

"Could you explain who was behind the Shadow State cabal?" Darsh asked.

Singh elaborated. "A handful of world leaders led the Shadow State. Two of them were former US President Kenneth Hill and the top leader, Richer, codenamed Black Sparrow Zero. They worked together with the help of the CIRB, working against our superagency at every turn."

"How did the operations against the Shadow State end?" Darsh asked.

Singh was hesitant to answer the question initially, but he felt comfortable sharing his plight with Darsh in hopes of resolution and comfort from his friend.

"The TAC Team involving Abhu, Raj, and myself, were successfully able to eliminate Alicia Blaze, Kim's imposter, and restore Judson Clayborn to his original identity after we waged war against Vritra's spirit consuming Judson's soul," Singh explained.

Still, he knew that the lighter mood in the room was about to darken.

"Unfortunately, after Hill was impeached and convicted for his treasonous ways, Hill managed to escape execution, and he captured my father, Khali. Hill threatened to ruin my father's face and kill my dad if we tried stopping him," Singh elaborated woefully.

"Hold on, Singh." Darsh paused the recording session.

"I was afraid of divulging this information during the debrief because I knew it would set off a chain reaction, one that could lead to an outcome that I regret," Singh continued off-camera.

Darsh was stunned by the revelation that Singh shared with him.

"Singh, I'm so sorry that this has happened. But we need to track down Hill and rescue Khali," Darsh said.

"It's not that simple, Darsh. If Hill knew that I had outed him, he might kill my father. I can't accept that," Singh argued.

"Who else have you told about Khali?" Darsh asked.

"Abhu, Raj, and Sharma, but you know what they say: Word gets around fast," Singh retorted.

Singh was barely able to maintain the façade of levity. After realizing that everyone in the EJFS might know why he had not been himself lately, he soon became emotionally distraught.

"Oh, Singh. I'm terribly sorry," Darsh comforted Singh, rising from his seat and wrapping his gargantuan arms around Singh for a healing embrace.

"Thank you, Darsh," Singh said.

"What are you going to do about Khali's disappearance?" Darsh asked candidly.

"I don't know. I have one more day to contact Hill to see my father again. But Hill is using him as a bargaining chip. I don't see any likelihood of rescuing my father unless we give Hill something of great value," Singh spoke woefully.

"This is terrible to hear, my friend. But, if you want to hear my advice, I implore you in the strongest possible terms: Call Hill back and discover your options," Darsh suggested.

Singh sighed heavily, feeling an unbearable weight on his shoulders.

"I don't know what options Hill will offer at this point. I am hoping and praying that my dad can withstand him and his wicked ways," Singh moaned. He held his face in his hands in unbearable grief.

Darsh felt quite pained upon seeing Singh's anguish.

"In light of what you've revealed to me: I feel it would be best to suspend the remainder of your debrief for another week or until we can resolve this crisis," Darsh spoke with heavy sorrow for his friend.

Singh was somewhat comforted that he was left off the hook for some time. But his heart was still heavy with immense sadness.

"Thank you for your empathy, Darsh. I'm glad to be surrounded by loving and caring agents like you," Singh commented.

"It's the right thing to do at this juncture. We'll worry about fulfilling our procedural mandate later." Darsh concluded before dismissing Singh.

Singh left the area and returned to his quarters, still suffering tremendous heartache for his father's plight.

He lay in bed, overwhelmed with worry and sorrow.

***

Meanwhile, in Belfast, Northern Ireland, the Siberia King had reached the Port of Victoria's docking point.

Hill's henchmen assembled near the docks to serve as the reception committee for the captured Khali.

Several men shouted commands to open the rear hatch. The ramp was extended toward the port side of the large cargo ship.

Khali was shackled and chained by every limb, and he was pumped with enough tranquilizers to bring down a strong stallion.

Khali's chains were carried by six powerful henchmen keeping Khali vertical during his transfer to an Apache helicopter.

Khali was slightly disheveled, and his face was severely bruised.

Kenneth Hill remained listless in his facial expression while he accompanied Khali to the chopper.

Dusk fell over the skyline in Belfast as the group escorting Khali to the military aircraft continued their rough treatment of him.

Robert Manning spoke to Hill. "It's been almost three days since you have talked to his son. Should we disregard the resolve of Khali's compatriots to come to his rescue?"

Hill scoffed. "Don't be ridiculous, Manning. Singh is biding his time, and nothing will change with his father. If he tries to pursue us, his father will ultimately perish."

Manning replied. "Remember what Pam told us about the EJFS. They are not to be underestimated."

Hill responded. "I'm not worried about the EJFS anymore, and neither should you."

The gathering that escorted a bound Khali reached the helicopter departing to a Siberian prison facility in Northern Russia.

The group boarded the high-speed chopper bound for Siberia, and Khali was left to rot in a cold cage with other henchmen containing his subdued strength and energy level.

That night, the helicopter sped above the Trans-Siberian airspace to the isolated prison in Northern Russia, where Khali would be confined for an indefinite amount of time.

4: Singh Makes the Call: Hill's Parting Shot

Singh's Quarters, Unit 11

Sapphire Quadrant – Level Five

Main Building

EJFS Thunderhead Palace Complex – Atlanta Branch – Eastern US Division

November 5, 2024

1:40 PM EDT, Tuesday Afternoon (Election Day)

Singh was restless in his quarters, knowing that the deadline for him to contact Hill to inquire of his father, Khali, was running out.

Raj and Darsh were due to meet with Singh regarding Khali's capture.

Abhu and Sharma sat with Singh in his quarters to provide as much support as possible for the long-time stellar EJFS agent. For them, they could not afford to see Singh remain in his current condition any longer. Singh must decide soon.

Abhu and Sharma were silent as they could not find the words to articulate how horrible they felt for Singh, but they continued to encourage Singh with words of hope with choice phrases such as "Don't lose heart" and "Stay strong."

For Singh, words offered truly little solace in his anguish about his father's possible fate.

Soon enough, Raj and Darsh reached Singh's quarters. They pressed the call button to request permission to enter.

"Come in," Singh responded.

Raj, accompanied by Darsh, joined Singh, Abhu, and Sharma to call convicted ex-President Kenneth Hill.

Raj spoke in a comforting yet firm tone. "Hello, Singh. I know this has been a stressful week for all of us, but the time has come for you to contact Hill. We need to find out where Khali is located and his current condition."

Darsh encouraged. "All of us will be here every step of the way, Singh."

Raj continued. "I have instructed Basu to patch you through our ghost line. You'll use one of our burner phones to speak to Hill for up to ten minutes without him being able to detect your location. We need you to keep Hill on the phone for at least 90 seconds for us to pick up a signal trace on him."

Singh experienced a wide array of emotions, ranging from stress to fear.

"I don't know if I am in any condition to perform this action. I am afraid I might be the reason that my father may disappear out of our reach," Singh said.

Sharma interjected, "Singh, you can do this. Remember that we are counting on you to reach Hill and determine the whereabouts of Khali. I know this is extremely difficult what we're asking of you, but you have no choice."

Singh sighed heavily. His courage increased after the quick pep talk from Sharma to boost his self-confidence.

"You're right, Sharma. We cannot afford to procrastinate any longer. I am ready," Singh stated.

Raj smiled and handed Singh a burner phone. Singh calmly and methodically spoofed his usual phone number to give Hill the false impression that Singh was calling from his smartphone device.

***

Meanwhile, Khali was being booked into solitary confinement at a Siberian prison center, usually a punishment reserved for the worst criminals on Earth.

Suddenly, Hill's smartphone rang, and he noticed that Singh was contacting him.

Hill promptly answered the call.

"You finally called me, Singh. That is highly suspect for someone who claims to love their father dearly. I would have expected you to call me much sooner," Hill taunted.

"Let us get to the point, Hill. Now, what do you want? Why are you holding my father as a bargaining chip?" Singh demanded answers.

"I want you to hand over your agency's roster list, all of them. If you turn over that information to me, I will let your father go free," Hill proposed.

"Why would you want our roster list? That is something that we keep highly confidential," Singh countered.

"Singh, you don't need to know the rationale behind my demands. If you want your father to be returned to you without any further harm, then obey me," Hill demanded angrily.

"Even if I were to request the list, I don't have the permission or the means to send it over to you. It is under the highest form of military-grade encryption known to man. My superiors would have me removed if I were to give you this list," Singh contested.

Hill frowned, yet he was impressed with Singh's loyalty to the EJFS.

"I underestimated you, Singh. Based on what my cohorts learned about you, I never thought that you would resist my demands. I will modify my request: I ask that you send your friend, Abhu is it? He may take Khali's place of incarceration," Hill continued.

Basu was on the other end of the line, monitoring the call on the triple-point subnet.

"20 seconds to location lock," Basu spoke discreetly.

Abhu overheard the call while the audio was filtered into his headset. He shook his head, signaling that he would not take Khali's place as a political prisoner.

Singh replied. "I know Abhu won't agree to that. There must be something else we could offer you. Maybe we could provide you protection from the public eye. You could live somewhere in total anonymity with a new identity," Singh offered.

Hill scoffed and chuckled malevolently.

"I find your attempts to circumvent my demands patronizing and yet humorous. If you think I have not taken the necessary precautions to protect myself, then you greatly insult me and underestimate how far I will go to get what I demand of you," Hill mocked.

"Ten seconds to triangulation," Basu noted on Singh's earpiece.

"What if I were to offer myself as your prisoner?" Singh suggested.

"What? You?!" Hill barked.

"That's correct, my life for my father's life," Singh confirmed.

"I refuse to believe what you are offering. I think this is some sort of ploy to buy time to find your father," Hill roared.

"Honestly, I don't care what you believe! I am telling you that I will give myself over to you so that my father will go free," Singh retorted.

"We got him! He's in Belfast, Northern Ireland, near the Port of Victoria!" Basu indicated with excitement.

Singh's mouth was slightly agape with a sense of relief.

There was a pause at the other end of the line.

"That will not be necessary, Singh. I see you have tracked the locator on my last phone that I left in Belfast. All deals are rescinded. But, before I go, I will send you one final memento of what shell of a man is left of your father," Hill fumed.

Hill prepared a pair of photos showing Khali's mugshot and the interior of his cold, dank, solitary confinement cell. Hill attached both media items to a text message and transmitted them to Singh's burner phone.

"Consider this the last time you'll ever see your father in one piece. Goodbye, Singh!"

Hill ended the call right before Singh saw the photos. He viewed them with horror.

"NO!" Singh shouted emotionally, and he crumbled into a blithering mess.

Raj, Darsh, Abhu, and Sharma rushed to console Singh in his traumatic moment, but Singh was nearly inconsolable.

Singh's father was out of reach.

***

Meanwhile, in Northern Siberia, Russia, Hill observed Khali's placement into the solitary confinement cell and approached Khali before sealing him away from all human interaction.

"Stop!" Hill ordered his men.

Hill spoke to Khali intently through the peephole in the door.

"Khali, your son Singh, tried to track us down. Because of this, you are indispensable to us now. You are going to be locked away forever, and I promise you, this will be the worst time of your life," Hill vowed and slammed the peephole shut.

Khali was left entirely alone. He was cut off from his friends, agents, and the rest of the world, never to be seen or heard from ever again.

After Hill concluded his interaction with Khali, he speed-dialed Secretary of State Pamela Harsh for an update.

Harsh was at her office when Hill called. She promptly answered her phone.

"This is Pam."

"Pam, it's Hill. Khali's in prison where he belongs. I suppose you have a place where I can go to stay off the radar for six months," Hill hinted for a quid pro quo.

"Yes, Mr. Hill, your safehouse in London, England, will be ready to occupy upon your arrival. Thank you for bringing Khali down. I will make sure that the EJFS cannot locate him, so you won't have to worry about them any longer," Harsh assured him.

Hill grimaced wickedly. "Thank you for saving my hide from execution back in the states. I don't know how to repay you."

Pam smiled. "Maybe one day you'll be free to return to the US Mainland again. But not yet. I will do my best to keep the EJFS at bay."

"Goodbye, Miss Harsh, until we meet again," Hill concluded.

"Be well, Mr. Hill," Harsh ended the phone call.

Kenneth Hill slipped into his long coat, gathered his belongings in a suitcase, and left to take another train to Koltsovo Airport bound for Heathrow Airport in London, England.

***

Later that night, there was an unplanned ritual where Agent Raj was being sworn in as the new Master and Head of the EJFS. Singh was not able to attend the ceremony due to his troubled emotional state.

All agents were left to ruminate on what happened to Khali and why Raj assumed headship over the entire EJFS.

Raj addressed his subordinates as the head of the illustrious superagency.

"My fellow EJFS agents, tonight is an especially dark night for all of us. I have been appointed as the new leader of the EJFS from now on. Khali has been captured by Hill, and what we assume are holdovers from his crooked administration. We do not know their current location, but we have detected a GPS transponder in Belfast, Northern Ireland, where the trail ends. With a heavy heart and terrible regret, we must suspend all active searches for Khali effective immediately. However, we will continue to monitor any new information and leads that may help us locate Khali. All usual procedures and protocols will remain in effect until further notice. Thank you, and may God be with us all!"

A moment of silence was observed for Khali's capture, followed by quiet prayer.

With the EJFS missing an influential leader in Khali, Raj led the superagency following the tremendous loss. Khali was in custody at a Siberian prison with no contact with the outside world.

Night fell over the US East Coast on Election Night, when it was later announced on the evening news that Republican Presidential nominee Wes Grisham easily defeated the lone holdover from Hill's failed administration, Peter Drake, in a landslide victory.

A time of uncertainty became apparent to many across the globe as Drake was poised to finish his term in late January 2025.

The End?